"Feel, *bella*. Feel ~~how much you're~~ **exciting me." X**~~a~~**hand all the way** ~~to~~ **pounding of his** ~~heart beneath her~~ **palm. "This isn'**~~t anything I've ever~~ **experienced either."**

Her scalp tingled. She dropped her champagne, ignoring the delicate breaking of crystal, wanting too badly to touch him with both hands. She slid her fingers to the back of his neck and raised her mouth, inviting him to kiss her. It was pure instinct and he didn't hesitate, covering her parted lips as though he'd been let off his leash after being tempted too long.

The world stopped, then spun the other way, dizzying her. She made one whimpering noise, astonished by how thoroughly such a thing could devastate her, wilting all her muscles.

She distantly heard another delicate glass shatter and then he picked her up, lifting his head to reveal a fierce expression. Victory? Not quite, but there was something conquering there. Something exalted.

Yet his bright gaze asked a question.

She nodded, unable to speak, and just gave herself up to it—to him. She knew when to fight her body and when to surrender. Perhaps it was the silver lining to all those years of having to accept that physiology trumped logic. This was bigger than anything she could make sense of.

The Sauveterre Siblings

Meet the world's most renowned family...

Angelique, Henri, Ramon and Trella—two sets of twins born to a wealthy French tycoon and his Spanish aristocrat wife. Fame, notoriety and an excess of bodyguards is the price of being part of their illustrious dynasty. And wherever the Sauveterre twins go, scandal is sure to follow!

They're protected by the best security money can buy—no one can break through their barriers... But what happens when each of these Sauveterre siblings meets the one person who can breach their heart...?

Meet the heirs to the Sauveterre fortune in Dani Collins's fabulous new quartet:

Pursued by the Desert Prince

His Mistress with Two Secrets

Bound by the Millionaire's Ring

Prince's Son of Scandal

Available now!

Canadian **Dani Collins** knew in high school that she wanted to write romance for a living. Twenty-five years later, after marrying her high school sweetheart, having two kids with him, working at several generic office jobs and submitting countless manuscripts, she got The Call. Her first Mills & Boon novel won the Reviewers' Choice Award for Best First in Series from *RT Book Reviews*. She now works in her own office, writing romance.

Books by Dani Collins

Mills & Boon Modern Romance

The Secret Beneath the Veil
Bought by Her Italian Boss
Vows of Revenge
Seduced into the Greek's World
The Russian's Acquisition

The Sauveterre Siblings

Pursued by the Desert Prince
His Mistress with Two Secrets
Bound by the Millionaire's Ring

The Secret Billionaires

Xenakis's Convenient Bride

The Wrong Heirs

The Marriage He Must Keep
The Consequence He Must Claim

Seven Sexy Sins

The Sheikh's Sinful Seduction

Visit the Author Profile page
at millsandboon.co.uk for more titles.

Back in 2012 I received a call—*The Call*—from editor Megan Haslam, telling me she wanted to buy my book. It was my first sale and terribly exciting. I have since worked with some of the other fabulous editors in the London office, but with *Prince's Son of Scandal* I came back to working with Megan. I'd gone so far down a rabbit hole with Trella in the first three books of this quartet I really wasn't sure I could pull off her story. Megan offered just the right feedback to help me make it work. We're reunited and it feels so good!

I'd also like to dedicate this book to you, Dear Reader, for your wonderful letters and support for the Sauveterre Siblings. I'm so glad you love these characters as much as I do.

CHAPTER ONE

Six months ago...

WHEN THE GREETER at the ballroom entrance asked Trella Sauveterre for her name, she nearly gave an arrogant "you know who I am."

She bit it back. Her sister was never acerbic. Not with strangers, and definitely not with underlings. Her twin was perfectly capable of terse words and might even hurl some blue ones at Trella when she learned what she was doing right now, but Angelique's personality was one of sensitivity and empathy. Gentleness and kindness.

Trella? Not so much.

"Angelique Sauveterre," Trella lied, wearing her sister's polite yet reserved smile. She ought to feel more guilty. She ought to feel like an overused cliché from a children's movie, but she didn't.

She felt *alive*.

And apprehensive. Terror could overcome her if she let herself dig deep enough. This was like swimming toward the middle of a lake, where the bottom was too deep to imagine. Who knew what dangers lurked in those dark watery depths? Monsters. They existed. She had met them. Had nearly been consumed by them.

But she wouldn't think about that.

Nothing in her outward appearance revealed the way her heart bounced and jostled in her chest, fighting internal battles. She moved gracefully, even though her muscles felt stiff and petrified, twitching to run.

Because, along with the trickles of fear, a tumbling waterfall of joy rang through her. It was all she could do to keep tears from her eyes or laughter from escaping her throat.

I'm doing it! she wanted to call her family and cry. *Look. I'm in public. By myself. I'm not shriveling like a vampire in the sun.*

But they didn't know where she was and it was best to keep it that way. This was the sort of sneaking out a window she should have done years ago, when she'd been an adolescent. Instead, she'd been a grieving survivor with an eating disorder and more baggage than a passenger jet.

Still was, if these people only knew.

She quashed the negative self-talk and moved like a normal person through the crowd. Gazes lingered, noting Angelique Sauveterre had arrived. Her bodyguard kept anyone from approaching, though. Maybe that wasn't normal for everyone, but it was for the Sauveterre twins, even the eldest set of brothers.

With her sister's aloof nod, she returned a few greetings to people she imagined she was supposed to know.

In a few weeks, she would come out as Trella and have nothing left to hide behind. No more walls, literal or technical. No broad-shouldered brothers. No playing her sister to avoid being herself. She had determined, had sworn on the blood she had shed when she nicked her ear cutting her own hair before Christmas, that this was the year she would free herself from the prison she had created.

For now, she was still hiding behind Angelique. She had impersonated her sister a few times recently, with her sister's permission, escorted by their brother Henri to watch his twin, Ramon, race. They'd also taken in a fellow designer's latest collection during fashion week. It had been spectator stuff where they didn't interact with anyone and kept to places her sister had been seen with their brothers before.

Trella had never walked out in public alone. In her entire life, she had rarely done anything alone. As a child, Angelique—Gili to her family—had been the needy one and Trella, the protector. She had held Gili's hand so her sister wouldn't tremble and cry at the attention they had received. Their brothers had barely given them breathing space even before Trella's kidnapping at age nine, always ready to catch a tumble from a swing or to keep them from wandering too far from the group.

Then she'd been stolen and had *wished* that her captors had left her alone.

She swallowed and veered her mind away from those memories. They were guaranteed to bring on an attack and she was doing far too well. It was coming up to two years without one.

The attacks had manifested years after her rescue, when she should have been finding her feet and moving on with her life. Instead, she had become a horrible burden. Her siblings would never say so, but they had to be sick of being on call for her. She was certainly tired of being the weakest link. She *had* to change.

Tonight was another step toward that. The press would go mad when she finally came out of seclusion at a friend's wedding in a few weeks. She had to be ready, but she had to *know* she was ready.

So she was testing herself, if somewhat impulsively, because this charity dinner hadn't been on her agenda at all when she had arrived in Paris.

She had been beside herself with pride when she'd landed, high on travelling from the family home in

Spain—by private jet with trusted guards, always—but without her mother or siblings. It had taken her newfound independence to the next level.

So, when Gili tentatively had asked if she could run to London for a hot secret weekend with her new paramour, *of course* Trella had told her to go. Her sister had looked incandescent when she'd spoken about Prince Kasim. He was clearly something special.

Trella wanted her sister to be happy, wanted to quit holding her back. Spending a night alone at their tightly secured living space above their design house, Maison des Jumeaux, had seemed a perfect cherry on top of Trella's already sweet split from old fears.

As the evening stretched on, however, she had restlessly poked around the flat, picking up after her sister and teetering on feeling sorry for herself. Wistfulness had closed around her.

Would *she* ever have a romantic liaison? Her feelings about men were so ambivalent. At fourteen, she'd had the usual rush of hormonal interest, even shared an embrace with the gardener's son behind a rosebush. Then their father had died and the most terrifying predators had emerged online, threatening her in vile ways. Her fear of men, of *everything*, had compounded a hundredfold. As her panic attacks escalated, the deepest fear of all had crept into her very soul—that she was so damaged and broken, no one would ever want her.

For years, she had barely allowed men near her, interesting or otherwise. She slipped from one secured location to another through shielded walkways, accompanied by a mostly female guard detail. Occasionally, her brothers introduced her to a friend, but even if she had wanted any of those bankers or race-car drivers to make a pass, Ramon and Henri wouldn't have allowed it.

Their dearest family friend, Sadiq, was the only man she'd spent real time with and theirs had never been a romantic relationship. He was the shy, heart-of-gold computer nerd who had helped the police locate her, returning her to her family. She loved him, but as her savior, not as a man.

Which was why his engagement had shaken her out of her ivory tower. She would do anything for Sadiq. If he wanted her at his wedding, of course she would attend, even though it meant overcoming her demons and returning to the public eye.

It had been a struggle to come this far, but now, as she stood on the cusp of achieving something like a normal life, she found herself resetting the goalposts.

She wanted her sister's anticipation for a weekend with a man. She wanted to be the person she would have been if she hadn't been stolen and assaulted, stalked and bullied, but it would never happen if she kept living behind these damned walls!

A disgusted toss of the latest fashion magazines onto the coffee table had sent a pile of paperwork sliding to the floor, revealing an invitation to this ball.

The fundraiser benefited orphaned children, something that would go straight to Gili's tender heart. Even if Gili had sent regrets, the Sauveterre checkbook was always welcome.

Not letting herself overthink it, Trella had briefed a security team and slipped on one of her sister's creations.

Where Trella loved powerful touches like strong shoulders and A-lines, along with eye-catching beadwork and bold colors, her sister's style was gentler. The champagne gown had a waifish quality in the way the sleeves fell off her shoulders. The bodice and torso were fitted to her figure, but the ruched skirt across her hips created a sensual impression of gathered satin sheets around a nude form.

She added her sister's earrings and a locket with a panic button, but kept the look simple, arranging her hair into a fall of dark locks and painting her lips a soft pink.

Now she was here, breathless and petrified, yet filled with more optimism than she'd experienced in years. She moved to speak to the aloof Russian host and his much warmer British wife, Aleksy and Clair Dmitriev.

"I'm so glad you came," Clair said, drawing her aside in a confiding way that revealed Clair had no idea she was talking to Gili's twin. "You're not my only supporter who comes without a date, but you're the only one who won't be silly about my guest of honor. Don't even ask how I got him here. I was hideously shameless, interrupting their trade talks and putting him on the spot in front of everyone. I talked him into auctioning himself for the first dance."

Trella scanned for a glimpse of this exalted personality. Clair continued her confession as she wound them through the crowd.

"Aleksy said at least I use my power for good instead of evil, but I feel a little evil because the ravens surrounded him the minute he arrived. They'll back off if you're there, though. I know you'll put him at ease. Everyone loves you. Do you mind?"

Trella could see how Clair got what she wanted, sounding sincere in her flattery as she took agreement for granted. Still, she was curious enough to murmur, *"Bien sûr,"* in her sister's preferred French.

Clair beamed and gently pushed into the thicket of gowns.

The mystery man turned, revealing a red sash beneath his black tuxedo jacket. He was tall. Intimidatingly tall, with broad shoulders and an economy of movement, suggesting a huntsman's physique lurked beneath his sophisticated attire. The blond glints in his light brown hair looked natural, given the hint of gold in his eyebrows.

Those eyes. They were such a piercing blue they struck like slabs off a glacier, peeling away to fall and rock the world. The rest of his features were precisely carved in sweeps of long cheeks under sharp cheekbones, a jaw hammered square and a mouth of two perfectly symmetrical peaks over a full but uncompromising bottom lip.

He was so compelling a force, so beyond her experience, the room faded from her consciousness. They became trapped in a noiseless, airless bubble as they took each other in.

Had she really longed to be seen as a woman? Because it was happening. He skimmed his gaze down in unabashed assessment. She saw the flash of interest in his gaze as it came back and locked with hers. He liked what he saw.

He saw Gili, though. Sweet Gili who was used to being in public, where men routinely sized her up as a potential conquest.

The strangest reaction slithered through Trella. She ought to have prickled with threat, or acted like Gili and let his male interest drift past her as if she didn't notice or care.

Instead, she took issue with her sister being seen as a trophy. Protective instincts honed since birth pushed her confrontational personality to the forefront of the image she presented.

You'll have to go through me, she projected, tucking Gili safely behind her.

His stare intensified. *Burned.* He saw *her.* Whatever shields she had walked in here holding—including her sister's persona—were gone. She felt completely unprotected against his thorough exploration of her face, his gaze touching each curve and dip of her features.

It felt like a spill of magic, making her cheeks tingle. She had to disguise a rush of unprecedented sensual awareness. Men didn't affect her, but the spell he cast sent invisible sensations from her throat to her nipples and her pelvis, into her thighs and terminated in a paralysis that nailed her feet to the floor. All the while, delicious stirrings swirled upward through her, making her feel drawn toward him.

"Your Highness," she heard Clair say from what seemed like another universe. "Have you met Angelique Sauveterre?"

"Ms. Sauveterre, the Crown Prince of Elazar, Xavier Deunoro."

Xavier had known exactly what he was doing when Clair Dmitriev had cornered him into making an appearance at her charity event. He was buying a future favor from her powerful husband, a man who was notoriously difficult to influence.

He had also known it would be an evening rife with what he had before him: Women in daring gowns, swishing their hips in enticement, sweeping lashes in false shyness while they twisted their hair in invitation.

As Europe's most eligible bachelor, he was used to having his pick from such an array. He only needed to drop a claw and let it pick up one of the brightly colored toys before him. It didn't matter which one fell into his hands. They were all the same, providing brief entertainment and something soft to embrace for a night, before forgetting them in the hotel room when he left the next morning.

Given the news he had received this morning, tonight's plaything would be his last before his royal duty took precedence. It was another reason he had agreed to this ridiculousness. At least he had a decent selection for his final visit to the amusement park.

He was taking his time singling out his companion. They all had their charms. Was he in the mood for voluptuous or fair? Should he be practical and choose the one wearing enough gold not to covet his own? Or go with the one who promised some spark as she set her chin and glared at the rest?

Then his hostess presented a newcomer like a gift, one who made the rest of the women take sharp little breaths and step back.

She was taller than most, with divine features that matched her name. Her skin was soft and flushed, too warm to be called cream yet not dark enough to be olive. Golden as a sunrise glancing off a snowy peak.

A muse, clearly, since he felt poetic stirrings just by gazing at her. How could he not admire her? Her figure was goddess-perfect, her mouth sinful, her eyes fey and mysterious, colored somewhere between gray and green. If he pulled her from the cloud of perfume surrounding them, he bet she would smell like mossy forest and clean cold streams.

That was what she presented on the surface, at least. In a blink, she had shifted ever so slightly and it was as if she'd hit exactly the right angle to catch and reflect the sun. Something less tangible than external beauty seemed to concentrate and strike out in a sharp white light that pierced his eyes, like a star being born.

She was the diamond in a bowl of imitations, a woman of facets and contrasts, infinitely fascinating and priceless. If recognizing that caused him a stab of regret because he didn't have time to fully explore her depths and contradictions, he ignored it. Such was his life. He took what he could, when he could.

Tonight, he would take her, *grazie mille*.

"Good evening." He bowed over her hand, letting his breath warm her knuckles and feeling the tiny flex of her reaction. "It's an honor to meet you."

"A rare treat indeed." The tilt of her lips suggested an inside joke. "The honor is mine."

"I've seated you at the VIP table," Clair said. "Please find your way when you're ready. Has everyone seen the silent auction items?" Clair broke up the knot of disgruntled women, most of whom drifted off.

A few opportunists remained, one being the redhead with the determined chin. He sighed inwardly as the redhead flashed a too sweet smile before asking, "Angelique, how is your sister? Still keeping to herself?"

Ah yes. That's why the name had struck him as familiar. The family had a tragic history. One of the twin girls had been kidnapped as a child. She was rumored to be batty, so they kept her out of sight. As someone who had been reported as everything from born of an alien to outright dead, he put little store in such gossip, but did wonder how she would respond to such a blatant intrusion. It was clearly meant to disconcert.

She swung a scythe-sharp glance at the redhead, revealing the compressed carbon beneath her sparkle.

"She's excellent." Her tone struck him as ironic. "What's your name? I'll tell her you were asking about her."

"Oh." The redhead was startled, but flicked him a glance and decided to take a final stab at snaring his interest. "*Lady* Wanda Graves."

"I'll be sure you're added to our list." She smiled distantly and turned to him. "Shall we find our seats?"

She didn't see the redhead brighten briefly before a darker thought struck, one that tightened her mouth. The other women who'd been standing by widened their eyes then averted their gazes before they scurried off.

He offered his arm and dipped his mouth to her ear. "You have a blacklist?"

"Nosy people do not wear our label."

Catty, ruthless, or both? Either way, he was entertained.

And now he was reminded that the sisters had some kind of design house. Women's fashion was last on his list of interests, but he took a fresh assessment of her gown, appreciating the peek of thigh exposed by the slit and the gather of strapless satin that left an expanse of upper chest and breast swell to admire.

"This is one of your creations? It's pure artistry."

"I can tell when I'm being patronized," she warned.

"Then you'll know I'm sincere when I say the dress is lovely, but I see the woman inside it. Which is the point, is it not?"

"Do you?" She tilted a considering look up at him, something dancing in the elfin green of her eyes. He could have sworn they were gray a minute ago. Her gaze dropped to his chest, where the band of silk slashed across his heart. "I see the crown, not the man. Which is what this is meant to convey, isn't it?"

Astute, but a woman who made her living with clothing would understand such nuances.

The sash in question felt unaccountably restrictive this evening. Duty hovered in his periphery, set there by a brief news item passed along from his PA about Bonnafete, a small principality in the Mediterranean. The reigning prince's daughter, Patrizia, had called off her marriage to an American real estate mogul.

Patrizia was a longtime acquaintance. Xavier was not as sorry as he had implied when he had sent his condolences. He was in need of a titled wife. His grandmother wanted him married so she could step down. Patrizia was infinitely suitable.

He had asked that his grandmother be made aware of the broken engagement. It was an acknowledgement of his responsibility toward her, their bloodline and the crown.

Loath as he was to marry, he preferred to spearhead such actions himself, rather than wait for her to issue orders. She might be the one person on this earth with the power to govern his actions, but he didn't have to encourage it. He was confident she would approve and God knew she would let him know if she didn't.

"Is it heavy?" his final sown oat asked of his sash. The levelness in her tone told him she didn't mean physically, proving she was even more perceptive than he'd imagined.

Compassion was not something he looked for in anyone, though, least of all his temporary companions. There was no room for any weakness in his life. No one saw him flinch. No one was privy to his bitterness at the hand life had dealt him.

It was a wasted emotion to feel.

So he ignored the chance she might understand him in a way no one else ever had and held her chair. "Nothing could weigh me down while I'm in your beguiling company, *bella*."

She froze and looked over her shoulder. "Why did you call me that?"

"It's an endearment. Elazar's official language is an Italian dialect, though French and German are commonly spoken along with English." He adjusted her chair as she sank into it then leaned down to speak against her hair where it fell in loose waves against her nape. "Why? Don't you like it?"

Tiny bumps lifted on her skin in a shiver of reaction. Her nipples tightened into peaks against the silk that draped over them, making him smile. She liked it.

Awash in more sexual anticipation than he'd felt in a while, perhaps ever, he seated himself, pleased he would end his bachelorhood with such a terrific bang.

* * *

Trella was a natural extrovert. The chatter and color around her, the voices and music and attention, was like standing in the sunshine after years in an *oubliette*.

But to have this man glance at her with that admiring look on his face as he seated himself next to her was a deliciously sweet accompaniment. He was clearly an accomplished seducer, wearing charm and entitlement as comfortably as his sash, but she was excited to be singled out by him all the same. It was the flirtation she had yearned for.

"What brings you to Paris?" he asked.

Although, if she was going to do this, she wasn't settling for plain vanilla.

"Surely you can do better than asking what a nice girl like me is doing in a place like this?"

"Let me consult my app." He glanced at an imaginary phone. "How about... What sign are you?" He affected sincere interest.

Her mouth twitched. "Gemini. Twins. Obviously. You?"

"No idea. August sixth."

"Leo. The lion. King of the jungle."

"Obviously," he said, with a self-deprecating tilt of the corner of his mouth.

She bit back a smile, intrigued by his position, but only because she knew what it was to be in the spotlight. He'd glossed over her query about the weight of his crown, but surely he wearied of attention and responsibility.

"You take horoscopes seriously?" he asked, nodding at a server who offered them champagne.

"Not as a belief system, but I used it as inspiration for a collection a few years ago. *We* used it," she amended quickly, clearing her throat over the white lie and sliding her gaze to ensure the people searching for their seats hadn't overheard her. It was well known in fashion circles that *Trella* had designed that particular line.

"How?" He seemed genuinely curious. "The patterns in the fabric?"

"Not that literal. More how the nature of each sign is perceived. They fall into different qualities, like fixed or mutable, and elements, like air and fire. There's a lot to play with. I work better with deadlines so I approached one sign a month. It was an interesting exercise." She leaned closer, wrinkling her nose. "Also a terrific marketing hook."

The corners of his mouth deepened. "Beauty *and* brains. Always an irresistible combination."

This prince, causing her heart to thud-thud under a simple compliment, should have sent her running. She had learned healthy caution from her childhood, but even though most men put her on edge, this one filled her with a giddy *lack* of fear. It was like breaking out of a shell. Like discovering she had the ability to fly.

She definitely wanted more time with him before this evening ended.

On impulse, she motioned for her guard, who was actually one of Gili's, and quietly gave him an instruction about the silent auction. He melted away.

Was she being too forward? Reckless?

Their table filled up, forcing her to wait to find out. Dinner passed in a blur of neutral conversation. Someone asked the Prince about his country's foray into green energy. She vaguely recalled his mountain kingdom between Italy and Austria had been accused of providing a tax haven during the world wars. Elazar sounded very modern and self-sufficient now. He spoke about exporting hydropower, since rivers and streams were one of their few natural resources. There was also a decade of investing in education, attracting engineering and technology start-ups, solar and wind power.

Her inner businesswoman should have been taking mental notes, but she was mesmerized by his casual command over his audience and subtly seduced with how close his sleeve came to touching her arm. Beneath the table, she imagined she could feel the heat from his thigh mere inches from her own. All she could think about was dancing with him.

Dancing. Tears pressed the backs of her eyes. She ached for that simple pleasure.

This adolescent reaction was ridiculous, but she let it happen. Embraced it. This is what she should have been doing at twenty, not hand-sewing sequins on mini-dresses for other young women to wear to exclusive clubs, killing hours with concentrated work so she could get through one day, one more hour, without a breakdown or the drugs that were supposed to prevent them.

Then Prince Xavier turned his terrifically handsome face toward her, bathing her in the light of his regard. "You must travel a great deal for your work? What drew you to fashion?"

He had given each of the others a moment in his attentive sunlight. Now it was her turn. He must engage in small talk with a thousand people a day, at ribbon cuttings and children's hospitals, but she would have sworn on her life the tension around his eyes eased as he met her gaze. He'd been doing his duty, impatiently waiting to get back to her. She felt delirious even as she prevaricated her way through her reply.

"Both of us are quite creative." Gili more so. She was the artist who designed out of love and ran the business out of necessity. Trella was the ambitious one, determined to turn a healthy profit. Practicality, not passion, had driven her into making her own clothes, because she couldn't bear being judged by trolls for merely *buying* something, let alone how it looked on her.

"We had some start-up help from our brothers but surprised them and ourselves with our success." Another fib. She wouldn't have rested until they were making buckets of money. She was competitive and driven by an I'll-show-you desire for revenge against those who had thrown shade.

"It can't be an easy field. I'm sure your success is due to hard work as much as anything else."

He was trying to get her into bed. She knew that with the brains he'd said he admired, but his flattery *worked*. She was ridiculously affected by his compliment. She wanted to say "It was a ton of work. Thank you for noticing." Gili was the face of Maison des Jumeaux, which meant she received the bulk of the credit—not that she didn't deserve a lot, but Trella worked just as hard and was not a naturally humble person. Hearing his praise went into her like a transfusion, tipping her further under his spell.

Their hostess moved to the podium to make a short speech, thanked the guests for their donations then announced the winners for the auction items. Trella grew increasingly self-conscious as the moments ticked down, certain she had truly lost her mind this time. Maybe she should leave before—

"Finally, our most coveted prize, a dance with the Prince of Elazar, has been won by... Angelique Sauveterre!"

The applause was polite, the knives in her back proverbial, but she felt them. She privately smirked, then blushed as Xavier showed no surprise. Was he so sure of her?

"I'm flattered."

"You should be. I promised to double the next highest bid. You had better dance well enough to be worth it."

"I do," he assured her, rising to help with her chair, doing that erotic thing of speaking against her hair so tingles raced all over her skin. "For that sort of generosity, *bella*, I'll give you the whole night."

Oh, he was good. Lightheadedness accosted her every time he called her *bella*, the same nickname her family called her. Her pulse pounded so hard she thought it would bruise her throat, but it fed the thrilling excitement washing over her. He made her feel so alluring. *Sexy*.

He made her feel as though he wanted *her*.

That was beyond captivating. She had spent a lot of dark nights telling herself how flawed she was, how she didn't want men anyway, so she didn't care if they didn't want her. She did want, though. She wanted to feel normal and alive. Happy and desirable.

The touch of his hand on the small of her back had a terrific effect on her. The awareness that had been teasing her all evening became a suffusion of deeply sensual lethargy. Dear Lord, was she becoming *aroused*?

It was what she'd envied her sister for—which was when it struck her what was happening. She and Gili had a twin connection. They didn't read each other's thoughts or anything so intrusive, but they picked up hints of the other's emotions despite whatever physical distance might separate them. The preternatural sense was stronger on Gili's side. Trella had been so messed up for years, taking antidepressants to quash anxiety attacks, she hadn't been as receptive to her sister's moods.

Lately, however, she'd become more aware, particularly if Gili was restless or having an off day. Tonight, her sister was with a man who truly excited her. She was usually so careful, so rarely selfish, yet she was basking in something that made her incredibly happy.

Her sister's buoyant heart lightened Trella's. She was

happy for Gili, happy her sister wasn't weighed down by all the things Trella had put her through. It added another lift of carefree joy to her own evening.

"You dance well yourself," Xavier said as he spun her in a waltz.

She was too exhilarated to respond. The sparkling ballroom circled around her in a kaleidoscope of colors. His embrace was confident and reassuring, making her feel light as a fairy.

"I feel like Cinderella." It was too true. She was the smudged sister who had escaped from the attic, wearing borrowed clothing to dance with a prince.

"You look like something out of a fairy tale." The line of his brow twitched and the corner of his mouth deepened, like he both surprised and disparaged himself for saying. "You're very beautiful," he added gruffly.

Gili was the beautiful one. Trella had fought hard to get back to the same weight as her sister, wanting to feel as good as Gili looked. She had let her hair grow out to her sister's length so she could impersonate her for her dry runs going out in public, but she never thought of herself as beautiful. She too often thought of herself as broken.

Not tonight. She diverted herself away from any thoughts other than how *glorious* this was. Around and around they went. His thighs brushed hers, his fingers splayed as though trying to touch more of her. She let her fingers trail closer to his collar so she could rest the side of one finger on the hot skin of his neck. It was electrifying. The magnetic sensations grew as he kept her dancing into the second song, tugging her toward an unknown crescendo. When someone tried to cut in, Xavier shrugged him off.

"The privilege of position?" she teased.

"I've never seen anyone glow like you. I'm enthralled."

Again, misgiving seemed to flicker like a shadow across his face. He didn't like admitting to whatever he was feeling, but it added to her own exuberance.

"I feel like… I can't even describe it. Like it's Christmas. Like anything is possible." She brought her gaze down from the chandelier into the turquoise blue of his eyes.

She reminded herself that becoming over-excited could have a rebound effect. She didn't want to backslide. It would be a long fall from this height.

Then she forgot any sense of caution when he said, "I need to kiss you." The desire in his words was a sensual squeeze that stole her breath.

A very long time ago, she had been quick to agree to anything that sounded adventurous. A dungeon full of shackles and bars had kept her grounded since then, but somehow, with a few words, this man reached past all the darkness and invited her into the light. To be the impulsive, audacious person she was in her heart.

"Me, too," she said through sensitized lips. *It's only a kiss.*

His sharp gaze moved beyond her. The next thing she knew, he had her off the dance floor, through a small break in the crowd and into an alcove hidden by the giant fronds of a potted plant.

She wasn't given time to decide whether she'd been too quick to agree. His arm tightened across the small of her back, pulling her in, arching her against the layers of his tuxedo. He was steely beneath his civilized covering. He knew what he wanted. His hot mouth covered hers without hesitation.

For a second, she was terrified. Not of him, but of how she would react. Would she panic?

Then her senses took in the way his mouth fit against

hers, moving to part her lips, questing for her response. Something primitive moved in her, shaking her foundations, waking the woman she might have been if her life had been different, drawing her beyond old traumas into a place she barely understood.

Pleasure flooded her, making her stiffen, wary of such a strong reaction, but primal need quickly took over. Her brain might not be able to process what was going on, but her body knew how to respond.

Rather than put the brakes on, her hands went behind his neck. She found herself running her fingers into his short hair, shaping the back of his head as she drew herself up, parting her lips so he could plunder at will.

His arms tightened around her and she thought he made a growling noise. It should have scared her. Male aggression, especially the sexual kind, was something she'd taken pains to avoid.

Strangely, with excitement pulsing through her, she found herself thrilled by his response. She kissed him back with abandon, just as if she knew what she was doing.

Something flashed behind her closed eyes and he abruptly lifted his head.

"That was a camera," he muttered, fingers digging in near her tailbone as he pressed her close enough to feel the thick shape straining the front of his trousers. "Let's find some privacy."

Her analytical mind urged caution, but her old self, her true self, trusted her instincts. She released a breathy, "Let's."

CHAPTER TWO

HE DIPPED HIS head to lightly scrape his teeth against her neck, urging against her ear, "You leave first. I'll follow you upstairs."

She gasped, mind going blank before a million thoughts rushed in.

"You have a room here? In the hotel?" What had she thought when he had said *privacy*? Was the idea of being alone with him intriguing or alarming?

"The penthouse, yes."

"Is it safe?"

"Of course." Good gracious he was handsome, even when he frowned. His features weren't too refined. There was just enough toughness in the intensity of his gaze, just enough stubbornness in the square of his jaw to make him look stern and rugged.

As he read her hesitation, his hand cupped the side of her head while his gaze flicked with irritation at the noise around them. "I want you to myself."

Empathy panged within her. She knew the wear and tear that being in the spotlight took on a person. She instantly wanted to give him the break he needed. He was a sophisticated man. She had nothing to fear from him physically, but was compelled to say, "I have guards. For a reason."

She was using her sister's tonight, both to give her own

a much-deserved night off as well as to maintain the illusion she was her twin. *She should tell him who she was.*

"The room is completely secure. More secure than here," he added, mouth twisting in dismay at their having been photographed. He led her back to their table. "I won't keep you waiting long."

Voices of caution crowded into her head, but when would she have a free pass like this again? When would she meet a man who made her feel anything like this? It wasn't just physical, although that part was so heady she felt drunk, but there was a rarity, too. There were other men in the world who were a safe bet, men vetted by her brothers, but when would she feel this pull? This compulsion to know more about *this* man?

Before she talked herself out of it, she let her finger press *up* for the penthouse. It wasn't that she didn't have misgivings, or that she ignored them, she *overcame* them. It was different. It was another small triumph that had her stepping lightly off the elevator onto thickly carpeted floor.

It was easy to spot the Prince's room. Two guards were stationed outside the door. Her own accompanied her as she approached them.

"Mademoiselle Sauveterre," one greeted with a respectful nod. "We were notified to expect you." He stepped inside and invited her guard to sweep the rooms.

Both men behaved with the utmost professionalism, not betraying a hint of judgment about what they must know was a preliminary for seduction.

A smile touched her mouth as she thought about how her brothers would blow their tops if they knew where she was right now, even though they had both been on the Prince's side of this equation hundreds of times, the hypocrites.

Then she was left alone and she took in the elegant shades of ivory and sage green on the walls and the furnishings. A glass of watered-down Scotch had been abandoned on an end table, ice long melted. She sniffed, then dared a sip, thought about looking at the view, then decided to leave the drapes closed.

The double doors to the bedroom stood open. She stared at the bed, taking another quick sip of liquid courage just as the main door opened. His star power impacted her anew, making her heart skip.

"You made yourself comfortable. Good."

"This is yours." She tilted the glass, then set it aside, instantly wishing she'd kept it to keep her hands busy.

"I'll make you a fresh one. Or, how about champagne?" He moved to the bar. As he peeled the foil from a bottle, the crinkle seemed overly loud.

This was the moment she should have admitted she was Trella.

A very real fear sat within that admission—that he would develop his own misgivings. He would either want explanations she didn't care to give, or he might jump to conclusions that made him averse to being with her. In no scenario did she imagine this exciting, lighthearted atmosphere would continue.

"You're nervous," he noted as he popped the cork.

"You're observant," she said, compelled to at least confess, "I don't do this."

It was true no matter which twin she represented. Gili running away for a weekend with a prince was as out of character as her being here with this one.

"I already guessed that." He set two glasses as he poured, canting his head to eye her. "You're not a virgin, are you?"

She choked. "No."

True again for both twins, but she had to look away, mind skipping off the dark memory like a stone off the water's surface.

No, that was another reason she was here. Being alone with a man was another snapped link in the chain that bound her to the past. She was really, really proud of herself right now. Even though her proffered excuse of "I'm just out of my comfort zone" was the understatement of the year.

He brought the glasses across the room to her and offered her one. *"Saluti."*

"Salud."

They sipped, gazes locked, unspoken expectations hovering between them. Her throat grew abraded by the bubbles.

"What if I change my mind about being here?" she asked in a soft rasp.

"Then I will be disappointed." His intent expression didn't change.

"Angry?"

"Disappointed. Very disappointed, *bella*." His gaze acted like wildfire, igniting her blood as he swept it across her cheek and down her throat.

He turned away to set music playing. The notes were low and sultry, matching the thick feeling in her veins, the sensual throb of her pulse.

"Either way, I'm pleased to have you to myself." He came back to her, steps laconic, touch smooth and confident as he looped his arm around her. "Whether you want to talk or dance or…pass the time in other ways."

He swayed them into a dance that was really just the press of two bodies. Foreplay. They both still held their champagne flutes. Held gazes.

"I wasn't in the mood to fight other men for your attention."

"Was anyone else even trying? I hadn't noticed." She batted her lashes.

His mouth tilted. "I like that wit, *bella*. I find myself regretting we only have tonight."

She tucked her chin and gave him an admonishing look. "You're patronizing me again. I don't need the rules spelled out. I'm not *that* green."

"See? Such sharp intelligence is the sort of thing that holds my interest longer than a few hours."

"Is that how long your liaisons usually last?"

He stopped dancing, arm remaining across her back, but loosely. "That's probably not a good topic of conversation."

"I know." Bubbles tickled her nose as she sipped, trying to wash away a strange bitterness on her tongue. It shouldn't matter what his past looked like. Whatever man eventually attached himself to her wouldn't come to her pristine. She couldn't expect it when she had such a complicated history herself. "I think I'm looking for reasons not to like you so I won't feel so…"

She frowned. The hand she'd rested on his shoulder slid down to splay on his chest as if she had the right to touch him with such familiarity, but touching him felt very natural. Her fingertips dipped beneath the ribbon of red, sliding the tips of her polished nails beneath it as she ever so slightly lifted it off the crispness of his shirt.

"I'm not a pushover. I'm normally the most contrary person you could imagine. A fighter." Her family told her that all the time, so why was she letting this happen? Her usual streak of rebellion was absent.

Actually, she realized with a spark of insight, it was directed against the life she'd been leading, pushing her to break free of old restraints. No one was stopping her from spending a night with a man except her. All she had to do was *choose* to.

"I'm not trying to pressure you. I'm sincere that I wish we had more time to get to know one another, but my life has never allowed for long term relationships." His hand shifted to splay in a warm brand against her lower back, offering a soothing caress. "For what it's worth—" He bit the inside of his cheek, seeming to weigh what he was about to say. The shadow moved behind his eyes again, telling her that he was uncomfortable with how revealing his words were. "If you walked out of here right now, I wouldn't go looking for someone else. You're the only woman I want to be with tonight."

"Why?" It came out of her with a pang of disbelief. "Please don't say it's because you like the way I look." She didn't want him to want Gili. It would break her heart—it really would.

His breath came out in a soft snort of disbelief. "Because of the way we make each other feel."

He lowered his head to graze his damp lips along her jaw and down to her neck, making her shiver. Her nipples pulled tight so quickly they stung. He chuckled softly at the way she audibly caught her breath.

"We're positively volatile." His hot breath bathed her ear before his teeth lightly closed on her lobe, nearly causing her knees to buckle.

She pressed her hand more firmly to his chest.

"No?" He drew back, but held her close. Held her up, if she was honest.

"I'm trying to think," she gasped, nearly overwhelmed by sensations that were the furthest thing from fear.

"And you can't? Then we feel the same." His tight smile only made the edgy fist of need inside her clench harder. "Feel, *bella*. Feel how much you're exciting me." He moved her hand all the way under the sash, so the pound of his heart slammed into her palm. "This isn't anything I've ever experienced, either."

Her scalp tingled. She dropped her champagne glass,

ignoring the delicate break of crystal, wanting too badly to touch him with both hands. She slid her fingers to the back of his neck and raised her mouth, inviting him to kiss her. It was pure instinct and he didn't hesitate, covering her parted lips as though he'd been let off his leash after having been tempted for too long.

The world stopped then spun the other way, dizzying her. She made one whimpering noise, astonished by how thoroughly such a thing could devastate her, wilting all her muscles.

She distantly heard another delicate shatter, then he picked her up, lifting his head to reveal a fierce expression. Victory? Not quite, but there was something conquering there. Something exalted.

Yet his bright gaze asked a question.

She nodded, unable to speak, just gave herself up to it, to him. She knew when to fight her body and when to surrender. Perhaps it was the silver lining to all those years of having to accept that physiology trumped logic. This was bigger than anything she could make sense of.

He set her on the bed and she watched him throw off his jacket, shaken by the feelings that were carving a valley through her. He joined her and dragged her half under him, kissing her again. Thorough, drugging kisses that set her alight, yet she felt stiff and frozen.

"What's wrong?" He lifted his head, proving himself to be attuned to her in a way that was reassuring and disturbing all at once.

"I'm shy," she admitted, ducking her head as she said it because that wasn't her at *all*. Her eyes stung with emotive tears at how monumental this was. She was alone with a man, on a *bed*, and he had set the sun inside her. He made it radiate outward, filling her with such heat and joy she was going to burst. "I want to touch you, but I don't want to make a fool of myself. I don't know if I can contain myself."

"Don't even try." His voice brimmed with graveled warning, which might have made her chuckle, but she released her breath and let her hands move to greedily stake a claim.

He was firm everywhere, taut and strong. Hot. Her fingers discovered the textures of his clothes, then slid beneath his shirt as he yanked it free of his belted pants. He made an approving noise as she found satin skin and the tension of his abdomen, then the shape of his rib cage and the sleek muscles across his chest. The sharp beads of his nipples fascinated her.

She made her own appreciative noises, utterly rapt with the contrast of his body to her own, all flat planes and crisp hair and indomitable strength.

He released her zip and dragged down the loosened front of her dress. As he bared her breasts, something elemental gripped her. The spirit of womanhood. She melted onto her back and arched, emphasizing their differences, liking that he made a noise that sounded almost suffering, yet growly and ferocious. He opened his mouth and engulfed her in such a place of earthy pleasure, she released her own cry of agonized joy.

Volatile. Was that what this was? She hadn't known she could feel like this, frantic yet intoxicated. Impatient yet timeless. She wanted to stay like this forever, running their hands over each other, kissing, mouths needing to fuse and breathing be damned. But as his hands moved on her, shifting silk with a touch so hot it burned her through the fabric, she wanted more. So much more.

His fingertips grazed the slit in her gown and she found herself offering more of her leg then trembling in anticipation, waiting for the feel of his touch on her skin. The pet of his hand on the outside of her thigh made her shiver. She gloried in the way he kissed her harder, deeper, hand shaping her hip, exploring her belly, then tracking to her other thigh. He squeezed the taut muscle then moved with delicious confidence to cup the center of her.

Breath stalling, eyes opening, she waited for panic, but before she could entertain a grim memory, he firmed his touch and rocked his hand, sending a jolt of incredible pleasure through her pelvis. Her eyelids grew heavy again and she found herself lifting, spellbound by the lightning bolts of sensation that grew in strength as they kissed and he caressed her.

How could anything feel this good?

She wanted to touch him as intimately, but she could hardly think of anything but how he was making her feel. Just as she tried to shape him through his pants, his touch changed, exploring beneath silk with knowledge and intention.

She bucked in reaction. "I can't—My heart is going to explode."

She moved a reflexive hand to cover his, not quite stopping him, because the slide of his fingers against her was so mesmerizing, but so sensitizing she almost couldn't bear it. Her entire focus narrowed to that delicate circle and stroke.

"I want to be inside you, but I don't want to stop touching you. Like that?" He pushed a long finger into her.

She couldn't speak, could only hear a keening noise that came from her as he penetrated and circled where she was so sensitive and molten that she ached. She tightened, trying to savor, trying to hold back the build, but wanton mindlessness took over. Her hips danced against his hand, the pleasure growing too acute to bear, tension growing and growing until she couldn't stand it—

"*Oh!*" Her world exploded in a sudden release that had her shaking and shuddering, flesh pulsing and eyes tearing at the absolute beauty of it.

She pressed his hand still, trying to ease the sensation, trying to catch her breath.

He kissed her, tongue questing for hers, and continued to gently caress her, soothing and teasing so her level of arousal didn't fade, only edged into deeper desire.

With a groan, she rolled into him, strangely ravenous. She wanted the barriers between them gone. Wanted *all of him*. What was he *doing* to her?

He made a feral noise and they tugged at each other's clothing, stripping in seconds, then rolled back together, naked, gloriously naked. Now he was hers, all hers. She swept her hands over him, enamored with his broad shoulders but equally fascinated by his rock-hard biceps and the way his Adam's apple bobbed in a swallow.

When she cradled the fiercest part of him in her palm, she wasn't frightened at all. She felt powerful, especially when he looked agonized and closed his eyes and breathed, *"Bella."*

With a smile, she pressed her mouth to his throat and tried to roll him onto his back. He rolled her beneath him instead, pressing over her as he kissed her, letting her caress him as he used his tongue to mimic what he wanted to do until she couldn't take it and tore her mouth from his. "I need—"

She didn't know what she needed. She was restless and urgent, loins feeling achy and neglected. Empty.

He reached over to the night table then rose over her, knees sliding between hers and parting her legs with effortless strength.

She felt so many things in that moment. Vulnerable, yes, but strangely trusting. It didn't matter if she didn't particularly enjoy this part. She wanted to know she could take a man—

"Oh."

He paused, tip pressing for entry, the invasion startling enough that she tensed.

His head came up. His whole body was taut, his cheeks flushed, his eyes glittering, but there was a shred of man still governing the animal. "I might literally die if you've changed your mind."

Maybe that's what made her smile. Maybe it was the fact her body was so eager for his. Maybe it was simply the joy of this crazy, magical night.

With a little arch, she invited him to complete his thrust and he did with a shudder, sinking deep, gaze never leaving hers, but glowing hot as the center of a flame as their flesh melded.

To say she became a woman under his possession was silly, but she *felt* like a woman in that moment. Mature and whole and *sacred*. She was responding exactly as nature intended under the advances of a mate. *Her* mate. With this act, he gave her back her sexuality, her desire. Her *self*.

She closed her eyes against something too big to contemplate, but it only made the sensations intensify as he took a testing withdraw and return. She shivered as though velvet passed over her skin.

"Yes?"

"Yes," she moaned, savoring the deliciousness that lingered with anticipation for another stroke. "More."

Lucidity faded as he did it again. And again.

He began to thrust with more purpose. She found her hips rising to meet his, longing for the return of his. Needing it. The dance delivered such acute pleasure, she released a strangled groan of enjoyment.

He picked up the tempo and magnificent sensations ran through her. She wanted to tell him but couldn't speak, as she was too enraptured. Tension gripped her. A kind of tortured ecstasy—her body searching for an answering call in his.

She needed him to be as driven beyond himself as she was. To come with her to this place where nothing existed but this new being they had become with their joining. Scraping her nails down his back, she grasped at his buttocks and pulled him into her. Into the eye of the storm.

They struck the pinnacle together, the climax so intense, she opened her mouth in a soundless scream. Pleasure like she had never known flooded in, drowning her as he held himself magnificently deep inside her, throbbing in her jubilant grip as he released a ragged cry of exhilaration and shuddered with completion.

Xavier swore.

"What's wrong?" Trella murmured, hands moving with endless appetite over his damp shoulders.

He withdrew and rolled away. "The condom broke."

She was glad it was dark now. After the first time, they had turned out the lights and slid under the covers to fondle and caress for ages, barely speaking, just kissing and enjoying. Bonding, she might have been tempted to think, yet something in his silence, and the condoms in the night table, told her he had done this a lot.

She had suffered a hollow ache as she'd forced herself to accept that, despite his sweet words, she was merely the woman *du jour* for him. A lady of the night, really.

Whether he had sensed her withdrawal, or she was just that easy, he had grown more passionate. The second time had been even better than the first. Her inhibitions were gone and he held out, giving her two shattering orgasms before taking her on a third ride that nearly killed her, their shared climax being so powerful.

She was too sweaty and lethargic to be triumphant, but she was pretty darned smug at having taken a lover. She had distantly been hoping she had rocked his world as thoroughly as he had rocked hers, but reality struck like a brick through a window at his words.

"It's okay. I won't get pregnant." She swallowed, trying to clear the thickness that gathered in her throat.

"You're on the pill or something?"

Or something. "Yes."

"I have physicals all the time."

"I'm fine, too." Did people really have these conversations? It scraped the romance off a wonderful evening, leaving her thinking about the rest of reality. Guilt crawled in. She had kept secrets from him and—far worse—from her family. They'd be worried sick if they knew where she was.

As if on cue, her phone plinked with the harp notes of her sister's ringtone. Like some kind of empath, Angelique was picking up on her sudden discord.

"I have to get that," Trella murmured, then she groaned. Her muscles ached as though she'd run a marathon. She forced herself to rise and move naked across the shadowed room, finding her clutch where she'd dropped it in the lounge, then came back to the bedroom door.

She stayed there, slyly hoping he was looking at her, silhouetted by the lamplight. In a quick exchange of texts, she reassured her sister she was fine. Gili knew something was up, though. Tendrils of misgivings began working through Trella's system. It was time to call it a night. She needed to hole up at the flat where she knew she was completely safe and process all of this.

"I have to go." She clicked off her phone and sent him a smile of cheerful resignation.

"Is everything all right?" He rose to pull on his pants, not bothering with underwear, which pleased her for some reason, but he didn't invite her to stay, which depressed her as well.

"Just my sister. She needs me to get home." She texted her guard that she would be ready in fifteen minutes and stepped into her thong.

Xavier shook out her gown and brought it to her, then moved behind her as she stepped into it. Hurrying her? She pulled up the gown then lifted her hair while he zipped.

His hands lingered on her skin, not moving, not holding her in place, but his grave words pinned her motionless. "I remember her kidnapping."

She dropped her arms, letting her hair fall over his hands, as helpless and as terrified as she had ever been. Her breastbone turned to ice and her ears strained to hear what he would say next.

"I was fourteen. My father was renouncing the crown. My mother was already gone, exiled by my grandmother for their divorce. I was feeling very sorry for myself. Then I saw photos of this little girl, so pretty and happy, stolen. I stopped worrying what would happen to me. I was so relieved when she was recovered."

His fingertips stayed across her shoulders, not caressing, just resting in small hot prints. She thought she would bruise from the contact. Not in a painful way. It was the opposite of injury. Healing?

He drew in a sharp breath and pulled his touch from her skin. "I don't know why I said that. It was far too personal for both of us. You're clearly still worried about her if you're rushing off." He bent to retrieve her shoes. "I hope she's all right."

It was me. She should have said it, but her throat was too tight.

She knew there were people who had rooted for her family all the way along, but it was so wrapped up in their notoriety, she didn't differentiate the kindly meant from the intrusive or downright cruel. Her family hadn't asked to be famous for the odd trick of nature that had created two sets of identical twins. They were just people, perhaps better looking by certain standards, definitely richer than average, but regular humans.

Yet the world was insatiably curious about what brand of soap they used and held strong opinions on how they should conduct themselves.

To have this man, who was completely removed from it, reveal such a personal memory connected to her affected her, changing the careful constructs inside her. Defenses that held darkness at bay while keeping her open to the people who loved her shifted and angled to provide space for him to enter.

No. She couldn't let him in! Tie herself to a man? Lose herself behind someone else's goals and wishes and expectations when she had so many unreached aspirations of her own? She couldn't attach herself to someone whose life was bigger than hers. She was trying to escape all the restraints that had bound her for so long.

Shaken at how vulnerable she was to him, she jiggled her bodice against her breasts, then perched on a chair to strap on her shoes, hands trembling.

"Is she really as beautiful as you?" He watched her with his fists pushed into his pockets. His naked shoulders were relaxed and outlined in pale gold while the shadows in his face suggested a brooding expression. The dark patch of his chest hair narrowed to a suggestive line, arrowing to his navel, then lower.

He was the beautiful one. She memorized this last intimate glimpse of him.

"Exactly as beautiful." She smiled, amused with her own joke, then poignant gratitude accosted her. "Thank you for tonight. I—" She stopped herself from saying something truly gauche.

She wanted to ask if he'd meant it when he'd said it wasn't always like this for him. She wanted to tell him what he had given her. She wanted to get out of here before she revealed too much.

She glanced at the clock. If she didn't show her face promptly, her guard would knock and enter. They were paid very well to be diligent and investigate when she wasn't where she said she would be.

Xavier moved to offer a hand, helping her to her feet. "Thank *you*. This was lovely." The words came off lighthearted, punching into her as she imagined the legions of other women who had heard such offhand praise. Not even, *I won't forget you*. Just, *this was lovely*. A pleasant meal. Nothing life-changing.

He brought her hand to his mouth, exactly as he had when they'd met, except this time he turned her hand over and kissed her palm.

Trying to hide how deeply that affected her, she said, "Goodnight, sweet Prince."

He snorted. "I could have you beheaded for that."

With a lightning move, he pulled her close and wove his fingers into her hair, planting a real kiss, a final one, on her mouth. It was painfully sweet. Thorough, yet tender. Oddly heartbreaking.

For her.

And even though she was the one to draw back, her lips clung to his. Temptation to stay, to say more, gripped her, but he distracted her.

"You've lost an earring." His fingertip flicked at her lobe.

"No!" Both hands went to her ears, finding one empty. "Here? In the room? Did you notice if I had both while we were downstairs?"

"I'll buy you new ones," he offered with an offhand shrug.

"They're sentimental. A gift from my father." *To Gili.* She clicked on the lamp and flung back the bed covers, searching.

A polite knock tapped on the main door, her guard telling her the car was in position. They avoided waiting whenever possible. It drew a crowd.

"I'll find it and send it to you at the design house."

"Promise?" She looked from his muscled chest to the sheets to his eyes. Oh, he was spectacular in the golden light, emptying her brain all over again.

"I only make promises I can keep."

"Thank you." She didn't bother worrying about him addressing it to Angelique. She would intercept it or come clean if she had to. "I really did, um, enjoy this."

His eyes warmed with laughter. "My pleasure, *bella.*"

She was starting to sound like the neophyte she was. Definitely time to make her escape. She ducked her head and made for the coach before she turned into a pumpkin.

CHAPTER THREE

Present day...

COMMUNICATIONS FROM PRINCE XAVIER'S grandmother fell into three categories. All were delivered by the palace's Private Secretary, Mario de Gaul.

"Your grandmother requests a meeting to discuss..." Fill in the blank. Those were routine and benign. She listened to her grandson's opinions and they worked together on a strategy for whatever event, negotiation or dignified visitor stood on the horizon. They were equals, more or less.

The second, more ominous type of appointment began with "Her Majesty invites you to join her at..." Fill in the meal. Those were more dictatorial instructions on how she wanted something handled. A parliamentarian or ambassador needed massaging. A high-level staff member needed firing. He was doing her dirty work.

Then there was—

"The Queen is in her receiving room. She expects you."

Mario entered with that missive on the heels of Xavier's Personal Assistant, who still stood before him, his speech bubble of grim news dissolving in the air above his pleading don't-shoot-the-messenger expression.

"Of course." Xavier rose from his desk. It was the appropriate response. One didn't refuse the Queen. One certainly didn't leave her waiting.

Still, his agile brain leapt to all the triage he needed to accomplish in the next few minutes, not least of which was to reassure his new fiancée, Patrizia, before she saw the headlines herself.

Switched Before Birth!
Future King an Expectant Father?
Trella Tricked Everyone—Including the Prince!

He should have said something a few weeks ago, of course, when the first bomb went off. Trella Sauveterre, lately returned to the public eye, had turned up pregnant. The reaction had been loud enough to shake the world off its axis, forcing him to reach out to her, again, much to his dismay. He didn't want anything to do with her after realizing how thoroughly she'd duped him.

Why had she done it?

The sting of chasing her to Berlin a week after Paris, like a fool with his first crush, came back hot and fresh under his skin. He'd had a very real duty to meet with Patrizia, but he had put it off, stealing an extra few days of bachelorhood, inventing excuses so he could…what? Have sex with a stranger once more?

Sex was sex. He'd had many lovers over the years and experienced varied degrees of pleasure. He put down the better experiences to chemistry, the less satisfying ones to inhibitions and incompatibility.

That night in Paris had seemed extraordinary while it was happening. She hadn't been a virgin, but she'd made sex feel new again. She'd been so responsive. So sensual. So *abandoned*. His stomach tightened just remembering it.

So what? He knew from his father's history that letting the brain below his belt do his thinking was disastrous.

Nevertheless, a day later, when he had read that *Angelique* would be in Berlin, he had reconfigured his entire schedule. Rather than courier her earring as promised, he had sought her out—only to find her with another man.

It had been the most lowering of moments, not because his ego was dented, but because he had revealed something of himself to her. Somehow, she had tricked him into believing they had a connection that went beyond the physical. What had possessed him to talk of those dark hours when his parents had been banished?

He didn't form intimate friendships. He was an only child raised by a grandmother whose life was too demanding to offer affection. Yet, for some reason, he had entrusted a one-night lover with his private thoughts.

He had trusted *her*. When she had said she didn't sleep around, he had believed her.

Judging by what he found in Berlin, however, she'd moved on very quickly. The innocent act was part of her routine, he had concluded, castigating himself for acting so callow as to follow her.

Nevertheless, when he had the chance to catch her alone, he approached, waiting for the catch of excitement she had kindled in him the week before.

Nothing. She was desirable the way all beautiful women were, but whatever he'd felt in Paris was gone. It had perplexed and annoyed him, made him doubly irritated with himself for thinking they'd had something special.

He's stood there searching for whatever it was that he'd found so enthralling and she had pretended she didn't even know him, staring blankly as though he had broken into her bedroom and stolen the diamond hoop earring he was returning.

In those seconds, he had felt as though she was even more of a stranger than she had been before they'd made love—which she was, he promptly learned. He hadn't slept with Angelique. He had slept with her twin, Trella.

The revelation had been welcome and infuriating. He didn't care for dishonest people, but his desire to see Trella had renewed itself. He had asked Angelique to pass along his contact details, wanting an explanation. Wanting something he refused to acknowledge, but...

Nothing.

Not one returned call, message or text.

What did it matter? He made himself get over her, focusing on more important things, primarily his duty to marry.

He had made a concerted effort to avoid all headlines containing the name Sauveterre, which wasn't easy. First, the mysterious, reclusive Trella had come out at a friend's wedding. That had kept the gossip industry booming through spring and summer, along with other news within the family, making it a challenge for him to change channels or flick screens fast enough to avoid catching sight of her.

Then, just as things seemed to have died down, she'd been caught climbing from her brother's car looking less svelte than in previous photos. *Pregnant*, the avid Sauveterre watchers speculated.

So what if she was? It didn't make a hill of beans difference to anyone's life, least of all his.

Still, Xavier had looked closely at the photos that emerged, one showing her in a stunning maternity gown at her brother's engagement party. She didn't look *very* pregnant. She had said she was on the pill. If she was carrying his child, she would have returned his calls. He didn't have anything to worry about, he assured himself.

This latest inflammatory sound bite was more of the same. Had to be. He had a walk-on part in the episodic drama that was the Sauveterre serial. He had slept with her *one night*. He resented being drawn into scandal for it. He was now engaged. That made besmirching his name unforgiveable. Immediately after allaying his grandmother's concern, he would insist Trella clear him of involvement so he could reassure Patrizia their marriage plans could continue.

Damn it, he had completely forgotten about Patrizia. He paused to text.

I'll have this cleared up shortly.

Their match was perfect in every way. Not only would it strengthen both of their countries, but they liked each other. Neither had unrealistic notions like love and passion to muddy the waters. She was nursing a bruised heart and was keen for a stable, reliable situation. A civilized relationship, she kept calling it.

He was pleased to perform his duty in a way he could stand. Patrizia was intelligent, attractive, well-bred. She would have children for the same reason he would: They were expected to. They respected one another. They were on the same page.

He wanted this marriage.

Mario paused with him and knocked, then announced him.

His grandmother didn't rise as Xavier entered. She didn't even look up from whatever she was writing with her antique silver pen. The crackle in the fireplace became the only sound along with the scratch of her pen.

He took the bull by the horns. "I'll refute it and press charges against the source."

The pen went down and she peered at him over her glasses. She was a well-preserved seventy, her eyes were the same Deunoro blue as his own, her hair more iron than silver. She was overdue to start her morning audiences, which always made her salty.

"The Queen Mother of Zhamair is the source."

Xavier's PA had also pointed out that the story had stemmed from Angelique's soon-to-be mother-in-law. "I haven't had a chance to confirm that. If she made a statement, I'm sure it's in reaction to some online nonsense."

"She is reacting, I am informed, to remarks made about her son and his fiancée. She wanted to set the record straight that Angelique was not the woman kissing you in the photos that emerged some months ago from Paris. Angelique has always been faithful to King Kasim. Is that true?"

"I couldn't say whether she's been faithful, but I'm told I was with Trella."

"You were *told*?"

"They're twins." He shrugged, not bothering to feel awkward discussing his sex life with his grandmother. She had had "The Talk" with him herself when he was an adolescent, explaining in no uncertain terms that royalty did *not* produce bastards and had offered explicit tips on how to prevent such a thing.

"That particular twin is pregnant." She used her most imperious tone. "A source intimately connected to her family has stated you were with her at an appropriate time for conception. Did you take precautions?"

"Of course."

The condom broke. Are you on the pill?
Yes.

"She would have told me if there were consequences." Tension gathered in the pit of his gut. He didn't know which one of them he was trying to convince. "Any woman who sets out to trap a man does not hide it for six months. Even if it was an accident, there's no reason to keep it from me. She might be pregnant, but *it's not mine*."

Her brows went up in regal disdain. "Perhaps you should confirm that."

As if that hadn't occurred to him? "Of course," he said. Dutifully.

"Because it would be a shame if this were to cause any delay in our schedule." She intended to step down the minute he was married. To Patrizia.

"Understood."

It was hot in Innsbruck, despite the elevation and the calendar showing the last days of summer. But maybe the heat was caused by this extra human she was carrying.

Trella lifted her face into the gentle breeze, enjoying the sweet scent of it. She was six months along and felt it, even though she wasn't showing much. Her mother had possessed the same tall, model-slender figure and had barely shown with twins until the very end. This was only one and with the right clothes, she barely looked pregnant.

She needed that ambiguity. Prince Xavier's texts had devolved to the two-word kind.

Call me.

She had ignored the latest, received this morning, exactly as she'd ignored every other text and call she'd received from him, the first immediately after he'd met Angelique in Berlin, and most recently after she'd been exposed by her sister's soon-to-be mother-in-law as the twin in his arms at the ball in Paris.

She had her reasons. That's what she kept telling herself, even though it was pure emotion that drove her and that emotion was cowardice.

"They're blocked by a service vehicle," her guard, Benita, said of their car, lifting her gaze from her phone to continue her scan of the street. "Let's wait inside."

Benita was as tall as Trella and had a mannish demeanor when she was on the job. No nonsense, no makeup, hair scraped into a bun, communications terse.

Trella didn't mind. She wasn't the most cooperative principal. To her occasional chagrin, she was a high maintenance person in every way. Acknowledging that about herself didn't stop her from saying, "I'd rather stay out here."

The day was gorgeous and she would be on bed rest soon. She wanted to enjoy the outside world while she could.

"Killian said—"

"I know. Take extra precautions." She scoffed at a lot of things, but not security reports. "I spoke to Sadiq. He's the one who discovered the hack and restored all the firewalls. No one even knows I'm here."

Except the handful of people inside the building who had just taken selfies with her. They were no doubt posting those as she spoke. She was a celebrity, whether she liked it or not. It was only a matter of minutes before lookie-loos began pulling over, wanting their own photo with a Sauveterre, especially the elusive pregnant one.

"My gut doesn't like it."

"Because Killian trains you to be overprotective."

Benita had tried to cancel this trip as soon as the security bulletin had come through. Trella wasn't sure why she had insisted on making what amounted to a house call for a joint venture she wasn't sure she would pursue, but she had.

Ah, she knew why she had come. For starters, her sister

had been doing this kind of thing on her behalf for years. It was yet another burden she had placed on her twin and it was her turn to pay it back, now that Angelique was starting her life with Kasim.

Oh, her sister was in love. It was as majestic a sight to behold as the timeless sparkling peaks around them. Trella was deeply happy for her, but so very envious.

Her gaze tracked to the sharpest, highest peaks to the south. To Elazar.

Was he texting from inside that border, sitting in his palace office, cursing her for ignoring him?

A flutter in her midsection had her resisting the urge to press her hand across her belly. She didn't like to draw attention to her pregnancy when she was in public. Besides, it wasn't the baby that caused that stir in her middle. It was a complex mix of emotions.

She wanted to tell him she was grateful. She wanted to see him again, to discover if the magical connection she'd felt in Paris had been real or just a product of an exciting foray into independence. She wanted him to know they were expecting a baby.

She also wanted to hold their night in her memory as the ideal that it was. She didn't want the harsh fallout she would have to face once she acknowledged this baby as his. Most of all, she didn't want to be a burden on a man who had seemed too perfect to want anything to do with someone as flawed as she was.

Her expected black sedan with its darkened windows slid up to the curb.

"There. See?" Trella said, even as she noted a man approaching in her periphery.

"That's not—" Benita's voice cut off.

Perhaps Trella went deaf at that moment because nothing penetrated beyond the fact that the back door opened and the Prince of Elazar rose from the interior.

He was as remarkable as she remembered. Like a knight of legend, his hair shot with glints of gold, his visage sharp and stern, his air one of heroic power. He was so godlike, she couldn't move. She was too mesmerized.

Then reality rushed in as a scuffling noise and a grunt penetrated. She swung her gaze to see Benita in a fight. A *fight*. With a *man*. He tried to twist Benita's arm behind her back as she bent forward, trying to use leverage to flip him.

Training, the kind Trella had attended to daily until pregnancy had sent her into yoga and water aerobics, jolted her into action. As Benita's attacker pulled back his weight, dragging Benita off her feet, Trella stepped in and nailed him with a solid, knuckle-bruising punch, right in the nose.

The man grunted and Benita twisted, nearly escaping.

"What the *hell* are you doing?" That *accent*. Strong hands grasped her upper arms and pulled her away from the struggling pair.

Trella turned into him, stomach flip-flopping in response as she felt his solid abdomen against her bump. Adrenaline coursed through her, but she only felt reassurance as he drew her protectively close. Her gaze stayed over her shoulder, fixed on the fight, which seemed to be more of a wrestle for dominance. A bloody nose wasn't slowing down the man and Benita wasn't giving up, biting out in Spanish, "Run."

"Help her—Wait. What are *you* doing?" Trella cried as she realized she was being shoved into the back of the car.

Xavier easily overpowered her, pushing her in and following without ceremony.

She was so shocked that it took her a moment to resist.

By then his big body had created a wall of shoulders and chest that were impossible to get past.

Before she could touch the door on her side, he pulled his own closed and the locks clicked. The car pulled away, leaving her guard scrapping on the sidewalk with a brute whose shirt was the same color as both men in the front of this car.

Far too late, she realized what was happening.

She was being kidnapped. *Again.*

CHAPTER FOUR

"Stop this car. *Now*."

Xavier respected her ability to sound so authoritative, but he ignored her and opened the privacy window long enough to accept an ice pack from his physician, Gunter, then tapped the button to close it.

"Hello, Trella. Have I got that right?" He knew he had the right one. It was impossible to explain, but the minute he had seen her, he had known.

He pushed aside the ridiculous high that rocketed through him as he finally had her alone and held out his palm. He wiggled his fingers, urging her to release the pendant she was pinching and let him examine her hand.

"What were you thinking, getting involved in that?" The mix of rage and fear he'd experienced at seeing her step into the fight was reflected in his tone. Even if she wasn't pregnant, it would have been a foolhardy, danger-ous thing to do.

But she was pregnant. There was no denying it. The narrow waist he'd held in the crook of his arm had thick-ened with an undeniable bump. Her breasts…

He dragged his gaze up, refusing to let fantasies side-track him, but her features were a distraction all on their own. Her face was rounder, her mouth lush and pouted. The urge to kiss her struck him with a fierce pull.

Damn it, what *was* it about her?

He met her glare with his own, thinking that he would have sworn her eyes were green, but they were steely. Bright as a cornered cat refusing to stay that way.

"I thought I was preventing myself from being kidnapped. Once again, I have trusted the wrong person." Her unpainted lips seemed bloodless, which gave him a moment of pause, but too much of his life had been set off balance by her. He wanted answers. Today.

"It's not a kidnapping." He set the ice pack near her thigh. "It's an improvised meeting to discuss mutual business, so drop your pendant. I know it's a tracking device. Your guard won't be harmed, only delayed. Your car can't chase us. It's still blocked."

"Which sounds a lot like a kidnapping." A harsh ringtone emanated from her purse. "That's for you." She pulled out her phone and used her thumbprint to accept the call then handed it to Xavier. Her hand might have trembled.

Desperate times called for desperate measures, he'd told himself when he'd concocted this intervention. As he picked up on Trella's shaken nerves, he wondered if he was using a sledgehammer to kill a fly. It hadn't occurred to him she might be anything but angry at having her timetable interrupted. He couldn't be happier if he inconvenienced the hell out of her. He was beyond incensed at the way she was impacting his life without any attempt to mitigate it.

Explaining that would have to wait. He'd been warned to expect this video call. He took the phone and met the formidable expression of a man who resembled Trella. Henri, Xavier suspected, since the other brother was in Brazil.

"Your demands?" Henri asked without greeting.

"A blood sample for a DNA test."

Trella made a strangled noise. "Like hell."

He glanced at her. "I would accept her word as to

whether she's carrying my heir, but she's lied to me more than once already."

Xavier willed her to lash out with denials of his paternity. With an explanation. An *apology*.

She hitched her chin and turned her face to the window.

"Return her to where you took her. I'll see what I can do about the blood test."

"You can't even get her to return a call. I can't wait any longer."

Trella's silence was gut-knottingly damning. Whatever lingering favor he had felt toward her went ashen and bitter. A jagged lump hardened in his throat. He swallowed it, but the acrimony only moved to burn as a hot knot behind his collarbone. Each minute that she failed to deny his paternity was a tiny, incremental progression toward accepting what he had been refusing to believe. What he still didn't want to believe.

"I have your coordinates," Henri said, dragging Xavier back from staring at the woman who was ruining his life. "A team has been dispatched. We don't need an incident. Return her to Innsbruck."

"If you're tracking us, you know we'll be in Elazar soon." Xavier leaned toward the window to see a helicopter chasing from the distance. "I'll close the borders if I have to, but she's perfectly safe, especially if that's our future monarch inside her. Stand down from trying to stop us."

"Unless my sister gives me her safe word, this escalates."

Xavier handed her the phone. "Your move, *bella*."

She flashed him a sharp glance then looked at her brother.

"We're coming," Henri said.

"I know." She nodded, pale and grave, then said, "Begonia."

"Vous êtes certain?"

"*Sí.*"

"That's tomorrow's word," Xavier said.

She shot him a startled frown.

He shrugged. "I do my homework."

"Then you'll know I'm buying you twenty-four hours." She turned back to her phone, expression haughty. "I'm sure Killian knows by now who hacked him. Ask him to drop a virus into the Elazar palace networks, won't you?"

"Killian has Elazar's Minister of Foreign Affairs on the phone, along with a more aggressive team assembled."

Xavier suspected that remark was more for his benefit.

"*Gracias.* Tell him I'll handle it."

"Will you?"

A leaden silence followed where she only gave her brother a tight-lipped look.

Xavier wondered if others were also frustrated by the avoidance game she had been playing.

"*Bien,*" Henri said. "If I don't hear from you every hour, your prince may expect a gun against his temple. *Je t'aime.*"

"*Te amo.*" She ended the call and slipped her phone back into her purse, then folded her hands into her lap. "Why did you say I lied to you more than once?"

Xavier admired the way she attempted to take control of the conversation, but he was not prepared to give her any concessions until he had what he wanted.

"Why did you speak Spanish and he, French? Was it code?"

"Habit."

She tried to leave it there, but he lifted a skeptical brow.

"It's true. Our father was French, Mama is Spanish. We grew up speaking both. I only told one lie."

"That you were on birth control."

"That I was Angelique. You asked if I was on the pill

or something. I said yes because that was true. At least, I thought it was." She bit the corner of her lip.

"Your *or something* failed?"

She flinched, making him realize his voice carried a thickness close to contempt or even hatred.

He grappled to hang onto his temper. "You assured me pregnancy wasn't possible. How have we arrived at having this conversation?"

Dumb question. They both knew how babies were made. They'd made love. She had come apart in his arms again and again. He'd been greedy as a starved beast certain he would die from the pleasure of being inside her when she shattered around him like that. Then, when he couldn't hold back any longer, he had joyously thrown himself into the small death of simultaneous orgasm.

In that post-climactic moment, when her breaths had still been jagged and his heart had pounded against her sweating breasts, he had felt...restored. Not just a release of tension but as though deeper needs had been met. Withdrawing had provoked a painful, abandoned sensation he had impatiently tried to forget.

"*Is that my child?*"

She jolted at the grate in his tone. "You said you wouldn't believe me no matter what I said."

"You'll submit to a blood test, then?"

Her eyes narrowed in mutiny.

"You can submit nicely or I can pin you down while my doctor takes it." He was clearly a sadist because something in him longed for her to push him into restraining her.

"Touch me and I'll break *your* nose." She started to lift a threatening fist and flinched, quickly cradling her right hand—which is what she'd been doing since her hands had gone into her lap, he realized.

He caught her wrist and held on when she tried to pull

away. The backs of her fingers were an angry red, her knuckles puffy.

His heart lurched.

"Did you break any bones? Can you move your fingers? That's what this is for." He picked up the ice pack, incensed all over again that she had waded into the fight.

"I know how to throw a punch." She took the ice and flexed her fingers against it, showing only a wince of discomfort so he presumed she hadn't fractured anything.

"What were you thinking? It's a damned good thing his reflexes didn't take over. You would have been on the ground."

"My bodyguard was being assaulted."

"No, *my* bodyguard was moving into position to cover *me*. *She* attacked *him*. Then you did. Do you understand what bodyguards are paid to do? There is no reason you should have involved yourself."

Her brows flicked in dismissal of his concern.

Was this really the mother of his heir? If he'd gone to a brothel and bought a *man*, he couldn't have picked someone less suitable.

"A simple blood test could prove I'm not the father. We could have it done before we cross the border." He pointed at the sign they passed that stated they were less than a mile away.

"I'm afraid of needles."

"Be afraid of *me, bella*."

Her flat smile died. Something vulnerable flashed in her expression.

His conscience pinched.

"Is that the problem?" His voice still sounded gruff and aggressive. His animosity hadn't evaporated just because he was finally getting answers. He didn't want to soften toward her at all. She was far too dangerous. But fear was an explanation he could understand.

"Have you been afraid of my reaction? I'm not happy." That was a gross understatement. A well-practiced aloof demeanor had always served him well, but it was impossible to find in the face of this life-altering situation. Still, he tried to reassure her. "Nothing bad will happen if the baby is mine. I'll recognize him or her as our future monarch. We will marry so it's legitimate. That's all. No stake burnings or feeding to dragons. Were you afraid I'd pressure you to terminate? Is that why you've kept it from me?"

Silence. She turned her attention out the side window again, so he couldn't read her expression.

"Do you not *know* who the father is? How many contenders are there?"

Her glare swung like a blade to slice through him.

"I don't *care* how many men you've slept with." Much. He was disturbed to realize he did, actually. It wasn't because of the paternity question, either. The passion between them had been unprecedented. He didn't like to think she reacted that way to every man she slept with. It would have made all of this even more intolerable.

"How pregnant are you? Let's see if that eliminates me, shall we?"

"Pregnant enough to need a pit stop. Can we stop here?"

"No." The border guard waved them through with only a very minor slowing of their speed, recognizing the plates. "We'll be at my chalet shortly."

The car sped along the pass that formed part of the border between Austria and Elazar. As they rounded a bend, the valley opened, allowing a glimpse of Lirona, the capital, once a modest fiefdom, now a thriving city of culture, intellect and wealth. It sat like a heart against the shore of

Lac Lirona, the arms of the mountains stretching out to embrace the blue water he loved with everything in him.

Over the centuries, his ancestors had fought to maintain their governance over this small kingdom many times. His great-grandmother had taken up with one of Hitler's top advisors to keep the Nazi invasion at occupation rather than annihilation.

That is where the bar is set when it comes to duty, his grandmother had extolled as a history lesson, explaining why Xavier's father was unfit to rule. *We are custodians. We do what we must. To put yourself before Elazar is treason.*

This, because his father had followed his libido into a high-profile affair with a topless waitress from Amsterdam then married the woman's aunt, owner of a drug café. His divorce from Xavier's mother had already been ugly and, even worse in his grandmother's eyes, *common*.

His grandmother was a hard woman—her father, King Ugo, hadn't forgiven his wife and Queen Julia had grown up in a harsh climate of blame and sacrifice. If her spare had survived, things might have been different. Instead, she had forced her only son to renounce the throne, disowning him and keeping her grandson as Elazar's future.

It was all on Xavier to perpetuate the monarchy into the next generation. He had planned to do so through an elegant association with Patrizia, a respected princess with a degree in social justice and a pedigree that couldn't be faulted.

Instead, he had behaved as impulsively as his father, tangling with a fashion designer whose life was stained with one scandal after another.

He was running out of hope that her child was not his. Whether his grandmother could find it in her to forgive him for this transgression didn't matter.

He would never forgive himself.

CHAPTER FIVE

AS SOMEONE WHO had grown up in obscene wealth, Trella didn't bat an eye at the chalet that turned out to be a three-story modern fortress with a nod to its rustic ancestors in its gables and tiered verandas.

She was more interested in counting pairs of eyes—one at the gate, two at the door, the physician who followed them into the house, the chauffeur who took the car around to what she presumed was the garage, a butler who greeted them and a woman named Inga who was asked to prepare tea.

"Powder room?" Trella clung by her fingernails to control.

Ghosts—terrible, terrible ghosts—were creeping in at the edges of her consciousness, but something pressured to diamond brightness inside her kept her from becoming hysterical. *This time she would get away.*

As each of the Prince's attempts to draw her out had pulled at her laser-like focus, she had resentfully allowed that she was taking the rough road, not the high one. She could still call in a team to break her out if she wanted, but a furious, too often helpless, part of her demanded she prove she could rescue herself.

Over the last months, she had come close many times to calling him. The problem was, she wasn't as stupid as many would conclude from her behavior. She knew what would happen and he had confirmed it. He would marry her.

Which meant a profile in the public eye that was even higher than the one she already occupied. One from which she couldn't retreat at will.

Worse, it meant being honest with him. She would have to reveal exactly how crazy she was. She would have to explain these ghouls tickling across her skin, making her want to scratch herself all over. The nightmare could spring to life with a beat of her heart, the cold sweats and shaking, the profound helplessness…

She hadn't suffered an attack since well before their night in Paris, but one ticked like a bomb inside her. She could feel it. But *no*. She wouldn't succumb, even though fighting it made it worse. She knew that.

With a dry mouth, she locked herself into a bathroom that smelled of potpourri. The small space was pristine, with a porcelain sink in a cherry wood vanity. She glanced from the full bath and shower to the frosted window that, once carefully opened, looked out onto the woods at the back of the house.

No balcony below this window, but it was big enough to allow a woman with a modest six month swelling in her middle to crawl through, and close enough to the nearby balcony she could swing a leg that direction and clamber across.

Not a kidnapping? Damned right it wasn't.

"I'm sure she'll come around," Xavier told Gunter. He hadn't lied when he had threatened to hold her down, but he didn't want to. It wasn't his habit to manhandle any woman, pregnant or otherwise. "Did she look six months to you?"

Gunter shook his head. "It's difficult to say. Every woman carries differently. The fact she was able to hide it so long leads me to wonder, but…"

They needed a blood test.

"And this?" Xavier waved to where she had disappeared to use the toilet.

"Extremely common. Although…" He glanced at his watch.

That's what Xavier had thought. He hadn't taken his eyes from the closed door and she was still in there. He didn't want to be indelicate, but he moved to knock.

Silence.

Fainted? His heart swerved.

"Trella." He tried the handle, found it locked and rattled it. "She wouldn't have—" The window dropped about thirty-two feet to the ground. That's why he hadn't bothered assigning someone to watch that side of the chalet.

"I'll send someone to check." Gunter hurried away, moving through the kitchen as Inga appeared with keys and a concerned expression.

Xavier gave the key a hard twist and walked into an empty powder room. A fresh breeze came through the open window. He glanced out to see Gunter below, holding Trella's clutch, a grim expression on his face as he tracked the distance to the nearest balcony.

At least *she* wasn't lying in the dirt below. Tramping through the alps in trendy heels wasn't much better. Damn it, this woman was turning into a nightmare.

"Alert security," he told Inga, and he strode outside to join the search.

Crammed beneath the sink was a little too much like the horrid cellar she'd been locked in during her first kidnapping. The shelf had easily moved to the bottom of the vanity, making room for her to curl herself on top of it, but she'd had to cover herself with the towels and was overheating.

Panicking.

No. One minute at a time. *Uno naranjo, dos naranjos...* She counted the seconds, counted the oranges, a scent she always associated with family since they had a grove of them at Sus Brazos. She would get through this. It was another test of her ability to move on from her past.

She did her breathing exercises while she listened for footsteps. When she was confident everyone had moved outside, she carefully opened the cupboard door and groped her way out of the small space, thankful for her yoga practice.

Carrying her shoes, she paused at the door. There were security cameras. She had noted one in the foyer as they'd entered. Someone would be watching the screens. She had to move fast, but—*thank you, Killian*—she had what amounted to an SOS flare in her phone. It was supposed to be for signaling help, but she hoped it could have another use.

She took the device from her bra, turned on the blinding white light, and walked into the hall, aiming the beam directly at the first camera she came to. It sat like a brilliant spotlight on the dark orb. She prayed it blinded the lens as she hurried through the house to the garage.

There was no one in the kitchen and keys hung neatly on the hook beside the door. She tucked her phone back into her bra and took all the keys, deducing from a keychain which one belonged to the top-down cobalt blue Audi.

Outside the garage doors, she heard footsteps jogging across gravel.

Her entire body trembled, but she fought to keep a focused mind. She *wasn't* helpless. She *would* get away.

She set all the keys on the passenger seat and climbed behind the wheel of the Audi, then hit the button on the visor to open the garage door, ready to start the car as soon as the door climbed high enough.

There was a click, the hum of a motor and a rattle of effort, but the door didn't budge. She jabbed her finger onto the button again, glancing at the jumble of keys. Should she take a different car?

The door to the interior of the chalet opened and Xavier came into the shadowed garage.

Nooooo! She jabbed again and again at the stupid button, then started the car with a roar of its high-performance engine.

"The house is locked down. Don't try to drive through the door. It's reinforced. You'll hurt yourself. And my car." He moved past the other three vehicles with smooth steps, pausing beside her to lean in and turn off the engine, pocketing the key. "But that was a very good try. I'm impressed."

She gripped the steering wheel, staring straight ahead, concentrating on not revealing the tears gathering hotly behind her eyes.

"Come back into the house."

"No."

"We'll talk here then." He moved to flick a switch on the wall. A fan came to life with a low drone, quickly sucking away the lingering exhaust.

He came back to set an elbow on the top of the windscreen. She felt his eyes studying her, but kept her nose pointed forward.

"I'm trying to be patient, *bella*, I really am, but I don't understand why you're being so combative. This doesn't have to be a fight."

"I could drive this, you know. Probably better than you."

"Not without keys."

"You'd be surprised." She worked her hands on the steering wheel's soft leather, more than a little enamored with cars, thanks to Ramon. "I can hotwire and drive anything. I've been up to two hundred and twenty on a closed circuit in my brother's Pur Sang. The Gs nearly crack my ribs when I brake from that speed, but it's quite a rush. Have you ever driven this the way it was designed to drive?"

"No." His tone was one of forced patience.

"Ramon got into racing after taking evasive driving lessons. We all had to take them." Like Ramon, she had tried to outrun herself on the track more than once, but it was never a permanent solution. At some point, she had to park the car, take off the helmet and face reality. "Because of my kidnapping."

She sensed him grow very still, indicating she had his full attention.

Had he thought that wouldn't come up? She hated that it defined her, but it did. She worked around it as often as she could, but when she did have to face it, she did it head-on with her foot to the floor, even though it also had the power to crack her ribs and shatter everything inside her.

As the silence lengthened, she suspected he was reviewing what he had said in Paris—when he had thought he was talking about her but had been speaking *to* her.

"You think *you* were worried when I was stolen." Her voice trembled against her will. She soothed herself by running light fingers across the bumps in the bottom of the steering wheel, playing over them like keys on a piano, but her hands shook.

His voice was grave. "If I was triggering you today, you should have said."

"Really?" A smile touched lips that felt so dry they

might split. Her body vibrated with fight-or-flight. She was going to crash hard after this, but she couldn't think about that yet. "Because I did tell you to take me back and you ignored me. Which is exactly what happened the first time."

Her knuckles whitened where she grasped the wheel again, trying to keep a grip on herself. It was time for the head-on collision.

"I said *stop*, and *no*, and *please* so many times I lost count. I said it when they threw me in their van and I could see Ramon running after us. I said it when one of them pulled me onto his lap and shoved his hand under my skirt and *hurt* me. I said it when he slapped me because I was fighting him. I said it when he locked me in a cold, dark cellar and I said it a lot when he let me out three days later, only to put me on a filthy stinking mattress and call me lucky. *Lucky.* Because he was going to show me what men liked."

She knew it was an assault to throw that at him. It was one of the reasons she rarely spoke about it, but she wanted to hurt him. She wanted to *scar* him.

"I should check with my therapist, see if my experience of being assaulted might create a profound desire to control my own destiny. Gosh, what an enlightening moment of self-discovery you've provided, Xavier. Yes, I'm quite sure that's why I'm *combative*."

He couldn't move, wasn't even sure he was breathing, as he tried to un-hear what she'd said. Who would do such a thing? To a *child*?

He didn't have a particular affinity for children, not having had a childhood to speak of himself. Royal duties took him into contact with them, but children were just one more foreign culture with whom certain rituals were observed. He didn't live among them or desire to.

What he did understand was that they were vulnerable. Those who exploited the weak were beneath contempt. Only a true monster would hurt someone as helpless as a nine-year-old girl, especially sexually.

"I didn't think I could get pregnant." Trella's thin voice echoed off the concrete and steel of his garage, underpinned by the drone of the fan. Her profile was pale and still, grayed by the half-light beyond the row of windows in the doors. "The damage he did was that bad. Do you understand what I'm saying? Because I don't want to get any more specific."

A twisted, anguished feeling struck his middle, clenching talons around his chest and squeezing his throat, pushing fear and helplessness to such heights inside him, it became a pressure he could barely withstand. He knew his heart was beating because it throbbed with painful pounds that rang in his ears, but he couldn't move or speak.

There were no words, no reactions, that fit this situation. Only a primal scream that would have no effect whatsoever. It wouldn't reverse the past, wouldn't erase her dark memories. He was at a complete loss.

"When I realized I was pregnant, I had to give the baby a chance. Even though the odds were against it. I've been expecting a miscarriage every single day. What was the point in telling you if I was only going to lose it? Even now, I'm terrified of becoming too attached in case something happens."

It was his. The knowledge crashed over him like a wave, bringing a sharp sting of heightened awareness to his whole body. It changed everything. His entire life, every decision and action, filtered in a blur through this lens of a new life they had created.

The cogs in his brain finally began turning, but with a rustiness that scraped at his detachment.

"So this is…delicate?" What if she lost it? For some reason, neat as that solution might sound, the idea appalled him. "Are you all right?" He should have asked these questions the minute he'd had her alone. "Has this put you into labor? Are you in pain?"

"No." She skimmed her hair out of her eyes and let herself relax into the seat of the car, hands settling over her bump. Her complexion was pale, but she sounded calm. "We're both quite healthy, all things considered. But I see a specialist in London and she wants me on bed rest for the third trimester. She was an intern in Spain when I was a child and knows everything I've been through. I'll let your doctor take my blood, but I'm not giving some stranger my medical history. He touches my arm. That's *it*."

He nodded, still trying to put the pieces together.

"I know I should have told you sooner, but I also knew that if I carried this baby to a stage where it could survive birth, then I would have to marry you. I don't want to."

Her gaze finally came up, striking into him like a harsh winter wind. Bleak.

"I thought if I ever married, it would be for love." Despondency pulled her brows together and her thick lashes swept down to hide her eyes again. "That makes me sound like a romantic and I'm not. I just don't want to be something taken on in sufferance. My sister fell in love. I know it's possible."

Her elbow came up to rest on the door and she set her teeth on her thumbnail.

"Plus, my life is already high profile. Yours is worse." Her hand dropped away and she flashed him a look of blame. "Why can't you be a mechanic or something? Your life comes with even more restrictions than I imposed on myself. Why would I sign up for that? Of course I avoided telling you."

He certainly wouldn't live this life if he had a choice, but it struck him as odd that she disparaged his station. Every other woman aspired to be his queen.

"So, yes, I've handled this badly. God knows I've been informed of *that* more than once." She rolled her eyes. "I probably owe you an apology."

"Probably?" Did she have any idea the damage she had caused by avoiding him?

"I'm not sorry. I will never be sorry that I'm trying to have our baby." Her chin came up, defiant and fierce, but with deep vulnerability edging her unblinking eyes.

Something stirred in him. Gratitude? How? This baby was a disaster.

As if she read his mind, the corners of her mouth went down. "And I think we'll do enough damage to each other in the next while that if we start apologizing now, we'll be peaking way too early."

Never trust anyone who can't make or take a joke, his father had told him once. *Your grandmother, for instance*, had been the rest of the crack.

His grandmother. Yes, indeed, there would be hell to pay and many, many apologies to make.

Before he could fully grasp the scope of impact, a dull buzz emanated from the front of her shirt. "Goodness, an hour gone already?" She reached inside her collar to bring her phone from her bra, voice shaken but trying for light-hearted. "*Hola*, Henri. I'm fine. Just congratulating the father of my child. Does he look green to you?"

Trella could ignore the signs for only so long. The nausea churning in her belly, the heart palpitations, the hot and cold sweats. An attack was upon her. Of course it was. This was one of the most stressful days of her life and she was doing everything wrong, making it worse. Maybe she *did* self-sabotage, the way her brother Ramon sometimes accused, but she would rather eat live worms than admit he was right about anything.

She hated to admit any sort of weakness, because she knew, deep down, that she *was* weak. There was no hiding it from her family, but few others knew exactly what a basket case she was. That's why she'd spent so many years sequestered in the family compound. It had provided the security and stability she'd needed to overcome the worst of her issues, but it had kept her pride intact, too.

Ridiculous pride that kept her from admitting she was falling apart to Xavier and his doctor.

Gunter took her blood then her blood pressure, which he noted was elevated. He frowned and began asking pointed questions about her pregnancy.

She clammed up. The truth was, she wasn't combative as a result of being kidnapped. She'd been born that way, much to her family's eternal frustration. Her experience only gave her an excuse for it.

At her silence, Xavier turned from the window where he'd been standing in quiet contemplation. "Pass the readings to her specialist. She can determine if further action is necessary and advise a treatment plan. Request her doctor come to Lirona as soon as possible and stay for the duration of the pregnancy."

"She has other patients," Trella pointed out.

"None so important as you," he stated with a humorless smile.

"Flatterer," she tried, but her own sense of humor was buried beneath an onslaught of sensory overload ticking toward detonation.

"Sir, I've performed many deliveries," the doctor argued. "There's no need—"

"Sweeten the deal however you must. Our women's

health initiative is due for an upgrade, I'm sure. Expenses won't be spared."

"Very generous, sir," the royal physician said more firmly. "I'm sure many Elazarians would benefit, but…" He cleared his throat. "Perhaps such an undertaking should wait until DNA results are received."

"The results are for the Queen. I'm confident this is my heir. But I do have to inform her. *Bella*, please advise your brother we'll be on the move again, but not for long. The palace isn't far."

That was when she should have said, *I can't*.

She knew what kind of self-care was needed. A quiet, dark room. A sibling holding her hand, talking her down from her mental ledge.

She didn't say anything. Her stupid, tender pride, knocked to the ground so many times, locked her teeth while the rest of her began a slow collapse.

Now she sat in the back of his sedan, gripping her elbows as the ghouls came for her. It was going to be a bad one. She could taste it. The sheer frustration of not being able to stave it off made her eyes sting. Her mind spun down ever more scary avenues. Dark, harmful thoughts crowded in, feeding the anxiety.

This is my life now.

There would be no escape from the attention. It would be worse. Harsher. More judgmental. All the things she had tried to avoid by keeping her pregnancy secret and withholding the father's name were going to come true now.

The pressure in her chest grew worse, suffocating her, and even though her specialist had assured her from the beginning that suffering an attack wouldn't hurt the baby, she was convinced it would, *knew it*. She was going to lose her baby because she couldn't control these awful spells.

While Xavier watched her lose *everything*. He would

reject her for being the disaster she was. Even if she managed to keep his baby and deliver it some weeks from now, he would take it from her. He might have her locked away.

She needed Gili. She took out her phone and gripped it so hard her hand ached. Where were Henri and Ramon? They wouldn't let anyone take her baby. They would always keep her safe.

No. She couldn't keep expecting them to turn up and save her from herself.

"Why are you breathing like that? Are you asthmatic?"

She shook her head and turned her face to the window, wanting to die because now he'd noticed she was off and was staring at her.

"I'll ask Gunter if he reached your doctor." He started to lean forward.

She grabbed his sleeve. "Don't."

"You're flushed." He touched the backs of his fingers to her cheek then her forehead, making her flinch. "Sweating."

"It's nothing," she lied in a strangled voice, and was both relieved and horrified that her phone began to ripple with the heavenly notes of a harp.

It took two tries to open the call. When her sister appeared, she wasn't in focus. Tears of homesickness and failure filled her eyes. "Gili."

"I know, *bella*," she sounded equally anxious. "I can feel it. Where are you? Still at the Prince's chalet?"

"I don't know." The realization that she was in a strange land had been stalking her. Admitting it made it real and added to her terror. Her heart was so tight, she feared it was going into arrest. She clutched at the front of her shirt. "We're driving. How will you find me if we're moving? I'm so scared, Gili."

"I know, *fillette*. Breathe. Count your oranges. I'm coming. See, I'm going through the door. Henri has been tracking you all day. We'll always find you, you know that. Are you still with the Prince?"

Trella looked up and saw Xavier staring at her like her hair was made of snakes.

It was the most humiliating moment of her life. She couldn't make it worse by having her sister come to her like she was a child. *Couldn't*.

"No." She turned back to her phone. "You're married now. You have to stay with Kasim."

"He understands. I've already sent someone to tell him and prepare the helicopter."

It sounded so outlandish. What other person had family flying in from all corners to save her from imaginary threats?

"No, Gili." She managed to sound firm, even though turning away her sister felt like plunging a knife into her own chest. "I don't want you to come. I mean it."

"*Bella*," her sister breathed as though she'd felt the knife, too, in the back.

"I have to learn, Gili. I *have* to. I'm going to hang up and I'll call you later—"

"Wait! Let me speak to the Prince. He needs to understand."

Since there was no way Trella could explain it herself, she pushed the phone toward him.

"It's a panic attack," Gili said. "She doesn't need drugs or a hospital or strangers making her relive why this is happening. She needs to feel safe. Is there a hotel where you can secure a room? I don't mean book one. I mean *secure* it."

"We'll be at the palace in ten minutes."

"Good. Get her into a quiet bedroom, keep the lights low, blinds down, guards at the door. She needs to let it run its course without fearing people are going to see her. Keep her warm and whatever she says, remind her she's safe. If you can't stay with her, I'll come."

"I'll stay with her." His voice was grim. He handed back the phone.

She ended the call, mortified by how needy her sister had made her sound. Appalled because it was true. She hadn't tried to weather a spell on her own since they had first started. It had been a disaster.

Nevertheless, she screwed up her courage, pressed the phone between her breasts, and spoke some of the hardest words that had ever passed her lips. "You don't have to babysit me."

She held her breath, dreading the prospect of going it alone.

"I'm not letting you out of my sight until that baby is born."

The harsh words jarred, taking her brief flash of gratitude and coating it in foreboding.

CHAPTER SIX

XAVIER HAD THE car drive to the postern gate, where delivery trucks and other utility vehicles came in. They took a lane through the back garden to the private apartments. It was a longer, slower, but much more discreet entrance into the palace built by a king three hundred years ago.

Did coming in this way also allow him to avoid Mario and any mention of his grandmother's expectation that he present himself? A man did what he had to for the mother of his unborn child.

Xavier didn't *do* emotion. Fits and tempers were signs of poor breeding. He'd been taught that from an early age. When women became histrionic, he offered space.

Not possible today. And as much as he wanted to hold himself apart from the way Trella was behaving, he couldn't. She was shaking, hair damp at her temples, eyes darting. When he helped her from the car, she clung to his sleeve and looked to every shadow.

It was unnerving. Even stranger, her sense of threat put him on guard.

He kept reminding himself this was a panic attack, something he knew very little about except that it was a false response. Nevertheless, her fear provoked a very real primal need in him to offer protection. His heart pounded with readiness and he scanned about as they moved, fingers twitching for a weapon. He'd never experienced such an atavistic, bloodthirsty reaction. He was not so far removed from his medieval ancestors as he had imagined. He was completely prepared to shed his cloak of civility and slay if necessary.

Staff leapt to their feet as they walked through the kitchen. He said nothing, only pulled her into the service elevator.

Gunter came with them, frowning as he saw how distraught she looked. "Are you in pain?" He tried to take her pulse.

Trella shrank into Xavier.

"Leave her alone." He closed his arms around her. Her firm bump nudged low on his abdomen, reminding him that her panic attack was only the tip of the iceberg where this confounding day was concerned.

His valet, Vincente, met them as they entered his apartment. Xavier had moved into his father's half of the rooms when he'd finished university and never even glanced toward the adjoined feminine side, but it was kept dusted for the ghosts of past queens.

He pressed Trella toward the canopied bed of gold and red then started to close the doors, telling Vincente, "I'm locking us in. Leave sandwiches in my lounge. If I need anything else, I'll text. No one comes in here. *No one.*"

"Of course, sir." He read Vincente's apprehension. "But I believe the Queen—"

"Inform her I'll be along when I can, but it will be some time."

Xavier did as he'd promised, moving to lock each door and close all the drapes, turning on one bedside lamp as he went. Then he shook out a soft blanket from a chest and brought it to where Trella sat on the edge of the bed.

She clutched the blanket around her, back hunched, still trembling.

All he could see was a nine-year-old girl. Was this what that experience had left her with? He had a thousand questions, but heeded her sister's advice and only said, "You're safe, *bella*. This is my world. Nothing can harm you here."

Tears tracked her cheeks and she swiped the back of her hand along her jaw, skimming away the drips.

"I didn't want you to see me like this." Her voice was thin as a silk thread. "I wanted you to think I was Gili. She cries at proper things, like weddings and stubbed toes. She's afraid of real things, not stuff she makes up in her head."

Was it made-up? He used the satin on the corner of the blanket to dry her cheeks, not sure where the urge to comfort came from. It wasn't taught or ingrained. Manners and platitudes got him through displays like this, not affection.

But he felt responsible for her and her attack. "I only wanted to talk to you. I didn't expect things to go off the rails like this."

"Don't blame yourself. I take everything further than it needs to go." She drew in a shaken sigh. Her eyes filled again.

"Is this what you were hiding, staying out of the spotlight all those years?"

She nodded jerkily. "It started after Papa died. We were fifteen. I was starting to feel like I might be able to go back to school and have a normal life. But we were seen as sex objects, I guess, because the most disgusting men found us online. I'd already been through an eating disorder and trolls mocking me for it. Then all these men started sending photos and telling me what they wanted to do to me. It hit a switch."

A streak of impotent fury lodged in his chest. His entire life, he had struggled against this particular irony. He was a future monarch, charged with great power and responsibility, godlike in some eyes, but he couldn't control how people treated each other. He couldn't prevent the kind of harm that had Trella drawing up her knees so she was a ball of misery. His inability to help her struck at the deepest part of him.

"I'm a woman of extremes. You might as well know that about me. Give me that pillow."

He dragged it closer and she fell onto her side and buried her face in it. She sobbed so deeply, was in the throes of an anguish so terrible, he was stricken witnessing it. How did she withstand it?

Let it run its course, her sister had said. That seemed cruel.

He settled on the bed behind her, rubbed her arm and soothed her shaking back. It took several minutes for her crying to subside. She lifted her head and breathed as though she'd been running for miles.

"I keep worrying I'll have an attack while I'm in labor. My doctor says this won't hurt the baby, but I'm so scared all this adrenaline is causing damage. What if we go through all of this and our child isn't fit to reign? What if that's my fault because I can't control this?"

"Is there nothing you can take? Something safe during pregnancy?"

"No. I mean, maybe, but I can't. *Won't*." She threw her arm over her eyes. "I tried drugs years ago. They made me depressed and dependent. I was close to taking a whole bottle just to end this."

She dropped her arm and twisted to stare at him from between matted lashes.

"I shouldn't have told you that. You'll declare me unfit and take our baby away. Oh, God…"

She rolled around the pillow again, dragging the blanket with her and pulling it over her head.

"Trella." He was no mental health expert, but he knew a tailspin when he heard one. He settled on the mattress behind her, propped on an elbow, letting his body heat penetrate the blanket as he gave rubs of reassurance against her shoulder and arm. He wanted to fold right around her, absorb whatever had such a terrible grip on her.

"Let's take this one thing at a time. Hmm? The baby is well. Your doctor said so, yes? Do you know the sex?"

It took a minute, but her breathing settled to something more natural.

"I've been afraid to ask, thinking it would make me more attached. I'm so scared I'm going to lose it." She shifted, pushing away the blanket to reveal her face, then peeled the blanket all the way back, piling it on him as she exposed her bump. She smoothed her shirt over the roundness. "It's moving. Do you want to feel?"

He stalled, reality hitting him like a train. He let her draw his hand across the tense swell of her midsection. He had thought it would feel like an inflated beach ball, but she was warm and there was give within the firmness. A shape. Something that felt no bigger than his knuckle pressed outward, moving across the palm of his hand.

He almost jerked back, yet he was too fascinated and kept his hand in place, waiting to feel it again. "Does that hurt?"

"It reassures me. *Hola, bebé. Cómo estás?*"

Another tiny kick struck his hand, prompting a soft noise of amusement deep in her throat. She turned her head to look at him. Her eyelids were red and swollen, but her smile was so filled with joy and wonder, she took his breath away.

The moment snaked out like a rope to encircle and draw them together, binding them, inexorable and eternal.

He sucked in a breath, drawing back as he tried to pull himself free of what threatened to carry him into deep waters like a deadly riptide.

"How are we even here? How—Why me, *bella*?"

"Why did I sleep with you? I didn't plan to sleep with anyone." She curled around her pillow, rubbing her face against it, drying tears. "I only wanted to practice being in public. I was so proud for having the courage to talk to a man, then to be alone with one. You made me feel normal. Safe. I needed that. I was using you. I admit that. But sleeping with you?" She craned her neck to look at him, her expression helpless. Anxious. "I couldn't help myself. You said we were volatile. That…"

He knew what he had said. It had been true. He'd never experienced anything like what he'd felt with her that night. Despite his best efforts, the memory haunted him. He wasn't a dependent person, but he was disturbingly gratified to be this close to her again. The animal inside him had finally stopped pacing with restless frustration.

He was loath to admit any of that, though. Her power to still affect him unnerved him. "It was my last night before I got engaged. We were both attributing significance for our own reasons."

The light in her eyes dimmed with hurt. She withdrew, turning away again.

He closed his fist in the tangle of blanket across their hips, lungs turning to lead.

"Either way, it gave me hope that I could *be* normal. Maybe fall in love and get married, someday. That's all I've ever wanted. To be normal. Now I never will be, because I'm carrying a royal baby and I was so happy to be pregnant, but I knew this was a disaster. You have your life and I've never had any life at all. I deserve a chance to be single and free. Free of *this*!"

Her tension returned in a contraction of her muscles that drew her in like a shrinking bloom, fists coming up to her clenched eyes.

"I told Gili I would run Maison des Jumeaux. When we were little, she was able to count on me. I want to be that person people can rely on, but I'm always going to be this pathetic—"

"Trella. You *have* to stop escalating."

"Do you think I can control it?" Her hands went into her hair, clenching handfuls. "I try. I really try, but the fear *grips* me. Now we have to get married and you don't want some crazy burden of a wife. You'll hate me. I'm *so scared* of what will happen."

"Stop." He couldn't stand it. He pressed his body heat around her, held her in sheltering arms and willed her back to calm. "Hatred is a wasted emotion. It closes all pathways to resolving a conflict. Our situation is difficult, but hating each other won't make it easier."

Her trembling continued, but he felt the moment his words penetrated. Her hands loosened in her hair.

"That sounds very wise," she said on a sniff. "Do they teach you that in monarchy school?"

"Divorce class. My mother was a great believer in practical demonstrations."

She unfolded a few increments more. "When we were in Paris, you said your mother was sent away by your grandmother because she wanted a divorce?"

He eased his embrace, regretting his loose lips. He had learned out of necessity to be comfortable with his own thoughts, never needing confidantes, but keeping her mind engaged seemed to forestall her emotional downtrends, so he answered.

"She made a commitment then didn't accept her lot. Unhappy wives move into the dowager wing. They don't reject royal life altogether. My mother tried separation, but my father and grandmother pressured her to have another baby. Since their marriage was over, she refused. She was granted a divorce on the grounds that she left Elazar. She had family in Germany so she moved there."

"Exiled, you said. But you still saw her? How old were you?" She tried to twist enough to see him.

He used the weight of his arm to keep them spooned. Her hair tickled his lips while the scent of her went straight to the back of his brain, finding where she had imprinted herself in Paris and settling like a puzzle piece matched to its empty space.

He shook off the notion. "I was eight. At boarding school. My life wasn't affected much. We exchanged a few letters, but what was there to say?"

"You didn't see her *at all*?" She tried harder to twist, rolling onto her back and forcing him to meet her gaze. "Do you see her now?"

"We send Christmas cards." He shrugged off the jabs of rejection that still came alive when he revisited the memory. "Chosen by our personal assistants. We're not sentimental people."

Her expression grew appalled. "What about your father? You said you were young when he abdicated?"

"Renounced," he corrected, regretting this. It was becoming too intimate. Too uncomfortable.

"Do you see him?"

"It was best we didn't communicate." *This* communication ended here, he conveyed by drawing back.

"But—" She groaned and rolled to face him fully. He could see a fresh wave of emotion taking its grip on her. Her hand closed on the front of his shirt, catching at a few chest hairs, making him wince. "Now I'm worried you'll drop out of our child's life like that. Swear to me you won't."

He covered her hand, loosening her fist and holding her slender fingers. He had to consciously overcome an urge to draw her hand to his mouth and kiss her bruised knuckles, even as he acknowledged she was far more likely to disappear than he was. Royal life was not easy, especially when shoved to the fringes as his mother had been. He didn't blame his mother for extricating herself, and wouldn't censure Trella when she did it, especially if the stress of life in the public eye put her in paroxysms like this.

"Duty may have skipped a generation, but it is firmly drilled into me. I will never forsake my obligation to our child."

"Obligation." Her brow furrowed. "What about love?"

He dried her cheek with his thumb. "Love is a problem not a solution."

"Who told you *that*?"

"It's an observation. My mother loved my father, which is why she couldn't bear his cheating. My father loved the woman who cost him his kingdom. Duty is more reliable."

She shook her head.

"I don't have to argue with you, *bella*. Time reveals all. Now, let's stop talking about things that upset you. What did your sister say about counting oranges? Tell me why she said that."

Xavier hadn't had his backside handed to him on one of the palace's sixteenth-century gold platters since his teen years. He refused to allow it today.

He had had plenty of time in the night, lying awake making decisions between comforting Trella through crying spells and nightmares, until she fell deeply asleep in the early hours.

He rose to put his plans into action and by the time the Queen summoned him, he was able to preempt a shred-

ding of his character by proving what he had told Trella—
he adhered to duty above all else.

"She has agreed to that?"

"She will."

"And you?"

"Of course. Why wouldn't I?"

The Queen cocked a skeptical brow. "You spent last
night with her. That implies…preoccupation."

"You think we were having sex? No." Despite having
few secrets from his grandmother, her intrusive remark
grated. "She was upset."

"Gunter said she's fragile." Her mouth pursed with disdain. Ruling required strength of every kind, especially
emotional.

He frowned, annoyed that Gunter's report had preceded
his own, especially because it was off the mark. Trella was
besieged. It was different.

"She held off telling me because her pregnancy is high-
risk."

"So, it would seem, is she."

An urge to defend her stayed lodged in his throat. She
was a threat—one he was mitigating to the best of his
ability.

"When would you like to meet her?" he asked instead.

"Perhaps after the baby is born?"

He hadn't slept. That's why the snub struck him as un-
conscionably rude.

Before he could react, Mario entered. "Deepest apologies, your Majesty, but Ms. Sauveterre's brother insists on
seeing her. We've stalled him as long as possible."

"He's *here*?" Xavier's heart lurched with protectiveness
and a jolt of alarm. Trella was catching up on much-needed
sleep. More importantly, "We both spoke to him yesterday.
She told him she was staying for the foreseeable future."

She couldn't leave.

"I believe it's the race-car driver. She has agreed to receive him. I thought you would wish to—"

"I would." Xavier strode from the room. When he heard raised voices as he approached the apartment they now shared, his aggression increased. With a snap of his fingers, security personnel fell into step behind him. He pushed into what had once been his mother's parlor.

Trella was red-faced as she confronted a man who looked like Henri but emanated a hot-tempered demeanor that was in complete contrast to his brother's air of aloof control. "No, *you* shut up—" Ramon was saying to his sister.

"Leave quietly or I'll have you removed." Xavier would do it himself. He was in that kind of mood.

Ramon snorted as he gave Xavier a measuring once-over, hands on his hips, looking willing for the fight Xavier promised.

"Don't." Trella threw herself against her brother's side, looping her arms tight around his waist. "I was saying things he didn't want to hear."

Despite the animosity that had been flaring between them seconds before, Ramon curled a shielding arm around his sister, even as he frowned at her, concern evident beneath his glare of impatience.

Trella looked as rough as the night she'd had. When Xavier had left her, she'd been subdued and exhausted, falling back asleep within seconds after he'd woken her to tell her he was leaving. She still had dark circles under red eyes and hadn't changed out of the silk pajamas he'd given her to wear to bed. In fact, she'd raided his closet for a thick cardigan to belt over them.

Xavier snapped out of searching her expression to realize she was bickering with her brother, refusing to go with him.

"All those times you showed up when I called makes

it possible for me to work through this. I know you *will* come if I ask. That means everything. But until I ask, you *have* to *butt out.*"

With a resigned scowl, Ramon dropped his arm from around her. "*Bueno.*"

"And be nicer to Iz—"

"No. Butting out goes both ways. And you *will* introduce me to your host."

"Did you call me a *virgin*?" Xavier asked Trella in an ominous tone as they entered his suite hours later. "You switched between French and Spanish so often, I might have heard wrong."

She tried not to snicker. "I told you it was a bad habit. Ramon and I are the worst because we get heated and grab the first word that comes in any language."

Ramon had joined them for a meal that might have been pleasant if so many questions hadn't been hanging over her like a guillotine blade. If he'd caught her alone again, he would have skewered her with all of them, she was sure, but he'd behaved. They had played verbal tennis as they always did, sticking to neutral topics like films and current events.

Sparring with her brother always helped restore her confidence. Where Gili was her security blanket and Henri was her rock, Ramon was her worthy adversary, keeping her sharp and forcing her to hold her own. She was tired and stifling yawns, but her lingering melancholy had lightened. As she looked into the cloudy crystal ball that was her future, she was thinking, *I can do this.*

Especially because, like her, Xavier seemed to be experiencing the same threads of attraction they'd felt when they had made this baby. A selection from her closet in Paris had arrived earlier and she now wore a dark blue skirt and a white maternity top. It draped her breasts in such a flattering way, she'd caught Xavier eyeing her chest more than once while they ate, making her tingle and giving her hope.

She turned her back on him and lifted her hair, silently requesting he release the tiny clasp at the top of her spine, realizing she hadn't properly answered his question. "And yes, I did. Ramon asked me how you did with looking after me through my attack. I said pretty well, for a virgin."

"Lovely. I hope the dining staff enjoyed that." His breath warmed the back of her neck along with the light brush of his fingertips, making her shiver.

"I said worse. I called Ramon a—"

"I heard that one. Very clearly," he cut in dryly, motioning her to lead the way to her side of the apartment. "Because of his engagement to 'Izzy.'"

"Isidora, yes. She's a dear friend. Her father handled our media for years. Aside from Gili, she was my *only* friend for a long time."

Her heart dipped and rolled when he turned, locking them into her bedroom. Despite her rough night, sleeping with him had been more than comforting. She had liked the brushes of contact and the inherent intimacy, the way his strong arms had made her feel so safe. It had given her that bonding feeling she had felt in Paris, one that was incredibly bolstering.

His efforts to comfort also gave her hope for their marriage. All her flaws had been laid bare, yet he had stayed with her. She was deeply gratified. Touched.

Now all she had to explain was that, as much as she might like to, she couldn't make love. Practically blushing at the mere thought, because she was so deeply tempted, she moved to take up her brush and began working it through her hair, trying to act casual as nerves accosted her.

He moved to lean on the footboard of the bed, appearing in the mirror behind her. The way he watched as she stroked her hair made her feel as though she was enticing him. The crackle of tension on the air was exciting, giving her that sense of power in her sexuality he'd instilled the first time. Oh, she wished their timing wasn't so far off.

His expression tightened before he jerked his gaze away, clearing his throat. "If she's such a good friend, why don't you approve of her?"

"Who? Oh. Um." She blushed at having her mind fixated on intimate acts while he was clearly not. "I approve of Isidora completely, but Ramon is sleeping with her."

"Stickler for waiting until after the wedding, are you?" He dropped a pointed gaze to her middle.

"Ha-ha." She tapped the brush against her thigh then set it aside. "No, their engagement is a publicity stunt. Earlier this year, Isidora took over her father's position at Sauveterre International." Trella took off her earrings and bracelet. "You'll notice Ramon's very public proposal coincides with the first photos of my pregnancy showing up online. He does that all the time, takes the spotlight off the rest of us. Izzy is so loyal she went along with it, but she had a terrific crush on Ramon when we were young. He never returned it and shouldn't sleep with her if he has no intention of marrying her. She's going to get hurt. That makes me mad."

"I see. Well, kindly convey that we would prefer fewer stunts in future. My team will handle—" he indicated her middle again "—this."

She blinked, not expecting him to be worried for Izzy, not really, but his cool attention to his own interests sent a premonition down her spine like a drip of icy water.

It occurred to her that he had closed the door not because he wanted to nurture the growing trust between them. He wanted to have a conversation that was best held within the gilded cage he'd assigned her.

Logically she knew she had imprinted on her first lover like a baby duckling emerging from its protective shell. She'd spent weeks reliving Paris and imagining this reunion, dreaming up scenarios where he was as happy about her pregnancy as she was.

It was delusional. She had known that, but apparently she was still building castles in the sky because a minute ago, she had been okay with his knowing all her worst secrets. Now a grossly naked sensation accosted her, like he had leverage on her.

She tried to disguise her apprehension with a tough smile. "It's time to discuss *this*. Isn't it?"

The barest flicker of emotion reflected in his blink. He folded his arms and tilted his head in assent. "Gunter informs me your doctor has accepted my offer of a residency at Hospital del Re, with a mandate to ensure our obstetrics wing is the best in the world. She'll be here tomorrow and has requested a private room be prepared for you."

"Bed rest." Trella had known it was coming, but still made a face of dismay.

"You'll fight it?"

"No." She wasn't able to keep the dread from her voice, though. "It's for the best."

"It is."

Something in his tone, in the subtle shift of his expression, pricked up her ears. Relief? His approval of her going into the hospital had nothing to do with the health of their unborn child. He was protecting his own interests again!

An ache of hurt spread through her until all her sweet imaginings had been pushed out and she was left with the ugly reality. She really had been deceiving herself all these months.

"Keeps me out of sight, does it? Is that the Queen's

preference? Or yours?" Behind the stir of their child, her abdomen tightened.

His expression grew even more shuttered. "It's expedient for all. You said you don't want the attention our association brings."

"Don't pretend you're doing me a favor. Are we not marrying, then?" Clearly not, if he was hiding her away.

Her arms pulled into a defensive fold across her front. Her shoulders grew rock hard while she ignored the creep of anguish that began working in tendrils through her core. What did she care? She didn't want a husband anyway!

Right?

"Of course we'll marry." He mirrored her posture, arms folded, seeming relaxed in the way he leaned on the footboard, but there was a stillness to him, an implacability in his tone. "Elazar had a bastard monarch in the 1700s. It was a bloody fight to keep the reign. We've been sticklers for legitimacy ever since."

She understood she was speaking to a future king now, not the charming prince who had lulled her with something that had resembled caring. Twice.

"Our marriage will be a private ceremony. Announced, but without fanfare. No formal photos. We'll keep it brief."

"The ceremony? Or the marriage?"

"Both."

The tendons in her neck flexed as she fought a choke, doing her best to hide how deeply he was striking against her hard-won self-worth. "How brief?"

"We'll divorce by the end of the year."

Her teeth closed on the inside of her lip, biting down harder and harder until she had to consciously remind herself not to break the skin.

What had she expected after showing him her true colors? A declaration of love? A desire to live out his life with *that*? Well, she knew exactly how much *duty* he felt toward her, didn't she? Not even four months' worth.

"That's quite the virgin birth you're orchestrating."

His eyes narrowed at her shaken tone. "Is this conversation going to bring on another attack?"

Oh, she hated above all things to be managed like she was too delicate for honesty.

"I do better when I know what's coming." Her voice only trembled a little, mostly from the effort to hide the burn of disgrace sizzling under her skin. "Is this room a time machine, by the way? I feel we've gone back to your 1700s and I'm something shameful you're sweeping under the rug."

"It isn't about hiding you." He showed the barest hint of discomfort by dropping his hands to the footboard and pushing to stand. "I'm acknowledging you and the heir you're providing me, but it would be helpful if your role was downplayed, so as not to overshadow Patrizia's."

"You're still *engaged*?"

"It's been called off, since I'm marrying you, but—"

"She's still willing to marry you?" The news pushed her into falling back a step. Maybe it was the realization that he still wanted that marriage himself. Why did that hurt? So much?

"Unless a better offer comes along, she is not averse to reviving our plan after you and I divorce." He must have read the incredulity in her expression, because he said, "We're friends. Both ruled by duty. The fact we *don't* have strong feelings for each other and she's *not* hurt by this—" again with the generic wave at her middle "—is the reason we're a good fit."

"But her child won't be first in line! Or is she hoping mine's a girl?"

"Gender isn't an issue in Elazar. First born is first in line, but…" He seemed to debate whether she could handle his next words before he said, without emotion, "Until you deliver a healthy baby, many aspects of this situation remain fluid."

Trella sucked in a gasp so sharp it went down the back of her throat like a spear, sticking in her heart and pinning her motionless. She tried telling herself the shivery clamp around her was anger, but it was anguish. Dark, blood-red betrayal.

"How *dare* you give someone *hope* that I'll lose our baby."

"It's not hope." He strode away from the foot of the bed in a sudden rush, making her jerk back another step and keep him in her line of sight. "It's caution. You said this will be your only pregnancy. There is a reason for an heir and a spare. If my uncle had lived, this conversation wouldn't even be happening. If my mother had done her duty, I would have other choices. I don't. I will accept what comes of this pregnancy, but I have to ensure there are alternatives."

She was so appalled that she wasn't even sure what the cold feeling against her lips was. Her fingers? All of her felt cold and empty and deeply furious.

She barely tracked that his hand flicked the air. Through her own haze of emotion, she had a brief impression of bitterness before he turned his back on her.

Anything close to suffering on his part was imagined, though. Had to be. Everything she had shared with this man was imagination and faulty memory. A wish. Girlish daydreaming. A rescue fantasy.

He was a spoiled prince who had sullied a maiden and was tidying up that mess the most pragmatic way possible.

"This really is medieval times, isn't it? Women have come all this way, yet I'm still just a vessel. A faulty one." She knew she was broken. It shouldn't surprise her that she was being rejected. She had thought she had prepared herself, but she hadn't. She was gutted and had to fight with everything in her not to reveal how devastated she was.

So many times, she'd wished she could go back to that moment as an impetuous girl, when Gili's math tutor had called out to her. She had run to tell him he had the wrong twin, *that's all*. It had been one second of impulse and she was still being punished for it.

Xavier's head tipped back as he aimed his gaze at the portrait of an ancestor surveying them from high on the wall.

"If I don't produce our next ruler, the crown passes to a family living in America for the last two hundred years. Rather than let that happen, our neighbors would squabble to take control of Elazar. Instability would ripple across Europe. The globe. We're a small country, but a pivotal one. I need more than one child to ensure Elazar's future. I need a wife with connections that cement our alliances."

His voice held not one iota of regret or even concern for how his plan would affect *this* child. Or her.

"Spell it out for me." She grappled for her most pragmatic tone. "Exactly how is this to work? Because I am not allowing some strange woman to raise my baby."

"Our child will be raised by nannies, tutors and servants, same as you and I."

"*I* wasn't!"

"You left for boarding school at *seven*. If you hadn't been kidnapped, you would have grown up there. Your brothers did."

"My parents traveled, but they were very involved. We knew they loved us!"

As she stared into his half-lidded eyes and read indifference, it struck her why he was being so dispassionate rather than weighing his decisions through his heart.

"You don't know what that's like, do you?" She felt

cruel saying it, but everything he had told her about his parents came back to her, bringing his brutally logical plan into focus.

His brow went up in arrogant query. "What?"

"Love."

He might have flinched, but it was gone so fast that she wasn't sure. His sigh was pure condescension as he pushed his hands into his pockets. "I told you last night—"

"I'm not talking about romantic love. *Family* love."

"Love of any kind isn't real." His voice slapped her down for being so gullible. "Look around. Is it here? Keeping anyone in my life but my grandmother? Loyalty. Obligation. Duty. Those are real."

She would have argued that her family loved her, but something else struck with brutal force. "Are you saying—"

She had a flash of her mother crying with joy because Trella was pregnant. Elisa Sauveterre was worried sick and had strong opinions on how Trella had avoided telling Xavier, but beneath all of that was pure, over-the-moon love for her unborn grandchild.

"Is your grandmother happy we're having a baby?" Her voice quavered with strain.

His jaw set. "That is not the word I would use, no."

"Wow." A jagged laugh clawed inside her chest. "Just wow." How did one survive such an emotional desert?

The answer was before her. They turned into this—an image of a man with a heart, but one who was actually incapable of deeper feelings. One who scoffed at love.

A fierce gleam—torment?—flashed in his gaze before he steeled himself behind a visage of hammered armor. "But she recognizes we have a responsibility toward it."

"Precious obligation," she said shakily. "Here's some news for you. I will *not* be shut out of my child's life and replaced by nannies and tutors. I'll call in the rescue team right now and barricade us in Sus Brazos for the rest of our lives if that's what you're thinking."

"Dramatics will not be necessary," he said with pithy disdain. "We'll share custody, fifty-fifty. Aside from security and education, how you meet the needs of our child is your business. Visitations to Spain or elsewhere can be worked out as they arise. But our child lives in Elazar." He pointed at the floor. "I will provide you with a home here in Lirona as part of our divorce settlement."

She shouldn't care how quickly he got rid of her. He was being so cold, acting so far removed from the man she had wanted to believe he was, she could hardly endure facing the next minute in his company let alone four months of marriage.

It still took effort to say, "Well, that's a relief." She held his gaze, saying goodbye to those moments when he had held her and touched her as if there had been more between them than obligation. "I can move on then, too."

His eyes narrowed with warning, gaze so hard and devoid of feeling she struggled to hold the contact. "You can."

How foolish of her to try getting under his skin. She looked away, thinking that she couldn't stay this close to him with her defenses annihilated the way they were.

"Where is this dowager wing of which you spoke?"

"You'll sleep where I can keep an eye on you. You were difficult enough to track down as it was."

"Confinement. How apropos. And *familiar*."

"I won't apologize. We've agreed it's wasted."

"I still won't forgive you."

"Because I'm not upending my life?"

"Because you don't want our baby!"

"I don't want our *situation*."

You don't want me! She didn't say it. She was appalled she had thought it and turned her face away, boiling in humiliation. Pressure filled her throat and sat livid behind her eyes.

Into the thick silence, he sighed. "What I want has never mattered, *bella*. Duty to the crown takes precedence. I learned that a long time ago."

His voice was surprisingly gentle, which made the lash of the words all the more cutting and intolerable.

"Don't call me that. It's a family nickname and implies we're closer than we are, but it's just something you say when you can't remember the name of the woman you're sleeping with."

Another loaded silence filled the room like an acrid cloud.

"Explain to me how sniping at each other will make this easier."

"It's the *truth*." She swallowed past the ache in her throat, but it only lodged deeper in her chest. "You called me that in Paris and it made me think you saw *me*, not my sister, but all you saw was a willing partner. I need to stop thinking we're friends. Stop acting like we are."

They were still strangers and would remain so. He kept his heart behind thicker walls than she had ever hidden behind.

"If you insist. Trella."

"Thank you." She wasn't grateful. She was shattered. "Can you—" She waved at the door. "I'm tired."

"Will you be all right alone?"

She had thought he couldn't hurt her any further, but that did it. After rejecting her so roundly, did he really think she would want to cling to *him* through another emotional storm? How did he manage to sound like he *cared* if she suffered alone?

"I have to learn to be, don't I? I've known that for a long time. Goodnight."

CHAPTER SEVEN

I NEED TO stop thinking we're friends.

There was no reason he should have lost sleep over that. Perhaps the *bella* endearment *had* always rolled off his tongue very easily around women, but for some reason knowing it held a more intimate connotation for her made it something he wanted the right to use. He doubted he would ever use it again with anyone else. It was hers now, which made it doubly frustrating she refused to hear it from him.

He went into his first meeting of the day, unrested and gritty eyed, only to face the woman still torturing him. They were about to negotiate their prenuptial agreement.

He introduced her to the palace attorney who fell under her spell at the first flash of her smile. She wore a pin-striped sky blue jacket over a white shirt that draped untucked over her matching skirt. It made her look smart and capable, yet sensual. Achingly vulnerable.

"I should have invited your brother to stay for this," he said as he directed her into a comfortable armchair.

"Why?" She cooled when he touched her arm and delicately removed her elbow from his loose touch, adjusting a cushion behind her back as she sat.

"To protect your interests."

"You can email the draft to him," the attorney said with

a magnanimous smile. "If he has concerns, we can address them before you sign."

She sat back and folded her hands on her lap, smiling in a way that could only be called patronizing.

"Gentlemen. Along with our mother, my siblings and I jointly own Sauveterre International. Ramon votes Gili's share and Henri votes Mama's because they don't take an interest. I vote my own, thank you very much. Maison Des Jumeaux is not the only enterprise I've asked SI to underwrite. One hundred percent of my initiatives have turned a profit because I have a brain and use it. So…" She cut a glance toward Xavier. "The Prince may show the draft to his grandmother before *he* signs, to ensure *his* interests are protected, but I'm confident I can look after my own."

The attorney cleared his throat and shuffled papers.

Xavier held her lofty stare.

He should have been affronted. It was a well-executed burn in front of the attorney and his PA, but he was darkly thankful for that scorn in her.

He had watched her all through their meal with her brother yesterday, captivated by her rallying spirit. The glimpse of her family dynamic and the new facets in her personality had only made him want to know her far better than he would be allowed to. It had taken genuine effort on his part to stick to the plan and outline how they would proceed. If he had had a choice—

He didn't. So he had said what needed to be said.

She'd been angry. Injured. She *was* sentimental. And despite his claims to be anything but, he didn't take pleasure in hurting others. If things were different…

Wistfulness was a useless emotion. He steeled himself against futile *if only*s. "Let's get started."

As promised, Trella protected her abundant interests with pointed questions and clear language. The details were hammered out with very little fuss until the attorney asked, "And the dissolution of the marriage? Midnight, December thirty-first?"

"That's fine. But if I lose the baby, the marriage ends immediately."

Her statement was jarring. Xavier swung his head to regard her, disturbed.

"There would be no reason to draw it out," she said stiffly. White tension ringed her mouth.

A strange void opened in him. Why? She was right. What else was there between them besides the baby?

You don't know what that's like, do you?

Her disturbing accusation last night kept ambushing him, but his parents had been disruptive forces in his life, dividing his loyalty, creating nothing but turmoil and disappointment. If that was love, he didn't need it.

His grandmother's levelheaded reason and clear outline of what was expected from a future monarch had been a welcomed relief. Taking responsibility meant taking control.

Like love, Trella was an unpredictable influence. Too much was at stake to indulge any latent desires for either. She was right. Without the baby, they had nothing holding them in their union.

He lifted a finger, indicating the attorney should record that their marriage would end if the pregnancy did. He ignored the grate in the pit of his stomach.

They signed the contract a few days later, once the DNA results had been confirmed. Afterward, Trella hurried to greet her mother, who had arrived for the ceremony that would be held in the palace chapel.

"We agreed on a private ceremony," Xavier said when she informed him her mother would attend.

"She's giving me away." Trella hadn't mentioned her sister had cried over missing the ceremony. "All of my family wanted to be here, but neither of us is getting the wedding we wanted, are we? Well, I guess you are. Later."

His expression had hardened as he looked away.

She wasn't trying to be "combative," just stating fact. She had hoped she and Xavier would have something to build a family upon, but they didn't.

That made her sad, but all her soul-searching had been done in the months of keeping her pregnancy under wraps. Xavier had given her a chance at motherhood that she had believed was out of reach. For that, she would always be grateful.

But he saw her as, at best, one of the many staff who would tend to his offspring so he wouldn't have to. They might marry, but she wouldn't be his wife.

He didn't want *her*.

She had to ignore how spurned that made her feel. She already had people who loved her, after all.

"*Mi niña hermosa*," her mother exclaimed as she finished buttoning the gown and Trella turned to face her. "Truly, this is your *pièce de résistance*."

Trella had been working on the gown in secret, not even showing it to her mother or Gili. It was understated, like her makeup, with a high waist to cover her bump and a simple bodice with cap sleeves. The seed pearls and crystals had been the time-consuming work and she was proud of how it had turned out.

Her hair was in a loose chignon. Her mother placed a bridal comb over her ear in lieu of a veil. The brushed silver flowers with pearls and diamonds was a family heirloom, not ostentatious, just right for a small afternoon wedding.

They followed the ever-efficient Mario to the palace chapel.

Xavier was already there, speaking to the bishop. He wore a bone colored tunic-style jacket with dark gold epaulettes and gold leaf embroidery at the cuffs and hem. His royal red sash sat across it, decorated with a number of pins, including a key and a family shield. A sword hung off his hip.

My prince, she thought, and ached inside.

He wasn't, and he never would be.

Xavier turned and splendor kicked him in the stomach.

Her dress was white, which somehow wasn't ironic despite being a maternity gown. Perhaps it was the fact her bump was still modest, or the way the gown drew his eye to the beading at her neckline and across her shoulders. The detailing resembled angel wings but also projected strength. Delicate armor.

The rest of her was incandescent. Her skin held the warm glow he had noticed the night they'd met, as if firelight reflected off a creamy nude. She was both waif and warrior. Goddess and maid. Infinitely fascinating.

She came forward, expression guarded as she introduced her mother.

Elisa Sauveterre was a tall, elegant woman of Spanish ancestry with sensual features and a single streak of white in her black hair.

As she held his hand in both her warm ones, shadows in the misty depths of her eyes told him she had feared this day would never come for her daughter. It made him feel churlish for bristling when Trella had informed him her mother was coming.

"It's an honor to have you here." He was embarrassed now that his grandmother wasn't attending, and that they hadn't extended an invitation for Elisa to stay at the palace. His impatience with himself sharpened his tone as he told Trella, "You look beautiful."

Her mouth tightened. "Thank you." But she might have been speaking to Mario who handed her a bouquet.

Mario was Xavier's witness, which suddenly felt like a disregard for the significance of the occasion. Xavier understood ceremony. His entire country was up in arms, wanting to witness this moment. The least he could have done was invite a friend to be his best man. He might not have many friends, but he had some.

Friends would come next year, though, when he married Patrizia in a spectacle he already dreaded.

Today's occasion was far more to his liking, even though the exchange of words seemed to hold extra power when spoken in such an intimate setting, heard only by the three witnesses. Even those few extra pairs of eyes and ears fell away as he spoke directly to Trella, losing himself in the shift of gray and green in her irises.

When she said, "I do," it reverberated within him, so visceral he knew that he would feel bound by this promise his entire life. She was his responsibility now, but he would have to turn away from her to perform the rest of his obligations. The war of dueling duties already hammered a crack into his psyche, causing a schism that would never heal.

"Do you have the ring?" the bishop asked.

"I'll only have to remove it when I go into the hospital." Trella waved off the case.

It was an unexpected swipe of claws at a part of him Xavier hadn't realized he'd exposed. What did he care that she didn't even glance at the ring he'd spent more than an hour dithering over, wanting it to match her sparkling, multi-faceted personality?

Her mother's tiny sniff broke the silence. Mario smoothly

withdrew the ring. The bishop quickly finished the ceremony.

"You may k-kiss the bride…" Everyone had got the memo this was not a conventional marriage.

Her wary gaze grew even more vulnerable.

Should he have forgone this custom? Probably. But he set his hand at her waist and drew her toward him.

She braced her forearm along his and clenched her fist into his jacket sleeve, leaning on him for balance as she offered her mouth.

He brought his hand to the side of her neck, felt the cool tickle of a few strands of hair, and reminded himself not to make a fool of himself. Keep it brief.

He nearly groaned at the onslaught of sensation when his mouth covered hers.

As tenuous as everything else might be, in this second, they were as united as they'd been in Paris. Everything in him wanted to deepen and ravish, requiring all his willpower to keep the kiss short and sweet.

Her mouth moved under his with equal restraint, but he tasted the desire for more in the way her lips clung to his. Paradise hovered like a promise, but he couldn't surrender to whatever this thing was between them. All he could have was this. One kiss.

And it was already over.

"Mario tells me you wish to cancel Australia." The Queen looked up from her breakfast. "Why?"

He *had* cancelled, if Mario had done his job. Xavier filled his plate and gave the butler a nod, sending him from the room so they could speak in private.

"Don't play dumb," he said as the door closed.

"It's an important initiative."

Unlike some of his counterparts, the royals of Elazar

took specific, active roles in government. His entire year had been a series of trade talks in various regions. It wasn't appearance for the sake of it, but business meetings and presentations to push for expansion of existing agreements that would keep his country from going bankrupt.

"She isn't due for weeks," his grandmother continued. "Even when she goes into labor, what help do you think you will be?"

"She's alone in a strange country, stuck in the hospital. I'm not leaving for a month of press interviews where the first question will be, 'Why aren't you with your wife?'"

"Is that why you visit her every day? Because I'm told she keeps herself amused. Drawing. Chatting to family. You wouldn't be missed."

Perhaps not. Even Trella had asked if he was only visiting for appearances' sake.

The press release on their marriage and impending parenthood had been short and vague, playing to concern for a successful pregnancy without going into detail. It had made Xavier sick to hear his team discuss how spinning the pregnancy as a miracle would create a groundswell of support, overcoming judgments about a scandalous, ill-timed affair.

Trella hadn't reacted beyond a remote, "I've played this game a long time. Say whatever you have to."

She had played the isolation game as well and did know how to amuse herself. He wasn't needed and didn't know why he counted down the minutes until he could dodge the paparazzi on the hospital steps and enter the guarded sanctum of her room.

Her prison was as cozy as it could be made. Monitors and equipment feeds were tucked behind panels. The walls were a comfortable mocha, the blankets printed with Elazar's national pasqueflower—the white buttercup that grew wild in their alpine meadows. Trella even wore regular clothes rather than a functional hospital gown.

But she reclined on the bed twenty-four-seven. Rising to use the toilet or shower was all the activity she was allowed.

Because of potential rupture.

Her doctor had scared the hell out of him when Trella had been admitted, explaining the need for such vigilance.

Trella had been stoic. She had checked into Hospital del Re the night they'd married and, despite only having resided in his apartment for a week, he'd felt her absence. Why? She'd been angry with him, cool when she'd been forced to speak to him, but somehow she had infused a sense of liveliness to the palace. The sound of her laugh in another room, or even just the splash of color from an abandoned scarf, made it less of a museum and more of a... Hell, it had always been his *home*. How could it suddenly feel like one?

He shook off the impression.

"You're very well-informed," he said, realizing the silence was stretching. "Yet you've never once asked *me* how she is."

"How is she?" She used her among-the-people tone of fabricated warmth, smile inching toward supercilious.

Anxious, he wanted to say. Trella *was* keeping herself busy, but he read the stress that lingered in the corners of her mouth and the tension between her brows.

"As well as could be expected."

"Then you should be able to leave her."

"I know what you're thinking." He shook his head. "I'm acting like a decent human being, not becoming attached."

Yet he was indulging himself with the visits. She hadn't asked him to come.

I've done this before, she'd said of her seclusion, then

had revealed her best coping strategy. She was an accomplished sketch artist.

Practice, she had dismissed when he went through her book. He'd been taken with each image. Some were graceful gowns, some intricate patterns for beadwork. Some were colored as brightly as a children's book and others were shades of gray.

Then he had found one of their wedding day, copied from a photo her mother had taken. Trella's hint of a smile as she gazed up at him held shy awe. He wouldn't call his expression tender, but there was no hiding that he was absorbed by her doe-eyed stare. The captured moment was uncomfortably revealing, yet honest enough he couldn't be ashamed.

"I meant that for Mama, but I think you should hide it in the palace, to be discovered a hundred years from now. Give the art historians something to get excited about." She tore the page from the book and signed it. Her conspiratorial grin as she rolled it had tugged at him to play along.

It had been the first time she'd warmed up to him since their marriage, eyes sparkling with the vivacity that had first ensnared him in Paris.

He'd accepted the drawing with the strangest tingle of pleasure, liking the idea of her being resurrected generations from now, pulled from the footnotes and celebrated.

For a moment, there'd been nothing between them but this frivolous secret they were planning to keep. Then, as their gazes stayed locked, sexual awareness had crept in. The attraction was still there, ignored and subverted, but in those seconds, he felt the lava churning below the surface, swirling and burning, building with pressure against the cracks.

"Surely you can make arrangements with one of her

family members if the round-the-clock care at the hospital isn't sufficient?"

He snapped back to the breakfast room and his grandmother's facetious tone. The heat in him faded.

"I've discussed that with her." He had suspected Trella was homesick after catching her tearily viewing photos of her infant nieces. "Her brother and his wife are tied up with their new twins. Her mother is on hand to help them. Her sister can't leave her new husband." They were trying to get pregnant, if Xavier was reading the subtext correctly. "And something has gone off the rails with the brother who was engaged. She'd rather not speak to him, so..."

"You're being manipulated."

"By whom?" He held her gaze, turning one of her best weapons—barely disguised derision—against her.

"You have obligations," she began in a very quiet voice that held no hint of a tremble. It was the very lack of emotion, the stamp of inarguable logic, that made her words so powerful.

The splinter he had experienced on his wedding day rent deeper, ringing with agony as he felt himself stretched on the rack of conflicting duties. Wife. Crown. Temporary commitment. Eternal service.

A sharp rap on the door had them turning their attention to Mario as he stepped in without waiting for an invitation.

"Apologies, Your Majesty, but the Prince is requested to go the hospital. Immediately."

"They're prepping her for surgery," he was told when he called from the back of his car. He broke into a sweat and urged his driver to hurry.

He was shown to a lower floor when he arrived. She was in pre-op, flat on her back in a hospital gown, hair covered in a blue cap, lips white, tubes taped to her arm.

"You made it." She held out her free hand.

He grasped her fingers, disturbed to find her grip clammy and weak. "What happened?"

"Pain. Tearing. They scanned and said it has to be now." Her mouth trembled.

Thirty-four weeks. So early.

"Shh." He leaned to shelter her, trying to smooth her tense brow with his thumb, but feeling the trembles coursing through her. "Are you having an attack?"

"No," she choked. "This is real fear, Xavier."

"It will be okay," he insisted, undone because she had every right to be scared and there wasn't a damned thing he could do. *He* was scared. "I'll come in with you."

What help do you think you will be?

"You can't. I asked."

How did that reach inside him and squeeze his lungs dry? Her wanting him with her spun and wrapped and pierced his heart like a barbed hook, deeply uncomfortable, but inexorable, tethering them together. "I'll come in anyway."

"You *can't*, but listen. I asked them to wait until you were here so I could ask... I've texted my family. Tell them how it goes as soon as you can. If I don't make it—"

"Of course you'll make it." He closed his ears against any other outcome.

"*Listen.* If I don't, swear to me you'll give the baby fair time with them. They'll need it." Her eyes filled. "Our baby deserves to know what love is."

Her words punched a hole clear through him, leaving an expanse of emptiness that was replaced with agony. The gentle rebuke in her eyes was another blow, searing and brutal, too painful to withstand, too impactful to avoid.

"You're going to come through this," he managed. What if she didn't? He couldn't even.

"Promise me on everything you hold sacred. Your crown. Everything." Her nails dug into the back of his hand.

"If you need to hear it, yes. I'll take the baby to your family myself." He would promise anything to ease that terror in her eyes. To ease his own sense of failure. Of being so lacking she had no faith in him to give their child what it needed. Their baby *did* deserve to know what love was. If she wasn't here to offer it...

"Sir, we have to take her now."

"Kiss me goodbye," Trella whispered.

He swooped without hesitation, felt the tremble in her pouted lips, thought he ought to be gentle, but he took. Ravaged. He invaded her mouth with his tongue and drowned in all she was, trying to slake a hunger he feared would last all of eternity. Her lips opened, surrendering, even as she responded, flavoring the kiss with sweetness amid the shared desperation.

He kissed her as though it was the last one they would ever share. He couldn't bear the thought that it might be.

"Sir—"

He straightened abruptly, feeling the loss like he was torn away by a tornado, hating that he was forever doing what *must* be done.

Trella covered her mouth with her wired hand, eyes blinking above her white fingers. She kept her grip on his fingers until she was forced to let go.

"Sir, there's an observation room for students. Let me show you."

A nurse showed him to a small room with a window. Beyond, he saw Trella nod at the anesthesiologist before her face was covered with a mask. Her doctor motioned gloved hands to the team then everyone moved into place so all he saw were backs clad in scrubs.

"It shouldn't take long," the nurse said. "If you feel lightheaded, there's a chair."

He ignored her, all his attention on the surgery.

"They're waiting for confirmation she's out," the nurse said. "There they go."

They began to move in a controlled, efficient way and the nurse was right. In a very short time, the doctor was handing a tiny, naked infant to the nurse standing by with a towel. The nurse angled the baby to the window, showing him it was a boy.

The anguish in the small face at being separated from his mother pierced Xavier unexpectedly. He felt ridiculously helpless, wishing he could comfort the boy.

"We've been preparing for a premature birth. He's small, but that attempt to cry is a good sign. That's the pediatrician who's taking him. He'll run tests and place the Prince in an incubator then come speak to you. You'll probably be able to hold him. Your son, I mean," she said with a wry attempt at humor. "Not the pediatrician."

Son. Xavier nodded and texted Trella's family, including his grandmother.

A boy.

It seemed such an inadequate few letters for the magnitude of what was happening to him. He had a child. A son.

His phone buzzed with returned texts from Trella's siblings, congratulating him and asking after her.

He glanced up and something had changed. The team around Trella had snapped into frantic action. The anesthesiologist was clearly alarmed and the surgeon's movements became agitated. Through the glass, he heard raised voices issue sharp commands.

"What happened?" Xavier slapped his hand to the window, even as his gaze looked for the door to enter the room.

"Sir, I—" The nurse made as if to close the curtain.

"Find out what's happening."

"Of course." She hurried away.

He pressed his forehead to the cold glass, terror snaking to squeeze his heart. He strangled on the one word he managed to whisper.

"Bella."

CHAPTER EIGHT

TRELLA CAME TO in a blurred awareness of voices and stark white. Even Xavier looked carved from pale marble, his blue eyes translucent as antique glass. Bottle blue, she wanted to call it. She should use that shade in next season's collection.

Why was he leaning over her like that? So close and grim?

"Baby?" She tried to say, but there was no sound. Her voice had evaporated.

"Fine. Really well, considering how small he is." He backed off as a nurse picked up her wrist, but his eyes stayed locked on her.

He. "A boy?" That came out in a raspy whisper.

"Yes."

She blinked heavy eyelids and tried to smile. "Sadiq."

"What?"

"He saved me." She was becoming aware that she was stoned. Recreational drugs weren't her thing, but she'd been prescribed so many pharmaceuticals to quell her panic attacks that she knew what this foggy haze was. She hated it and fought to think through it. "I wouldn't be here without him."

"Dr. Lagundo saved you," he snapped.

"Why are you mad?" She frowned, startled to find the

nurse was still beside her, fussing with her arm. Whatever she did hurt, but distantly. "Can I see him?"

"Soon." The nurse seemed familiar. Her smile was nice, but Trella couldn't recall her name.

She hated drugs. Hated being dopey and disassociated. She ought to be upset as Xavier's remark belatedly penetrated. "I almost died?"

"There were some tense moments," the nurse said. "Your doctor will tell you more. I'll let her know you're awake."

She left and Xavier came back to her side, mouth pinched.

"Are you angry that I pulled through?"

"What? No! Why would you think that?"

She tried to think through a brain made of cotton balls. "You don't like me. You're mad about the baby."

"None of that is true." He loomed over her again, very intimidating. If she wasn't so spaced-out, she would think he sounded tortured. "You scared the hell out of me."

Was he holding her hand? Something cupped her fingers in warmth. It was nice. She liked the gentle stroke across the back of her hand.

"But it would have been easier for you." She was briefly thankful for the drugs because despair didn't overtake her. "I make things harder. I don't mean to. My family forgives me because... I don't know. They love me, I guess. But you don't, so it's okay if you wish I had died."

"Stop saying that. What would Tyrol do without you?"

"Who's Tyrol?"

"Our son."

She frowned. "I expected a girl."

"I texted you the name a couple days ago." He sounded disgruntled. Maybe self-conscious. "You said you liked it."

"When? I hate drugs. They make me so stupid. Is it Tuesday or Wednesday?"

"Wednesday. I texted on Monday and asked what you thought of Tyrol or Trentino." He seemed to be petting her arm, combing his fingers into the gaps between hers. "They're family names. You said you liked Tyrol. We're *not* naming him Sadiq."

"But picture your grandmother's face if we did."

He choked out a laugh, turning his face away, shoulders shaking. "You're funny when you're high, I'll say that much."

"You should laugh more."

He looked back at her with an expression she couldn't decipher. Regret maybe, but something like appreciation?

She closed her eyes against his sorcery.

"Did you know, *bella*? Is that why you said those things before you went in?"

"I don't get into trouble on purpose," she grumbled, ignoring the number of times Ramon had accused her of doing exactly that. "And I don't apologize when I do. It makes people feel good when they help me. My whole medical team is feeling super heroic right now."

He let out another incredulous laugh. "That is some seriously backward logic. Exactly how ripped are you?"

"Admit it. This morning you were ambivalent about having a son. Now you're grateful. You're welcome for the clarity."

Stunned comprehension seemed to blank his face, but she didn't gloat.

"I want to see him." She weakly squeezed the hand that gripped hers. "Is he beautiful? Does he look like you?"

"He looks mad." His voice wasn't quite steady. More emotion shifted across his profile, things she couldn't interpret. Concern? "He wants you."

It's the drugs, she warned herself, even as her heart turned over with sweetness that he might feel something on their son's behalf. *Don't start seeing things that aren't there.*

She didn't doubt he'd been worried on some level when he thought she would *die*. He wasn't a monster, but he had made it abundantly clear that his heart was beyond reach. He was capable of kindness, but that was the limit.

His phone buzzed. "That's your family. I'll let them know you're awake. Smile." He held up his phone to take her photo.

She stuck out her tongue and crossed her eyes. "Tell them we named him Sadiq."

"That's the friend whose wedding you attended earlier this year, isn't it? His wife would object, wouldn't she?" He tapped the screen.

"She would stab me in the eye. That's why it's funny."

"I'll tell them his name is Tyrol." He leaned down to press a kiss between her brows. "I like your eyes the way they are."

"Xavier?" She touched the side of his head, keeping him from straightening. "It's really confusing when you're nice to me."

His thumb traced near the corner of her mouth. "I never said I didn't like you, *bella*. You do make things hard. All of this is hard. But I am grateful for our son."

And me?

His eyes were an endless blue that only grew more intense the further she fell into them, but even in her muddy-minded state, she knew better than to ask.

And he didn't say.

CHAPTER NINE

XAVIER LEFT FOR Australia ten days later.

Trella and Tyrol were released from the hospital and went directly to her family's compound in southern Spain. Her brother was in residence with his four-month-old twin girls. Her mother was there, along with a team of nannies and servants and guards. Xavier could not have arranged better, safer care for either of them.

Trella had bounced back from near-death with startling cheer, pouring such tenderness and joy over their son Xavier almost thought it was fake; it was so far removed from anything he had ever experienced himself. Her words from pre-op kept echoing in his head. *Our child needs to know what love is.*

Did he? Because the limited feelings Xavier had allowed himself to feel toward her had amplified his fear when her surgery had gone sideways. This level of concern for someone wasn't comfortable. Was he a bad parent for setting up his son to love and possibly to lose?

He needed distance as a buffer against becoming more deeply invested in both of them so he went to Australia as scheduled. He hated every single one of the thirty days he was gone, which only underscored why the separation was necessary, he supposed.

It didn't help that things went exactly as he had warned

his grandmother they would. He answered the same question so many times he muddled his lines at one point.

"The plan was tripped last year."

The blond newscaster tittered.

"The trip was planned," he corrected, yanking his mind back from Spain to Adelaide and the trade talks he'd been in. "The early birth made it possible for me to travel as scheduled. I was on the brink of canceling, which would have been a shame."

Several handshake deals were already moving toward more formal agreements. His adherence to duty was producing much-needed results.

"But you must miss him!"

"Technology is a wonderful thing. We check in often. He's thriving and Trella is recovering. That's the most important thing." He flicked a glance at one of his handlers, silently conveying that if they didn't swerve back to topic, this interview was over.

The newscaster took the hint. "We wish them well. About your meeting with the state representative today…"

Did he miss his son, Xavier wondered later? If such an emotion had never been acknowledged, internally or externally, did it register with anyone if it somehow manifested today?

How *could* he miss the boy? Tyrol was an infant who wanted to suckle and sleep. Trella was adept at keeping Xavier apprised of their son's progress, such as it was. She texted often, telling him about a gain of an ounce or other small milestones. She sent him photos—probably half a dozen a day. A more pragmatic man would say one was plenty, but Xavier found himself studying each one, fascinated by tiny eyelashes and miniature fingernails. The boy's eyes looked like his own, but his mouth was definitely Trella's.

One grim night, Xavier let himself recall that for a few moments, this boy's resemblance to his mother had been all that might have been left of her. The despondency that had engulfed him at the thought had had him placing a video call to her.

She had been surprised since she usually initiated the calls if she happened to be nursing and the time was right on his end. She had asked him about his day, which he didn't care to talk about, and he had listened to whatever she volunteered, silently mocking himself for being riveted by small talk about her family and a few shower gifts.

There shouldn't have been any holes of curiosity or unmet sense of obligation within him. His wife and child were well. He was getting on with his life exactly as he should.

So why did he nearly go through the roof when he woke to a fresh message from her?

Ramon and Izzy are getting married! The wedding is at the end of the month, in Madrid. We decamp to the family mansion the day before I'm due to return to Elazar. I'll extend our stay until after the ceremony since it's only an extra weekend.

On the surface, it was a perfectly reasonable assumption. Moving her and Tyrol with the rest of the staff to Elazar for a few days so she could turn around and go back was a needless expense. Royal detractors would have a field day. She was nursing, so she couldn't leave Tyrol in Elazar while she attended the wedding. Xavier had no reasonable basis to refuse her request.

Nevertheless, the only word that came to mind was, *No*. He didn't analyze it, he only knew he would not go back to the palace and wait for her.

* * *

As the youngest, Trella sometimes thought she had received all the leftover DNA after her siblings had taken the best of it. Henri had their father's sense and logic. He was stubborn, yes, but *she* was outright obstinate. Ramon had their mother's passion and determination, but Trella was an opinionated hothead. Gili scooped up all the sensitivity and generosity while Trella selfishly stole all the attention with her nervous breakdowns.

None of them were small-minded or jealous, but Trella—the baby who was spoiled and deferred to all the time—was drowning in envy of all of them.

Why couldn't she have a partner in parenting like Henri had with Cinnia? Why couldn't she have a big wedding that had everyone buzzing with excitement, like Ramon was planning with Isidora? Why couldn't she have a husband who not only couldn't keep his hands off her, like Kasim with Gili, but refused to have any other woman by his side as he took the throne of his country?

Why did she have so much negative self-talk eating away at her self-esteem? *They* didn't. They were all better and smarter than that.

She was the broken one.

With her arms braced on the side of the pool, she gave desultory kicks behind her while watching Cinnia hand off a freshly fed Rosalina to Henri.

"I'll put her down and work through siesta. You'll finish your lunch then rest before we travel?"

"I will," Cinnia promised, smirking at Henri's overprotectiveness before he erased it with a tender kiss. "Thank you, darling." She gave her wrap dress a final straighten and turned back to the salad she'd been picking at while nursing.

Henri glanced at Tyrol, asleep in the cot in the shade.

"Do you want me to take him up? You should sleep before we leave, too."

The flight was an hour and Trella was five weeks postpartum, but her scare during delivery had set them all back to watching her like she was made of spun glass.

"I'll take him when Cinnia goes up. The weather won't be as warm in Elazar. I want to enjoy the pool while I can."

"I'm going to miss you when you go back to Elazar," Cinnia said as Henri left.

"I know. This has been really nice."

Quite by accident, Cinnia had been the first to know Trella was pregnant, when she had been hiding her own pregnancy from Henri. They had become very close in those early months and sharing these weeks of new motherhood had deepened their sister-like bond.

"Is it going to be okay living there, do you think?" The simple question was the reason Trella loved Cinnia. Her sister-in-law invited confidence but didn't intrude.

Trella sighed, daunted enough by the future to admit, "I have no idea. I feel good. Physically, I mean. And stable, mentally. But I'm *here*. That always helps."

"At least I knew Henri when I was in your shoes." Cinnia had been Henri's mistress for years before her pregnancy tore them apart and drew them back together. "It must be hard, having a baby and still being at the getting-to-know-you stage. You two haven't had a proper chance, have you?"

"No." Two nights and daily hospital visits that she'd said she didn't need.

She had, though. She'd soaked up his duty visits like sunshine, trying not to read into the kiss they'd shared when they wed. He'd seemed to be pretending it hadn't happened, sticking to chatting very generally about whatever meeting he'd been in or whatever political scandal was trending.

When he'd gone through her sketchbook, she'd felt very vulnerable, especially when he found the one she'd done of them. Why had she thought it was a good idea to give it to him? He'd probably thrown it out, but she had longed so badly for him to feel *something* about their wedding day.

He'd looked…touched? Whatever the softening in his face had been, it had caused her to moon so obviously, he'd flinched and looked away.

She was such an idiot. He was probably feeling put-upon. When they did connect over the tablet, he had seemed remote. He wasn't impatient, but she had the sense his prevailing mood was resignation.

She was trying to resign herself as well. Years of therapy had taught her to focus on one small piece of the future at a time. When he had crushed her soul with his news that their marriage would be temporary, she hadn't tried to imagine what her life would look like after their divorce. She had focused on making it to term with her pregnancy.

Once Tyrol had arrived, she'd come here, where she'd been able to focus on Tyrol and her recovery. Returning to Elazar and her looming divorce wasn't something she was ready to contemplate. She didn't even know how to handle the two and a half months left in their brief marriage!

Making a concerted effort to include Xavier in Tyrol's progress had seemed like the right thing to do. She told herself it was her way of encouraging a bond between father and son, but she knew there was a part of her that liked having an excuse to reach out to him. She was still trying to push for something that was futile.

But just when his reticence had her convinced he felt nothing, he would surprise her by phoning to ask how things were going. He would linger on a video call after she'd run out of things to say, seeming content to stare at a sleeping baby over a screen.

Such a confounding man.

She glanced to where Tyrol slept; the one thing in all of this that made her unspeakably proud. If everything she'd been through in her life, all the pain and traumas and anguish had had to happen in order to bring her son into this world, so be it. She accepted all of it.

"Has your doctor really forbidden you to have another?"

"We talked it over several times through the pregnancy. It was my idea that she would tie my tubes during delivery, so I wouldn't need another surgery in the future. She did. I'm not sorry, or even very sad. I resigned myself a long time ago to not being able to get pregnant. He's truly a miracle. The delivery was such a near miss, though. I wouldn't want to push my luck, especially now he's here and needs me."

Cinnia nodded. "What about a surrogate? I'm sorry. Maybe that's not something you'd consider?"

"Gili told me years ago she would be my surrogate, but that was before Kasim." She tucked her chin. "Can you imagine his reaction?"

"He gives her anything she asks for." Cinnia closed her grin on her fork. "His head would literally explode trying to decide whether to be possessive or indulgent."

"Right?" They both chuckled, then Trella sobered. "They would want to secure his heirs before even thinking of it, anyway. I don't see Xavier wanting to wait." *There is a reason for a spare.* "Maybe I'll find a surrogate someday, but I don't think that would change Xavier's mind about us. It's not just about another baby. We're not you and Henri." Or Gili and Kasim. Or Ramon and Isidora. "He has other considerations."

He doesn't want me.

She *had* to accept that.

It made her chest grow tight, though. Her throat ached.

She ducked under the water to hide how she was tearing up. She stayed there, diving deep and crawling along the bottom until her lungs were about to burst, only coming to the surface when she reached the stairs.

"Pah!" She stood and wiped the water from her eyes.

Cinnia had come to her feet and was saying hello to someone.

Henri had returned with a striking blond man in tailored dark gray pants and a collared T-shirt that hugged the fit muscles of his shoulders and revealed his tanned gorgeous biceps.

The newcomer glared at her from his familiar, laser blue eyes. "Should you be *swimming*?"

Suddenly dizzy, Trella panted, "*Hola, cariño.* I missed you, too."

Xavier was distantly aware of Henri retreating with his wife, but if the woman had a name, he had already forgotten it. His entire focus was eaten up by the way Trella rose from the water like Venus herself.

Water sluiced down her body, washing away the grinding aggravation that had propelled him here. He had needed to see her without understanding why. He might have labeled it homesickness if that wasn't such a juvenile emotion and he was in Elazar, not a part of Spain he'd never seen before.

But he'd come here with single-minded determination and when he'd finally clapped eyes on her, she'd been on the *bottom of the pool*, trying to give him a heart attack all over again.

All his concern, pining and every other thought in his head drained away, however, as she walked toward him.

Coming here was a mistake. He saw that as clearly as he saw she wore a red bikini, the triangles of fabric tied off at her hips and between her breasts. She had been quite comely with the weight of a baby distending her middle, always turning herself out stylishly, even when she'd been in the hospital.

Keeping his mind off sex while she'd been in a delicate condition had been, if not easy, at least quickly forestalled by worst-case scenarios. He had told himself any attraction he still felt was a byproduct of his not having had sex since they'd made the baby sleeping in the cot to his left. Maybe the two kisses they'd shared had ambushed his memory when it was least convenient. Definitely, he relived their night in Paris far too often.

It all added up to an obsession he should have put behind him by now.

He hadn't.

Her approach coiled him tight. He hadn't seen her naked since Paris and her hourglass figure was as spectacular as his libido recalled. Better. Glittering droplets sparkled on her golden skin and her breasts were positively voluptuous, swaying as she padded toward him, bare feet slapping the tile.

His mouth watered. A distinctly male pulse tugged behind the fly of his pants. He had to resist a telltale swallow and consciously regulated his breathing. The animal, that restless beast that had been scratching and digging inside him, howled as she drew near, wanting to leap on her. Reunite.

"What are you—?" She was squeezing water from her hair, but as she met his gaze, her eyes widened in reaction, pupils exploding like fireworks. Her breath caught, expanding her chest and drawing his attention to her nipples, already sharp from the chill, but poking even harder under his gaze.

"Wh-what are you doing here?" Her hand went to a nearby chair back as if she needed to steady herself.

He was acting directly against his responsibilities, despite the rationalizations he'd concocted. Angry with himself for the hunger clawing through him, he searched his brain for the reasons that underpinned his arrival.

"I'm taking you to Madrid. You'll stay with me there."

Her shoulders fell. "You don't trust me?"

That wasn't it, but he didn't want to admit—even to himself—that he hadn't been able to wait three more nights to see them. Not just his son. Her.

He found his gaze straying to the curve of her hips and the dip of her navel and forced his attention to drag across to the infant in a pale green onesie. The strangest yank in his chest had him stooping to pick up the boy.

The sleeping baby gave a small start of surprise, fingers splaying, then relaxed into a warm ball against the hollow of Xavier's shoulder. He felt heavier. Sturdier.

"He's growing."

"He is." She wrapped a towel around her middle, hands shaking. "Xavier, I swear I wasn't trying to avoid coming back. The wedding is a rushed thing. Izzy's father has been ill. It's a big deal for him to be able to walk her down the aisle so they're indulging him. It's also the only chance for the bunch of us to be together for the foreseeable future. That's why I need to be there."

"I'm not saying you shouldn't go. But it's your first public appearance since we married. We should be seen together."

"Well, of course you were invited. I just didn't think…" She was taken aback, which was justified, he supposed. "Doesn't it send the wrong message?"

Because of the way their press release had been worded.

Given Ms Sauveterre's preference for avoiding the spotlight, the marriage is a formality to ensure the legitimacy of Prince Xavier's heir and won't be continued in the new year.

"I've spent a month having my devotion to my family questioned. I'd like to change the optics." There. That was the excuse he had given his grandmother and he stood by it. Their countrymen were going mad over the three photos he'd released of the young prince, but they were questioning why he wasn't spending more time with him.

Trella understood how the PR game was played. She wouldn't fault this move.

The warmth that had pinkened her cheeks drained away, though. Her expression stiffened. "Of course. And we both know how unimpeachable your sense of obligation is. Most of my packing is done. I only have to shower and change. Shall I send a nanny to take him? After you've had time to post some selfies, of course."

He had set himself up for that, but it still landed on target. "I'll keep him," he said in a tone that let her know she was walking a fine line.

She flipped her wet hair and walked away.

Trella fell asleep on the flight so they were in Madrid before she was alone with Xavier again. Physically she was recovered, but Tyrol was so little he needed to feed often, even if that meant waking him. She was up several times a night so tended to nod off midday. But rather than dozing, she would have preferred to spend the time working through Xavier's surprise appearance.

Optics? Really? It was incredibly insulting. Her entire family had been used a million times over to sell magazines and promote products, all without their consent. She was tempted to tell him what she thought of him, but part of her disbelieved him.

For a minute, as they'd stood by the pool, she'd thought—But, no. His carnal look had been gone once he'd picked up Tyrol. She had imagined it. What kind of wanton did it make her that she had responded to blatant lust, anyway?

She *had* responded, though. She had run to the shower to cool off, slowing the race of her pulse and willing away the thrumming awareness in her loins.

Fat lot of good it did. Flutters of intrigue were still playing like butterflies in her middle, gaze straying to the cut of his pants over his butt and the sculpted muscles beneath his shirt as he paced in front of her. She had missed him!

Tyrol finished nursing and was fast asleep so she unlatched him and handed him off to a nanny, then she struggled to put herself together behind the screen of a receiving blanket that didn't want to stay in place.

Yes, I'm half-naked under here. *Stop staring.*

A flush of heat went through her. It was a lusty reaction that had simmered at merely sensual while she'd been feeling squat, scared and vulnerable in a hospital. Or when he'd been on the other side of the planet.

Now she was more confident on so many levels, but still unsure of herself with her husband. This was as bad as his ambush in Innsbruck when he'd left her with nowhere to hide.

"Ready?" he said, tucking away the phone he'd been tapping while she'd nursed.

"For?"

"I've been waiting to look around. I haven't seen the house, either."

"Oh. Um, sure." The mansion was on a small estate in La Moraleja, farther out of the city from the historical home in the Salamanca neighborhood that had been in her mother's family for generations. This house was built with old-world touches like columns and wrought iron rails, but it was very modern, perhaps only a few years old.

"Did you lease it? Or…?" Surely he hadn't purchased something for a long weekend?

"It belongs to a friend. We studied architecture together. He showed me the plans a few years ago. I'm interested to see how it all came together."

He waved for her to lead him from the lounge to a small dining area that was likely used for intimate lunches. The gallery that overlooked the main door was above them. A row of tall windows afforded a view of the landscaped grounds.

"I didn't know you were interested in architecture." She watched him take in the elevator, set in a convenient location, but made unobtrusive by disguising it with the rise of the stairs. Why did a bit of small talk make her so nervous?

"I'm an architect."

"Really! What have you designed?"

"My chalet." He bypassed the entrance to the kitchen and opened a door to the patio, inviting her to exit ahead of him.

"You did well. I liked it." A wind had come up beneath the overcast skies, making her hug her arms and try to tuck her wayward hair behind her ears as they walked past flower pots that lined the covered pool.

He was looking sideways at her.

"I wasn't trying to escape because I didn't like the floor plan."

He rolled his eyes, which made her smile, but self-consciousness stuck like a burr, prickly and sharp. It was strange to be with him again, in person, alone, without nurses or valets hovering. With sexual awareness sizzling within her.

"I'm serious," she said, trying to hide her nervousness. "I know you don't need my approval, but I thought it felt cozy despite the open plan. You obviously placed the windows very carefully. Each view was a well-framed photograph of the natural world—what?" she demanded as his look grew penetrating. "I'm an artist. I notice when care has been taken for a particular effect. Don't you? Look at these stairs."

She waved at the way they curved down from the upper terrace.

"Most people see convenience, but the placement balances the turret on the other side, which is probably the master bedroom, situated to overlook—" She turned to look across the expanse of grounds, charmed as she noticed the brook and the wooden bridge. "Oh, that's lovely, isn't it?"

"He wanted to put the master bedroom on this end," Xavier said. "At the top of the stairs, closer to the pool. I suggested the turret and told him to curve the stairs."

She pivoted to face him, watching his gaze track the upper terrace, profile dark with critique, but also...envy?

"What else have you designed?"

"Nothing. My attention is needed elsewhere." He said it without emotion, but she felt the pang that he refused to betray.

"You're frustrated."

His lids came down so the heat of his gaze glowed fiercely behind the veil of his spiky lashes. "We're talking about that, are we?" His attention dropped to her mouth.

Suddenly they were poolside again. Such a hard streak of sexual heat shot through her, it physically stung from the base of her throat, behind her breastbone, sank like a hot coal in the pit of her belly and radiated warmth into the juncture of her thighs. Her heart took off at a gallop while birds took flight in her midsection.

"I meant as an artist!" She blushed, embarrassed at how quickly and blatantly she reacted to a simple look.

His mouth deepened at the corners. He pushed his hands into his pockets. "There are many ways to apply form and function to the role I occupy. I don't have to design something."

"It's not the same." She was still flustered, stewing in heat and being confused by it. "I told you about the time I was depressed? It was because the medication made it impossible for me to create. The need was there, but when I sat down to draw or sew, it was like sending a bucket into an empty well. I wasn't having panic attacks, but I didn't see any point in being alive if I couldn't..." She held up her hands.

"I'm not depressed."

"But you're denied."

"So what?"

"It's something you need."

"It's something I *want*. Desire can be ignored in favor of more important things."

"We're not talking about architecture, are we?" She let her hands fall and blinked, eyes watery from the wind. Or so she hoped he believed.

A long silence followed where only a distant wind chime rang.

"Are you really here because of optics?" It made her lungs feel heavy and raw.

He hissed out a long breath. "I came because I wanted to." He set his teeth after he said it, as though absorbing some inner thought that displeased him, then said in a voice rife with subdued turmoil, "But we don't get everything we want, *bella*. You know that as well as I do."

He wasn't mocking her. He was saying it with deep understanding of the things she would never have—a carefree childhood, another pregnancy. She choked up, wanting to ask if he had come because he'd wanted to be with her, but she was too scared of the answer.

So she only said, "Have you forgotten my name? You're calling me *bella*."

"It's not an endearment. It's who you are. It's what you are." The last bit sounded as though it came out against his will.

She wanted to believe him, but her misshapen heart was so very conscious of her flaws. Of the fact he had rebuffed her.

"I've never felt beautiful." She toed a pebble. "I was the messy one, always grass-stained and needing my hair combed. After my kidnapping, the press called me 'the fat one,' because I comfort-ate. I starved myself in retaliation and cut my own hair and looked like a Goth for years, dark circles under my eyes, makeup smudged and face pale from not sleeping properly. It took ages after I got my panic attacks under control to look as healthy and happy as my sister."

She squinted as she looked up, startled to find she had his full attention. That wasn't pity in his expression, though. He was engrossed, which made a squiggling sensation tremble in the pit of her stomach.

"You asked me that night in Paris, remember? You asked if I was as beautiful as my sister. I thought it was funny to say yes because I was impersonating her. The only time I feel beautiful is when I look like her." She knew better intellectually, but deep down, she still had a lot of demons.

"You were stunning when you were pregnant. You're beautiful now. When I saw your sister in Berlin, I thought she was beautiful because she looked like you."

She shook her head. "You didn't even know—"

"I *knew*. I could tell the second I saw her. I just didn't believe it. I thought—"

"What?" She held her breath, brimming with dread and hope, not sure what she wanted to hear.

He grimaced. "I thought I'd been a fool. That the way we'd reacted to each other had been a one-off thing."

She swallowed. "It wasn't?"

His gaze slammed into hers, pupils expanding the way a cat's dilated before it pounced. Lines of tension pulled the rest of his face into the harsh countenance of a barely restrained barbarian. "Clearly."

She stood on a tipping point, vibrating under the strain, drawn, drawn, drawn. The pull in her chest was nearly irresistible. A prickling wash of sensations made her hyper aware of everything around her, the pale heat of the sun, the scent of the grass, the dampness in the air and, most especially, the way he was looking at her mouth. At the way such a tiny expression of interest from this man could send wildfire through her whole body.

She tore her gaze from his, seeing only a blur of green and blue.

"Please be careful, Xavier." She scraped at the hair tickling her cheek, shaken. "My self-esteem is full of holes. Don't give me hope if there is none."

"For what? You don't want to be married to me. You said so."

"I don't want to be married to a man who doesn't want me." She had to press her lips tight so they wouldn't tremble. Meeting his gaze was hard. She couldn't hide the struggle, the longing, that was eating her up. "If you do…"

"I don't *want* to want you," he ground out.

She jerked back as though he'd struck her. He winced. "I mean I can't *afford* to want you. My father followed where sexual interest led. It was a disaster. I didn't expect this," he grated. "I wouldn't have come."

She breathed through each of the blows, eventually able to ask, "That's all you feel?" The question was too revealing. She regretted it, even before he answered.

He took a long time, then, "Don't hope, *bella*. You know my views on love."

His gentle reply broke her chest open, leaving her heart pulsing like an open wound. *This* was what she had been avoiding accepting. This was why she couldn't bear to look into her future. He was never going to love her.

Engulfed in agony right to the backs of her teeth, she nodded dumbly. "Will you listen for Tyrol when you go in? I want to see the bridge."

She didn't notice the hand he reached out as she walked away.

CHAPTER TEN

HE HAD HURT HER. He hadn't wanted to. Cruel to be kind, he had thought, and he had regretted it immediately. What could he do, though? Admit that what he felt was not purely sexual. Even if he was capable of love, which he wasn't, they had no future. He couldn't lead her on.

He hated that he'd returned her to that stiff wariness, though. The woman who had texted without hesitation for the weeks they'd been apart suddenly had a full schedule and little to say. By the time they were at a dinner hosted by the bride's parents the next evening, the tension between them was palpable. Her family smiled around it.

Angelique hadn't arrived yet, Henri was there with his wife and twins along with her mother, and Trella spent most of the evening needling Ramon.

Xavier tried to intervene at one point. Ramon wasn't above getting personal in retaliation and neither was Trella. It was escalating, but the bride, Isidora, tugged him aside. She was a stunning woman with auburn hair and a smile that put anyone at ease.

"It's a rookie move to get involved. Better to ignore them. Trust me."

He waited until they had left to ask Trella, "Why were you being so contentious with Ramon?"

"I wasn't. That's how we communicate." The passing streetlights flicked over her stoic expression.

"I thought you might bring on an attack."

"No." She sounded petulant. "We fight like that all the time. It's fine."

"It wasn't because you're angry with me?"

Silence, then, "I'm not angry. I'm hurt."

He should have left it there, but said, "Either way, you should take it out on me, not him." *Punish me.* He couldn't stand the guilt he was carrying.

"I'd rather fight with Ramon." Her hands twisted in her lap. "I know he won't let me win. Any points I score, I've earned. It builds my confidence. And no matter what I say, he'll still love me. I don't have that kind of trust with you."

Be careful what you wish for, Xavier thought, flayed to the bone. He didn't speak of it again.

Trella was a dam filled to the brim, gates stuck. When Xavier bowed out of joining Ramon and his racing friends at a sports bar the next evening, the pressure inside her climbed a notch higher.

"The bar isn't Kasim's thing, either. I invited him to come over with Gili for the evening after they see Mama. Cinnia wants to give the girls a quiet night so she's staying in." Trella desperately needed time with her sister. "Do you mind?"

"You're not going clubbing with the bridal party? I'll stay with Tyrol."

"Isidora will have enough paparazzi as it is. If Gili and I went? We're doing her a favor staying away."

"I see. Of course. Invite them. That's fine." They were being exceedingly agreeable and polite since she'd admitted to her hurt feelings last night. It was horrible. She kept wondering how she would endure two more months of this. A lifetime, really. Would it be worse or better when they divorced and lived apart?

She was so caught up in her own turmoil, she completely forgot that Xavier had met Gili before. *Gili* hadn't, the darling. She rushed him when she arrived, taking both his hands to say beseechingly, "I'm so glad we have this chance to clear the air. I can't imagine what you thought of me in Berlin. You must have been so shocked. But I hope we can be friends because I already adore your son."

Her sister's warmth could melt glaciers and Xavier's expression eased in a blink. "It's already forgotten," he assured with his patented charm.

Trella felt a stab of jealousy. Why couldn't she win him over as easily?

Gili turned to her then, concern in her eyes, because of course she had picked up on Trella's distress. At the same time, something glowed from her like a beacon, a happiness so bright, it blinded.

Oh, Gili. Anytime Trella thought she couldn't survive whatever anguish was gripping her, her twin found a way to lift her out of it. Smiling tearily, she hugged her pregnant sister tight.

Xavier was glad to have an evening with the King of Zhamair. Asking Kasim about a complex situation in one of his neighboring countries was a welcome distraction from his struggle between duty and desire. Between wanting to mend fences with Trella and letting her bruised feelings keep her at a distance.

Thirty minutes in, he realized the women hadn't come back from fetching Tyrol. "Did we bore them? I'll find—"

"Please let them be," Kasim said. "She needs time with her sister."

"Which one?" Xavier asked dryly, hoping Trella wasn't shedding tears over him.

"A fair question." Kasim took up his drink. "Their interdependence takes getting used to, doesn't it? But this…" He chucked his chin toward the ceiling, where the women were likely in Trella's room. "She was bursting at the seams."

"Pregnant?" A surprise rush went through Xavier. He was astonished to realize he was pleased for the couple. Why? It had nothing to do with him.

Except that he knew how good it felt to have a child. It struck him then how important Tyrol had become to him. Not because he secured Elazar's future, but because Tyrol was… Tyrol. Not an insurance policy for the future, a relation.

Disconcerted, he had to clear sudden emotion from his throat as he rose to shake Kasim's hand. "Congratulations."

"Thank you." Kasim darkened with a flush of pride and hitched his pants to sit again. "It's very early days, only confirmed the day before we left Zhamair. Not something we're making public."

Xavier fetched his own drink and offered to tap glasses, experiencing envy as he thought of Kasim sharing the moment of discovery and every single day of the pregnancy, along with the birth. Feeling robbed was not a new sensation for him. He got over it quickly, but he wondered if Kasim realized how lucky he was, able to go through this process as many times as his wife was up for.

He could, too, he supposed, with Patrizia.

His brandy tasted like snake venom. He abandoned it.

"I'd like you to consider something," Kasim said, sounding like someone unused to requesting favors. "Closer to the birth, I'd like Trella to come to Zhamair."

A strange void opened in Xavier. "We won't be married any longer." It took enormous effort to state that with equanimity. "Trella may go where she pleases." The knowledge knotted his gut.

Kasim's smile tightened. "I expect she'll want to bring Tyrol. I know Angelique will want to see him by then."

Which would require Xavier's permission. He instantly rejected the idea. He had sent Trella to Spain while he'd traveled Australia before he'd realized how unbearable it would be. The King of Zhamair was not plotting to steal his son, he was sure, but at least if Tyrol stayed in Elazar, he knew Trella would come back.

He looked away, disturbed by the dependence that train of thought suggested.

"It was very hard on Angelique to be apart from Trella when Tyrol was born." Kasim took a healthy sip of brandy, like he needed it, and hissed out his breath. "She fainted when Trella flatlined. Then your text came through and I realized why. She was hysterical until Trella was revived."

So was I, Xavier could have said, but they were already sharing far past his usual level. He loathed thinking about those long terrifying minutes. It put him in a cold sweat.

"I'll see what I can do," he said woodenly, mostly to end the discussion. Doing a favor for one of the most powerful men in the Middle East was a smart move, he reasoned, but was repelled by the idea of using his son for political gain.

Duty. It wasn't a double-edged sword. It was two branding irons pressing him front and back, pinning him in place, allowing no escape and only sinking deeper into his flesh when he tried.

Much later, when the couple had left, he was still thinking about where the line was drawn. Would his grandmother say Tyrol was doing *his* duty by going to Zhamair, cultivating warm relations with a foreign entity?

The poor boy didn't even know what he was in for. He lay unswaddled in Trella's lap, gaze wandering the ceiling, arms flailing and fingers catching in the curtains of her loose hair as she looked over him.

"Who gets another cousin?" she asked the boy with soft excitement.

Xavier sat with his feet propped on the ottoman. Her top afforded him a lovely view down her cleavage and her gentle laughter was as erotic as her tickling hair might feel, sweeping across his skin. It was sheer torture to sit here, wanting without having, but far too soon he wouldn't even have this much so he savored the pain.

"Did you know she was pregnant? Before she told you? Kasim made it sound like you have a supernatural link." He was skeptical, but Angelique had called her that time in the car, seeming to know Trella's panic attack was upon her.

"Was he worried I spied on them while they were making that baby?" She lifted her head, so stunning, with amusement curving her lips, that his heart lurched. "No, it's nothing like that. More an emotional thing." Her smile faded. "I should have realized how happy she was, but I've been distracted."

Pensive because of him. Upset. At least she was talking to him again.

"Do you feel it with your brothers?"

"They're too pigheaded, especially Ramon. Isn't he?" she said to Tyrol. "*Tío* Ramon is a *toro*." A bull.

"But you still love them." Xavier was beginning to see how love wasn't just a romantic notion, or even a desire, for her. It was as vital to her as oxygen. It drove the very blood in her veins.

"I love them very much," she agreed, sober and ultra-gentle as she kissed Tyrol's bare feet. "They got me through my darkest times. I hung on because of them. Pushed through *for* them. Now I have Tyrol." She dipped to nuzzle his tummy, making his little arms jerk.

You have me, Xavier thought, but thorns had invaded his windpipe. He was starkly aware he couldn't pledge anything more than the pittance he'd already offered.

"You never wished for brothers or sisters?" Her head came up. "Your mother didn't have more children?"

"My father has a daughter. Maybe three or four years old by now? My mother has two boys. Teenagers, I think."

"You've never met them?"

"There's no place for them in my life." That's what he'd always thought, but he heard how cold it sounded, especially as she looked so askance.

"You could have made one."

"What would I have in common with them?"

"*Parents*?"

"They didn't act like parents." He shook the cubes of ice in his glass, wondering if he could judge when he'd barely grasped the ropes himself. "Neither were a great example of the importance of sibling relationships, either. I was young, but I picked up on jealousy and resentment between my mother and her sister. Because of her marriage into royalty, I suppose. And my father lost his brother."

"It wasn't his fault, was it?" She gathered Tyrol to her shoulder, tucking his blanket around him. "How old was he?"

"He was sixteen, his brother was eighteen. It was just a bad wind that came up while he was sailing. My father didn't talk about him often, but when he did..." Xavier swallowed, still affected by the memory of his father growing teary. "He missed him. Made me think I was better off without that kind of risk."

"But you'll give Tyrol a sibling."

"I have to." It was the stark truth, but again he heard how indifferent it made him sound when really his emotions on the matter were so tangled he couldn't even begin to name them.

Her brows pulled together and her mouth pouted. "I'll do it because I *want* to."

Without his need for biological children, many options were open to her, adoption among them. He suppressed a flinch, surprised how much it hurt to think of her starting a family with another man.

"You should," he made himself say. "You're a natural at motherhood. Family is clearly your source of strength."

She stared at him like he was a dog that had been hit on the highway.

"Are you going up?" he asked, trying to change the subject. "Leave him with me. I'll put him down when he falls asleep."

Her mouth twitched, but if she was surprised at his desire to hold his son, it was quickly blinked away. He let out a breath as she placed the boy's warm weight in his hands, relaxing as he embraced one of the few responsibilities he was pleased to have.

Trella hovered, watching Tyrol rub his fist against his cheek, chasing it with his mouth. They shared a chuckle at his efforts, but Xavier's was bittersweet.

"My family was not yours, *bella*. The way you are with them is a foreign culture to me. I can't emulate something I never had. But I do want Tyrol to be happy. Happier than I was."

Her hand settled on his shoulder. It was unnerving not only because they hadn't touched since she'd been in the hospital, but because she gathered the torment rippling through him into a hot ball in the corner of his chest, so it pulsed under the feathery weight of her fingers. He held very still, as if her hand was a shy bird and he didn't want to startle her into flitting away.

"I know." Her thumb moved in a brief caress. "And I know you're starting to love him. I'm glad."

His heart swerved as her hand lifted and he watched her retreat.

* * *

Trella was trying hard to resign herself to Xavier's limitations. Gili had hugged her and wiped her tears and said, "Give it time." Things had been rough between her and Kasim before they'd married. *She* wasn't ready to give up on Trella finding happiness with Xavier, but that was Gili. She wanted to believe the best of everyone and everything.

Trella wasn't so sure, but she took heart from the way Tyrol had begun prying himself through Xavier's defenses. Xavier took every opportunity to hold his son. Not for optics. No one was seeing him walk down the hall in the middle of the night. He *wanted* to hold him. He expressed concern about a little spit-up, then worried the damp patch would make Tyrol uncomfortable and changed him. He talked to his son about architecture, for heaven's sake, then broke off when he realized Trella was listening.

Still, when she had accused him of starting to love his son, she suspected he had been more surprised by his capacity to do so than she was.

And therein lay the problem. She had told him she didn't want to be married to a man who didn't want her. She had meant a man who didn't *love* her. If there was a chance he might develop feelings for her, surely she owed it to Tyrol to give their marriage a chance?

Or was that a foolish rationalization because she was smitten?

Either way, she had to keep the struggle off her face and smile for the wedding photos. Ramon and Isidora's marriage should be perfect, even if hers wasn't.

The ceremony was held in a five-hundred-year-old cathedral, conducted by an archbishop, witnessed by royalty, aristocrats, heads of state and celebrities from film, stage and the athletic arena. The route to the hotel, where the reception was held, had been blocked off and was lined ten-people deep with bystanders, photographers and even television cameras. Drones buzzed between the cars and a helicopter pattered overhead.

They hurried from the cavalcade up the red carpet, past the deafening cheer of the throng behind the velvet ropes, through the security checkpoint and into the relative peace of the ballroom where they finally caught their breath.

Mirrored tabletops reflected the lush floral arrangements of orchids and roses. Wisteria dripped from the ceiling along with crystals that glinted like snowflakes. A harpist's delicate notes welcomed them along with uniformed staff carrying trays of gold-rimmed glasses of champagne.

"That was insane," Xavier said, not dropping his protective hold across her back.

"Small wonder I've never been on a date before, isn't it? We're a nightmare to take anywhere."

Surprise loosened his clean-shaven jaw. "You never dated? *At all*?"

"Well, there was this one stranger I met in Paris." She gave him a cheeky wink and made a tiny adjustment to his boutonniere. It was a delicate creation of spotted feather and red-throated orchid with a lacy fern frond behind it. She deliberately avoided looking at the red sash that scored his chest, announcing his station—the role that was more important than she could ever hope to be.

"Seriously? I'm the only one?"

She shrugged. "One of Ramon's friends recovered from a crash at Sus Brazos two years ago. I ate dinner with him by the pool a few times. We kissed once, but it was…"

"What?" His fingers dug into her hip, something flashing in his eyes as his expression grew unreadable. She wouldn't let herself believe it was possessiveness.

"Nothing. Over before it started. Like you and me." Affair, pregnancy, marriage. They were all slipping like sand through her fingers, refusing to be slowed. "But thank you for coming with me tonight. I should have said that before. I was dreading coming alone and having to dodge awkward questions about our marriage."

She made herself smile and meet his eyes as she started to step out of his embrace. His arm hardened.

"The things I'm still learning about you," he muttered. The fingers of his free hand looped around her wrist. He looked across the room, expression tight then came back, fierce and hot. "I hate this, *bella*. We had one damned night that was perfect. The only regret I had was that I didn't have more time to get to know you better and now we have time and we're wasting it."

Edginess came off him in waves, rattling whatever defenses she still managed to hold up against him. Her bottom lip grew wobbly and she had to tuck it between her teeth. "I thought you were just putting the time in, waiting for us to be over."

"No." He shook his head, voice deepening. "No, I'm... I'm trying to protect you."

"Oh, Xavier." She sighed. "I'm *tired* of being protected. That's why I slept with you. I wanted to feel what other people feel. The ones who aren't sitting in a vault waiting for their lives to start. I wanted to flirt. Feel pretty. Dance."

"Go on a date?"

"Yes."

His thumb stroked the thin skin inside her wrist. "This is a date."

Not a real one, she thought. People who went on dates were hopeful of a future. But beggars couldn't be choosers. She forced herself to make a face of forbearance as she said, "It's not dinner and a movie, but I suppose it will do."

His expression relaxed, lips twitching. "Too cliché. I've

brought you star gazing." He deliberately let his attention scan the growing crowd of celebrities.

Relief as much as amusement sent laughter bursting out of her. She slid her arm around him, hugging herself into him as lightness filled her. "If you promise to have me home by curfew, then yes, I would love to be your date."

Over before we started.

These last few days had given Xavier an unprecedented glimpse into Trella's world. She was right. All too soon they would be strangers again. He couldn't countenance it. Like his last night of freedom in Paris, he was compelled to grasp this chance with her.

Unlike Paris, he couldn't steal her away and it was delicious torture standing beside her, setting a subtly possessive touch upon her, but unable to do more. All the while, he fell under her spell, as did everyone she spoke to.

It was humbling, in a good way, to be with a woman whose attention was as valuable as his own. Rather than having to consciously include her in a conversation, they operated as a unit. One minute she introduced him to a family friend with a pedigree that matched his own, the next he was catching up with a diplomat he'd dealt with in the past whose wife was a client at Maison des Jumeaux.

Then they were interrupted and she threw herself into a man's arms. "Sadiq!"

The man's wife, who happened to be Kasim's sister, Xavier learned, was clearly a close friend, too. They spoke with the couple for a long time, until Xavier couldn't wait to dance with Trella again.

"Explain to me exactly how he saved you?" He prompted when they were on the floor.

"Hacking." She glanced around as she said it. "We're not supposed to talk about it. He still does some high-level work on the side. He found out where I was being held and alerted the police."

"How old was he?"

"Fifteen. Crazy to think of, isn't it? He didn't know us very well, either, just had some classes with the boys. I think it was the challenge of it. He's stubborn that way. It definitely wasn't a desire to be a hero because you can see how self-effacing he is. But he wanted to help and persevered until he had something. Every time I see him, I'm reminded that he gave me this life and I should be grateful for it. Not waste it."

She met his eyes as she echoed what he had said earlier, but he read the deeper question in the longing look she gave him. They'd been engaging in subtle foreplay all night, not pawing each other, but neither shy about taking the other's hand or pressing close. He'd watched her nipples harden and heard her breath catch and felt the goosebumps that rose on her arms under the brush of his hand.

God knew he was aroused just by her nearness, never mind the scent that had hardwired itself into him or the way watching her quick mouth as she talked and laughed made him want to kiss the hell out of her.

He touched her chin then couldn't resist letting the backs of his fingers slide down the heat of her soft throat. As he let two fingertips rest on her pulse, the one that confirmed she was alive when she might very well have been lost and he never would have known her at all, he wondered how the hell he was ever going to say no to her again.

CHAPTER ELEVEN

TRELLA CHECKED ON Tyrol as soon as they arrived at the mansion. He was sleeping soundly, completely oblivious to the potential shift in his parents' relationship.

As she stood over him, she thought of all the reasons her marriage was impossible. Progeny, publicity, even Xavier's rejection of love over duty. His refusal to open himself *to* love.

She thought of all the ways she was broken, but miracles happened. This tiny boy, for instance. She owed it to him to try with his father, didn't she? Really try to reach his heart?

Was it a rationalization? Perhaps. She couldn't deny that lust was alive and well inside her, but so was something deeper and more nascent. She didn't want to believe it was love. Not yet. Not when she was about to risk rejection. Not when there was every chance she would have to spend her life yearning for a man who might very well be incapable of the emotion.

"How is he?" Xavier asked in a whisper, coming up behind her.

His need to see his son fed her hope that he was more than capable of deeper feelings.

"Perfect," she answered, watching his profile soften as he looked at Tyrol.

"He is," he agreed, turning up the flame of desire inside her.

She led him from the room, heart hammering, and went to his room, not her own.

"Bella," he protested as he followed, but stayed in the open door, backlit by the light from over the stairs.

"Close the door, please."

He sucked in a long breath, like he needed it to face a Herculean task. "I can't. You know I can't."

"I don't want to make a fool of myself in front of the guard in the hall."

He pushed the door shut and leaned on it, breath hissing out. He was a dark shadow in the unlit room. She saw his fist close against the hardwood next to his thigh.

"Can you even make love?"

"As of midnight, yes," she said ruefully.

His head thumped back against the door. He swore. "You know this is impossible. You know—"

"I do." She went to him and picked up that rock hard fist, gently rubbing his fingers, trying to coax the tension from his hand. "But who else am I going to have sex with? Hmm? Who else do I trust with myself?"

"I still don't understand why you ever did."

She kissed his fingers. "Because no one else makes me feel like this." She set his open hand above her breast, where her heart raced. "If it's not the same for you—"

"It is, damn you." He hooked his hand behind her neck and dragged her closer, voice growing hoarse. "No one else has *ever*—"

He covered her mouth with his, cutting off whatever he'd been about to say.

She didn't care. All she cared about was being up against his lean, powerful body, feeling him devour her mouth as though it was the only thing he would ever need.

It was an onslaught, his hand shifting to her hair to drag her head back. His other arm crushed her into him while his lips ravaged and his tongue invaded.

Her heart knocked into her rib cage, sending sweet pulse beats through her arteries, weakening her limbs. She felt helpless, but not to him. To this yearning. Lethargy stole her strength when she longed to cling to him. All she could manage was to crush the edges of his jacket in her fists and moan into his mouth.

He made a jagged noise and dragged his teeth along her generous lower lip, tugging then releasing. "I'm being too rough."

"I need to know you feel the same. I want you so *bad*. You have no idea."

"I do." Another rough noise scraped from his throat. He dragged up the skirt of her gown, so when he picked her up as he pushed off the door, her legs were free to twine around his waist.

"But it's only lust, *bella*. Tell me you understand that."

She was on the verge of laughing, loving his easy strength. Her self-assurance slipped a notch, but she could feel him hard and straining between her legs. It was too beguiling to ignore, making her tighten her arms and legs, trying to increase the pressure there. "Whatever it is, I need it."

He walked her unerringly to the bed and came down to settle his weight on her, mouth sealing to hers again. Writhing under him, she tried to touch all of him with her whole body, tried to drag his clothes out of the way while searching for hot naked skin.

"Slow down." He grabbed her hands and pinned them over her head, then dragged his mouth along her jaw, down her throat and bared her breast for his fierce gaze. "This will *not* end before it starts." He used his teeth on the swell of her breast, making her shudder. "I've fantasized about it too many times to rush now that I have you where I want you."

A surge of moisture hit her loins. "I think about us when I'm in the bath."

He lifted his head and with a hiss said, "You witch." He levered up and rolled her over, swept her hair out of the way then slowly tugged open the ties behind her neck. "Tell me exactly what you do when you're in the bath." He set kisses down her spine. "Be specific."

"I could show you." She lifted into his hardness.

He grasped her hip and met her pressure with thrusts of his own, breaths thick and animalistic as he ground his erection into her soft cheeks. Then he slid a hand under her bunched skirt and across her stomach, fingers delving beneath her silk panties as he settled on her again. "Keep moving," he said, gently sawing two fingertips between her damp lips, mouth planting wet kisses on her nape. "Show me how much you want me."

She did. She rocked herself between his hand and his heavy hips until she was trembling with desire. She stopped, shaking with arousal. "I'm so close. I want to feel you inside me."

"Not yet." He shifted and settled his hand deeper, so his fingers slid inside her, so satisfying yet maddening. "Keep going."

Helpless to her own body, she did, until she was releasing broken cries, fists clenching the blankets, body clasping uncontrollably at his penetration, shivering and completely lost. Utterly his.

"So good," he said, licking between her shoulder blades, still mimicking lovemaking with light thrusts of his hips, drawing out her orgasm as he kept his hand in place. "I want you in a thousand ways. There will never be enough time for how much I want you."

And he called it *only lust*?

She pushed against the mattress, trying to twist beneath him. He withdrew his hand, but hooked his fingers in her panties and pulled them down and off, sitting up on the edge of the bed to throw them away, then he shrugged off his jacket and kicked off his shoes.

She knelt behind him and reached to work down the buttons of his shirt. He turned his head to catch at her mouth with his, easily distracting her. Their tongues met and the heat kept growing, not appeased in the least. She sobbed and he turned to scrape his hands down her shoulders, brushing her gown away so she knelt in a puddle of near-black velvet.

He stood then, chest expanding in deliberate breaths between the edges of his open shirt, as if he strained to keep control of himself. "Don't ever ask me again if you're beautiful. Know it, *bella*. You are the kind of beautiful that could topple a kingdom."

He reached out and wound her hair around his hand then bent to kiss her.

She tried to balance the bitter with sweetness in her own kiss, but her desire was too potent. It was all lust. He pulled back to yank his pants open then stripped, checking for a moment with one hand and reaching toward the night table.

"I can't get pregnant," she reminded.

He snorted and found a condom anyway, tearing it open with his teeth.

It shouldn't have made her want to cry, but it did.

"Bella," he chided as he pressed her flat and used a knee to part her legs, "I'm protecting *you*."

It didn't feel like it. But when he stroked his tip against her, hot and beguiling, he seemed to send electric lines of pleasure radiating through her. She forgot to be outraged or hurt. She set her hands on either side of his head and kissed him. Extravagantly. Invitingly.

And when he sank into her, it was her turn to bite his lip and groan.

"I'm going to make it last," he said into her mouth. "All night."

"Yes, please…"

Mario met them as they entered the palace. He smiled benignly at Tyrol, who was fussy after the travel, and said to Xavier, "The Queen expects you. She'd like to hear about Australia."

Completely attuned to her husband after their night of lovemaking, Trella felt his surreptitious sigh.

"Of course." He glanced at Trella from eyes bruised by their sleepless night. "Eat. Get some rest."

She nodded and followed his retreat with her gaze, feeling as though he took her heart and spun it out like twine behind him.

All of her felt undone and achy. They'd had one conversation in the dawn light, bodies still damp with exertion, while her nerve endings had still been singing with joy.

"You know this doesn't change what has to happen." His voice had been grave, his body steely against hers.

She had shifted her head on his shoulder. "I know. But I'm not sorry. Are you?"

"I'm trying to be."

She had turned her lips in to his throat and they had started all over again.

"Gerta can take the Prince up to the nursery, Ms. Sauveterre," Mario said as they arrived on the second floor.

Signora Deunoro, Trella longed to say, but it had been agreed from the outset that she would not change her name. After Tyrol's christening, she was to receive an honorific title of *Dama*, the lowest of Elazar's ranks. A future monarch could not have a parent who was common.

"I'll keep him. He's having an off day." And she was feeling neglectful after leaving him in Gerta's care during the wedding last night. "You go settle in," she said, since Gerta hadn't actually seen where she would be living in the palace. "I'll bring him when he's ready for a long nap."

With a curtsy, Gerta followed Mario's direction to the nursery level while Trella turned toward the room she'd occupied before she'd gone into the hospital, the ones adjoined to Xavier's.

Mario cleared his throat. "You're in the dowager's wing now, Ms. Sauveterre."

This doesn't change what has to happen.

Speechless, composure fraying, she let Mario escort her across the gallery, through a pair of doors, down a long hall where paintings of Xavier's ancestors watched her progress in silent judgment, and through another set of doors.

The temperature grew cooler as they walked. Tyrol's fussy cries echoed off the high ceiling with the sounds of their footsteps. She didn't try to soothe him, just let him express exactly what she was feeling, and was viciously pleased to see Mario's obsequious expression grow more and more strained.

She understood that the dowager's wing had been deliberately placed to provide as much distance as possible between former queens and new ones. It wasn't a horrible place. It had been prepared for her occupancy with cheerful floral arrangements, a new sofa and her very own lady's maid, Adona, who was eager to prepare her some soup.

Mario offered a quick tour, pointing to a bright, empty room as a potential studio, if she wanted to provide a list of items she would like placed there.

"A crib and a change table," Trella said, growing as fractious as her son. "Tyrol needs a nursery."

Mario tilted his head in a way that was unbearably condescending. "Royalty inhabits the royal wing."

"I see." She sat on the sofa and dug in her shoulder bag for the receiving blanket she carried. She shook it out with a snap then tucked a corner into her collar as she met Mario's gaze with a challenging one of her own. "And do I go on safari to the nursery to feed him? Or does he exercise his lungs through the palace every two hours as he is brought to me?"

Tyrol was showing off the growing strength of his lungs, recognizing the feeling of the soft flannel against his cheek as she draped it over him and growing frantic for her to open her buttons.

"It was understood the Prince was taking a bottle," Mario said, mouth pinched, gaze averting self-consciously while his whole face went red.

Oh, was he uncomfortable with her breastfeeding? What a shame.

"He'll *need* a bottle, won't he? Or he'll starve to death before we get to each other. Am I even allowed into the palace without an escort? He's *six weeks old*. Still a few days shy of his due date. He's not weaned and won't be for a *year*."

"As I see." Mario cleared his throat and turned to the door. "I'll leave you to it."

"Do."

This doesn't change what has to happen. Xavier should have told her *this* was going to happen. How *dare* he use her up last night, thinking this would be okay.

Trella woke thick-headed from a heavy nap to hear Xavier's hushed voice, "Give him a bottle if he needs it." A door closed.

She jackknifed to sit up and shot a look to the travel cot she'd had Gerta bring down from the nursery. It was empty.

Sucking in enough breath for a scream, she leapt from the bed and stumbled into the lounge, wearing only the oversized T-shirt she'd thrown on for sleep. Xavier was there, but no one else. No Gerta, no Adona, no *Tyrol*.

"Oh, *hell* no," she informed and rushed after her son.

"Trella." He caught her arm and reaction kicked in. She used the momentum to round on him, heel of her hand aimed straight for his nose.

He deflected, tried to catch her into a hold, but she expertly twirled out and broke his grip, the movements ingrained in her muscles from years of practice. Knocking a lamp in his direction to force him to leap back, she backed up too, out of his reach, neatly balancing on the balls of her feet, breathing in hisses as she gauged the distance between him and the door and how she would take him out in order to get there.

"I didn't *know*," he growled, holding himself in ready stance. "*Calm down*."

"Bring him back." She reached for a slender vase and flicked its three tall irises at his feet, spattering water on the bottoms of his pant legs, then tested the heft of the blown glass as a weapon.

"You're going back to the room you were in, next to mine. I sent him up because he needs a bath. I stayed to tell you that and keep you from throwing a righteous fit when you woke and saw he was gone. Calm the hell down."

"You should have told me last night this could happen. This, by the way, is how you put up a fight." She shook the vase at him, mocking his lame attempt to turn her away last night.

"This was always going to happen!" He pointed at the door. "If not today, soon enough. In a few weeks, you'll move out of the palace and he'll come and go between us. That is reality, Trella. I have damned well made that clear to you. More than once. *You* came to *my* room, last night, knowing that. Don't pretend this is news."

She threw the vase at the fireplace so it shattered and droplets of water made the dancing flames sputter and crackle. Then she stared at the destruction, chest heaving.

"Is this bringing on an attack?"

"Don't pretend you care if it does."

"I *care*," he bit out. "Why the hell do you think I'm here?" He looked positively tortured as the words escaped him. He wiped his expression away with a stroke of his hand, releasing a heavy sigh.

"I've just been raked over the coals for *one* photo." He held up his finger. "And because a debate has sprung up online. Team Trella or Team Patrizia. My fault." He turned his hand to tattoo his chest with his finger. "I promised to undo all of that, as if it's even possible, and walked back to my room to learn you'd been sent here. Do you know how much furniture *I* wanted to break? Do you understand what I'm doing, taking you back there? It's pure weakness!"

No, it wasn't. That's not what caring was. He wasn't ready to hear or believe it, though, and she was too angry and hurt to explain it.

"Why does she hate me so much? Why—?"

He closed his eyes. "I keep trying to tell you. Emotion has nothing to do with it. It can't. That's the point."

"The crown is all that matters."

"Yes."

"I hate your crown! I hate that our son will be raised with this same hard-hearted attitude."

"Hate away. It changes nothing."

"And you want me to come to your rooms again, anyway."

"Yes."

"Even though it won't change anything, either."

"Yes."

Mouth trembling, she knew that, like him, she didn't have a choice. She would go with him and believe what she believed, that he would change, and one of them was going to lose.

She nodded jerkily, but before she could step forward, he leapt to meet her, not letting her walk through broken glass to get to him. Then he was cupping her cheek, tilting her lips up to the hungry weight of his own. She moaned, knowing what that taste was now. That narcotic that filled her with hope when he kissed her. *Love.* She was madly, deeply, hopelessly in love with him.

CHAPTER TWELVE

"YOU'RE NEGLECTING YOUR DUTIES. The Australian agreements have completely fallen apart." His grandmother had called him on the carpet before he'd even digested his breakfast.

"Both parliaments have risen for the year. The committees adjourned," he said.

"Yet I am informed the deadline is the end of the year. If it's not finalized, we start over in the new year." She held out a missive.

He took it and quickly gathered how certain opportunistic corporations were manipulating the fine print, trying to push Elazar into a stress position and a renegotiation that would be advantageous to their own interests. She was right. He should have caught on when the meetings had begun experiencing delays two weeks ago.

"This is the first I'm hearing of this," he muttered.

"Because you've been distracted. Dating. *Shopping*."

He gritted his teeth. Trella was preparing to move her design house's head office to Lirona. The fashion industry was waiting with baited breath for her to purchase her property. Real estate and tourism would boom the minute the new fashion district was born. Squiring her to potential locations, ensuring the choice worked as well for

Elazar as it did for her, fell right into Xavier's trade negotiation bailiwick.

His grandmother ought to be thanking Trella, but she only said, "Mario has set up an emergency meeting of the council. You're expected at ten o'clock. We cannot afford to lose this, Xavier."

Duty. It was killing him. Quite literally chipping away at his flesh. His belt had had to go in an extra notch and the scale had him four pounds under his usual weight. He had no appetite. Of course, he was on his wife like a stallion with a mare every chance he got. No wonder he was skin and bones.

Bristling with culpability, he returned to his apartment. He would have to hurry to make the meeting, but he was more aware of the clock ticking down on his marriage.

In a few days it would be Christmas, his one and only with his son's mother. Then their marriage would melt away like snow under rain. Gone, gone, gone.

He nodded at Vincente to leave his jacket on the bed and dismissed him, then he went through to Trella's room, where he slept every night with her naked body resting against his. They tried to keep a low profile but were fooling no one, except possibly themselves. Despite the intensity and excruciating pleasure and profound satisfaction they gave each other, they had to keep rising and moving apart.

Soon that would be permanent.

Not yet. His hand closed in a tense fist. He wasn't ready.

"I have to run to a meeting—" he began as he entered.

She sniffed and turned with surprise. She had showered while he'd been to see the Queen and wore only a slip. She was on the phone.

"*Esta bien, Mama. Te amo,*" she finished and signed off, then swiped her cheek.

His heart lurched. "What's wrong?"

"Nothing." She turned away for a tissue. "Ramon and Isidora arrived safely at Sus Brazos. Gili and Kasim will be there tomorrow."

And this was her first year apart from them. She was homesick. She didn't have to say it. He watched her wither daily, saying nothing because they both left many things unsaid, aware their days with each other were numbered. They didn't want to waste them with animosity and problems they couldn't solve.

Guilt assailed him, though. He was *stealing* time with her. Neglecting his duties while he neglected her needs. He pinched the bridge of his nose. "If you want to spend Christmas with them, you should."

"With Tyrol?" She brightened.

"Bella." He hated saying no to her, but it echoed in his voice. "You're upset. You miss them." She was going to need them more than ever soon.

"I can't leave him! He's still feeding in the night. I would miss *him*." She waved in the direction of the nursery, where a nanny took him for a bath every morning while they ate breakfast and started their day. She softened her tone, her expression so vulnerable she put an ache in his chest. "You could come."

You're neglecting your duties.

"No, I can't." This was it, he realized. The fracture that had begun working its way through him on their wedding day began to cleave open, tearing him apart. *But he had no choice.* "The Deunoros spend Christmas here."

"And I'm not a Deunoro. Why should he spend Christmas with her? She hasn't even looked at him since—"

"Leave it."

She buttoned her lip, but the glare she sent dropped the room temperature lower than it had been on the sleeting day of Tyrol's christening.

He couldn't let her bring it up because he was ashamed of his grandmother's behavior. Rather than the traditional pomp of open-topped carriages and a public stroll with the future monarch back to the palace, they'd all traveled by car. His grandmother had come in her own, arriving last and leaving first. Exactly one photo had been taken of Queen Julia standing with her grandson at her side and her great-grandson in his bassinet. Trella had been left out of the picture.

He closed his eyes, afraid he couldn't do this if he looked at her. His voice was hoarse with strain. "You should go see your family and come back to the new house."

He heard her breath suck in, sharp and mortal. "No, Xavier. Not yet."

"I was hoping we could get through Christmas, but we're only putting off the inevitable."

"What about…" Her voice faded. "What about a surrogate?" He had seen her afraid before, but not like this, with her throat exposed while she offered a knife.

He had to consciously remember to breathe. "It's not about another baby, *bella*."

His own composure threatened to crumble as her chin crinkled and her eyes filled. She caught her mouth into a line to hide its tremble, then that glorious Valkyrie in her came forward, steeling her spine and refusing to be cowed.

"I'm not leaving Tyrol. I'll move into your stupid ugly house if you make me, but I'm taking him with me."

That stung more than it should. He hadn't been able to design a home from greenfield for her, which felt like a breach of duty in itself, but he'd personally overseen all the renovations and security upgrades to the one he'd bought. He'd taken the utmost care with every detail.

"Don't make this ugly. The agreement is three and a half days each." That was not renegotiable.

"You're *busy*. Why should someone else feed him a bottle when he could be with me?" Oh, she was fierce when she wanted to be. Flushed, with her eyes glimmering, she threw the forces of nature at him. "At least I *love* him."

"So do I!" It exploded out of him. Within him. *Nothing* would come between him and his son.

She threw her head back, fury fading into sorrow. "But you don't love me. I can live somewhere else."

He jerked his head to the side, slapped by the torment in her voice.

"Say it," she choked. "Tell me these last weeks of..." She waved at the bed where they had writhed with passion. "I have tried *so hard* to show you we could make this work. Every breath I take is carefully measured to make sure I don't impinge on your role in any way. I should bite my tongue right now. You have a meeting to get to, right? I give and give and you can't offer me a crumb? A maybe? A *chance*?"

"You think I like seeing you holding back, afraid to laugh too loud, keeping to these rooms when you should be able to say and do whatever the hell you please? I hate what I'm doing to you. You never wanted this."

"But if you *loved* me—"

"I *can't* love you! I've upended my world as far as I can. Things are tipping off. *This has to end.*"

She rocked as if buffeted by a hurricane wind. He watched her lips go white with the rest of her. Her fingers twitched at her sides and she swayed again then locked her knees.

"Bella." He reached out, feeling the chasm in him widen to a canyon, pushing her further and further beyond him.

She drew a jagged breath and leveled her shoulders. "You should go. I don't want to be blamed for you missing your meeting."

* * *

Had that really happened?

One minute she had been feeling sorry for herself over her siblings getting together without her, the next her tiny nascent family of three had been torn down to one and a half.

How had she not fought hard enough? Aside from viewing a few buildings for Maison des Jumeaux, she had lived as a shut-in again, not wanting to make headlines. As painful as she'd found it when he disappeared for a few days on palace business, she had never once complained. Even his grandmother's frosty behavior at the christening had gone unremarked until today.

All the while, she'd been aware of the days lifting off the calendar like ravens, one by one, swooping away and forming a black, jeering cloud on the horizon. They'd mocked her for loving him despite his lack of commitment. For waiting so patiently for words of love that were never going to come.

Did she regret trying to make their marriage work? No. But failing despite leaving her heart wide open was liable to kill her.

Shaking, she pressed a fresh tissue to her closed eyes, soaking up the leak through her lashes, taking a slow breath and consciously softening her shoulders.

Uno naranjo, dos naranjos...

It struck her what she was doing. *Oh, no.*

She pressed the tissue harder into her eyes, becoming aware of the sensations pinging to life in her. A roiling stomach, a creep of foreboding down her spine. Cold specters began to float in her periphery, voicing the ugliest of thoughts. *Why would he want you? You're the broken one. You're soiled.*

"No," she whispered, certain that being susceptible to

these attacks *proved* how unworthy she was of love. Was that the ghouls talking? Or the unvarnished truth?

"*Dama*?" Her maid knocked, making her heart leap. Adona entered. "The Private Secretary is here. Her Majesty wishes to see you."

Not now. She couldn't. Not with a spell coming on. All of her went rigid while her blood moved like acid in her arteries.

Why did the Queen even want to see her? Her mind raced, trying to think of an excuse, but what could she say?

"Please give me a moment to dress." *Uno naranjo, dos naranjos...*

She chose the dress she'd worn to the christening, since its red and gold were Elazar's national colors and quietly proclaimed her station as the mother of a future monarch. Adona gave her hair a twist while Trella dabbed on light makeup, even though it didn't matter if she put on clown pants or a G-string with water wings. She was going to the guillotine.

As if that were true, the flutters deep in the pit of her belly grew worse. Mario's dour face made his silent escort that much more ominous. Her feet felt like they didn't belong to her. She couldn't make her throat swallow.

The ghouls chuckled as they stuck to her clammy skin, following her into a stately room of powder blue and white striped wallpaper.

The Queen wore a dark green sweater set and a severe expression. She was seated and Trella was not invited to do so.

Trella ordered her fists to loosen and clasped them in front of her. She took measured breaths, nodded in greeting as the door behind her closed, shutting her in with what she had long suspected was an enemy.

"I'm a woman of well-cultivated patience, but mine

has run out," Queen Julia stated. "It would benefit all if you went to Spain for Christmas and did not come back."

Her nails dug into her palm beneath the cover of her other hand. "Xavier suggested the same thing."

Surprise flickered in the Queen's face before she blinked it away. She nodded. "Good. He's finally showing sense."

"I said I'd go if Tyrol came with me." She wanted that so badly, she would buckle into the carpet if the Queen agreed.

The older woman hardened before Trella's eyes. "*No.* But allow me to lend my voice to my grandson's. You do more damage than good by lingering."

The words hit so hard, Trella had to press into her toes to stay on her feet. Still, her inherent streak of bellicosity reared its head. Another woman would have taken this chance to make a good impression and reason with the woman. She wouldn't pour gasoline over the one bridge open to her and light a match.

"Is that what you said to *his* mother when you exiled her?"

The Queen's eyes were so much like Xavier's, it was sheer agony to look into the contempt they held.

"I was told you have a predilection for dramatics." She was like a cat that knew its prey's weakest spots, but took her time piercing them, preferring to terrorize before putting a creature out of its misery. "Xavier's mother has always had access to him. He chose not to pursue a deeper relationship."

"Because you didn't approve of one. Did you? And he couldn't afford to alienate you. He didn't have anyone left." She showed the Queen how she had won more staring contests than she'd lost.

After a moment, the Queen reached very casually to

polish her glasses, then perched them back on her nose. "*My* relationship with my grandson is not up for discussion. But if he's asked you to leave, yours with him is clearly over."

Breathe. Uno naranjo, dos naranjos...

"Xavier has been conditioned to believe that people who love him leave and don't come back. I plan to show him that's not true." Would it work? She couldn't think about that right now.

"What he *knows* is that a country can't maintain stability when it's ruled by emotion. Scandal and division among its people are poison. How can he be regarded as a man of integrity when he's with a woman who is nothing but racy headlines?"

"I can't control my headlines!"

"No. You can't. That's why removing yourself is the least you can do. If you care anything for him and your son, protect them."

Score one for the Queen. She knew it, too. She didn't move, but her verbal rapier kept whipping the air, cutting into Trella with casual ease as she spoke again.

"You have no idea the strength required to hold this position. Your weaknesses would become theirs, undermining what has taken five hundred years to build."

"Loving is a weakness?" Where had she heard that before?

The Queen narrowed her eyes. "Your background, your extensive need for therapy and your delicate mental state are weaknesses."

It was as if she saw into Trella's soul where the specters were swirling and cackling, dragging icy fingers over her bones. *She sees you. She knows.*

"The toll of the throne would break someone like you. This is a marathon that lasts a lifetime. What are you going to do when it becomes too much? Retire behind closed doors and burden the palace with making explanations? If that's to be the end result, do it now. Fade into the background before you do any more damage."

"Someone like me," she repeated darkly.

They won't come for you. They won't want you after this. It was the oldest, darkest, ugliest voice. The one that made her eyes sting and her heart shrink.

She hadn't come back to her family in pieces because she had passively accepted her situation, though. She had fought with every ounce of will she possessed, from the first moment through all the other struggles to today.

"You know *nothing* about me and what I can endure. Do not confuse my capacity for love as an inability to stand and fight. In fact, love is my *weapon*. You want to go to war with me? Gird your loins. You might rule this country, but I rule the online world. I'm beloved by *billions*. You want to protect what's taken five hundred years to build? I belong to something that's lasted millennia. *Family*. When you die, do you think *duty* will squeeze a single tear from Xavier's eye?"

The Queen went white. "You're becoming hysterical."

"You unleashed this!" She stabbed the air between them. "Love is the only thing that pulls us through hardship. *I know that*. And your tepid love isn't enough to sustain him. Yes, you love him in your stunted way, but you're afraid to show it. Why? Because you might have to deal with grief again? Is that why you don't even look at Tyrol? You're afraid he'll die and you don't want to be attached? Now who's weak?"

Queen Julia gave her bell a resounding shake.

"What's wrong? This is what someone looks like when they're fighting for the people they love. Still think I'm not tough enough for the job?"

"*Get out.*"

"Ms. Sauveterre!" Mario entered. "Please."

She shot him a bitter look on her way past him then ran blindly to her room.

Voices were droning around him, but Xavier wasn't tracking. He was lost in a fog he hadn't experienced since childhood. Twice. The miasma was cold and gray and left him rudderless. His grandmother had been there to lead him along those other two times, but she was the last person he wanted to turn to right now.

Not because he blamed her. No, he blamed himself.

All he could hear was Trella saying, *If you loved me.*

He had said he couldn't love her as if he didn't have the capacity. For a long time, he had believed he didn't. The love he'd once felt for his parents had stagnated under their leaving, stunting him into an inability to feel anything beyond superficial liking.

And yes, Trella had been a distraction lately as they had tried to cram a lifetime into the short marriage they had agreed to, but the fact that their time was finite had put that pressure on them. Hell, he'd called it off and he was still distracted.

I can live somewhere else.

The doom he'd felt at that statement couldn't be measured. He tried to picture Patrizia in the room where he'd held Trella and bile rose to the back of his throat.

No, the real problem was that he was afraid to *admit* he loved her. Otherwise, he might feel like this when their marriage ended. But he did feel like this now, which must mean—

"You agree, Your Highness?"

"Pardon?" He sucked in a deep breath, like he was coming out of a coma. What the hell had he done?

"We were discussing where the tax rate should break."

He shook his head, taking in the dozen people slouched over a boardroom table, surrounded by laptops and scratch pads and coffee cups while snow fell beyond the windows.

"Get the Australians on the phone. We'll request an extension into January. We'd rather be with our families through Christmas and I'm sure their people would, too."

Screw duty. He had to fix things with the woman he loved.

He rose just as his PA slipped into the room and hurried across with a message that Angelique was trying to reach him.

Frowning, Xavier excused himself and turned on his phone. It lit up with missed calls and texts.

What happened?
Where is she?
Are you with her?

His heart lurched. He hit reply on a video call, moving farther down the hall to an alcove where he had some privacy.

Angelique appeared, her pinched expression deeply anxious. "Are you with her? She keeps texting that she's fine, but she's not fine. I can tell."

"I'm not with her—"

"Damn it, Xavier, you can't leave her alone when she's having an attack!"

Her tone made Xavier's scalp prickle. He only half-believed in the twin connection, but her alarm was genuine enough that he looked for his PA to signal for his car.

"Is there someone who could check on her and get back to us?" Kasim asked.

"She's really scared, Xavier." Angelique sounded half-hysterical herself.

"I'll try her right now. But if you two feed off each other's mood, you should try dialing back your worry and send her some calming thoughts." It came off the top of his head out of frustration and sounded too metaphysical.

Her wet face went blank with surprise. "I honestly never thought of that. God, I'm such an idiot. Of course. I'll text her that I love her."

His conscience twisted as he thought of his own refusal to say those words this morning. He ended the call and tried Trella. She declined to answer, but texted a moment later to say she was napping.

"Everything all right, sir?" his PA approached to ask.

Xavier held up a staying hand as he reached Vincente. "Have you seen Trella today?"

A brief hesitation, then, "Adona said she locked herself in her room after her audience with the Queen."

"She spoke with my grandmother? The car," Xavier snapped at his PA. "Now."

CHAPTER THIRTEEN

SHE WAS DOING this for Tyrol, she kept telling herself, as she bit down on one of his teethers and counted her oranges. Some women went through the pains of childbirth. Her lot was to weather waves of terror. The irrational, fearful thoughts would pass. The sweating and sobs of insecurity needed to run their course. She just had to breathe and count her oranges and wait it out.

It was easier when someone she loved and trusted sat with her and told her she was safe. She didn't feel safe right now. She felt very temporary and unwanted. Abandoned. Forsaken.

"Shh," she breathed, pushing those thoughts away.

I am strong. I am loved. I can do this.

She should have brought her phone in here. All the texting had been breaking her concentration. She had left it on the night table, but now she wished she was reading Gili's comforting words. It was almost as good as having her here.

"Trella!"

Oh, God. What was he doing here? She had locked up and told Adona not to let anyone in. Now he would see her like this and know how cracked she really was.

His footsteps crossed into her bathroom. There was a systematic banging noise. He was opening all the cupboards beneath the dual sinks, looking for her.

"You're sure she didn't leave?"

He had someone with him? And someone who saw him searching cupboards for her? She pulled her feet in tighter, driving the curve of her spine into the wall behind her.

The closet light flicked on, blindingly bright even against her clenched eyes. She made a noise of protest and ducked her head.

"Are you here?" he demanded.

She plucked the teether from her bite. "I don't want you to see me like this."

"Get out and lock the doors."

"Yes, sir." It was Adona and a moment later, a distant noise of a door closing sounded.

Xavier came to the back of the closet and swept aside the gowns. He swore when he found her huddled in the corner on the floor. He crouched and wiped her wet cheek with his hand, drying it on his thigh. "Why didn't you call me?"

"I have to do this alone."

"No, you don't," he said grimly and started to gather her.

"Don't." She pressed as hard as she could into the corner, holding him off with one shaking arm.

"What did she say to you?"

She didn't know if her mental state made him sound that lethal, or if he really was murderous.

"Nothing I don't say to myself." She clenched her eyes in anguish. "I am a detriment. A hindrance. You shouldn't be here. What are you going to do? Run out of every high-level meeting because I'm having an episode? This can't happen. You can't be here. I *have* to do this *alone*."

"Look at me," he said gently.

"No, *you* look at *me*. Is this a queen? It's *not*. I pretended for a while that we could find a way and you followed me through the looking glass because duty chafes and the sex is great, but we knew it couldn't last. You were right, Xavier. This was always going to happen. *This*—" she pointed at her position on the floor "—will happen when I can least afford it. I wish I wasn't this person, but I am. And if you stay in here and nurse me through this, you're only proving that I'm a burden. *I have to do this alone.* I'm an adult who will be a single mother. *I* have to know I can do it."

The mention of living alone sent a tumble of unvoiced fears through her head. Intruders. Kidnappers. A million bad, horrible, terrifying things.

"Bella," he said gently. "I want to talk to you about that. Come on. Come out of here."

"No." She slapped at his reaching hands and said very clearly, "There is no way. None. Just—go look after Tyrol. Please? I can't look after him when I'm like this. If you want to help me, go do that. Please?"

He stared at her, jaw clenched. "I'll bring him to you. Will that help?"

"I can't use him as a crutch. It would turn into me using him all the rest of my life. I won't put that on him. But I'll feel better if I know you're looking after him. Please?" She clutched his wrist. "Will you do that for me?"

"Trella—"

"I'm begging you, Xavier. *Please.*"

He left her in the closet like a child hiding from monsters, hating himself for abandoning her, but she'd knocked the wind out of him. Blind shock held him in stasis for long minutes outside her door.

She thought her attack made her unfit to be his wife?

This was his fault. Not just her breakdown, but her belief that she had to be perfect to be his queen. She was already perfect in the way of fierce storms and jagged mountains and a flower blooming on a broken stem. Her perfection was in her resilience. That's what was needed in his partner. He loved her for her strength and her ferocious capacity to love and her ability to move forward despite how many times she'd been knocked down.

With her emotional bravery top of mind, he strode to the nursery where Tyrol had just woken.

"I was about to bring him down for a feed—"

"Warm a bottle. I'll take him." He carried his son through the palace, pushing into his grandmother's parlor where she was meeting with Mario.

"Out," he said to Mario, and gave the door a light kick behind the man.

"Your meeting?" his grandmother prompted.

"My wife was indisposed. Someone upset her. I had to care for our son."

"We pay staff to care for him."

"He shouldn't need his parents because you and I didn't? We'll never know, will we?" He set Tyrol in her arms.

"What—"

"Hold him. Feed him."

"What do you think you're proving?" She lifted her brows and calmly silenced the boy with the nipple.

"What are *you* trying to prove? Look at your great-grandson. Can you honestly say you feel nothing toward him? Because that's certainly how you act."

She looked at the boy. His hand found her thumb and gripped it. A dribble of milk leaked from the corner of his mouth and his eyes were focused on her.

A flinch of anguish crossed her expression before her mouth softened in tenderness. "He looks like your father. Let's hope he doesn't have his temperament. Your father wasn't cut out for the crown. I let him go because I had to, Xavier." Her head came up, blue eyes clouded with sorrow and a pleading for forgiveness. "He wasn't his brother. He wasn't you. He was never going to survive the demands. I let him go and yes, you suffered, but I had already lost both my sons. I couldn't let you go, too."

It was the most sentimental thing he'd ever heard her say. Shaken, he lowered to sit across from her. "I'm a parent now. I do understand," he said at length. "I can't stomach the idea of his being across the city three and a half days a week, let alone not in my life at all."

"You shouldn't have agreed to share him."

"I intend to renege."

Her head came up, surprise in her lined face.

"They're both staying with me. I'm not asking you. I'm telling. If that means you stay on the throne the rest of your natural life, so be it."

"So she's won you over." She sniffed her disdain.

"No, it's up to me to win her."

Her gaze came up again.

"If I can't give the woman I love what she needs, how the hell can I give our country what it needs? She makes me whole. Stronger. I want to be a better man *for her*. That can only make me a better leader. A better king."

Tyrol finished his bottle. She set it aside and brought him to her shoulder to rub his back, exactly as if she'd been mothering infants all these years.

"After the risks she took bringing him into this world, how can you not want to know her? If you knew the things she's been through…" It was killing him, what she was enduring right now, but she seemed to need to prove something to herself and he had to give her that. "She's stronger and more determined than either of us can conceive."

"Her reputation, Xavier. Patrizia is such a good fit."

"I don't love Patrizia. I love Trella." It was conviction. Will. Fate. But he couldn't help pointing out, "So does everyone else, judging by the online polls. She's the more popular choice by a long shot."

"Don't be vulgar," she said crossly. "What about another baby?"

"We'll find a way. I am going to find a way to make it work. I have to. I can't live without her."

She let out a sigh of defeat. "Some monarchs would rather die than watch the next generation struggle to master the art of ruling. I've always thought I could give up the throne to you quite confidently. You rarely make mistakes. I will trust your judgment holds true in this instance."

He didn't need her approval, but he was glad to have it. Now he only had to convince Trella to stay.

Trella woke to bright light beyond the cracks in her blinds. She squinted gritty eyes at her clock. It was late morning. She had pumped milk a few hours ago when her swollen breasts had woken her, so she wasn't too uncomfortable, but she missed Tyrol enough that her chest hurt just thinking about him. She texted the nursery, then glanced at herself in the bathroom mirror, cringing.

She had done it. She splashed her face, brushed her teeth, then texted her sister.

It's over. I'm okay.

She earned a heart emoji in response.

The residual depression of an attack hovered like a cloud, though, along with profound loss as she accepted she and Xavier would never be. It had been a serious trip to hell and back, but she was *back*. That was something, she reassured herself. She had proved to herself she could not only grit her way through an episode, but that it wouldn't actually kill her.

Where was Tyrol? She checked her phone and saw Gerta had replied.

The Prince is with the Prince.

Xavier had had more meetings today. Was Tyrol sick?

She tugged a robe over her nightgown and yanked open her door—to find Xavier slouched in an armchair, clothes rumpled, eyelids heavy. Tyrol was fast asleep on his shoulder. It was such a tender scene, it pushed tears into the backs of her eyes.

"Is he okay?" She gently gathered the sleeping baby into her arms.

"Missing you, but otherwise fine. He just ate. That's purely for show," he added as Tyrol began to stir and fuss at the sound of her voice.

She sat to feed him, but Xavier was right. Tyrol nodded off before he'd taken more than a few gulps and she cuddled him instead. Oh, he smelled good and his skin was so soft. His hair was fine against her lips and his grip on her finger, endearing.

I'll always come back to you, my sweet, sweet boy. She had thought about him a lot last night. She had thought about Xavier and how delusional she had been, ever thinking she could be his queen when she had this awful shortcoming.

Fresh agony washed over her.

When she couldn't avoid it any longer, she looked at where Xavier hadn't moved.

"Was it a rough night?" she asked.

"For him? Not particularly. For me? Yes."

With a lurch in her heart, she noticed the glass on the table beside him. "Are you hungover?"

"No. I poured it, then thought I'd prefer to be sober if you decided you needed me."

"Were you worried? I'm sorry."

He snorted and reached for the glass. "Now, she's sorry." He made a face at his first sip and clunked the glass back onto the table. "Mostly water now. How was your night?"

"Awful."

He nodded in grim agreement.

"Why are you angry? Xavier—"

"I'm not angry." He shot to his feet, though, and paced a few steps only to turn back abruptly. "I am angry. I respected your wishes because fine, I accept that you had to feel you could get through an attack alone. But I have issues, too. *Because* of you. You ignored my texts for months before you admitted you were pregnant. Then you locked me out of a delivery room while you *flatlined*. We've been apart more than we've been together. You damned well need to stay accessible to me. I need to know you're alive, even if you're not at your best."

That was the problem. Sometimes she was at her absolute *worst*.

And she really wasn't up for a scolding over it. Or facing how she was supposed to be accessible from across the city. Much as she had given his grandmother a show of bravado, that's all it had been. She couldn't be his wife. She knew that now and it hurt so badly; she had to escape to hide how anguished she was.

"I want to shower. Can you take him and order breakfast?"

He said nothing as she handed him Tyrol again.

Swallowing, heavy with a melancholy that would never lift, she went back to her room and started the shower, blinking hot eyes as she did. She wasn't ready. If she hadn't had that stupid attack, if they hadn't had that big fight yesterday, they could still play alternate universe a few more days. Why had she shortchanged them like that?

She stepped under the spray and turned to see Xavier had come in behind her.

"Where's Tyrol?"

"Nursery." He peeled off his clothes, dropping them to the floor as the glass walls gathered steam.

"What are you doing?"

"What does it look like?" He opened the door and came in, crowding beneath the head that rained from the ceiling.

They'd showered together before, daily, but that was *before*.

"Xavier, I can't." Her heart was too tender, still pulling at all its old fractured lines and itching from fresh stitches.

"What did I just say about locking me out?" He cupped her wet head and planted a single kiss on her mouth, hot and possessive. Oddly tender.

She moaned and ducked her face as soon as he let her, tucking her forehead into his collarbone. Her vision filled with the golden skin she loved, taut and smooth over hard muscles. He was growing aroused, which always excited her.

"You know we're just putting off the inevitable. You were right all along," she muttered.

"You're staying here. We're staying married."

For a couple of heartbeats, she thought she'd imagined it, then she jerked back her head and looked at his implacable expression. The wetness in her clenched eyes wasn't from the water raining on her face.

"The future king decrees it? We both know I'm not a suitable queen."

"You are."

"You saw me last night!"

"And I see you this morning, having survived it. That's who and what you are, *bella*. You survive. You push through hardship to come out the other side, bruised maybe, but you make it. You don't give up on yourself, you would never give up on Tyrol and I won't let you give up on us."

Her mouth trembled. "If you loved me—"

He made a noise of imprecation. "If? *If?*" His hands cupped her face again. "You put a spell on me the first time we met. You gave me a son and helped me kick-start my heart so I could give him the love he deserves. Of course I love you, you infernal woman. How the hell else are we here?"

"You don't have to yell about it. What about Patrizia?"

"Are you seriously worried about a woman you have never met? You've ruined her life, *bella*. Just as you have ruined mine. But you won't feel bad about it because you've saved us both from a terrible mistake."

"Tyrol did. Lay the blame where it belongs."

"I thought I just did. God, I love you." He kissed her and this time he meant it, fusing his mouth to hers and letting her taste his desperation.

She grasped his wrists and pulled away, gasping, trying to speak from soul to soul. "Do you mean it? Because I don't think you understand how much it means to me that you can accept me, with all my breaks and imperfections. Don't say it unless it's true."

"You are flawed. You're unpredictable and defiant and shameless. You're also brave and creative and you love with everything in you. If you can rise out of your past and risk your heart, what kind of coward would I be if I refused to do the same? I'm privileged to be one of the people you love, Trella. I know what an exclusive club it is."

They kissed again and this time they didn't stop. The water rained down, washing away any ghosts that lingered, leaving only the love they had for each other.

Her body melted against his and she found herself pressed into the wall by his flexing muscles.

"Mine," he growled, kissing and licking at her neck and shoulders, across her breasts then between them. "There is no more locking yourself away. Understand? Not from me." The kisses continued, down her arms, across her hips.

She needed this doting attention. This all-consuming passion from him. It soothed and healed and made her feel cherished. By the time he knelt and hitched her thigh onto his shoulder, she was nearly weeping at the sweetness of him pouring such love all over her.

Her stomach jumped in reaction at the way he claimed her. He pleasured her until she was delirious, crying out with abandon. Then he stood and took her where she was, against the hard tiles, naked and slick as he drove into her, hard and deep. It was lust and bonding and naked unabashed love. When the climax came, they were in it together, trying to meld their slippery bodies into one being so they could never be separated again.

Then they leaned there, panting and wrung out, the water cooling, barely able to find the strength to get to the bed. They fell asleep in each other's arms, waking to make love again without the frantic pace driving them.

"We have time, *bella*. All our lives," he murmured, rocking lazily within her.

She released a shaken sigh, combing her fingers through his hair and was astonished at the lightness in her. The breadth of view. Years and years to come of this.

"I love you. You're the only man who could have given me this."

"You're the only woman I want or need. The only woman I could love so much."

Later that evening, he placed his rings on her finger as they dressed for dinner. The Queen wasn't one for making apologies, either, but she invited them to dine with her and suggested Xavier take his son and wife to Spain the day after Christmas if it was something Trella wanted.

It was, he did and it was wonderful.

EPILOGUE

Press release five years later...

Inconceivable Twins!

The Deunoro Palace surprised the world today by announcing that King Xavier and Queen Trella are celebrating the arrival of their daughter, Vivien.

Queen Trella's sister, Queen Angelique of Zhamair, also celebrates with her husband King Kasim the arrival of their third child, and first daughter, Genevieve.

While it was widely reported that Queen Angelique was carrying twins, it has now been revealed that, with the help of the world-renowned fertility clinic in Lirona, Queen Angelique was implanted with one egg from each set of parents.

Mother and babies are in excellent health.

The Queens' brothers, Henri and Ramon Sauveterre, were on hand with their own growing families to welcome this latest and most unusual pair of Sauveterre twins.

* * * * *

"I understand that you're used to ruling everything you see, but I took care of your company and your family and this whole great mess just fine when you were gone. I don't need you. I don't *want* you."

"Then why did you go to such trouble to find me?" Leonidas demanded, and the force of it rocked Susannah back on her heels. "No one else was looking for me. No one else considered for even one second that I might be anything but dead. Only you. Why?"

Susannah hardly knew what she felt as she stared at him, her chest heaving as if she'd been running and her hands in fists at her sides. There were too many things inside her. There was the fact that she was trapped in this marriage and in this family and in this life that she'd wanted to escape the whole time she'd been stuck in it. More than that, there was the astounding reality of the situation. That there was *life* inside her. That she'd found her husband on a mountaintop when everyone had accepted that he was gone, and that she'd done more than save him. They'd made a *life*.

One Night With Consequences

When one night…leads to pregnancy!

When succumbing to a night of unbridled desire
it's impossible to think past the morning after!

But, with the sheets barely settled,
that little blue line appears on the pregnancy test and it
doesn't take long to realise that one night of white-hot
passion has turned into a lifetime of consequences!

Only one question remains:

How do you tell a man you've just met
that you're about to share more than just his bed?

Find out in:

The Guardian's Virgin Ward by Caitlin Crews

A Child Claimed by Gold by Rachael Thomas

The Consequence of His Vengeance by Jennie Lucas

Secrets of a Billionaire's Mistress by Sharon Kendrick

The Boss's Nine-Month Negotiation by Maya Blake

The Pregnant Kavakos Bride by Sharon Kendrick

A Ring for the Greek's Baby by Melanie Milburne

Engaged for Her Enemy's Heir by Kate Hewitt

The Virgin's Shock Baby by Heidi Rice

The Italian's Christmas Secret by Sharon Kendrick

A Night of Royal Consequences by Susan Stephens

Look for more One Night With Consequences
coming soon!

A BABY TO
BIND HIS BRIDE

BY
CAITLIN CREWS

First Published in Great Britain 2017
By Mills & Boon, an imprint of HarperCollins*Publishers*
1 London Bridge Street, London, SE1 9GF

© 2017 Caitlin Crews

ISBN: 978-0-263-93515-8

Our policy is to use papers that are natural, renewable and recyclable
products and made from wood grown in sustainable forests. The logging
and manufacturing processes conform to the legal environmental
regulations of the country of origin.

Printed and bound in Spain
by CPI, Barcelona

USA TODAY bestselling and RITA® Award–nominated author **Caitlin Crews** loves writing romance. She even teaches her favourite romance novels in creative writing classes at places like UCLA Extension's prestigious Writers' Program, where she finally gets to utilise the MA and PhD in English Literature she received from the University of York in England. She currently lives in the Pacific Northwest, with her very own hero and too many pets. Visit her at caitlincrews.com.

CHAPTER ONE

"THEY CALL HIM the Count," the gruff man told her as he led her deeper and deeper into the wild, wearing more flannel and plaid than Susannah Betancur had ever seen on a single person. "Never a name, always *the Count*. But they treat him like a god."

"An actual god or a pretend god?" Susannah asked, as if that would make any difference. If the Count was the man she sought, it certainly wouldn't.

Her guide shot her a look. "Not sure it really matters this far up the side of a hill, ma'am."

The hill they were trudging up was more properly a mountain, to Susannah's way of thinking, but then, everything in the American Rockies appeared to be built on a grand scale. Her impression of the Wild, Wild West was that it was an endless sprawl of jaw-dropping mountains bedecked with evergreens and quaint place names, as if the towering splendor in every direction could be contained by calling the highest peak around something like Little Summit.

"How droll," Susannah muttered beneath her breath as she dug in and tried her best not to topple down the way she'd come. Or give in to what she thought was the high elevation, making her feel a little bit light-headed.

That she was also breathless went without saying.

Her friend in flannel had driven as far as he could on what passed for a road out in the remote Idaho wilderness. It was more properly a rutted, muddy dirt track that had wound deeper and deeper into the thick woods even as the sharp incline clearly indicated that they were going higher and higher at the same time. Then he'd stopped, long after Susannah had resigned herself to that lurching and bouncing lasting forever, or at least until it jostled her into a thousand tiny little jet-lagged pieces. Her driver had then indicated they needed to walk the rest of the way to what he called *the compound*, and little as Susannah had wanted to do anything of the kind after flying all the way here from the far more settled and civilized hills of her home on the other side of the world in Rome, she'd followed along.

Because Susannah might not be a particularly avid hiker. But she was the Widow Betancur, whether she liked it or not. She had no choice but to see this through.

She concentrated on putting one booted foot in front of the other now, well aware that her clothes were not exactly suited to an adventure in the great outdoors. It hadn't occurred to her that she'd actually be *in* the wilderness instead of merely adjacent to it. Unlike every person she'd seen since the Betancur private jet had landed on an airfield in the middle of nowhere, Susannah wore head-to-toe black to announce her state of permanent mourning at a glance. It was her custom. Today it was a sleek cashmere coat over a winter dress in merino wool and deceptively sturdy knee-high boots, because she'd expected the cold, just not the forced march to go along with it.

"Are you sure you don't want to change?" her guide had asked her. They'd stared each other down in his ramshackle little cabin standing at lopsided attention in an overgrown field strewn with various auto parts. It had made her security detail twitchy. It had been his office, presumably. "Something less...?"

"Less?" Susannah had echoed as if she failed to catch his meaning, lifting a brow in an approximation of the ruthless husband she'd lost.

"There's no real road in," her guide had replied, eyeing her as if he expected her to wilt before him at that news. As if a mountain man or even the Rocky Mountains themselves, however challenging, could compare to the intrigues of her own complicated life and the multinational Betancur Corporation that had been in her control, at least nominally, these last few years, because she'd refused to let the rest of them win—her family and her late husband's family and the entire board that had been so sure they could steamroll right over her. "It's off the grid in the sense it's, you know. Rough. You might want to dress for the elements."

Susannah had politely demurred. She wore only black in public and had done so ever since the funeral, because she held the dubious distinction of being the very young widow of one of the richest men in the world. She found that relentless black broadcast the right message about her intention to remain in mourning indefinitely, no matter what designs her conspiring parents and in-laws, or anyone else, had on her at any given time.

She intended to remain the Widow Betancur for a very long while. No new husbands to take the reins and take control, no matter how hard she was pushed from all sides to remarry.

If it was up to her she'd wear black forever, because her widowhood kept her free.

Unless, that was, Leonidas Cristiano Betancur hadn't actually died four years ago in that plane crash, which was exactly what Susannah had hauled herself across the planet to find out.

Leonidas had been headed out to a remote ranch in this same wilderness for a meeting with some potential investors into one of his pet projects when his small plane had gone down in these acres and acres of near-impenetrable national forest. No bodies had ever been found, but the authorities had been convinced that the explosion had burned so hot that all evidence had been incinerated.

Susannah was less convinced. Or maybe it was more accurate to say that she'd been increasingly more convinced over time that what had happened to her husband—on their wedding night, no less—had not been any accident.

That had led to years of deploying private investigators and poring over grainy photographs of dark, grim men who were never Leonidas. Years of playing Penelope games with her conniving parents and her equally scheming in-laws like she was something straight out of *The Odyssey*, pretending to be so distraught by Leonidas's death that she couldn't possibly bear so much as a conversation about whom she might marry next.

When the truth was she was not distraught. She'd hardly known the older son of old family friends whom her parents had groomed her to marry so young. She'd harbored girlish fantasies, as anyone would have at that age, but Leonidas had dashed all of those when he'd patted her on the head at their wedding like she was a puppy and had then disappeared in the middle of their reception because business called.

"Don't be so self-indulgent, Susannah," her mother had said coldly that night while Susannah stood there, abandoned in her big white dress, trying not to cry. "Fantasies of fairy tales are for little girls. You are now the wife of the heir to the Betancur fortune. I suggest you take the opportunity to decide what kind of wife you will be. A pampered princess locked away on one of the Betancur estates or a force to be reckoned with?"

Before morning, word had come that Leonidas was lost. And Susannah had chosen to be a force indeed these past four years, during which time she'd grown from a sheltered, naive nineteen-year-old into a woman who was many things, but was always—*always*—someone to be reckoned with. She'd decided she was more than just a trophy wife, and she'd proved it.

And it had led here, to the side of a mountain in an American state Susannah had heard of only in the vaguest terms, trekking up to some "off the grid" compound where a man meeting Leonidas's description was rumored to be heading up a local cult.

"It's not exactly a doomsday cult," her investigator had told her in the grand penthouse in Rome, where Susannah lived because it was the closest of her husband's properties to the Betancur Corporation's European headquarters, where she liked to make her presence known. It kept things running more smoothly, she'd found.

"Do such distinctions matter?" she'd asked, trying so hard to sound distant and unaffected with those photographs in her hands. Shots of a man in flowing white, hair longer than Leonidas had ever worn it, and still, that same ruthlessness in his dark gaze. That same lean, athletic frame, rangy and dangerous, with new scars that would make sense on someone who'd been in a plane crash.

Leonidas Betancur in the flesh. She would have sworn on it.

And her reaction to that swept over her from the inside, one earthquake after another, while she tried to smile blandly at her investigator.

"The distinction only matters in the sense that if you actually go there, *signora*, it is unlikely that you'll be held or killed," the man told her.

"Something to look forward to, then," Susannah had replied, with another cool smile as punctuation.

While inside, everything had continued that low, shattering roll, because her husband was alive. *Alive*.

She couldn't help thinking that if Leonidas really had repaired to the wilderness and assembled a following, he'd been trained for the vagaries of cult leadership in the best possible classroom: the shark-infested waters of the Betancur Corporation, the sprawling family business that had made him and all his relatives so filthy rich they thought they could do things like bring down the planes of disobedient, uncontrollable heirs when it suited them.

Susannah had learned a lot in her four years of treading that same water. Mainly, that when the assorted Betancurs wanted something—like, say, Leonidas out of the way of a deal that would make the company a lot of money but which Leonidas had thought was shady—they usually found a way to get it.

Being the Widow Betancur kept her free from all that conniving. Above it. But there was one thing better than being Leonidas Betancur's widow, Susannah had thought, and it was bringing him back from the dead.

He could run his damned business himself. And Susannah could get back the life she hadn't known she wanted when she was nineteen. She could be happily divorced, footloose and fancy free by her twenty-fourth birthday, free of all Betancurs and much better at standing up for herself against her own parents.

Free, full stop.

Flying across the planet and into the Idaho wilderness was a small price to pay for her own freedom.

"What kind of leader is the Count?" Susannah asked crisply now, focusing on the rough terrain as she followed her surprisingly hardy guide. "Benevolent? Or something more dire?"

"I can't say as I know the difference," her guide replied out of the side of his mouth. "One cult seems like another to me."

As if they were a dime a dozen in these parts. Perhaps they were.

And then it didn't matter anyway, because they'd reached the compound.

One moment there was nothing but forest and then the next, great gates reared up on the other side of a small clearing, swaddled in unfriendly barbed wire, festooned with gruff signs warning intruders to Keep Out while listing the grisly consequences of trespassing, and mounted with aggressively swiveling video cameras.

"This is as far as I go," her guide said then, keeping to the last of the trees.

Susannah didn't even know his name. And she wished he could come with her, since he'd gotten her this far already. But that wasn't the deal. "I understand."

"I'll wait down by the truck until you need to go down the hill," the man continued. "I'd take you inside…"

"I understand that you can't," Susannah said, because this had all been explained to her down in that ramshackle cabin. "I have to do the rest of this alone."

That was the part that had given her security detail fits. But everyone had agreed. There was no way that Susannah could descend upon some faraway compound with an entire complement of Betancur security guards in tow when it was likely her husband was hiding from the world. She couldn't turn up with her own small army, in other words. Even a few hardy locals would be too much, her guide had told her, because the sort of people who holed up in nearly inaccessible compounds in the Rocky Mountains were usually also the sort who didn't much care for visitors. Particularly not if said visitors were armed.

But a young woman who called herself a widow and was dressed to look as out of place on this mountain as Susannah felt was something else entirely.

Something wholly nonthreatening, she hoped.

Susannah didn't let herself think too much about what she was doing. She'd read too many thrillers while locked away in the Swiss boarding school where her parents had insisted she remain throughout her adolescence, and every last one of them was running through her head on a loop this afternoon.

Not helpful, she snapped at herself. She didn't want to think about the risks. All she wanted—all she'd ever wanted—was to find out what had happened to Leonidas.

Because the sad truth was, she might be the only one who cared.

And she told herself that the only reason *why* she cared was because finding him would set her free.

Susannah strode toward the gates, her skin crawling with every step she took. She knew the video cameras were trained on her, but she was worried about something worse than surveillance. Like snipers. She rather doubted anyone built a great fortress in the woods like the one she saw before her, sprawling this way and that, if they didn't intend to defend it.

"Stop right there!"

She couldn't see where the voice came from, exactly. But Susannah stopped anyway. And raised her hands up, though not entirely over her head. There was no point coming over completely submissive.

"I'm here to see the Count," she called into the silent, chilly forest all around her.

Nothing happened.

For a moment Susannah thought nothing would. But then, slowly, a door at the side of one of the great gates before her swung open.

She held her breath. Would this be Leonidas after all this time?

A man came out through the door, but it wasn't Leonidas. This man was much shorter than the husband she'd lost, with an alarming semiautomatic rifle slung over his shoulder and a distinctly unfriendly expression on his round face.

"You need to get off our mountain," he told her, waving the rifle as punctuation.

But he was frowning at her as he spoke. At her clothes, Susannah realized after a moment. Because she certainly wasn't dressed for an assault on a compound. Or even a walk in the woods, for that matter.

"I have no particular desire to be on this mountain," she replied crisply. "I only want to see the Count."

"The Count sees who he wants to see, and never on demand." The man's voice throbbed with fervor. And more than that, fury. As if he couldn't believe Susannah's temerity in suggesting she should have access to a being of such greatness.

It was possible she was imagining that part. What did she know about cult members?

She inclined her head at the man. "He'll want to see me."

"The count is a busy man," the man scoffed. "He doesn't have time for strange women who appear out of nowhere like they're begging to get shot."

That would be a direct threat where she came from,

Susannah reflected, while her heart beat out a desperate tattoo in her chest. She reminded herself that here, in the middle of this vast and dangerous wilderness, the people who held these places had a different relationship to their weapons. And to threats, for that matter.

The man before her was perhaps being nothing but matter-of-fact.

"I'm not looking to get shot," she told him as calmly as possible. "But the Count will want to see me, I'm sure of it." She wasn't sure of any such thing. The fact that Leonidas had locked himself away in this place and started calling himself something so ridiculous suggested that he had no desire to be located. Ever. But she wasn't going to get into that with one of his wild-eyed true believers. She aimed a cool smile the guard's way instead. "Why don't you take me to him and he can tell you so himself?"

"Lady, I'm not going to tell you again. You should turn around. You need to get off this hill and never come back here again."

"I'm not going to do that," Susannah said, with that iron matter-of-factness she'd developed over the past few years. As if she expected her orders to be obeyed simply because she'd issued them. As if she was Leonidas himself instead of the young widow everyone knew he'd never meant to leave in charge of anything, much less the whole of his fortune. But Susannah had done exactly what her mother had told her to do. She'd taken Leonidas's name and gained his authority at the same time. She'd been confounding people in the corporate world he'd left behind with this exact same attitude for years now. "I have to see the Count. That's nonnegotiable. Whatever needs to happen so that I can do that is up to you. I don't care."

"Listen, lady—"

"Or you can shoot me," Susannah suggested coolly. "But those are the only two possible outcomes here."

The man blinked at her as if he didn't know what to do. Susannah didn't entirely blame him. She didn't cower. She didn't shift her weight from side to side or give any indication that she was anything but perfectly calm. She simply stood there as if it was completely natural that she should be thousands of feet high on the side of a mountain in the Idaho wilderness. She gazed back at the strange man before her as if she marched up to the doors of cults and demanded entry every day of the week.

She stared at him until it became clear that he was the one who was ill at ease, not her.

"Who the hell are you?" he finally demanded.

"I'm so glad you asked," Susannah said then, and this time, her smile was something less than cool. Something more like a weapon and she'd had four years to learn how to shoot it. "I'm the Count's wife."

CHAPTER TWO

THE COUNT DIDN'T have a wife.

Or he hadn't had one in as long as he could remember—but that was the trouble with everything, wasn't it? It was eating at him more and more these days that there were so many things he couldn't remember.

There were more things he couldn't remember than things he could. And all of them had happened in the last four years.

His followers told the stories of how they'd found this place. How they'd come here, each finding his or her own way up the mountain and proving themselves worthy of entry. They spoke of what they'd left behind. The people, the places. The things. The dreams and expectations.

But the Count knew only the compound.

His first memory was of waking up in the expansive set of rooms he still occupied. He been battered, broken. It had taken him a long time to return to anything approaching health. To sit, then stand. Then slowly, painfully, walk. And even when he'd been walking around of his own volition at last, he hadn't felt that his body was back to his standard.

Though he couldn't have said what his standard was.

It had taken him almost eighteen months to feel something like normal.

And another eighteen months to realize that no matter what he pretended because it seemed to make his people so nervous when he did not, he didn't really know what *normal* was.

Because he still couldn't remember anything but this. Here. Now.

His people assured him it was preordained. They told him that it was all a part of the same glorious plan. They had gathered, they had prayed, and so to them a leader had appeared in this same forest where they lived. The end.

The Count had agreed because there was no reason not to agree.

He certainly felt like a leader. He had since the first moment he'd opened his eyes. When he issued an order and people leaped to fill it, it didn't feel new. It felt deeply familiar. Right and good.

He rarely shared with anyone how much he liked the things that felt familiar. It seemed to shy too close to some kind of admission he didn't want to make.

His every need was attended to here, of course. His people gathered to hear him speak. They fretted over his health. They fed him and they clothed him and they followed him. What more could a man want?

And yet there was a woman in the compound, claiming she was his wife, and the Count felt as if something in him he'd never known was there had cracked wide open.

"She's quite insistent," his closest adviser, Robert, said. Again—and this time with more obvious disapproval. "She says she's been looking for you for some time."

"And yet I do not have a wife," the Count replied. "Have you not told me this from the start?"

Robert was the only follower with him then, watching

the woman in question on the bank of monitors before them. The Count waited to feel some kind of familiarity or recognition. He waited to know her one way or another, but like everything in his life, there was no knowing. There was no memory.

Sometimes he told his people that he was grateful for this blank canvas.

But then there were other times, like this, when the things he didn't feel, the things he didn't know, seemed to batter at him like a winter storm.

"Of course you do not have a wife," Robert was saying, sounding something like scandalized. "That is not your path. That is for lesser men."

This was a place of purity. That was one of the few things that had always been clear to the Count, and it was handy that he'd never been tempted to stray from that path. The men and women here practiced a version of the same radical purity that he did—with a special dispensation for those who were married—or they left.

But in all this time, the Count had never gazed upon a female and felt something other than that same purity, drowning out anything else.

Until now.

It took him a moment to recognize what was happening to him, and he supposed that he should have been horrified. But he wasn't. Lust rolled through him like an old friend, and he couldn't have said why that failed to set off any alarms within him. He told himself temptation was good, as it would make him even more powerful to conquer it. He told himself that this was nothing more than a test.

The woman who filled his screens looked impatient. That was the first thing that separated her from the handful of women who lived here. More than that, she looked... Fragile. Not weathered and hardy the way his people were. Not prepared for any eventuality. She looked soft.

The Count had no idea why he wanted to touch her to see if she could possibly be as soft as she looked.

She was dressed in clothes that didn't make any sense to him, here on top of the mountain. He could never remember being off the mountain, of course, but he knew that there was a whole world out there. He'd been told. And all that black, sleek and slick over her trim little figure, made him think of cities.

It had never occurred to him before, but he didn't really think about cities. And now that he had, it was as if they all ran through his head like a travelogue. *New York. London. Shanghai. New Delhi. Berlin. Cairo. Auckland.*

As if he'd been to each and every one of them.

He shoved that oddity aside and studied the woman. They'd brought her inside the compound walls and placed her in a sealed-off room that no one ever called a cell. But that's what it was. It was outfitted with nothing more than an old sofa, a toilet behind a screen in the corner and cameras in the walls.

If she was as uncomfortable as the last three law enforcement officials had been when they'd visited, she didn't show it. She sat on the sofa as if she could do it forever. Her face was perfectly calm, her blue eyes clear. She looked almost serene, he might have said, which only drew attention to the fact that she was almost incomprehensibly pretty.

Not that he had many other women to compare her with. But somehow the Count knew that if he lined up every woman out there in the world he couldn't remember, he would still find this one stunning.

Her legs were long and shapely, even in the boots she

wore, and she crossed them neatly as if she hadn't noticed they were splattered with mud. She wore only one rather large ring on her left hand that kept catching the light when she moved, and she crossed her fingers in her lap before her as if she knew it and was trying to divert attention away from all that excessive sparkle. Her mouth caught at him in ways he didn't entirely understand, greed and hunger like a ball inside him, and the Count wasn't sure he liked it. He concentrated on her remarkably glossy blond hair instead, swept back from her face into something complicated at her nape.

A chignon, he thought.

It was a word the Count didn't know. But it was also the proper term to describe how she had styled her hair. He knew that in the way he knew all the things he shouldn't have, so he shoved it aside and kept on.

"Bring her to me," he said before he thought better of it.

Then he thought better of it and still said nothing to contradict himself.

"She's not your wife," Robert said, scowling. "You have no wife. You are the Count, the leader of the glorious path, and the answer to every question of the faithful!"

"Yes, yes," the Count said with a wave of his hand. What he thought was that Robert didn't actually know if this woman was his wife. Neither did he. Because he couldn't simply have appeared from nowhere in a shower of flame, the way everyone claimed. He'd understood that from the start. At the very least, he'd thought, if he'd simply appeared one day in a burst of glory, he wouldn't have needed all that time to recover, would he?

But these mysteries of faith, he'd learned, were not something he could explore in public.

What he knew was that if he'd come from somewhere

else, that meant he'd had a life there. Wherever it was. And if this woman thought she knew him, it was possible she could prove to be a font of information.

The Count wanted information more than anything.

He didn't wait to see if Robert would obey him. He knew the other man would, because everyone did. The Count left the surveillance room behind and walked back through his compound. He knew it so well, every room and every wall built of logs. The fireplaces of stone and the thick rugs on the common floors. He had never thought beyond this place. Because everything he wanted and needed was right here. The mountain gave and the followers received, that was the way.

Sydney. Saint Petersburg. Vancouver. Reykjavik. Oslo. Rome.

What did it mean that he could suddenly *see* so many more places? Places not hewn from wood and tucked away in these mountains, with nothing to see in all directions but trees and weather? He wasn't sure he wanted to know.

The Count made his way to his own private rooms, set apart from the dormitories where the rest of his people slept. He kept his expression blank as he moved, as if he was communing with the Spirit the way he was supposed to do, the better to discourage anyone from approaching him.

The good news was that no one would dare. They watched him as he walked and the more attention-seeking among them pitched their prayers even louder, but no one tried to catch his eye.

When he got to his rooms, he waited in the outer chamber. When he'd first started to come into awareness, to become himself, he'd recoiled from the starkness of these rooms. It had felt like a prison, though he knew, somehow, he'd never been in one. But now he'd come to prefer it to the relatively cozier rooms on the other side of his doors. Stark-white walls. Minimal furnishings. Nothing to distract a man from his purpose.

It was between him and his conscience that he'd never quite managed to feel that purpose the way everyone assumed he did.

He didn't have to wait long for them to bring her in. And when they did, the starkness of the walls seemed to make the shock of her black clothes that much bolder in comparison. Everything was white. The clothes he wore, loose and flowing. His walls, the hardwood floor, even the chair he sat in, like an ivory throne.

And then this woman in the middle of it all, black clothes, blue eyes and unbent knees. This woman who stared at him, her lips slightly parted and a sheen in her eyes he couldn't quite read.

This woman who called herself his wife.

"I do not have a wife," he told her when his followers had left them alone at last. He told himself there was no reason his anticipation should make him so...restless. "The leader has no wife. His path is pure."

He stayed where he was, sitting on the only chair in the room. But if standing there before him like one of his supplicants bothered her—though, of course, his followers would all be prostrate before his magnificence rather than stand and risk his displeasure—she didn't let it show.

In fact, the look on her face was something that edged more toward astonishment. With an undertone he was fairly sure was temper—not that he'd seen such a thing with his own eyes. Not directed at him.

"You've got to be kidding."

That was all she said. It was a harsh little whisper, nothing more.

And the Count found himself fascinated by her eyes. They were so tremendously blue it made him think of the breathless summers here, and they were filled with a brilliant, diamond-cut emotion he couldn't begin to understand.

"I do not kid," he said. Or he didn't think he did. He was certain he never had, anyway. Not here.

The woman before him blew out a breath as if something was hard. As if she was performing some kind of physical labor.

"How long do you intend to hide out here?" She threw the words at him in a tight sort of voice that suggested she was upset.

The Count could not think of any reason at all that she should be.

"Where else would I be?" He tilted his head slightly to one side as he regarded her, trying to make sense of all the emotion he could see swirling around her, written into every line of her black-clad body. Trying to puzzle out its cause. "And I'm not hiding. This is my home."

She let out a sharp little laugh, but not as if she thought anything was funny. The Count found himself frowning, which never happened.

"You have many homes," she said in a voice that sounded almost…gritty. "I enjoy the penthouse in Rome, certainly, but there's something to be said for the New Zealand vineyard. The island in the South Pacific. The town house in London or the Greek villa. Or all those acres of land your family owns in Brazil. You have multiple homes on every possible continent, is my point, and not one of them is a sanitarium in a mountain tree house in Idaho."

"A sanitarium?" he echoed. It was another word he didn't know—and yet did, as soon as she said it.

But she wasn't paying attention to what he did or didn't comprehend. She was pivoting to take in the stark-white chamber, her arms crossed over her chest.

"Is this supposed to be some kind of hospital room?" she demanded. "Has this been a four-year mental health retreat from all your responsibilities?" Her blue gaze was even sharper when it landed on him again. "If you knew you were going to run away like this, why bother marrying me? Why not pull your disappearing act before the wedding? You must know exactly what I've had to deal with all this time. What did I ever do to you to deserve being left in the middle of that mess?"

"You're speaking to me as if you know me," the Count said in a low, dangerous voice that she did not seem to heed.

"I don't know you at all. That's what makes this so vicious. If you wanted to punish someone with the company and your horrible family, why choose me? I was *nineteen*. It shouldn't surprise you to learn that they tried to eat me alive."

There was something sharp inside him, like broken glass, and it was shredding him with every word she spoke. He found himself standing when he hadn't meant to move.

"I did not choose you. I did not marry you. I have no idea who you are, but I am the Count."

His hand had ended up over his chest and he dropped it, ill at ease with his own fervency.

"You are not a count," snapped the woman he was realizing, too late, was far more dangerous to him than he'd imagined anyone could be. And he couldn't tell if that was a kind of apprehension that worked in him then or, worse, something far closer to exhilaration. And she clearly wasn't finished. "Your family has certainly flirted with this or that aristocracy over the years, but you are not titled. Your mother likes to claim that she is a direct descendent of the Medicis, but I'm not sure anyone takes that seriously no matter how many times she threatens to commit a murder over a meal."

The Count's head was reeling. There was a faint, dull pain at his temples and at the base of his skull, and he knew it was her fault. He should have had her removed. Tossed back in that cell, or dropkicked down the side of his mountain.

There was no reason he should cross the room, his bare feet slapping against the bare floor, to tower there above her.

There was no reason—but she should have been concerned. If she'd been one of his followers she would have thrown up her hands in surrender and then tossed herself at his feet. She would have sobbed and begged for his forgiveness.

This woman did none of those things.

She tipped her chin up and met his gaze as if she didn't notice that he was significantly taller than she was. More, as if she didn't care.

"I would be very careful how you speak to me," he told her, managing to get the words out through the seething thing that had its claws in him and that broken glass inside.

"What is the purpose of this charade?" she demanded. "You know I'm not going to be fooled by it. You know I know exactly who you are. No threat is going to change that."

"That was not a threat. It was a warning." He realized he wanted to reach over and put his hands on her, and that threw him. But not enough to back away. Not enough to put a safe distance between them the way he should have. "There's a certain disrespect that I confess, I find almost refreshing, since it is so rare. And suicidal. But you should know my people will not accept it."

"Your people?" She shook her head as if he wasn't making sense. Worse, as if he was hurting her, somehow. "If you mean the cult on the other side of these doors, you can't really think they're anything but accessories to a crime."

"I've committed no crimes."

But he threw that out as if he was defending himself, and the Count had no idea why he would do such a thing. Nothing in his memory had prepared him for this. People did not argue with him. They did not stand before him and hurl accusations at him.

Everyone in this compound adored him. The Count had never been in the presence of someone who didn't worship him before. He found it...energizing, in a strange way. He recognized lust, but the form it took surprised him. He wanted to drag his hands through her neat, careful hair. He wanted to taste the mouth that dared say such things to him.

He wanted to drag out the broken glass inside him and let her handle it, since he might not know how or why she was doing it, but he knew it was her fault.

"You swanned away from the scene of an accident, apparently," she was saying, with the same fearlessness he couldn't quite believe, even as it was happening. And she was carrying on as if he was about as intimidating as a tiny, fragile female should have been. "Your entire family thinks you're dead. *I* thought you were dead. And yet here you are. Hale and healthy and draped in bridal white. And hidden away on the top of the mountain, while the mess you left behind gets more and more complicated by the day."

The Count laughed at her. "Who is it that you imagine I am?"

"I am not imagining anything," the woman said, and she seemed to bristle as she said it. Maybe that was why the Count found his hands on her upper arms, holding her there before him. Then dragging her closer. "I knew it was you when I saw the pictures. I don't understand how you've managed to hide it for so long. You're one of the most recognizable men alive."

"I am the Count," he repeated, but even he could taste the faintly metallic tang of what he was very much afraid was desperation. "The path—"

"I am Susannah Forrester Betancur," she interrupted him. Far from pulling away from his grip, she angled herself toward him, surging up on her toes to put her face that much closer to his. "*Your wife*. You married me four years ago and left me on our wedding night, charmer that you are."

"Impossible. The Count has no wife. That would make him less than pure."

She let out a scoffing sound, and her blue eyes burned.

"You are not the Count of anything. You are Leonidas Cristiano Betancur, and you are the heir to the Betancur Corporation. That means that you are so wealthy you could buy every mountain in this range, and then some, from your pocket change alone. It means that you are so powerful that someone—very likely a member of your own family—had to scheme up a plane crash to get around you."

The pain in his temples was sharpening. The pressure at the base of his skull was intensifying.

"I am not who you think I am," he managed to say.

"You are exactly who I think you are," she retorted. "And Leonidas, it is far past time for you to come home."

There was the pain and then a roaring, loud and rough, but he understood somehow it was inside him.

Maybe that was the demon that took him then. Maybe that was what made him haul her closer to him as if he was someone else and she was married to him the way she claimed.

Maybe that was why he crushed her mouth with his, tasting her at last. Tasting all her lies—

But that was the trouble.

One kiss, and he remembered.

He remembered everything.

Everything.

Who he was. How he'd come here. His last moments on that doomed flight and his lovely young bride, too, whom he'd left behind without a second thought because that was the man he'd been then, formidable and focused all the way through.

He was Leonidas Betancur, not a bloody count. And he had spent four years in a log cabin surrounded by acolytes obsessed with purity, which was very nearly hilarious, because there was not a damned thing about him that was or ever had been pure.

So he kissed little Susannah, who should have known better. Little Susannah who had been thrown to him like bait all those years ago, a power move by her loathsome parents and a boon to his own devious family, because he'd always avoided innocence. He'd lost his own so early.

His own, brutal father had seen to that.

He angled his head and he pulled her closer, tasting her and taking her, plundering her mouth like a man possessed.

She tasted sweet and lush, and she went straight to his head. He told himself it was only that it had been so long. The part of him that had honestly believed he was who these crazy people thought he was—the part that had developed the conscience Leonidas had never bothered with—thought he should stop.

But he didn't.

He kissed her again and again. He kissed her until the rest of her was as soft and pliable as her mouth. He kissed her until she looped her arms around his neck and slid against him as if she couldn't stand on her own feet. He kissed her until she was making tiny noises in the back of her throat.

He remembered her in a confection of a white dress and all the people their families had invited to the ceremony on the Betancur family estate in France. He remembered how wide her blue eyes had been and how young she'd seemed, the virgin sacrifice his brute of a father had bought for him before he'd died. A gift tied up in an alliance that benefited the family.

One more bit of evidence of the insupportable rot that was the Betancur blood—

But Leonidas didn't care about that.

"Leonidas," she whispered, tearing her mouth from his. "Leonidas, I—"

He didn't want to talk. He wanted her mouth, so he took it.

Susannah had found him here. Susannah had brought him back his life.

So he swept her up into his arms, never moving his mouth from hers for an instant, and Leonidas carried her into the bedroom he couldn't wait to leave at last.

But first, Susannah owed him that wedding night.

And four years later, Leonidas was ready to collect.

CHAPTER THREE

LEONIDAS'S MOUTH WAS on hers, and she couldn't seem to recover from the sweet shock of it. He kissed her again and again and again, and the only thing she could manage to do was surrender herself to the slick, epic feel of his mouth against hers.

As if she'd spent all these years stumbling around in the dark, and the taste of this man was the light at last.

She should stop him. Susannah knew that. She should step back and draw some boundaries. Make some rules. Demand that he stop pretending he didn't remember her, for a start. She didn't believe in amnesia. She didn't believe that someone like Leonidas, so bold and relentless and *bright*, could ever disappear.

But then, he'd always been larger than life to her. She'd known who he was since she was a child and had been thrilled when her parents had informed her she was to marry him. He'd been like a starry sky as far as she'd been concerned on her wedding day, and some part of her had refused to believe that a man that powerful could be snuffed out so easily, so quickly.

And before she'd had a chance to touch him like this, the way she'd imagined so fervently before their wedding—

She needed to stop him. She needed to assert herself. She needed to let him know that the girl he'd married had died the day he had and she was far more sure and powerful now than she'd been then.

But she didn't do any of the things she imagined she should.

When Leonidas kissed her, she kissed him back, inexpert and desperate. She didn't pause to tell him how little she knew of men or their ways or the things that lips and teeth and that delirious angle of his hard jaw could do. She met his mouth as best she could. She tasted him in turn.

And she surrendered.

When he lifted her up in his arms, she thought that was an excellent opportunity to do...something. Anything. But his mouth was on hers as he moved, and Susannah realized that she'd been lying to herself for a very long time.

She could hardly remember the silly teenager she'd been on the day of her wedding after all that had happened since. She'd known she was sheltered back then, in the same way she'd known that her father was a very high-level banker and that her Dutch mother loathed living in England. But knowing she was sheltered and then dealing with the ramifications of her own naïveté were two very different things, it turned out. And Susannah had been dealing with the consequences of the way she'd been raised—not to mention her parents' aspirations for their only child—for so long now, and in such a pressure cooker, that it was easy to forget the truth of things.

Such as the fact that when her parents had told her—a dreamy sixteen-year-old girl who'd spent most of her life in a very remote and strict Swiss boarding school with other heiresses to various kingdoms and fortunes—that she was destined to marry the scion of the Betancur family, Susannah hadn't been upset. She hadn't cried into her pillow every night the way her roommate did at the prospect of her own marriage, scared of the life spooling out in front of her without her permission or input.

On the contrary, she'd been delighted.

Leonidas was gorgeous, all her school friends had agreed. He was older than them, but much younger than some of her friends' betrothed, and with all his hair and teeth as far as anyone could tell. And she'd met him, so she knew firsthand that he was merciless and forbidding in ways that had made her feel tingly all over. Moreover, every time they'd interacted—as few and far between as those times might have been over the years, because he was an important man and she was just a girl, as her mother chastised her—he'd always treated her with a great patience even she'd been able to see was at complete odds with the ferocity of his dark gaze.

She forgotten that. He'd disappointed her on her wedding night, then he'd died, and she'd forgotten. She'd lost herself in the scandal and intrigue of the Betancur Corporation and all its attendant family drama, and she'd completely failed to remember that when it came to Leonidas she had always been a very, very silly girl.

Back when she was one, and again now. Clearly.

Say something, she ordered herself.

But then he was laying her down on the bed in the next room, and following her down to the mattress, and Susannah didn't have it in her to care if she was silly.

She'd been promised a wedding night. Four years ago, she'd expected to hand over her innocence to the man who'd become her husband and instead, she'd been left to years of widow's weeds and seas of enemies—not all of whom had come at her as opponents.

Susannah couldn't count the number of men who'd

tried to seduce her over the years, many related to Leonidas, but she'd always held firm. She was the Widow Betancur and she mourned. She grieved. That little bit of fiction had protected her when nothing else could.

But Leonidas wasn't dead. And more than that, as he sprawled out above her on that firm mattress and pressed her into it, all his lean, solid strength making her breathless with a dizzy sort of joy, it made her forget that he had ever disappeared in the first place.

As if this was their wedding night after all.

"This has been four years overdue," he said, his voice a low growl against her neck, and she could *feel* him just as she could hear him. There was something in his tone she didn't like—a certain skepticism, perhaps, that pricked at her—but it was swept away when his mouth fixed to hers again.

And Susannah did nothing to dig her feet into whatever ground she could find. She let Leonidas take her with a fervent joy that might have concerned her if she'd been able to think critically.

She didn't think. She kissed him instead.

His hands dug into her hair, tugging slightly until he pulled it out of the knot she'd worn the heavy mass of it in. He muttered something she couldn't quite hear, but she didn't care because he was kissing her again and again.

When he moved his mouth from hers to trace a trail down the length of her neck, she moaned, and he laughed, just a little bit. When he tugged on her cashmere coat, she lifted herself up so he could pull it from her body. He did the same with her shift dress, tugging it up and over her head. She had the vague impression that he tossed both items aside, but she didn't care where they landed.

Because she was lying beneath him with nothing on

but a bra and panties and her knee-high boots, and the look in his dark eyes was…savage.

It made Susannah shake a little. It made her feel beautiful.

Raw. Aching and alive.

As if, after all this time, she really was more than the shroud she'd been wearing like armor for all these years. As if she wasn't the little girl he'd married, but the woman she'd longed to be in her head.

"You are the perfect gift," he said, as if he really couldn't remember who she was. As if his amnesia game was real and he really believed himself some or other local god, tucked away here in the woods.

But Susannah couldn't bring herself to worry about that. Because Leonidas was touching her.

He used his mouth and his hands. He found her breasts and cupped them with his palms, then bent his head to tease first one nipple, then the next. Through the soft fabric of her bra, his mouth was so hot, so shocking, that she arched off the bed. To get away from him—or get closer to him—she couldn't quite tell.

He stripped the bra from her, then repeated himself, but this time there was no fabric between the suction of his mouth and her tender skin. Susannah had never felt anything like it in her life. She felt…open and exposed, and so bright red with too much sensation she might as well have been a beacon.

Her head thrashed against the mattress beneath her. She gripped him wherever she could touch him, grabbing fistfuls of the flowing white garments he wore at his sides, his hips, and not caring at all when her own gasps and moans filled her ears.

Then he moved lower. His tongue teased her navel, and then his big hands wrapped around her hips.

And he didn't ask. He didn't even move her panties out of his way. Leonidas merely bent his head and fastened his mouth to the place where she ached the most.

Susannah thought she exploded.

She was surprised to find, between one breath and the next, that she was still in one piece. That every bit of suction he applied between her legs made her feel like she was breaking and fusing back together again—over and over again.

She felt a tug at her hip, heard a faint tearing sound that she only dimly understood was him tearing her panties from her body, and when he bent his head to her once again, everything changed.

It had already been madness. And now it was magic.

Leonidas licked his way into her, teasing her and tasting her. It took her long moments to realize that he was humming, a low sound of intense male approval that she could feel like shock waves crashing through her body. It was like a separate thrill.

She felt his fingers tracing through her heat, and then they were inside her. Long and hard and decidedly male.

"My God…" she managed to say, her head tipped back and her eyes shut tight.

"That's what they call me," he agreed, laughter and need in his voice and his words like separate caresses against her soft heat.

He scraped the neediest part of her with his teeth, then sucked at her, hard—and that was it.

Susannah thought she died, but there was too much sensation. *Too much.* It broke her into pieces, but it didn't stop. It didn't ever stop. It went on and on and on, and she couldn't breathe.

She didn't want to breathe.

And she was still spinning around and around when

he pulled away from her. She managed to open her eyes and fix them on him, watching in a dizzy haze as Leonidas stripped himself of that flowing white shirt at last.

Susannah couldn't help the gasp she let out when she finally saw all of him.

His muscles were smooth and tight, packed hard everywhere in a manner that suggested hard labor instead of a gym. She might not have seen him naked four years ago, but she'd certainly spent time researching him online. She thought he was bigger now than he'd been when that plane went down. Tougher, somehow.

Maybe she thought that because he was covered in scars. They wound all over his chest and dipped below his waistband.

"So many scars…" she whispered.

Leonidas froze. And Susannah couldn't bear it.

She wasn't sure she'd thought much at all since the moment she'd walked through the doors to this chamber and had seen Leonidas sitting there as if he belonged on this godforsaken mountaintop. As if he wasn't a Betancur. Or her husband. Her mind had gone blank while her mouth had opened, and she saw no reason to reverse the not-thinking trend now.

Susannah reached up and traced the scars that she could touch. Over the flat plane of his chest. Across the ridged wonder of his abdomen. On the one hand, he was a perfect specimen of a male, lean and strong and enough to make her mouth water. On the other, he wore the evidence of the plane crash that everyone had said was too deadly for anyone to survive. It was as if two pictures tried to collide in her head, and neither one of them made sense. Not the Leonidas he'd been, who had left her so abruptly. Not the man who called himself the Count and hid away in this compound.

But her fingers didn't need pictures. They didn't care which version of him he was today. His skin was so hot and his body was so hard, and every time she found a new scar and ran her fingers over it as if she was trying to memorize it, he pulled in his breath with a sharp sound that she knew, somehow, had nothing to do with pain.

"Do they make me a monster?" he asked, his voice a quiet rumble.

Susannah opened her mouth to refute that—but then saw the way his dark eyes gleamed. And she remembered. This was a man who had considered himself something of a god even before he'd crash-landed in the middle of the Rocky Mountain wilderness and found some followers to agree with him.

He didn't think he was a monster. She doubted Leonidas Betancourt ever thought ill of himself at all, no matter what he was calling himself today.

She wrinkled her nose at him. "Do you care if they do? Or do you fancy yourself as much a monster as a man?"

And he laughed. Leonidas threw back his head, and he laughed and laughed.

Something speared through her then, part fear, part recognition. And something else she couldn't quite identify.

It was because he was so beautiful, she thought. There was no denying it. That thick, rich dark hair, shot through with a hint of gold and much longer than his austere cut back in the day. Those dark, tawny eyes that burned and melted in turn. His height and his whipcord strength, evident in everything he did, even sit on a makeshift throne in a white room in a guarded compound. All of that would have been enough to make him noticeable no matter what. To make him attractive no matter where he went.

He had turned her head when she'd been little more than a girl.

But he was so much more than that. It was something about the sheer, sensual perfection of his face. The way his features were sculpted so intensely and precisely, put together like an amalgam of everything that was beautiful in him. His Greek mother. His Spanish father. His Brazilian grandparents on one side, his French and Persian grandparents on the other.

He was glorious. There was no other word for it.

And when he laughed, Susannah was tempted to believe that he really was a god, after all.

"You are quite right," Leonidas said after a long while. Long after she'd been captivated by the way his laughter transformed him, right there where he sat astride her. Long after she'd lost another part of herself she couldn't quite name. "I don't care at all. Monster, god, man. It is all the same to me."

And this time when he came down over her, she was already shaking. A deep, internal trembling, as if a terrible joy was tearing her apart from inside out. Some part of Susannah wanted it no matter how she feared it, and because she couldn't tell if it was suicide or something sweeter, she threw herself into his hands.

Leonidas shifted. He kicked off his trousers, and then settled himself between her legs. He pulled her thighs up on either side of his hips while Susannah tried to make her whirling head settled down enough to accommodate him.

Then it didn't matter, because he kissed her. Again and again, he took her mouth until she felt branded. Possessed.

Taken. At last.

It made her wonder how she'd ever survived all this time without him. Without *this*.

In some distant part of her brain she knew she should tell him.

I'm a virgin, she could say. *Word of warning, our wedding really was a white one.* Maybe he would even laugh again, at the absurdity of a woman her age still so untouched. Whatever he did, whether he believed her or not, it would be said. He would know.

But Susannah couldn't seem to force the words out.

And she forgot about it anyway as his hands gripped her hips again, and he shifted her body beneath his in an even more pointed manner, as if he intended to take charge of this and do it his way.

Maybe that would be enough.

It would have to be enough, because she could feel him then. Huge and hard, flush there against the part of her that no other person had ever touched.

A different sort of shiver ran over her then. Foreboding, perhaps. Or a wild need she'd never encountered before, drawing tight all around her as if she was caught in a great fist. Again she opened her mouth to say the thing she didn't want to say, just to make sure he didn't—

But he thrust into her then, deep and sure.

Susannah couldn't control her response. She couldn't pretend. It was a deep ache, a burning kind of tear, and her body took over and bucked up against him as if her hips were trying to throw him off of their own volition. She couldn't control the little yelp that she let out, filled with the pain and shock she couldn't hide.

Though the instant it escaped her, she wished she'd bitten it back.

Above her, Leonidas went still. Forbidding.

His eyes were like flint.

And still, she could feel him there, deep inside her, stretching her and filling her, making her feel things in places she'd never realized were part of her own body. The fact she couldn't seem to catch her breath didn't help.

"It has been a while, I grant you," Leonidas said and he sounded almost...strained. Tight and something like furious at once. "But it's not supposed to hurt."

"It doesn't hurt," Susannah lied.

He studied her for a long moment. Then, not changing the intensity of his gaze at all, he lifted a hand and wiped away a bit of moisture she hadn't realized had escaped from her eye and pooled beneath it.

Leonidas repeated it on her other eye, still watching her intently.

"Try that again."

"Really." Susannah didn't want to move, possibly ever again, but there was something working in her she didn't understand. Something spurring her on, pulsing out from the ache between her legs that she knew was him, fusing with that breathlessness she couldn't control. A kind of dangerous restlessness, reckless and needy. She tested her hips against his, biting down on her lower lip as she rocked yourself against him. "It feels fantastic."

"I can see that. The tears alone suggest it, of course. And the fact that you're frowning at me proves it beyond a doubt."

Susannah was indeed frowning at him, she realized then, though she hadn't known it. She knew it now, and she let it deepen.

"Here's a newsflash," she managed to say. "Just because people worship the ground you walk on—literally—doesn't mean you can read minds. Particularly not mine."

"Tell yourself anything you need to, little one," he murmured, and that should have enraged her. But it didn't. If anything, it made her feel...warm. Too warm. Leonidas ran his hands down her sides. Once, then again.

He brushed her hair back from her face. She could still feel him inside her, so big and so hard, and yet all he did was smooth those caresses all over her. "I don't have to read your mind. Your body tells me everything I need to know. What I don't understand is how you've managed to remain innocent all this time."

She opened her mouth to answer him, but she was distracted by the way he touched her. Those big hands of his moved all over her, spreading heat and sensation everywhere he touched. He didn't move inside her. He didn't slam himself into her or any of the other things she half expected him to do. He only touched her. Caressed her. Settled there above her as if he could wait forever.

It made a little knot deep in her belly pull tight. Then glow as it began to swell into something far bigger and more unwieldy.

"I don't know what you mean," Susannah said at last, blinking more unwelcome heat from her eyes. "I am your widow. Of course I'm innocent. You died before you could change that."

If she had any doubt that he was pretending not to remember her before, it disappeared. Because the look he turned on her then was 100 percent Leonidas Betancur. The hard, ruthless man she remembered vividly, all ruthless power sharply contained.

The one who hadn't been in evidence when she'd walked into this place.

Had he truly forgotten who he was?

And if he had—when had he remembered?

"I find that hard to believe, knowing my cousins," he was saying, offering more proof. He tilted his head to one side, and his dark eyes glittered. "I would have thought they'd be on my widow like carrion crows."

"They were, of course."

"But it was your depth of feeling for me that prevented you from taking a better offer when it was presented to you?" Leonidas's voice was sardonic. The expression in his tawny dark eyes was cynical.

And that knotted thing inside her seemed harder. Edgier.

"It might surprise you to learn that I don't like your cousins very much," she told him, bracing her hands on his shoulders as if she'd half a mind to push him off her. But she didn't. Her fingers curled into him of their own accord. "I asked them to respect my mourning process. Repeatedly."

This time, when Leonidas laughed, it wasn't anything like sunshine. But Susannah still felt it deep inside her, where they were connected, and then everywhere else in a rolling wave of sensation.

"What exactly have you been mourning, little one?" he asked, that sardonic cast to his beautiful face. "Me? You hardly know me. Let me be the first to assure you I'm no better than my cousins."

"Maybe you are and maybe you're not," she retorted. "But I'm married to you, not them."

And something changed in him then, she could feel it. A deep kind of earthquake, shaking through him and then all over her.

But as if he didn't want her to notice, as if he wanted to pretend instead that it hadn't happened, that was when he chose to move.

Everything changed all over again. Because she was so slick and he was so hard, so deep. And Susannah had never felt anything like it. The thrust, the drag. The pressure, the heat. The pure, wild delight that seemed to pound through her veins, turning to a bright, hot liquid everywhere it went.

Tentatively, with growing confidence, she learned to

match his slow, steady rhythm. He was being something like careful she would have said with all her total lack of experience, but there was something in the slowness that tore her wide open with every intense stroke.

She felt it building in her all over again, that impossible fire she'd never felt before today, and she could tell from the deepening intensity on his face above her that he knew it. That he was doing this. Deliberately.

That this had been the point all along.

And something about that set her free. She didn't fight it. She didn't try to keep her body's wild responses in check. Maybe she would regret her abandon later, but here, now, it felt natural. Right. Necessary.

She simply hung on to him and let him take her wherever he wanted them to go.

This was her husband, back from the dead. This was overdue.

This was the very thing she'd wanted more than anything else in all the world, that she'd missed all these years, and Susannah hadn't known it until now. Until Leonidas had touched her and changed everything.

Until they were so deeply connected that she doubted she would ever be the same again.

He reached between them and found her center with his deliciously hard fingers, and then he made everything worse.

Better.

"Now," he ordered her, every inch of him in control of this. Of her.

And she obeyed.

Susannah shattered. She shattered and she flew, like a sweeping, sparkling thing, pouring up and out and over the side of the world.

And she thought she heard him call out her name as he followed.

CHAPTER FOUR

ALL THE CULTS Leonidas had ever heard of in his former life discouraged the departure of their members under any circumstances—sometimes rather violently.

But he had every intention of walking out of his.

He rolled out of the bed, leaving her there in this chamber of his that had somehow become most of his world, despite how tempted he was to taste her all over again. All her flushed and sweet flesh, his for the taking, as she'd curled up there and breathed unevenly into his pillows.

God, how he wanted more.

But he'd remembered who he was. And that meant he couldn't stay in these mountains—much less in this prison of a compound—another day.

He braced himself against the sink in his bathroom and didn't allow himself to gaze in the mirror that hung there above it. He wasn't sure he wanted to see what he'd become, now that he knew the difference. Now that he could remember what he had been like unscarred, unscathed.

When he'd been a different sort of god altogether.

He took a quick shower, trying to reconcile the different strands of memory—before and after the accident. Leonidas Betancur and the Count. But what he kept dwelling on instead was Susannah, spread out there in his bed with her blond hair like a bright pop against the cheerless browns and grays he'd never noticed were so grim before. She'd looked delicate lying there, the way he remembered her from their wedding, but his body knew the truth. He could still feel the way she'd gripped him, her thighs tight around him and the sweet, hot clutch of her innocence almost too perfect to bear.

Leonidas shook it off. He toweled dry, expecting he'd have to cajole her out of his bed. Or dry her tears. Or offer some other form of comfort for which he was entirely unprepared and constitutionally ill-suited. Leonidas had no experience with virgins, but conventional wisdom suggested they required more care. More…softness. That wasn't something he was familiar with, no matter who he thought he was, but he assumed he could muster up a little compassion for the young, sweet wife who had tracked him down out here in the middle of nowhere and returned him to himself. Or he could try, anyway.

But when he returned to the bedroom, Susannah wasn't still curled up in a replete, satisfied ball, like a purring cat. Nor was she sobbing into his sheets. She was on her feet and putting herself back together as if nothing had happened between them.

Nothing of significance, anyway.

That pricked at Leonidas. He opted to ignore it.

"We have to think about the optics of this, of course," his immensely surprising wife told him as she pulled her shift back on and then smoothed it over her belly and thighs with quick, efficient jerks that reminded him how she'd tasted when she'd come apart beneath him. "We can't have the lost, presumed-dead president and CEO of the Betancur Corporation shuffling out of a mountain hideaway like some kind of victim. And we can't allow anyone to suggest there was a mental break of any kind."

"I beg your pardon. A mental break?"

Susannah only looked at him over her shoulder, her blue gaze somehow mild and confronting at once.

Leonidas didn't know why he had that sour taste in his mouth. Much less why his body appeared not to mind at all, if his enthusiastic hardness at the sight of her was any guide.

His voice was stiff to his own ears when he spoke. "I have no intention of telling another soul that I lost my memory, if that's what concerns you."

"What concerns me is that we have to construct a decent narrative to explain where you've been for the past four years," she said evenly, turning around to face him as she spoke. "If we don't, someone else will. And surely you remember that you are a man with a great many enemies who will not exactly greet your return by dancing in the streets of Europe."

He didn't know who this *we* was. He hadn't known who *he* was for four years, and he certainly didn't know who Susannah was. His memories of her were so vague, after all, especially in comparison with the vibrant creature who stood before him in this room that had never held anything but his thoughts. He had a faint flash of their wedding, or the pageantry of it, and a flash of her blond hair above that theatrical dress she'd worn. He could hear the distant echo of the lectures he'd received from his mother on the topic of why it was necessary he marry a woman he had not chosen himself and what he owed the family as the acting head of it after his brutal, controlling father's death. His mother, selfish and deceitful and lavish in turn, who'd never sacrificed a thing for any reason—who had given her violent husband the son he'd demanded and then done nothing to protect Leonidas from the old man's rages. His mother, whom he'd loved despite all the evidence across the years that he shouldn't, and whom he'd obeyed because he hadn't had it in him to break her heart.

Or whatever passed for her heart, that was.

The actual woman he'd agreed to wed had been an afterthought. A placeholder. The truth was, he'd thought more about Susannah today than he ever had during the whole of their engagement or even the ceremony and reception where they'd united their two wealthy and self-satisfied families and thereby made everyone involved a great deal wealthier.

And he was thinking more about her right now than he should have been when there was a cult yet to escape and a whole life to resume. Almost as if he was the one who required cajoling and care, a notion that appalled him. So deeply it nearly made him shake.

Susannah twisted her hair back and secured it by simply knotting it there, and she frowned slightly at him when she was done. Her eyes moved from the towel knotted around his waist to the scars that tracked across his chest, and only after that did she meet his gaze.

"You're not planning to stay here, are you?" she asked, and though Leonidas looked, he couldn't see the note of doubt he heard in her voice on her face. "Not now that I've found you, surely."

And Leonidas didn't spare a glance for this room he'd spent entirely too much time in over the past few years. This room where he'd recovered from a plane crash and failed completely to recover his own mind. This room where winter after winter had howled at the walls and barricaded him inside. This room he'd once called a perfect place to clear his mind of everything but what mattered most. He'd thought he knew what that was, too. If he let it, the knowledge of how lost he'd been might bring him to his knees.

He didn't let it.

"I think not," he said.

He took his time dressing in what his followers—though it made Leonidas uneasy to call them that now that he remembered everything and found it all more than a little distasteful—would call his "out there" clothes. Meaning, something other than all that flowing white. Boots and jeans and a sweatshirt as if he was an interchangeable mountain person like the rest of them.

When he was Leonidas Betancur and always had been, no matter what the people here had told him about prophets falling from the sky.

But he remembered who he was now. And the fact that his wife—*his wife*, after all these years of chastity—stood opposite him in clothing far more suitable to their station than his…gnawed at him. The fact she'd put herself back together with such ruthless efficiency after what had happened between them, almost as if she was attempting to erase it, on the other hand, bit deep.

Leonidas didn't want her in tears, necessarily. But the fact Susannah seemed utterly unaffected by handing over her virginity to him in a cult's compound rankled. If he hadn't been watching her closely he might have missed the faintest tremor in her fingers. The hint of vulnerability in that mouth of hers he already wanted to taste again.

But he couldn't focus on that. He couldn't focus on her the way he wanted to do. Not in a place like this, where she could never be safe.

They needed to walk out of this compound before anyone in it discovered that the Count had remembered his true identity. And Leonidas needed to keep himself from burning it down on the way out. Somehow.

"Follow me," he told her when he was ready. "Do as you're told and we might just make it out without incident."

She looked startled. "Do you think there could be a problem?"

"Not if you do exactly what I tell you to do."

Leonidas cast an eye around the room, but everything in it belonged to the Count, not him. He wanted nothing that had been here.

His long, agonizing recovery. His acceptance of his role in this place. His acquiescence to the followers here, allowing them to make him into the god of their choosing. His cooperation. He wanted none of those things.

Leonidas wanted to be *himself* again.

And once he left the bedchamber, everything went as seamlessly as he could have wished. The people here had no idea that everything had changed. That their Count had woken up from the spell he'd been laboring under at last.

Leonidas told his followers that Susannah was chastened and humiliated after making such absurd claims against him, something she made believable by walking several steps behind him, her head demurely lowered, as if she really was. So chastened and humiliated, in fact, that the Count was taking her down off his mountain himself in one of his rare excursions from his sanctuary.

"In the future," he told Robert as the other man walked beside him, "we should not allow women making false claims behind our walls."

"She seemed so certain," the other man said, with that little gleam in his dark eyes. "And you seemed so intrigued, Count."

Leonidas smiled at him the way he always did, but this time, he saw what the Count never had. That Robert thought he was the leader here, for all his noisy, public piety. That perhaps he was, as he was the one who had found Leonidas and doctored him back to health. That Robert needed a prophet—because a prophet could so easily become a martyr.

Information he imagined American law enforcement might find useful when he got out of here.

"You should be more certain," he told Robert, enjoying the way the man's gaze turned defiant, though he kept his mouth shut tight in the presence of the Count. "Or perhaps you do not belong here."

And then Leonidas walked right out of this life he'd never chosen and didn't want, back out into the world he'd never meant to leave.

"The moment the press discovers you're alive, I expect they'll descend on us like locusts," Susannah said in that cool way of hers that made him wonder exactly what had changed her from the sweet little princess he recalled into this quiet powerhouse who walked beside him, out of the compound and down the mountain to where a local waited in a four-wheeled truck covered in mud. "If they discover you've been held here, that will be bad enough. But that you lost your memory? Forgot who you are and thought you were a—"

"Do not say 'god,'" he warned her in an undertone as they approached the waiting vehicle, because she wasn't the only one who worried about optics. And the press. And the consequences of these lost years, now that he could remember what he'd lost. "Not when there is the slightest possibility that someone else might hear you."

"We can't let anyone paint you as weak," she told him, with only a nod at the man waiting for them. Her blue gaze met Leonidas's and held. "That would have entirely too many repercussions."

She sounded like a perfect little bloodthirsty Betancur,

not the hesitant schoolgirl he remembered. It reminded him that while he'd been stuck in amber for years, she hadn't been. She'd been thrust into the middle of his family and all its tiresome intrigue and squabbling.

And Leonidas couldn't tell if that chafed at him—or if he liked that she was no longer so fragile. So frothy and breakable, all big white dress and wide eyes.

All he knew was that he wanted more. He wanted everything he'd missed. More of Susannah. More time with her, to probe that fascinating head of hers and take a whole lot more time exploring that perfectly lush little body. Just *more*.

He wanted back the four years he'd lost. He wanted to clear away all the shadows in his head, once and for all. He wanted to feel even an ounce as invulnerable as he had before that plane had gone down, or as he had as the Count—a man who knew his exact place in the world.

He wanted to be *certain*, and he could start with his wife, he thought. Because she was a sure thing. She was already married to him. She'd come and found him.

But first he had to play Lazarus and rise from the dead.

Just over three weeks later, Leonidas stood in Rome.

Where he belonged.

The Betancur Corporation offices were chrome and steel packed into a historic building in the bustling heart of the ancient city. He could glimpse his reflection in the glass of the great windows that rose before him, making one entire wall of his vast office a view of Rome spread out at his feet. He remembered this view just as he remembered the company and all the years he'd spent here, bolstering the family fortune and living up to his name.

But what he couldn't quite remember was the man who'd stood here four years ago, seeing what he saw.

He knew who he was now. He remembered the before, the after. His childhood, one vicious beating after the next as his father "prepared" him for life as the Betancur heir. His mother's carelessness and total lack of interest in protecting her child from these rampages, as none of it concerned her directly, she'd told him once.

"Your father is your problem," she'd said.

He was that all right. And more. Whether Leonidas had wanted everything that came with his position as the Betancur heir or not hadn't signified. No one had ever asked him what he wanted. His mother had abandoned him to his father's tender mercies, and Leonidas hadn't had any choice but to become the man his father wanted him to become.

He could remember everything now. The child who'd stopped crying out, hoping someone might save him, because no one ever had. The adolescent who had never bothered to step outside the lines drawn for him because the consequences couldn't possibly be worth surviving just to engage in a little pointless defiance. He'd grown into the life he'd lived according to his father's every harsh dictate until the old man had died—possibly after poisoning himself with his own evil, Leonidas had always thought, despite the medical authorities who'd deemed it an aneurysm.

He remembered it all.

Leonidas knew that if he turned around and sought out a mirror, he would finally look like himself again, despite the scars that told the story of that terrifying plane crash. His bespoke suits were flown in from Milan and tailored to his specifications in the privacy of his own home. He wore leather shoes crafted by hand for him by local artisans who thanked him for the honor. His hair was once more cut the way he'd always preferred it, short and neat and with the vaguest hint of the military, as if he was always on the verge of going to war.

He'd learned to sleep again in his own bed, a king-size monstrosity that sprawled across the better part of his penthouse and had been designed to work as well for intense play as sleep. Far better than the sturdy, efficient mattress in the compound.

He indulged in rich foods again instead of the bland rations of the compound. He rediscovered his family's wine labels and his own vast collection. He reintroduced himself to strong coffee and even stronger spirits.

It wasn't simply that he didn't belong in the cult—that he'd never belonged on that mountaintop—it was that the place where he did belong was almost unimaginably luxurious, and he could see that now in a way he'd never done before. He knew exactly how marvelous every bit of his life was, because he'd lost it for four years.

He kept telling himself he was lucky. That many people never got the opportunity to see life from more than one side, or if they did, it was usually a downward spiral with no possibility of return.

That notion had buoyed him for the better part of his reentry into the world. The long plane flight back, filled with phone calls to the Betancur legal teams across the planet, as well as the authorities back in Idaho about Robert's plans and goals. And then to his mother, who had performed her usual Maria Callas-like operatics at the sound of his voice but, of course, hadn't stirred herself to rush to his side from her current holiday in the South Pacific.

All excellent distractions from the fact that the last time he'd been on a private plane, it had exploded and very nearly killed him.

He'd reminded himself of his luck over and over

again during the press junket when he landed. During the speeches he gave in all the subsequent interviews, or the little myths he told anyone who asked about his time away. Every time he smiled and shaped those optics that Susannah was so concerned with—and that his board of directors had agreed were of paramount importance.

And then it had been time to go back to work, and that was where Leonidas had discovered that his memory was not all that it should have been.

He refused to admit it at first because he didn't want to believe it was possible, but it seemed as if he hadn't *quite* remembered everything when he'd regained his memory. Not everything.

He turned then, thrusting his hands into the pockets of his three-piece suit, keeping his face impassive as he looked out the glass on the other side of his office. This was the internal wall, and through it he could see the whole of the serenely lavish executive floor the Betancur Corporation offices.

More to the point, he could see Susannah.

He didn't know what he'd thought she did, back there in the States when she'd appeared at the compound. Perhaps he hadn't been able to consider it while he was so busy regaining his own identity. His own past, for good or ill. He'd first had an inkling on the flight back to Europe when she'd managed all the calls he'd had to make and had cut in when necessary with a quiet word that had always—always—stopped everyone else talking. Instantly. And he'd noticed it even more during that first press conference when they'd pulled up outside his building and she'd handled his reintroduction to life with such seeming ease. She used that smile of hers, cool and calm. She'd exuded that particular slickness, impressive and unmistakable, that seemed to define her these days—

because she hadn't dropped it when they'd finally made it past the throng of reporters and into the private elevator that whisked them from the street to the lobby of his penthouse.

Their penthouse, he'd had to remind himself. Because she lived here, too—and had, she'd informed him, ever since the wedding he'd forgotten for all this time.

"Have you taken over my position in the company, as well?" he'd asked when they'd stood in a silence he didn't want to consider awkward, not quite, in the great open room that soared up three stories and had been his pride and joy, before. His architects had made his vision real when he'd bought the building, making the top three floors of one of Rome's many ancient edifices so modern and airy within while still including elements of the historical details.

But that day, all he'd been able to focus on was Susannah. His throat had been dry from the press conference. He'd felt outside himself, as if he was recovering all over again from the accident that had struck him down in the first place. When what he really was doing was standing in the middle of what should have felt like home.

Then again, maybe nothing was going to feel like home anymore, he'd told himself. Maybe that was the trouble. There was not one single part of him that wanted to return to those Idaho mountains. But he didn't quite know how to be in Rome where he belonged, either.

In the fact that the wife he barely knew was more comfortable in his home than he was… Troubled him.

Maybe it wasn't that it troubled him. Maybe it was that it made him feel both fierce and something like lonely in a manner he didn't like at all.

"No one has replaced you," Susannah had replied in those first moments in the penthouse. She'd been standing there in another one of her sleek black ensembles. She seemed to have nothing but. The only color on her was the gold of her hair and the bright blue of her eyes. It made her something more than pretty. *Striking.*

He had the distinct impression that no one underestimated her twice.

"Do not attempt to placate me, please."

She'd raised one eyebrow, and he, in turn, had hated that he didn't know her well enough to read that expression on her face.

"You died before you could alter your will to reflect the changes everyone assured me had been agreed to before our wedding, Leonidas, which meant everything defaulted to me. And I saw no particular reason to appoint a new president or CEO, just to fill the position. There have been many candidates over the years, as you might imagine. But none have been you."

"It's been four years. That's an eternity."

She'd smiled coolly. "We've only actively been looking for replacement for…oh…the last eighteen months or so."

Leonidas had imagined he could feel the rusted gears of his mind start to grind together. "That makes no sense. Surely one of my cousins—"

"Your cousins have a great many ideas, and an even greater sense of entitlement, but what they do not have are the skill sets to back those up." She'd raised one delicately shaped shoulder, then dropped it. "And unfortunately for them, while they may be of the Betancur blood, I've been the one with the deciding vote."

No, Leonidas thought now as he had then, it would not be wise to underestimate his ever-surprising wife.

She was in the office, making her way down the center aisle of the executive floor with all its deliberate windows to let light pour into the company's highest offices. This afternoon she wore yet another dark wardrobe concoction, black boots and a dark dress he knew was an inky navy blue only because the color was slightly different from the boots. Today's boots boasted impressively high heels, but she seemed to walk in them just the same as she had when she'd been hiking up and down mountains. The dress had tiny sleeves that curved over her shoulders, somehow calling more attention to her feminine, elegant figure without actually showing too much of it.

He wanted to taste her. He wanted to test the difference between how delicate she appeared to be and how fierce he suspected she truly was.

He couldn't seem to get his need for her under control, but he told himself it was no more than a function of the time he'd spent away from the company of women. She'd reignited his thirst, that was all. It was nothing personal. It couldn't be.

Leonidas wouldn't let it be anything like personal.

He didn't do *personal*. He suspected that had been the first casualty of his father's style of parenting. Nothing was personal. Everything was the business.

He waited there as she made her way down the long hall, smiling and nodding to all she passed. Some in the hall itself, some through those walls of glass. Not quite friendly, he noticed. But cool. Direct and precise.

The Widow Betancur.

"I was barely more than a child when we married," she had told him, somewhere over the Atlantic Ocean. She'd curled her feet beneath her on the leather sofa in the private jet's living room area and managed to look nothing at all like small or vulnerable when she did it. The air steward had handed her a warm mug of something—and it ate at Leonidas that he didn't know what she drank, that he didn't know her preferences as well as the least of his employees—and she held it between her palms as she spoke in that smooth voice of hers, all those polished European vowels that could dance so nimbly from one romance language to the next. "For the first year after your disappearance, the only thing I had going for me was the depths of my grief."

Leonidas had let out a hoarse sound. A laugh, he'd told himself. "What grief? To my recollection we barely knew each other."

Her blue eyes had been frank. Assessing.

"But no one knew that," she'd said quietly. "Or if they did, it was their word against mine. And I was your widow, with your fortune and your power at my fingertips. So it didn't matter what people speculated. It mattered what I said. And I said my grief was too intense to even think about naming your successor."

He tried to imagine the company—his family—after his death. His scheming cousins would have seen it as divine intervention and a chance at last to take what they'd long believed was theirs. His manipulative mother would have moved to consolidate her power, of course, but would also have grieved him, surely. If only in public, the better to attract the attention she always craved. And Apollonia Betancur's public emotional performances tended to raze cities when she got going. Meanwhile, his greedy board of directors, each one of them so determined to squeeze every last euro out of any potential deal, would have formed alliances and tried to pulverize the competition in their race to take what had been Leonidas's.

All of them were jaded sophisticates. All of them were deeply impressed with their ability to manipulate any and all situations to their benefit. They were among the most debauched and pampered of the wealthy elite in Europe, and they exulted in the things they owned and the lives they ruined along the way.

And it seemed they'd all been bested by a nineteen-year-old.

He'd smiled at that. "So you mourned my untimely passing. You grieved for much longer than anyone could have expected after a marriage that lasted less than a day. Judging by your somber attire, you continue to do so."

"Grief squats on a person and stays until it is finished," Susannah had said softly, as much to the mug between her hands as to him. Then she'd lifted her gleaming gold head and she'd smiled at him, her clever blue eyes gleaming. "And who among us can say how another person grieves? Or when that grief should be finished?"

It had been clear to Leonidas that she'd outsmarted them all.

An impression that his weeks back here in Rome had done nothing to dissipate.

As if she could feel his eyes on her then, all the way from his end of the long hallway, she looked up. Her stride didn't change. Her expression didn't alter. Still, Leonidas felt sure that something in her had…hitched.

She pushed through his door when she reached it, letting it fall shut behind her. And then they were enclosed in the hushed quiet of his soundproofed space. A big smile took over her face and Leonidas felt that strange hitch again, but in him this time.

It took him longer than it should have to remember that his wife was entirely about *optics*. She was only putting on a show, he told himself sternly. She was smiling for the benefit of the people in the office around them who could look in through the glass of his wall and watch them interacting. This was for everyone out there who gossiped and wondered and whispered among themselves about the kind of relationship a man who should have been dead had with the wife he'd left behind.

He knew better than to give them anything. But keeping his expression impassive was harder than it ought to have been.

"Your secretary said you wished to see me," Susannah said. She didn't wait for his answer. Instead, she walked over to the sitting area nearest the big window with the sweeping views of Rome and settled herself on one of the low couches.

"I did indeed."

"I think it's going well, don't you?" She folded her hands in her lap, and Leonidas had the strangest flashback to the compound. To the way she'd sat there then, in that little cell with cameras trained on her, as calmly as she was sitting before him now. Exuding serenity from every pore. "I think your cousins found it a bit difficult to pretend they were excited by your resurrection, but everyone else is eating up the story like candy."

"By everyone else, you mean the world. The tabloids."

"Not just the tabloids. You are a major story on almost every news network in Europe. Returning from the dead, it turns out, is a feel-good crowd-pleaser for all."

He knew she was right. But something in him balked at her cynicism—or maybe it was something else. Maybe it was the fact that when she was close to him, all he wanted to do was touch her the way he had when he'd been the Count and hadn't known better.

And all she wanted to do was talk about narratives. Optics. Campaigns and complicated plots to secure his place here again.

She had been the virgin. But Leonidas was the one who couldn't seem to let go.

In all the time since they'd been back in Rome, she'd stayed out of his way. Available should he require her assistance, but back in the penthouse—where she had been sleeping in one of the guest rooms the whole time he'd been away, apparently—they hardly interacted at all. When he'd asked one night why she appeared to be avoiding him in the home they shared, she'd only smiled sweetly and told him that she was very cognizant of the fact that he needed to find his own way back into his life. That she didn't want to intrude.

The entire situation set his teeth on edge. And Leonidas didn't particularly care to investigate why that was.

"I'm glad you called me in," Susannah was saying. "Because I've wanted to speak to you, too. I didn't want to rush into this until you'd been home long enough to really feel as if you'd got your feet beneath you, but I also don't think there's any point in dragging things out unnecessarily."

Leonidas knew he needed to say what he'd wanted to say, or he wouldn't. Because he hadn't believed it was happening at first. He assumed it was stress, or that perhaps he was overwhelmed—though he couldn't recall ever being overwhelmed before in his life. Then again, his life had never included a lost four years and a cult before now.

Then this morning he'd sat in a meeting, listening to the discussion all around him and well aware that the people speaking were among those he ought to have recognized. He'd recognized the names on the memo that his secretary had handed him, but he hadn't been able to match names to faces.

"There are holes in my memory," he told her now, before he thought better of it. He stayed where he was. Tall and straight and with all that glass and Rome behind him, as if that would make a difference. As if that would make him whole.

Susannah blinked, and he thought she froze. "Holes?"

"I know who I am. I know you. I certainly knew my mother when she finally deigned to appear the other night, in all her state."

"Apollonia is not easily forgotten. Though one might have occasion to wish otherwise."

"But there is so much I can't remember. Too much."

There. He'd said it. He waited for it to hit him—for the fact that he'd admitted to such weakness to take his knees out from under him where he stood. The way his father would have taken his knees out for him, were he still alive.

But it didn't happen.

And it was because of her, Leonidas knew it. She was why he hadn't keeled over in the telling of this most disastrous of truths. She only gazed at him as if she was perfectly happy to wait as long as it took for him to tell her the rest of it.

"Faces. Names. Business decisions I clearly made years ago." He shrugged. "I don't have access to any of it."

She considered, her hands seeming to tighten in her lap. "Is this all the time?"

"No. But it's enough. I was in a meeting of vice presidents this morning and I didn't know a single person in the room. And not all of them were hired in the past four years."

"No, they weren't." She was frowning then, that gaze of hers fixed on his, and there was no reason Leonidas should have felt something like relief. That someone other than him knew. That it wasn't only his weight to carry. "Do they know you can't remember them?"

He let out a harsh sound without meaning to do it. "That would be bad optics, I realize," he said, perhaps more sternly than necessary. "I would hate to dilute the message."

Susannah didn't appear to move, and yet Leonidas was certain her back was straighter than it had been before.

"I was less concerned with the optics, or any message you might have sent, and more concerned with you." Her lips pressed together in a firm line, and Leonidas couldn't possibly have said why he felt chastened. "I expect you managed to cover it so no one could tell you didn't remember them."

"I did." He inclined his head. "But I worry it is only a matter of time before I find myself in a situation where covering it is not possible."

She appeared to mull that over. "What did the doctor say about any lingering memory loss? Did the subject arise?"

Leonidas had not been at all interested in seeing a doctor when he'd finally made it home, as it had seemed like yet another admission of weakness to him. But he had eventually succumbed to the family doctors who had tended to the Betancur family for years, because in the end, how could he not? Whether it was a weakness or not, there was no one more concerned with the four years he'd lost than him. He was the one who would had lived through them, convinced that he was someone else entirely.

There had been no small part of him that had worried he was damaged forever by that damned Count.

He blew out a breath now, and kept his gaze on Susannah. "It's possible I'll never recall the actual plane crash, but I imagine that is something of a blessing. The doctor was confident that more and more memories will come back with time, until there is very little, if anything, missing. But I don't have time."

A faint line appeared between her brows. "You have all the time you need, surely."

"Only as long as no one suspects the truth." He eyed her. "You are the only one who knows, Susannah. You and one doctor who I very much doubt would dare to disobey my order of silence. Not when his livelihood depends on me."

She no longer clasped her hands together in front of her like a latter-day nun. One had risen to her collarbone and she pressed against it, as if she was trying to leave her fingerprints against her own skin. There was no particular reason Leonidas should find that so maddeningly sexy. So alluring. It was as if he was helpless against the need to taste her. Just one more time. That's what he told himself, night and day when this craving hit him: one more time.

But not now.

"I need you," he said baldly. Starkly.

Leonidas didn't think he imagined the faint jerk of her body then. She flinched, then obviously worked to repress it.

"It's clear to me that you spent the past four years learning everything there is to know about this company," he said, as much to cover his own admission as anything else.

"I had no choice." Her blue gaze had gone stormy. "It was that or be swallowed whole."

"Then you will guide me," he told her, and he wasn't sure he was entirely concealing his relief. "You will cover for things I cannot remember."

The strangest expression flitted across her face. "Will I?"

He moved toward the sofa then, as if admitting what he needed had loosened his feet. "Under normal circumstances it would be strange to bring my wife wherever I went, but you have already served as a quasi-CEO. No one will think anything of it."

"And how will this work? Will we develop a system of touch? Will we rely on sign language? Or, I know, I will alert you to things you should know in Morse code. Using my eyelashes."

Her hands were back in her lap. It occurred to him that she did that when she was anything but serene. When she only wished to appear calm.

That shouldn't have felt like an electrical current inside him, but it did.

"Or you could simply greet the person in front of you, using the correct name, and I will follow suit." She didn't say anything. And yet somehow he had the distinct impression that that expression he couldn't quite read on her face was mutinous. "Will this be a problem for you?"

"It would be helpful if you knew the time frame for your memory to return."

"I'm told the human mind does what it will," he said coolly. Through his teeth. "I assure you, however inconvenient my memory loss is for you, I feel it more keenly." She nodded with that, and then swallowed, visibly. And something like foreboding wound its way through him. "What was it you wished to speak to me about?"

"Well," Susannah said quietly, her face calm. Serene. And yet Leonidas didn't believe it this time. "This feels awkward. But I want a divorce."

CHAPTER FIVE

SUSANNAH WAS CERTAIN that Leonidas could see how she shook where she sat, as his usual arrogant, haughty expression shifted to something far more lethal and dark.

He stood there, more beautiful than any man should have been, a dark and bold thrust of impossible masculinity in the middle of this glass office with the mellow gold of Rome behind him. She'd be lying if she said he didn't affect her. If she didn't shiver every time she was near him as if she was still that overwhelmed teenage bride from four years ago.

And it had been bad enough on that mountain. She'd been beating herself up for the way she'd succumbed to him ever since it happened. What had she been thinking? How had she toppled so quickly to a man she hardly knew? She'd called it her wedding night, but it hadn't been. The Leonidas she'd found in that compound, leading that cult, was more of a stranger than the convenient husband she'd barely known years before.

She had no excuse for her behavior. She knew that. Just as she knew that she could never let him know about the dreams that woke her with their potency, night after night, until she'd had to lock herself in her own bedroom in the penthouse they shared to make sure she stayed away from him in those dark, dangerous hours when she woke up alone and so very hungry.

For him.

Leonidas's return had changed everything, just as she'd imagined it would.

The world had gone mad when the fact he'd been found alive had hit the wires. Reporters and law enforcement and his board of directors had been in fits all around him, his family had hardly known how to process it and had acted out as they always did, but beneath all of that, the truth was that this homecoming was Leonidas's. Not hers. This had nothing to do with her.

Susannah had been a widow for all of her marriage. And she'd deliberately maintained that position these past four years because it was that or succumb to a far worse situation.

But with Leonidas home, she was free.

No matter that he was looking at her now with an expression she could only describe as predatory.

"I appear to have misheard you." His voice was nothing but cold warning, but she made herself meet his gaze as if she couldn't hear it. "Would you repeat that?"

"I think you heard me perfectly well," she said, as if that trembling thing wasn't taking her over. As if she didn't feel there was a very good chance it might sweep her away. But she told herself he couldn't possibly see that, because no one ever saw her. They saw what they wanted to see, nothing more. "I want a divorce. As soon as possible."

"We've barely been married for any time at all."

"Perhaps it feels that way to you because you can't remember it. But I can." She forced a smile and kept it cool. "Four years is actually a very long time to be a Betancur."

"That sounds as if you do not wish to be part of my

family, Susannah." He inclined his head in that way of his that reminded her that there were people out there in the world who considered him a god. And it wasn't a metaphor. "No one can blame you in this, of course. They are an unpleasant, scavenging, manipulative lot, and that is on a good day. But they are not me."

"Leonidas—"

"You are married to me, not them."

"That argument might have worked four years ago," she said faintly, because the truth was, it was working now and that was the last thing she wanted. She didn't understand herself. She'd worked tirelessly all these years to find him so she could escape and now she could do just that, her body was staging a rebellion. Her breasts hurt when she was with him. They ached so much it echoed low in her belly, and the fire of it made her feel entirely too hot. So hot she was afraid he could see it all over her. "I was a very malleable teenager, but that was then."

"And this is now." She didn't think he moved or did anything in particular, and yet somehow, there was no more air in the room. As if he'd taken it all and was holding it ransom right there in front of her. "And my need of you is dire. Would you refuse me?"

"I would like to," she told him, smiling to take the sting out of it. But the way he regarded her suggested she had succeeded.

"Tell me, Susannah, why did you track me down?" he asked after a moment. When the gold of the city outside had long since blended into the gold of his eyes and she worried she'd be eaten alive by the gleam. "Why did you come all the way to Idaho and climb up that mountain when it would have been so easy to stay right here? Everyone believed me dead. You could have left me there and no one would have been the wiser. Not even me."

"I really, really want that divorce," she told him as blithely as she could, but she could hear the catch in her voice. The breathlessness.

What she didn't want was this conversation. She'd naively assumed that there wouldn't be anything to discuss. Leonidas didn't know her. He couldn't possibly want any kind of relationship with her, and the truth was, he likely hadn't wanted one back when. She doubted that he was even the same man who had left on that plane four years ago. And it wasn't as if she would note the difference, because they'd been strangers thrown together in a marriage convenient to their families, and no matter that she'd had teenage fantasies to the contrary.

This was the perfect time to draw a line under their strange, doomed marriage, and go on with their lives. Separately.

Before she was forced to face the fact that after saving her virginity all this time—after turning away Leonidas's cousins one after the next and after shutting down each and every delusional suitor who'd tried to convince her that they'd fallen in love with her smile, or heard her laughter across a room, or found her unrelenting use of black clothing seductive—she'd thrown herself at this man.

Leonidas hadn't known who he was. But she'd known exactly who she was, and that was what she couldn't forgive.

It had taken every bit of self-control she had to act as if the loss of her virginity didn't affect her. But she was terribly afraid she'd used it all up back there in that compound she fervently hoped American law enforcement had since dismantled. Because the longer she was around this man, the less she thought she would be able to keep that control intact.

She wanted out before she broke. She wanted an escape at last from what she'd never wanted to accept would be the rest of her life, and she didn't care if her parents were disappointed. She refused to be a pawn any longer. She wanted no part of Apollonia's theatrics and schemes. She didn't want to be a bargaining chip between the grasping Betancur cousins. She was tired of all this corrosive power and all the greed everyone around her had for more and more and more.

All this time, she'd believed she had a responsibility to the husband who had died so suddenly. Maybe *because* of all her girlish fantasies about what could have been. Whatever the cause, Susannah had taken that responsibility seriously, and one of the reasons she'd been so successful was because she'd felt nothing. She'd understood exactly who her parents were on her wedding night when they'd had the opportunity to try to comfort her and had instead made her feel small. Soon after, she'd come to understand the intricacies of the Betancur family and its businesses in repulsive detail. The plane crash and its wake had showed her everything she needed to know about her in-laws.

She'd filed it all away, felt nothing besides the loss of her dreams that she'd convinced herself weren't real, and that had helped her become perhaps the most powerful widow in the world.

But then she'd walked into a cult leader's compound after all these numb, safe years, and she'd felt entirely too much.

The entire plane ride back she'd tried to convince herself that it had been a geographic problem, that was all. That what had happened in that compound had been a thing that could happen only in the Rocky Mountains out there in the midst of that unnervingly huge continent. And still she woke every night to find herself barricaded in her room in the penthouse, swaddled in her bedclothes with her heart gone mad and a deep wildness between her legs, alive with too much yearning. With too much intense hunger.

It wasn't going away. It wasn't getting better.

And Susannah had realized that the only thing worse than spending the rest of her life as the Widow Betancur was this. Longing for a man who she knew, even if he didn't—not yet, anyway—would grow out of his need for her. Fast. The way her mother had coldly told her men did, in her version of "the talk" the night before Susannah's wedding.

"Leonidas Betancur is a man of tremendous wealth and taste," Annemieke Forrester had told her only daughter that night, sitting on the edge of Susannah's bed in the hotel suite where they'd all been staying in anticipation of the grand ceremony. "You would do well to assume his sexual tastes are equally well cultivated." Susannah must have made some kind of noise to match her immediate reaction, a flush of confusion and something like shame, because Annemieke had laughed. "You are an untried, untouched teenager, child. You cannot hope to interest a man like Leonidas."

"But…" Susannah had been so young. It hurt to remember how young. How sheltered. "He is to be my husband."

"You will quickly learn that your power comes from the grace with which you ignore his dalliances," her mother had told her matter-of-factly. "It will make him respect you."

"Respect?" she'd echoed.

"Your job is to produce an heir," her mother had continued. "Your virginity is your wedding gift. After that, you concentrate on getting pregnant and staying pretty. Think *grace*, Susannah. No one values a shrill, embittered woman en route to a nasty divorce. You will live a life filled with comfort and ease. I'd advise you to make the best of what you have."

"I thought that marriage would be—"

"What?" her mother had interrupted scornfully. "A fairy tale? Leonidas will tire of you, girl, and quickly. Let him." She'd waved her hand in the air impatiently. "It doesn't matter where a man roams. What matters is the home he returns to. Over time, he will return to you more than he will leave you, and he will do this far more cheerfully if you have spared him the scenes and remonstrations."

Susannah had tried to take that to heart when her brand-new husband had left her on their wedding night, apparently already tired of her, though she'd been crushed. She wasn't as foolish these days as she'd been then. And the only reason he wanted her around now, she'd thought even before he'd told her that there were gaps in his memory, was because she was the one who had found him. The only one who knew where he'd been.

Leonidas Betancur was not a sentimental man. She knew that. Neither with his memory nor without it. The scars on his body hadn't made him into someone new, they'd chiseled him into a harder sort of perfect marble, that was all. He was more beautiful, somehow, for being tested—and surviving—but he was still made of stone.

She knew. She'd felt him surge inside her and send her shattering into pieces.

And Susannah wasn't a teenager anymore. She'd grown out of the fairy tales that had colored her youth because she hadn't known any better.

She knew better now. She wanted only to be free.

"You must know there can be no divorce," Leonidas said now. Darkly, that gaze of his still fixed on her. "Not so soon after my return." His hard mouth moved into something only an optimist would have called a smile. "Think of the optics."

"I'm sensitive to optics, certainly." She was proud of how even her voice sounded. How controlled. "But I also want my life back."

"What life do you mean, exactly?" He tilted his head slightly to one side and she felt that sense of disconnection again. As if they were in two places at once, and one of them was the compound where he had ruled supreme. "If memory serves, and of course it may not, the life you led before marrying me was little better than a prison. A pretty one, I grant you. And that was the appeal, of course. Your promised naïveté. You were more sheltered than the average nun."

She'd gone stiff and she didn't even know why. "What you talking about?"

"It is amazing what things stay in the memory, even when the chief financial officer's name has gone up in smoke." Leonidas wandered across the office, and that should have taken a bit of that predatory focus off her. He wasn't even looking at her, after all. But somehow, Susannah did not feel at all at her ease. "Your father promised you to me when you were very young, you must know this."

"Of course I know it. I never forgot it in the first place."

She regretted her petulance the instant she spoke, but if it bothered him, he ignored it. Which only made her regret it more.

"Your father is not a kind man, as I'm sure you're aware," Leonidas said in that same dark way. He poured himself a measure of something from his personal bar, dark and amber, but he didn't drink it. He only swirled it in its tumbler and stared at it as if he was studying it. "Nor is he a good one. He sought to sweeten the pot, you see, when I was less interested in the match than he wished me to be." His gaze rose from the crystal and met hers, and it took everything Susannah had not to flinch. "He wasn't simply selling his daughter, you understand. He promised me you would be untouched. Completely and wholly unsullied. That was meant to sweeten the deal. A virgin sacrifice, all for me."

There was no reason why Susannah's mouth should have gone dry. Why her heart should have pounded too hard and her eyes feel too bright. It wasn't as if any of this was a surprise, not really.

But on the other hand, he was talking about her life. And all those years she'd spent in her overly strict boarding school, forever fielding intrusive questions about her virtue. When there had been no moral reason for her to remain pure, the way her parents had pretended there was.

When there had never been anything to it but leverage.

"Whatever my father is or isn't is immaterial." She shrugged, and hoped she was managing to keep her expression clear, because there was no point mourning her parents when she already knew exactly who they were. "This is about me. This is not about what a teenage girl thinks she owes her parents. It's about what I want."

Again, he didn't appear to move. And still Susannah found it difficult to pull in a breath.

"And what is it you want?"

"Freedom," she replied at once. Perhaps a touch too intensely. "I want my freedom."

"And what do you imagine freedom looks like for a woman who was the Widow Betancur?" he asked quietly. "Where do you think you can hide from the influence of my name?"

She heard the trap around her. It was as if she could feel iron closing in on her from all sides, and the funny part was, though she knew she should get up and run while she could, she didn't move. There was something about that sardonic lash in his voice. There was something about the way his dark gaze met hers, and held.

"I am no longer a widow," she reminded him. "You are standing right in front of me."

"And yet you are still dressed in dark clothes that might as well be fully black, as if you anticipate a second funeral at any moment."

"Dark colors are very slimming."

"The world is not prepared to let go of such an icon as their favorite widow, Susannah. Surely you must know this. Where will you go? Your past will follow you as surely as a shadow. It always does."

"Says the man who took a four-year break from his."

"I'm not going to argue with you."

She recognized that voice. It brought her back to the conversation they'd had in the car that had delivered them from the church to their reception four years ago. To the pitiless way her new husband—a perfect stranger with a cruel mouth she'd found fascinating despite herself—had gazed at her from his seat.

It was not unlike the way the Count had gazed at her from his white seat in his bright white throne room.

"There will be no honeymoon," he had told her four years ago. "I cannot take that kind of time away from my business." And when she had reacted to that, when she had allowed some or other emotion to color her face, he had only grown colder. "I understand that you are young, but in time you will thank me for giving no quarter to your childishness. We all must grow up sometime, Susannah. Even spoiled little girls must turn into women."

She hadn't thought about that conversation in years.

And he was still talking now.

"You obviously hold a bargaining chip," he was saying, but in that merciless way as if no matter what she held, he was the one in total control. "I do not wish anyone to know that I lost my memory in the first place, much less that I have not yet gotten parts of it back. For all the reasons we discussed in Idaho that make what happened there so precarious. Optics, my cousins. All of the above."

"I sympathize, but that doesn't make any difference—"

"I'm not finished."

And there was no reason Susannah should feel duly chastised, but she did. And worse for her self-esteem and the strides she'd been so sure she'd made in his absence, she fell quiet.

On command, like a dog.

"If you wish to divorce me, Susannah, I have no objection to that."

His voice was so cool, so even and without inflection, that she wasn't sure she'd heard him correctly for one jarring beat of her heart. Then another. But then his words sank in.

And she had no idea why there was some perverse thing in her that very nearly wanted to…argue, perhaps? Or make him take it back. Almost as if…

But she didn't let herself think that through. She should never let him touch her, that was all. That was the beginning and the end of it, and that was what she kept returning to while she sat here, her fingers laced together lest they take it upon themselves to touch him again.

"Oh. I mean, good. We agree."

"I will give you a divorce," Leonidas told her. "But not now."

As if it was entirely up to him. Again, as if he was the god of everything.

"You can't bargain me into staying," she said, with entirely too much intensity once more.

It was a mistake. She knew it when something flared in that gaze of his, and the way he stood there, all that arrogance in a bespoke suit, seemed to blur a bit. Less a pointed weapon, somehow.

Leonidas only shrugged, but the tenor of everything had changed and seemed…almost lazy.

"You want to be free. I want your help and am willing to free you after you give it."

"Why does my freedom come with a price tag?" she demanded, because she couldn't seem to help herself.

"Because that is the world we live in, little one." He didn't shrug again, but the look in his dark eyes seemed to suggest it, all the same. "I don't see why we can't help each other. But if that is not possible, I will have no choice but to use what leverage I have."

She didn't ask him what leverage he had. Susannah knew that it didn't matter. He would come up with something, and if he couldn't, he would manufacture something else. Hadn't she seen this in action time and again these last years? That was what these people did. It was in their blood.

"This is a good thing," she told him after a moment, when she was absolutely certain that she would sound and look nothing but in complete control. As if she was made of the same stone he was. "I was tempted to forget, you see. I was tempted to think that you were a victim. I almost felt sorry for you, but this clears it up, thank goodness. It reminds me who you are."

"Your beloved husband?" he asked sardonically. "The one you have grieved with such dedication all these many years?"

"Not just a Betancur," she said, as if it was an epithet. It was. "But the worst of them by far."

Leonidas looked more than merely predatory, then. Something in his starkly beautiful face edged toward cruel, but it wasn't intimidating. Or it was—of course it was, because this was a man who couldn't help but intimidate as surely as he breathed—but Susannah was more focused on the melting sensation that swept over her, then settled low in her belly like a greedy pulse.

And the fact that she was almost 100 percent positive that he knew it.

"It sounds as if we have a deal," he said.

And then Leonidas smiled.

CHAPTER SIX

A LONG AND exhausting month later, Susannah sat in the back of a car careening through the wet streets of Paris, wishing her head would stop feeling as if it might split into pieces at any moment.

She wasn't particularly optimistic. A long evening loomed ahead of her, and she would have given anything to leap out of the car, race through the rain and the crowds of fashionable Parisians to tuck herself up in her bed and hide beneath the covers—but she knew that wasn't possible. Tonight was the Betancur Foundation's annual charity ball that this year would serve as Leonidas's formal reintroduction to society after all his time away.

That Leonidas had survived the crash had not been known to anyone at first, they'd told the press. His funeral had been a sincere gesture of grief and mourning, not a cynical spectacle while they waited to find out if he'd live. And when his survival had become known to them, his condition had been so extreme that everyone involved had kept it quiet rather than throw the corporation into turmoil.

"Of course, I wanted nothing more than to race to his side," Susannah had told a concerned American interviewer. "But my husband is a Betancur. I knew he would want me to take care of his company while the doctors took care of him."

His assumed widow's refusal to hand over the reins looked much less stubborn through this lens, of course, which had led to any number of think pieces celebrating Susannah's "iron will" and "clear-eyed leadership" from publications that had addressed her in far less friendly terms a few months back.

But the ball was a different animal. It was overwhelming at the best of times, so filled was it with the members of the Betancur family and all their usual drama and intrigue. Susannah expected that the return from the dead of the Betancur heir himself would make it all…insane.

Surely the prospect would make anyone tired. At least this year she wouldn't have to deal with marriage proposals over canapés and several attempts at a coup before dessert. Or so she hoped.

Leonidas sat beside her in the car's comfortable backseat as the driver navigated the Paris traffic, talking into his mobile in dark, silky tones that didn't require Susannah's fluency in German to realize were menacing in the extreme. His tone did it for him. It was something about one of the resorts the corporation ran in the South Pacific, but she couldn't quite summon up the energy to care about that the way she might have normally. She stared out the window as Paris gleamed in the wet dark and plucked a bit listlessly at the dress she wore. Not that it was the dress's fault. It was a stunning creation in a deep, mesmerizing green that had been presented to her like a gift by Leonidas's Milanese tailors when she knew very well it hadn't been a gift at all. It had been a command.

Leonidas didn't have to *say* that he didn't want her to wear black any longer. That she was no longer the Widow Betancur, but his wife, and should allow her wardrobe to reflect that reality. She'd understood the message.

It was the first time she'd worn a bright color—or any

color other than the darkest of navys and the deepest of charcoals—since her wedding, which seemed appropriate for their anticipated debut as an actual married couple, a whole four years later than planned.

No wonder her head felt so tender.

The city blurred into one long gleam of frenetic light outside the car windows, and Leonidas's voice was that same low murmur, all power and command, that Susannah could feel as much inside her body as with her ears.

The trouble was, she was just so *tired* these days.

It wasn't the dress. Or the rich shade of green that flattered her so well she'd been forced to consider the fact that Leonidas had selected it because he'd known it would, which made her...uncomfortable. Restless in her own skin. She'd have liked to blame something so relatively innocuous as her wardrobe, but she knew better.

Susannah told herself it was the charade itself that exhausted her. The difficulty of keeping one foot in the Betancur world when she planned to escape it as soon as possible. That would exhaust anyone, surely. The weeks since she and Leonidas had made their bargain had seemed to creep by, every day somehow harder than the last. After all those years of playing the Widow Betancur so well, it should have been easy enough for Susannah to continue along in the same role just a little while longer. But for some reason, this last month had been more difficult than any she could remember.

It's because you know this is temporary, she told herself now, watching the city melt from shadow into dancing light and back again on the other side of the glass. *When there was no escape, when you had no choice, it was easier to simply* do *what had to be done.*

Her headaches had only gotten worse as time went on. It seemed all she wanted to do was lie down and sleep, except even when she forced herself into a long and uninterrupted night's rest, she never woke refreshed. She felt thick all the way through. Underwater, somehow.

She'd been toying with the idea that she was allergic to Leonidas.

But the thing she felt when she was close to him, doing as he'd asked and helping him navigate the cutthroat world he occupied as if he'd never been away, was not an allergy. It had a great many similar symptoms. Breathlessness. A pervasive flush. A sort of restless, itchy feeling all over...

If it was an allergy, she could take decongestants and be done with him. With this. But there was no remedy for the intensity that Leonidas exuded the way other men wore cologne.

God help her, all she wanted was to be done with this.

She'd spent her entire life training to be married off to a man like Leonidas. Then the whole of her marriage training to be as ruthless and powerful as the husband she'd lost. Susannah had no idea what it was like to be on her own.

No one had ever asked her what it was *she* wanted. Which was probably a good thing, she thought wryly, because she had no idea.

"You seem drained yet again," Leonidas said from beside her, as if in answer to the question in her head, but she knew better than to think he could read her. Or would want to read her, for that matter, as if they shared some kind of intimacy. The truth was, she might be married to him, but he wasn't hers.

A man like Leonidas would never be any woman's.

Susannah hadn't realized he'd finished his call. She turned from the rain-lined windows and the gleaming lights of Paris just there on the other side, and tried to arrange her face into something pleasant. Or calm enough to be mistaken for pleasant, anyway.

"I'm not drained," she said, because it was polite. But he was watching her, his dark eyes brooding and entirely too close, there in the backseat of the car, and she didn't feel particularly *polite* after all. "I find I am less interested in this endless game of playacting with every day that passes, that's all."

His brows rose and she thought she saw something glitter there, deep in his dark gold gaze. But when he spoke his voice was even.

"I regret that my presence is such a burden upon you."

It occurred to her that he was playing a role just as much as she was, and she couldn't have said why that realization sent a bolt of something like shame spinning through her. But she didn't let it keep her quiet.

"Yes, thank you. It always helps to be sardonic, I find. It makes everything so much better."

"As does sarcasm."

"You asked me to help you, and I agreed to do that," Susannah reminded him tightly. "I could end that agreement at any time, and whether you recall the name of every assistant in the Malaysian office or not is no concern to me either way."

Leonidas didn't look chastened. But then again, he never did. He might not remember the many people who tried to speak to him over the course of a day, but he certainly seemed to remember that he was the one in charge. Of everything. It galled her that she'd allowed him to take charge of her as well, when surely she simply could have left.

Why hadn't she left?

"Let me hasten to assure you that this extreme torture will end soon enough," he told her, and there was a note in his voice she didn't like. One that made it seem impossible that he was doing anything but indulging her, with no intention whatsoever of keeping his promises.

But there was no point debating possibilities. And her head hurt too much anyway. Susannah didn't respond. She rubbed at her temples instead, listening to the music her bracelets made as they jangled on her wrist.

"If you continue to get these headaches, I think you should see the doctor," Leonidas murmured after a moment. In that way of his that would have made an apology sound like a command.

Not that Susannah could imagine this man apologizing for anything. Ever.

"I don't need a doctor to tell me that I'm under stress," Susannah said tautly. "Or that what I need to recover from such stress is a solitary retreat. Far, far away the intrigue and drama of the Betancur Corporation."

For once, Leonidas did not respond in kind. Instead, he reached over and took her hand in his. And Susannah wanted to pull it back instantly, rip her hand from his so that she wouldn't have to sit there and fight the surging sensation that rolled through her at even so small a touch.

As if they were naked again. As if he was braced above her and thrusting deep inside her—

That was what bothered her most about this extra and intense time with him.

She didn't hate him. She wasn't disgusted with him or even disinterested. On the contrary, she continued to find her husband entirely too fascinating by half. And every time he touched her, it set off the same chain reaction. Sometimes he took her elbow as they walked down a hall or through a press gauntlet. Sometimes he helped her in or out of the car, his hand so strong around hers she imagined he could use it to lift her straight off the ground if he chose. Sometimes he touched the small of her back as they entered the room, as if he was guiding her before him. It didn't matter what he did, how utterly innocuous it was—gestures knit together by old-world manners and inbred politeness, meaningless in their way.

And yet every single time his body touched hers, Susannah…ignited.

She felt it at the point of contact first, like a burst of bright light. Then it rolled through her, making her breasts feel heavy and aflame at once. Making the blood in her veins feel sluggish. And then all of that heavy ache and thick sweetness spiraled around and around, sinking down through her until it pooled deep in her belly. Low and hot and maddening, there between her legs.

She comforted herself with the knowledge that no matter what, Leonidas had no idea what he did to her. He couldn't. Of course he couldn't, because she went to such lengths to hide it. And soon she would be far away from him and only she would ever know the true depths of her own weakness.

But as the brilliant lights of central Paris danced over his bent head from beyond the car windows, as he held her hand between his and she felt as bright as the ancient city shimmering in the rain all around her, there was a shuddering part of her that wondered if any of that was strictly the truth.

Maybe he did know. Maybe he knew exactly what he did to her, just as he'd known exactly how to touch her back in that compound…

Not that she cared, because he was pressing his big, clever fingers into her palm.

"What are you doing?" she managed to ask, and assured herself he'd think the catch in her voice was from her headache, not him.

"I was taught that massaging pressure points eases headaches," Leonidas said with gruff certainty. More to her hand than her, she thought, dispassionate and distant, like a doctor. But then he glanced up to catch her gaze, a little smile flirting with his mesmerizingly hard mouth, and her heart slammed at her.

It took her a few moments to collect herself long enough to recognize that he was right. That the pain in her temples was receding.

"Your family obviously taught you more useful things than mine ever did," she said without thinking. "My mother believes in suffering, as she'd be the first to tell you."

"My father was a mean old bastard who relished the pain of others." Leonidas's voice was matter-of-fact. He exchanged one hand for the other, pressing down into her palm and alleviating the pain almost instantly when he did. "Particularly mine, as he told me every time he beat me bloody, which he did with great relish and regularity until I got too big at sixteen, at which point, he switched to psychological warfare. And you've met my mother. The only sort of pain Apollonia Betancur knows how to relieve comes back every morning-after when the night's intoxicants wear off."

Susannah was very still, and not only because he was still holding her hand with his. But because of that searing, dark undercurrent in his voice that told her exactly what it must have been like to be born a Betancur. And not just any Betancur, ushered into a life of privilege from the first breath, but the heir to the whole of the Betancur kingdom whether he liked it or not.

Of course they'd beaten it into him. How else would these people do anything? She already knew they were monsters.

But she also knew her husband well enough by now to know that he would hate it if she expressed anything like sympathy for the childhood he'd survived, somehow.

"I was glad they sent me away to that school when I was small," Susannah said softly. So softly he could ignore it if he wanted and better yet, she could pretend she wasn't saying it out loud at all. "For all that it was lonely, I think it was better than having to live with them."

But he didn't ignore her. "I wish they'd sent me away more than they did, but you see, there were a great many expectations of *the next Betancur* and none of them could be beaten into me while I was elsewhere."

Leonidas was no longer smiling when he let go of her hand and Susannah knew better, somehow, than to reach back over and touch him again the way everything in her wanted to do—and not with a meaningless little gesture. He looked carved from rock, as impossible as a distant mountain, and she wanted to…comfort him, somehow. Care for him. Do *something* to dispel the dark grip that seemed to squeeze tight around the both of them.

But she didn't dare put a finger on this man.

She kept her hands from curling into impotent fists by flattening them on her own lap.

"My headache is gone," she told him. "Thank you. You are a miracle worker, no matter where you learned it."

"The benefits of living off the grid, far away in the woods and high up on a mountaintop," he told her after a moment, when she'd thought he might not speak at all. "No one can run out to the nearest pharmacy to fetch some tablets every time someone feels a bit of pain. We learned other methods."

"I'm stunned," she managed to say. And she was aware as she spoke that she didn't sound nearly as calm as she should have. "I would have thought it would cause a full-scale revolt if you'd healed someone with anything other than the force of your holiness."

Leonidas let out only a small laugh, but to Susannah it sounded like nothing less than a victory parade.

"It's possible I was a terrible disappointment as a resident god," he said, his voice rich with something it took her entirely too long to realize was humor. At his own expense, no less. And she felt that like a new, different sort of touch. "But in the habit of most gods, I will choose not to inquire."

And it was lucky Susannah didn't have to summon up a response, she thought as the car pulled up to the entrance of the desperately chic Betancur Hotel. They had to get out of the car and acknowledge the waiting paparazzi. She had to steel herself against Leonidas's hand at her back when she'd barely survived the car ride over. And still, she could only count her good fortune that she was able to stand and walk at all—because the sound of real laughter in her husband's dark voice was enough to make her knees feel weak.

She was very much afraid of the things she might have said—or worse, done—if that car ride had lasted another moment.

And none of that could happen, because she wasn't staying. Not only wasn't she staying, she needed to hurry up her departure, she told herself as they walked into the hotel in a flurry of flashbulbs and the typical shouting of their names. The lobby was a riot of color, golds and marbles and sultry onyxes, but all Susannah could see with any clarity was Leonidas as he led her to the grand ballroom.

She needed to hurry up and leave before she couldn't. She needed to go before she found herself addicted to these small moments with him and stayed. Like an addict forever chasing that dragon and never, ever finding it.

"You look appropriately somber at the prospect of a long night with my family and all their works," Leonidas said as they made their way toward the gala, smiling and nodding at Europe's elite as they passed in the gilded hallways.

Susannah let out a small laugh. "I can handle your family. It's mine that makes me anxious."

"I don't remember much about our wedding," he said then, angling a look down at her as they reached the doors of the ballroom. She thought she could see too much in his gaze, that was the trouble. She thought there was more in all that dark gold than there was or ever could be.

And Susannah didn't understand where the forced calm she'd wielded like a sword these last years had gone. She only knew it had deserted her completely tonight.

"I don't think that's the memory loss acting up again," she said quietly, but not at all as calmly as she'd have liked. "I think it's that you didn't much care."

"I didn't care at all," Leonidas agreed, and whatever had afflicted her, she thought it was gnawing at him, too. And there was no reason that should bring her any sort of comfort. What did it matter what happened between them? This was temporary. This had to be temporary. "But I remember you. And your mother."

"Mother prides herself on being memorable, but only for the correct reasons. Namely that she is Europe's foremost gorgon."

She'd meant that to be funny. But her words hung there between them, and even Susannah could tell that they were something else entirely.

The hand at her back smoothed down an inch or two, then rose again. And all the while, Leonidas's gaze was fixed to hers as if he could see every last part of her. Because of course, he knew what it had been like to come of age in that chilly, remote boarding school, aware at all times that her only use to her parents was as a pawn to further their ambitions. To have no sense of *family* the way others did. To be so utterly and terribly alone, always.

Until now, something in her whispered.

He knew exactly what that was like.

But she reminded herself harshly that there was no *now*. There was no *them*. Leonidas wasn't simply a Betancur, he was the worst of them. He was what happened when greed and ambition was chiseled over generations into aristocratic blood and entirely too much power. If inconceivably wealthy families could create an avatar, Leonidas was the perfect choice to represent his. Hard and dark and utterly lethal.

And now risen from the dead, as if he needed to add to his mystique.

She told herself these things over and over, until it was like cold water in her face.

But it didn't change the way he'd touched her. Or the fact that somehow, the worst of the Betancurs—her husband—had managed to comfort her when no one else could. Or ever had.

Or had bothered to try.

Somehow he'd managed to soothe her on the night of the annual gala, when Susannah was used to facing nothing but fanged smiles and knives to the back all around. She would have said it was impossible.

"Ready, then?" he asked, in that low voice that did upsetting things to her pulse. And that look in his eyes was worse. It made something deep inside her melt.

"Ready," she said, as briskly as she could, but it didn't stop the melting.

Susannah was beginning to think nothing could. That she'd been doomed since the moment she'd walked up that mountain in farthest Idaho and had demanded to see the man they called the Count.

That the Count had been easier, because he'd simply kissed her. Taken her. Done as he wished. Which had allowed her to pretend that under other circumstances, she'd have resisted him.

When what these weeks had taught her was that she didn't want to resist this man, no matter what he called himself.

Leonidas inclined his head and offered her his arm, and Susannah took it. And for the first time since they'd entered their wedding reception four years ago, she entered a glittering, gleaming ballroom packed to the chandeliers above with the toast of Europe not as the rigidly composed, much-hated, always solitary Widow Betancur.

This time, she was no more and no less than Leonidas's wife.

And he was right there with her.

CHAPTER SEVEN

THAT SUSANNAH WAS used to the endless pageant and conspiratorial drama of the Betancur clan was immediately obvious to Leonidas—and likely to the whole of the gala, he thought as he stood near the high table some time later, because she remained so composed in the face of their antics.

He was the one having some trouble adjusting to life back in the fold.

Only a scant handful of his relatives actually stirred themselves to do anything resembling work, of course, so he hadn't seen much of them since his return as he'd been focused on the company and getting up to speed on everything he'd missed. But this was a widely publicized, celebrity-studded charity ball where they could all do what they liked best: lounge about in pretty clothes, exchange vicious gossip, and carry on theatrical affairs with whoever struck their fancies—from lowly valets to exalted kings as it suited them. Usually in full view of their spouses and the press.

Leonidas was used to the offhanded debauchery his cousins practiced with such delight. He remembered it all in excruciating detail when really, his cousins' behavior was something he'd happily have forgotten.

The Betancurs gathered the way they always did at

functions like this one, sulky and imperious in turn, making Leonidas wish he could rule here as he'd done in the compound. His cousins usually did as he asked because it was bad for their bank accounts to get on his bad side, but only after great productions of pointless defiance. Meanwhile, Apollonia held court the way she liked to do, carrying on about *her only child's* return from death when it suited her, and then ignoring him entirely when it amused her to harangue the guests instead, likely in search of her next lover.

That his mother valued only the fact that she'd borne him because of the access that granted her to the Betancur fortune and consequence should no longer have had the power to hurt him. He'd gotten over that when he was still a boy, he would have said. But it rubbed at him tonight even so.

"It would not kill her to at least put on a decent show of maternal devotion, surely," he said in an undertone to Susannah at one point.

And then asked himself what the hell he was doing. The woman wasn't his friend. She wasn't even his date. She was the wife he'd never wanted who, it turned out, didn't want him, either. Whatever else she was—including the only woman he could recall being so obsessed with it was becoming an issue he feared his own hand wouldn't cure—she was certainly no confidante.

"This is no show, it's what Apollonia's maternal devotion looks like," Susannah replied in that cool way of hers that he found he liked entirely too much, all smooth vowels and that little kick of archness besides. She stood beside him as they watched his mother berate a minor duchess, and Leonidas tried to channel a measure of her untroubled amusement. "It is only that she is devoted to herself, not you."

And that was the trouble, Leonidas knew. He'd been on that mountain too long, perhaps. But he hadn't expected to *like* the sweet little virgin his mother had insisted he marry to best honor his late father's wishes that the stodgy Martin Forrester be recognized for his hard work in turning at least three small Betancur fortunes into remarkably large ones, and then adding to them every year. Even from beyond the grave, his father's orders carried the weight of his fists.

But it had not occurred to Leonidas to revolt. Not then.

"Besides," Apollonia had said while sunning herself on one of the family yachts as the Côte d'Azur gleamed in the distance, some years before his wedding, "it will make you look more relatable."

"I hope not." Leonidas had been reading complicated work emails on his mobile instead of waiting attendance on his mother, but that was when he'd still shown up when she'd called—when he'd still felt some measure of obligation. "Why would I wish to relate to anyone?"

"Most men in your position marry cadaverous actresses or shriveled little heiresses, all of whom are notable chiefly for the breadth of their promiscuity," Apollonia had told him, glaring at him over the top of her oversize sunglasses. If the fact that she had been a Greek heiress with something of a reputation when his father had met her years ago struck her as at all ironic, she didn't show it. "This one is a merchant's daughter, which makes you look benevolent and down-to-earth for choosing her, and better yet, she's a guaranteed vestal virgin. People will admire you for your keen character judgment in choosing someone so spotless, and better yet, you won't be forced to make desultory chitchat with every man who's been beneath her skirts."

In truth, Leonidas hadn't expected to spend much time

with her at all. What access he had to the offhanded memories of the man he'd been back then assured him that he'd envisioned a comfortably Continental sort of arrangement with his new wife. He'd assumed they'd handle the matter of his heirs as quickly and painlessly as possible, appear at an agreed-upon number of social events together each season, and otherwise retreat to whichever Betancur properties they preferred to live out their lives as they saw fit, with as many lovers as they could handle as long as they were reasonably discreet about it.

This was the world they'd both grown up in. People organized their lives around money, not emotion.

But Leonidas found that as he watched his spotless wife navigate the toothsome sharks masquerading as the crème de la crème of Europe—to say nothing of the far more unpredictable members of his own family—he hated it. All of it.

The notion that they were destined to end up like all these people here tonight, full of Botox and emptiness. The idea that she was one of them, this forthright creature with the cool smile and the faraway eyes. Even the faintest possibility that the woman who'd gazed at him as if he'd cured her outside these very doors tonight could ever become a master manipulator like his own mother.

He hated this.

He was nothing like these parasites any longer. That was the trouble. The compound had changed him whether he liked to believe that or not. The Count had believed in something—and no matter if it was crazy, Leonidas couldn't seem to get past the fact that he didn't.

He'd done what was expected of him. But did he know what he wanted?

Susannah wasn't like the vultures in this hard, brittle world either, he reminded himself fiercely. She'd told him who he was and given him the one thing he'd never had in his whole life of excess. Her innocence. As a gift, not a bargaining chip.

In fact, unlike every other person he'd ever known, in this life or the one he'd thought was his for four years across the planet, she hadn't bartered with it. She hadn't even mentioned it, before or since. If he didn't know better—if he couldn't see her reaction every time his hand brushed hers—he might have thought he'd imagined the whole thing.

Most people he met used whatever they had as leverage to make him do something for them. Give them power, money, prestige, whatever. In the compound, access to the Count had been doled out like currency. It was no different in the Betancur Corporation. There was literally nothing people wouldn't do to get a piece of him.

Susannah was the only person he'd ever met who didn't appear to want anything from him.

And he found he could think of very little else but keeping her, whether she wanted to stay or not.

"What a glorious resurrection," his cousin Silvio interjected then, smiling to cover the sharpness in his voice and failing miserably as he came to stand beside Leonidas. Yet his gaze rested on Susannah. "You must be so happy to have your beloved husband back, Susannah. After you mourned him so fiercely and for so long."

Leonidas understood from his cousin's tone, and Susannah's deliberately cool response, that Silvio had been one of the cousins desperate to marry her himself. To take control of the Betancur Corporation, of course—but it was more than that. Leonidas could see it all over Silvio. It was Susannah herself. She got under a man's skin.

But the only man who had touched her—*or ever will*, something dark in him growled—was him.

You agreed to let her go, he reminded himself. *Who does or doesn't touch her has nothing to do with you.*

He jerked his attention away from Silvio and looked around at the rest of his assembled family instead. His few remaining aunts were clutching wineglasses like life vests and muttering to each other beneath pasted-on smiles. His single living uncle stood with a cluster of Italian celebrities, yet looked as dour as ever.

The rest of the cousins were up to their usual tricks. Gilded swans with murder in their eyes, they all smiled to Leonidas's face, exclaimed over Susannah when they could get her attention, and hardly bothered to do him the courtesy of hiding their plotting behind a polite hand.

And Silvio wasn't the only one who'd sniffed around Susannah, right in front of Leonidas. He might have thought it was nothing more than a test to see exactly what sort of marriage he and Susannah had—but he saw the way they looked at her. He knew that every last one of them would die to get his hands on her if they could.

The frostier she was, the more they wanted her.

The trouble was, so did he.

His entire family would be ridiculous if they weren't so dangerous at times, Leonidas thought as the night wore on. Some more than others, lest he forget that at least one of the sleek relatives smiling his way tonight was more than just teeth. One of them had arranged for that plane to go down.

He'd seen the reports that had led Susannah to his compound. He knew as much as she did—that the plane had been tampered with. He didn't have to cast around for a reason when he was the head of the family, the CEO and president of the company, and he was related to all these jealous snakes. He was sure it had made perfect sense to one of the jackals he called cousin to get rid of him before he could have his own children and complicate matters—and their own fortunes—even further.

It almost didn't matter which one it had been.

"Are you enjoying all this family time?" he asked Susannah during a lull in the forced family interactions.

"Are they a family, then?" she asked, but there was a smile in her blue eyes and that eased the weight in his chest he'd hardly noticed was there. "I rather thought I was being feasted upon by a pool of piranhas."

"Never fear," Leonidas said darkly. "I haven't forgotten that one of them wished me dead. Or I should amend that. I assume they all wish me dead. But I also assume that only one of them acted on that wish."

She tipped her head to one side, still smiling. "Can you really make such an assumption? They do seem to like gathering in groups."

"Indeed they do." Leonidas inclined his head toward his aunts, who had gone from conspiratorial whispers to gritted teeth and eye daggers, visible from halfway across the ballroom. "But teamwork is not exactly a Betancur family strength."

Susannah laughed, which Leonidas enjoyed entirely too much, but then stopped abruptly. As if it had been snuffed out of her. He followed her gaze across the room and found an older couple entering the room. The woman was tall and thin, with a haughtily sour look on her face, as if she'd smelled something foul—and continued to smell it as she swept in. The man was much rounder and wreathed in as many mustaches as chins, looking so much like a staid, plush banker that Leonidas would have guessed that finance was the man's trade even if he hadn't recognized the pair of them on sight.

Susannah's parents. His in-laws.

And his wife looked about as happy to see them as he was.

The older couple picked Susannah out of the crowd and started toward her as the band began to play again after a short interval. And to Leonidas's surprise, Susannah grabbed his arm.

"We must dance, of course," she said, sounding almost offhand when he could see that frantic gleam in her gaze.

"*Can* I dance?" he asked mildly, looking down at her. And the way she was still watching her parents approach as if she expected them to strike her down where she stood. "Or is it only that I do not wish to?"

That penetrated. She blinked, then frowned at him.

"Of course you can dance," she told him, with only a hint of frost. He admired her restraint. "You were taught as a boy, like every other member of your social class. And mine."

"I can't remember one way or the other, but I feel certain I detest dancing."

"Luckily for you, I can remember that you love it." She smiled at him, and no matter that it was a touch overlarge. "Adore it, in fact."

Leonidas did not adore dancing by any stretch of the imagination. But he'd walked into that one, he was aware.

"You cannot possibly wish to dance with me in front of so many people," he said as if they had all the time in the world to have this conversation. As if her parents weren't bearing down on them even now. And what was the matter with him that he vastly preferred her family troubles to his own? "How will you possibly extricate yourself from this marriage when there will be so many witnesses to our romantic waltz on this, our first night in society since my return?"

"That is a sacrifice I'm willing to make," she replied

sweetly. "Because you love dancing so much, and *of course* I want to help you return to the life you were denied all this time."

Leonidas eyed her, and tried to keep his lips from twitching. "You are too good to me. Especially when you have so little experience with formal dancing. To think, you could make a fool of yourself so easily."

Her sweet smile took on an edge. "I know how to dance, thank you."

"You can't possibly have practiced since you were in school. What if you've forgotten all you learned?"

"I don't know why you imagine yourself an expert on my dancing prowess," Susannah said loftily, "but for all you know I danced all night and day while you were gone."

"While draped in black shrouds to honor my memory? I doubt it." He smiled at her then, a bit lazily, and was astonished to realize that he was enjoying himself for the first time since he'd entered this ballroom and started wading through too many vipers to count. "As far as I can tell, that means the only real dance partner you have ever had is me. At our wedding."

He didn't know why he said it that way—as if he was staking a claim on her where they stood. Or why she took his simple statement of fact so seriously, her blue eyes turning solemn as she regarded him. That odd electricity that had nearly been his undoing in the car earlier, then again at the ballroom doors, coursed through him again then. Making him think that if he didn't touch her right now he might char himself from the inside out.

But he managed to keep his hands to himself.

"I said *you* love to dance," she said after a moment, and the smile she aimed at him then wasn't a fake one, all polite savagery. It was real. Wry and teasing and *real*.

And all theirs, here in a ballroom that might as well have been a goldfish bowl. "I didn't say I enjoyed it, only that I could. You know how it is. A single bad experience can ruin the whole thing and then you're left with a lifetime aversion."

"I'll assume we're still talking about dancing," Leonidas said mildly.

She laughed then, and Leonidas couldn't help himself. He told himself he was indulging her, but he had the sinking suspicion that really, he was indulging himself.

He took her hand in his and he led her out into the middle of the crowded dance floor, ignoring the couples who parted to let them through—as much to gawk at them as to show them any consideration, he knew. He didn't care. Just as he didn't care that she was melting into him and holding on to him not because she was as wild with need as he was—or not only because of that—but because she wanted to avoid unpleasant conversations with her own parents.

She was doing this only because it was easier. He understood that. It was a way to hide in plain sight, right out there in the middle of the dance floor, looking for all the world like a fairy tale come to life. The Lazarus Betancur and his lovely bride, at last. It provided the damned optics she loved so much, and in as perfect a form as possible.

But when Leonidas pulled her into his arms, bent his head to meet and hold her gaze, and then began to move—none of that seemed to matter.

There was nothing but the music, then. The music and the woman in his arms, the whisper of her rich green gown and those blue eyes of hers like whole summers in the sort of simpler times he'd never known. There was nothing but Susannah and the way she gazed up at him, the same way she had that day in the compound when he'd been so deep inside her he hadn't cared what his name was.

It was almost too much to bear.

He was used to waking up in the middle of the night with wildfire dreams of those delirious, delicious moments in the compound storming all over him like some kind of attack. She'd touched him a thousand times since then in those dreams, glutting herself on the hardest part of him, and even better, letting him take his time with her. Again and again, until she fell apart the way she had then.

And he woke every time to find himself alone.

He was used to handling his hunger as best he could, with his hand in the shower and the ferocity of his self-control throughout all the hours they spent together every day. But the scent of her skin was imprinted on him now. The sound her legs made when she slid one over the other to cross them. The sweetness of her breath against his neck when she leaned in to whisper something to him in a meeting.

This was something else. This was holding her against him, as if in an embrace, and for all that it was formal and right there in full view of so many, that was what it felt like.

The kind of embrace Leonidas didn't want to end. Ever.

And even as alarms went off inside him at that, at a notion so foreign to him, Leonidas couldn't bring himself to pull away as he knew he should have. He didn't do what he knew he should. The truth was, he feared he'd lost his sanity a long time ago and the only person who had tried to save him—from the compound, from himself, from that wall between him and his memories—was Susannah.

Then she'd surrendered herself to him, and he couldn't seem to get past that.

She'd given him a gift and yet somehow he felt as if she owned him. Stranger still, he didn't mind the feeling when he knew—he *knew*—everything in him ought to have rebelled at the very notion.

He couldn't find the words to tell her that. He wasn't certain he would have said anything even if he could. Instead, he danced.

They danced and they danced. Leonidas swept her from one side of the ballroom to the other, then back again. Whether he could remember how to dance or not was immaterial, because his body certainly knew what to do while he held her. And then did it well.

And all the while he held her in his arms and against his chest as if she was precious. As if she was everything.

As if she was his.

"Susannah…" he said, his voice low and urgent.

But there was something else in her gaze then. Something more than blue heat and longing. She swallowed, hard, and he watched as emotion moved over her face, then made her generous mouth tremble.

She looked miserable.

And Leonidas was such a bastard it only made him hold her tighter.

"You promised," she whispered, and he shouldn't have found a kind of solace in the catch in her voice. "You promised me that this was only temporary."

"Susannah," he said again, and there was an intensity to his own voice that he didn't want to recognize. "You must know—"

"I need this to end," she told him, cutting him off.

Her voice was like a blow, and he didn't know how

she could have spoken so softly when it felt as if she'd hauled off and struck him. Hard.

He told himself he was grateful.

The things he saw in her eyes were not for him. He was a Betancur. The worst of them, according to Susannah. The high king of the vipers, and nothing would ever change that. Not his so-called death and resurrection.

Not her.

"Of course," he said stiffly, all cut glass and stone. "You need only ask."

"Leonidas," she whispered then, her blue eyes filling with a different emotion he didn't want to see. He could feel it in the way her fingers dug into his shoulder and her hand clenched in his. "Leonidas, you have to understand—"

"I don't," he told her, and he willed himself to stone. To granite. To something impenetrable, even to a woman like this, who still smelled like innocence and still gazed at him like he might really be a god after all. "I don't have to understand anything. We had a deal. Even the worst of the Betancurs can keep his word, Susannah, I assure you."

She flinched at that. "I didn't mean that."

"I think we both know you did. Every word." He stopped moving, holding her against his chest as if he was turning the dance into something else, right there beneath the riot of chandeliers where everyone could see them. Her green dress pooled around his legs, and he had the fleeting thought that he was the one drowning. *Steel*, he ordered himself. *Stone.* "I am everything you think I am and worse, little one. I will eat you alive and enjoy every bite. Running away from me and this cesspool I call my business and family is the best thing you could possibly do."

"Leonidas, please."

"You were my widow for four years," he said with a quiet ferocity that left marks inside him with every word. "All I need is a few more hours. Can you do that?"

She looked helpless and he knew who he was then. Not that he'd been in any doubt. Because he liked it.

"Of course. And this doesn't have to end *tonight*. It just has to end."

Leonidas did nothing to contain himself then. The wildness in him. The darkness he feared might be lethal. The need and the hunger and all the things he wanted to do to her, all wrapped up in that howling thing that didn't want to let her go. That wanted more.

That *wanted*.

He knew exactly what he wanted tonight.

"It will be tonight," he growled at her, still holding her too close against him. "Or not at all. The choice is yours. But once you make it, Susannah, there's no going back. I am not a forgiving man no matter what identity I wear. Do you understand me?"

He could see her nostrils widen and her pupils dilate. He saw her pulse go mad in her neck. There was a faint flush turning her skin hot and red at once, and she wasn't doing a particularly good job of restraining her shudders.

But she didn't speak. It was as if she knew better. As if she knew exactly what it would do to him—to them both—if she did.

Instead she nodded once. Jerkily. Her gaze fixed to his as if she didn't dare look away.

And without another word, Leonidas turned and led her from the dance floor, like the gentleman he wasn't, not anymore.

Before he threw her over his shoulder and carted her

off to his lair, the way he wanted to do more than he wanted to draw his next breath.

And might do still, he told himself grimly.

The night was young.

CHAPTER EIGHT

SUSANNAH HAD FORGOTTEN about her parents.

The truth was, Leonidas had taken her into his arms and she'd forgotten everything. The charity ball all around them. The fact they were the furthest thing from alone. That there were smiling business rivals and leering paparazzi and everything in between, with his family's treachery and the inevitable appearance of her own parents, just to make everything that much more fraught.

It had all disappeared.

There was nothing but Leonidas. The music soaring and dancing along with them. And all the sweet and terrible things that swelled between them, making it entirely too hard to breathe.

She'd felt this way only once before, and it had been far more muted in comparison. What kept racing through her like a different sort of heat was that she was positive Leonidas knew it.

She had been such a confused jumble of feelings on their wedding day. She'd still had such high, silly expectations, of course, no matter how many chilly lectures her parents had given her to prepare her—but he had taken the knees out of each and every one of them. She'd been trembling as she'd walked down the aisle, but the cool, assessing look he'd given her when he'd swept back her veil hadn't assuaged her nerves any. And then when he'd pressed a kiss to her mouth at the front of the church, it had been little more than a stamp of acknowledgment. As if he was affixing a halfhearted seal to one of his lesser possessions. The things he said to her in the car, the way he'd called her a child, had rocked her. And his total disinterest in her at their own reception, too busy was he talking to his business associates, had hurt her feelings more than she'd wanted to admit even then.

A wise girl would have armored herself a little after all these clear indications that this man did not and would not care about her, and she'd tried. Susannah really had tried—but she'd been so young. So frothy and silly, looking back.

But then there had been that dance. That single dance. When Leonidas had held her in his arms and gazed down at her, something arrested and yet stern on his face that seemed to match the wildfire raging inside her. There had been nothing in all the world but the feel of his intensely strong arms around her and the easy way he'd moved her around the floor, as if he was giving her a preview of the way their life would go. Him, in complete control. Her, a little too captivated by the way he handled her and everything else.

And all of it distressingly breathless and dizzyingly smooth.

She shouldn't remember it the way she did, in vivid and excruciating detail. And it certainly shouldn't have played out in her head the way it had all these years, over and over. That dance had made her wonder about him, the man she'd lost so swiftly, more than she'd ever admitted to anyone. It had made her wonder what would have happened between them if they'd ever had a proper wedding night. If he hadn't gotten on that plane.

Now she knew.

And this dance tonight had made her heart hurt all over again, if for different reasons. Because she knew too much now. She knew him and she knew herself and she knew that no matter how precarious it all felt when she was in his arms or how badly she wanted to stay there, she had to go.

Or she wouldn't.

She was still sorting through the clamor inside her as Leonidas led her from the dance floor. His hand was still wrapped around hers, all that fire and strength making her feel entirely too hot and something achy besides. And Susannah knew she needed to jerk her hand away and step away from her husband.

Now.

Before she spent any more time noticing how perfectly her hand fit in his and how the enveloping heat of it seemed to wrap itself around her and hold tight—

But before she could do the right thing, they stepped into the throng and the first people she saw were her parents.

Her parents, who had not supported Susannah's transformation from biddable pawn into powerful widow—because they couldn't control her and oh, how they'd hated that. They'd urged her to remarry with all possible haste, preferably to a man of their choosing, and hadn't liked it when she'd told them that one marriage of convenience was enough, thank you. They hadn't much cared for it when she'd ignored their arguments in favor of various suitors anyway.

They'd liked it least of all when she'd stopped taking their calls.

"You ungrateful child!" her father had boomed at her only a few months back when she'd refused to attend a dinner party he was throwing, where he'd wanted to use her presence to impress some of his associates as all things Betancur did, and Susannah had foolishly allowed her assistant to connect his call. "You wouldn't be where you are if not for me!"

"If I'd listened to you I would have married Leonidas's dour old uncle when he demanded it three years ago," she'd replied, happy all of Europe sat between her and her parents' home outside London. "Somehow, I can live with the consequences of the choice I made."

The conversation had disintegrated from there.

But invitations to the Betancur Ball were highly prized and fought over across the world, and there was no keeping her own parents off the list. What Susannah couldn't believe was that somehow she'd forgotten they'd be coming tonight.

You've been so consumed with Leonidas you hardly know your own name, she accused herself. And she knew it was true.

It was one more reason she had to put distance between them. Because she knew all too well that the day was fast approaching when she wouldn't want to do anything of the kind, and then she might as well lock herself away in a tower somewhere before he grew bored of her and did it himself.

Leonidas came to a stop before her parents, and Susannah didn't know if it was because he recognized them or simply because they dared to block his path.

"You remember my parents, of course," Susannah said for his benefit. She thought perhaps Leonidas was lucky to forget so many things. She'd like to forget her parents herself. Particularly on a night like tonight when she knew that they'd come with every intention of cutting her down to size. Right here in public where she was unlikely to make a scene or even respond too harshly.

Leonidas inclined his head, but said nothing when Susannah slipped her arm through his. She felt the dark gaze he slid her way, but he still said nothing, so she moved closer to him as if she intended to use him as a human shield.

Perhaps she did.

"Your husband has been resurrected from the dead," her mother said coolly instead of condescending to offer a conventional greeting to either her daughter or the man whose funeral she'd attended. "I don't think it's unreasonable to have expected a call, Susannah. Or was it your intention that your only flesh and blood should learn of this miracle in the press like everyone else?"

"What my mother means to say, Leonidas," Susannah said in mild reproof, her gaze on her mother, "is 'welcome home.'"

Leonidas gave her another swift, dark look she thought was a little too much like a glare, but he didn't say anything. He certainly didn't indicate that their relationship had effectively ended just moments before on the dance floor.

Instead, he smiled in that way he did sometimes, that made it seem as if he was bestowing a great gift upon the receiver, and then he shook her father's hand. The two men started one of those endlessly tedious masculine conversations that purported to be about business and was in fact a clever little game of one-upmanship, which left Susannah to her mother's manicured talons.

But she still held tight to Leonidas's arm.

"Imagine my surprise to discover that the tabloids knew more about my daughter's life than I did," Annemieke continued, and Susannah doubted anyone would be fooled by the little trill of laughter her mother let out as punctuation.

"Given that you and Father were exhorting me to re-marry only a few months ago, I didn't think you would be the best person to take into my confidence on this matter."

Annemieke sniffed. "You knew he was alive all this time and yet you played your deceitful games. With everyone. You are a sneaky creature, aren't you?"

She raised her voice when she said it, because, of course, it was for Leonidas's benefit. And something swept over Susannah, hot and prickly. Because her mother didn't know that she was planning to leave this man who had only just returned to her. Her mother didn't have the slightest idea what their relationship was like. Even if she believed that Susannah had spent years knowing that Leonidas was alive and pretending otherwise, it was obvious they hadn't spent any time together. How could they have when the world thought he was dead and Susannah had been busy acting as the face of the Betancur Corporation?

Which meant her mother was deliberately trying to undermine Susannah in front of Leonidas. She *wanted* to malign Susannah in his eyes.

Of course she does, a voice deep inside Susannah said briskly, before that sad, silly part of her that always hoped her parents might act like parents despite years of never doing anything of the kind showed itself. *This is about power. Everything to all of these people is always, always about power.*

She'd had four years of it, and she was sick of it. More than sick of it. She could feel her aversion to the games these people played like a weight beneath her breastbone, doing its best to claw its way out.

But she refused to give her mother the satisfaction of seeing that she'd landed a blow.

"I haven't been feeling well," Susannah said as evenly as possible, before her mother could start in again with some new insult. "I keep getting terrible headaches. I suppose it's possible that the emotion of Leonidas's return has got to me more than I might have thought."

Leonidas moved beside her, letting her know that he was paying attention to her conversation as well as his own. She instantly regretted using the word *emotion* where he could hear it. And she hated that she was holding on to him in the first place. She'd been handling far more intense scenes than this all by herself for years. He didn't need to do anything to support her.

But before she could put the distance between them she should have, he shifted where he stood and then slid his hand to the small of her back as if they weren't strangers who happened to be married to each other, but a unit.

Suddenly Susannah was afraid of the emotions she could feel slopping around inside her as if they might flood her, then carry her away, if she gave in to a single one of them.

She needed to stop this. She needed to escape this gilded, vicious world while she still could.

And she needed to leave soon, before she forgot the way out.

Something in her whispered that the line was coming faster than she wanted to admit—and if she wasn't careful, she'd cross it without realizing it.

"Resurrection is a tricky business," Leonidas was saying to her mother, merging their two conversations into one.

"It could be that, I suppose," Annemieke said with a

sniff. "Though Susannah has never been a sickly thing, all fainting spells and fragility."

"This is where she calls me 'sturdy,' which is never a compliment," Susannah murmured, not quite under her breath.

Annemieke swept a look over her daughter, from her head all the way to her toes and then back again, in that pointedly judgmental way that always left Susannah feeling lacking. More than lacking.

Susannah reminded herself that she didn't send time with her parents for a reason. After tonight it would likely be months and months before she had to face them again and by then, who knew where she'd be? If she was divorced from Leonidas the way she planned, it was entirely likely that her parents would want nothing to do with her.

If she kept that happy day in mind, tonight didn't seem so bad. And there was no point indulging the part of her that went a bit too still at the notion of leaving Leonidas when she could feel all that warmth and strength from the hand he held at her back. No point at all.

She made herself smile. "It's only a little headache now and then," she said. "I'm sure I just need to drink more water."

"I only suffered from headaches once and it was very unpleasant." Her mother lifted a brow, and there was a gleam in the blue eyes she'd passed on to her daughter that Susannah did not like at all. "It was when I was pregnant."

And Susannah didn't hear if there was any conversation after that point, because everything seemed to... stop. Leonidas went very, very still beside her. His hand didn't move, and she suddenly felt it less as moral support and more like a threat. A terrible threat she should have heeded from the start.

A dark foreboding she wanted to reject swept over her. But she couldn't seem to speak, not even to deny what she knew—*she knew*—was completely false.

Especially not when she could feel all that lethal power emanating from the man beside her. The husband who had agreed to let her leave—but he was a Betancur. There wasn't a Betancur in six generations who'd been *laissez faire* about the family bloodline, and somehow she very much doubted that Leonidas would be the first.

Not that she was pregnant, of course, because she couldn't be.

She *couldn't* be.

"I'm nothing like my mother," she told him fiercely when he made their excuses in a gruff tone and led her away, his hand wrapped tight around her upper arm as if he expected her to bolt. "I never have been. I don't even look like her. It's ridiculous to assume that we would share anything."

He didn't stop moving through the crowd, inexorable and swift, towing her toward the doors though the party was still in full swing.

"Everyone gets headaches, Leonidas," she gritted out at him from between her teeth. "There's no need to jump to dramatic conclusions. It's as likely to be a brain tumor as it is that I'm pregnant."

But Leonidas only threw her a dark, glittering sort of look that made everything in her pull tight and then shiver. He didn't reply, he just slipped his phone from his pocket with his free hand, hit a button, then put it to his ear and kept walking.

Sweeping her along with him whether she liked it or not.

And everything after that seemed to happen much too fast, as if she was watching her own life catapult off the side of a cliff in front of her.

Leonidas whisked her from the ballroom without seeming to care overmuch that they had been expected to stay for the whole of the gala. He didn't even bother to make their excuses to his family. He had her in the back of his car and headed back to the soaring townhome he kept in Paris's Eighth Arrondissement, steps from the Avenue des Champs-élysées, without another word to her on the drive back.

And worse than that, when they arrived back in the glorious nineteenth-century dwelling in the sought-after Haussmann style, a doctor waited there in the foyer.

"This is ridiculous," Susannah all but sputtered, forgetting any pretense of calm, and who cared that the doctor was standing there as witness.

"Then it costs you nothing to indulge me," Leonidas replied, that same glittering thing in his gaze while he continued to hold the rest of his body so still.

As if he is lying in wait, something in her whispered. She repressed a shudder.

"I can't possibly be pregnant," she snapped at him.

"If you are so certain, you have even less reason to refuse."

Susannah realized he'd turned to stone. That there was no give in him at all. This was the Leonidas of stark commands and absolute power, not the man who'd touched her back, held her hand and made her heartbeat slow. She didn't understand how he could have both men inside him, but clearly he couldn't be both at the same time.

And she knew she'd surrendered to the inevitable— that it must have showed on her face—because the doctor smiled his apologies and led her from the room to take the test.

More astonishingly, she followed him.

Susannah had worked herself into a state by the time she found Leonidas again, waiting for her in his private salon filled with priceless antiques and bristling with evidence of the Bettencourt wealth at every turn. But she could hardly pay attention to that sort of thing when her life was slipping out of her grasp right there in front of her. He stood at the fireplace, one arm propped up on the mantel as he frowned at the flames, and he didn't turn to look at her when she came in.

"You are going to feel very silly," she told him. Through her teeth. And opted not to notice how absurdly attractive he looked without his coat and tie, his shirt unbuttoned at the neck so his scars showed. Or the way she melted inside at the sight of him, until she could feel that dangerous pulse between her legs. "This is embarrassing. That doctor will sell the story to every tabloid in Europe."

"I am not the least embarrassed," Leonidas replied, still not looking at her. "And if the good doctor dares, I will destroy him."

She felt dizzy at the mild tone he used, or perhaps it was the unmistakable ferocity beneath it. Either way, she took a few more steps into the salon and gripped the back of the nearest settee. She told herself it wasn't to keep her balance, because nothing was happening that should so unsettle her that she'd lose her footing. Because she wasn't pregnant. Her mother was waspish because she enjoyed it, but Susannah had long ago stopped listening to her when she was being provoking.

Leonidas would learn to do the same, she told herself piously.

Or not, a voice inside her remarked. *As you are so intent on leaving him.*

"I'm not pregnant, Leonidas," she said for the hundredth time, as if she could finally make it so if she said it fiercely enough. As if she might finally light upon the right tone that would make him listen.

Leonidas stood then. He turned from the mantel and regarded her for a moment in a manner that made every part of her shiver. And keep right on shivering.

"You are so certain, little one," he said after a moment. "But I can count."

Susannah flushed at that, as if he really had slapped her this time. She felt feverish, hot and then cold, and she gripped the high back of the settee so hard she could see her knuckles whiten in protest. She wanted to tear that damned Betancur sapphire off her finger and hurl it at him. She wanted to run down the grand staircase and out into the Paris streets, and keep on running until her legs gave out.

And while he stared at her, his gaze too dark and much too certain, she counted. The way she'd absolutely not done on the way here because it was impossible and she refused. But she did it now.

Seven weeks since that night in the compound and she hadn't bled in all that time. In fact, she couldn't remember the last time she had. It certainly hadn't been in the ten days before she'd left for Idaho to find him, because she would have remembered having to deal with that while pretending to everyone she knew that she was going anywhere but where she was really heading.

"I assumed this couldn't possibly be an issue," she said after a moment, aware she sounded more like her mother than herself. Harsh and accusing, and that was just to start. She couldn't imagine the expression on her face and wondered if she was more like her mother than she'd ever believed possible. "And I'm sure it won't be. But why didn't you make sure that something like this could never be in question?"

"Did you see a condom in that compound, Susannah? Because I did not. Perhaps I assumed you would be on birth control yourself."

"I find that hard to believe. I was the virgin in the scenario, not you."

"And I was a holy man who'd been on the top of a mountain for four years. How did I know how you'd spent your time out there in all that sin?"

"You're one to talk. My understanding is that the entire point of becoming a cult leader is to avail yourself of the buffet of attractive followers."

Leonidas smiled, and under the circumstances Susannah thought that scared her most of all.

"Did I not mention that I was entirely chaste that entire time?" His smile deepened, but it didn't touch his eyes. "Untouched and uninterested for four years. I have been entirely faithful to you throughout our marriage, Susannah. As you have been to me. Surely this is something to celebrate."

But she was sure that she could hear a steel door slamming shut as he said it.

"It was an accident," she said, but her voice was barely a whisper. "It didn't mean anything. It was only an accident."

And if he planned to answer beyond that enigmatic expression on his face, she would never know. Because that was when there was a discreet knock on the paneled door and the doctor stepped back into the room.

"Congratulations, *madame, monsieur*," the doctor said, nodding at each of them in turn while Susannah's breath caught in her throat. "The test is positive. You are indeed pregnant, as you suspected."

And this time, it was Susannah who turned to stone.

There was no other word to describe it. One moment she was standing there, furious and affronted and so very certain that this was all a mistake, and then the next she found herself a hard thing all the way through, as every part of her rejected the notion outright. Physically.

Because she couldn't possibly be pregnant.

But one hand crept around to slide over her belly and hold it, just in case.

She barely noticed when Leonidas escorted the doctor from the room. He could have been gone for hours. When he returned he shut the door behind him, enclosing them in the salon that had seemed spacious before, and that was when Susannah walked stiffly around the settee to sit on it.

Because she thought it was that or grow roots down into the black herringbone floor.

He crossed back to the fireplace and stood there again, watching her, while the silence grew fangs between them.

His dark, tawny gaze had changed, she noticed. It had gone molten. He still held himself still, though she could tell the difference in that, too. It was as if an electrical current ran through him now, charging the air all around him even while his mouth remained in an unsmiling line.

And he looked at her as if she was naked. Stripped. Flesh and bone with nothing left to hide.

"Is it so bad, then?" he asked in a mild sort of tone she didn't believe at all.

Susannah's chest was so heavy, and she couldn't tell if it was the crushing weight of misery or something far more dangerous. She held her belly with one hand as if it was already sticking out. As if the baby might start kicking at any second.

"The Betancur family is a cage," she told him, or the parquet floor beneath the area rug that stretched out in front of the fireplace, and it cost her to speak so precisely. So matter-of-factly. "I don't want to live in a cage. There must be options."

He seemed to grow darker as she watched, which she knew was impossible. It was a trick of the light, or the force of her reaction. He couldn't summon his own storm.

"What do you mean by that?" he asked, and this time there was something in his low, fierce voice that made her break out in goose bumps.

Everywhere.

"I have no idea," she said, sounding broken to her own ears.

Panic was so thick inside her that she was surprised she could breathe, much less speak, and scenarios drifted through her head, one more outlandish than the next. She could live abroad, in a country far from here, just her and the baby. So long as no one knew who they were or how to find them, they could live anywhere. She could raise a child in some protected mountain valley some-where and learn how to farm—perhaps in Idaho, for a little symmetry, where it was apparently perfectly easy to disappear into the woods for years at a time. She could relocate to any number of distant, unfashionable cities she'd never seen and work in an anonymous office some-where, raising her child as a single mother no different from all the rest.

"None?" The way Leonidas studied her did not make her goose bumps subside. She rubbed at her arms and wished she could stop that shivering thing down deep inside her. "No ideas at all?"

"Anything but this," she threw at him. "That's my idea."

"Define 'this,' please."

"*This*, damn you." She shook her head, only dimly aware that moisture leaked from her eyes as she did. "I've been a pawn in Betancur games for four years, and it's too long. I don't want to do it for the rest of my life. I certainly don't want to raise a child the way I was raised. Or worse, the way you were. This is a prison and if I don't want to live in it, I'm certain my child deserves better, too."

And she watched him change again, softening somehow without seeming to move. She didn't understand it. It wasn't as if it made him any less... Leonidas. But it was as if something in him loosened.

It occurred to her as she watched his subtle transformation that he might not have known what she'd meant by *options*.

Just as it occurred to her that it had never crossed her mind that she wouldn't keep her baby. She hadn't wanted to be pregnant, but the doctor had told her she was and all she'd thought about was escaping the Betancurs *with* her child.

She supposed that answered a question she hadn't known she had inside her. That she was already a better mother than her own, who had spent a memorable Christmas one year regaling Susannah with tales of how close she'd come to ending her pregnancy, so little had she wanted a child. Susannah had been twelve.

"You must know that I never wanted to let you go in the first place," Leonidas said now, drawing her attention back to him and that hooded, lethal way he was watching her from his place by the fire. And she should have been appalled by that. She should have railed against the idea. But instead there was something small and bright inside her, and it glowed. "I entertained the possibility because I owed you. You came to that mountain and you restored me to myself. I told myself the least I could do was grant you a wish. But you should know, Susannah, that there is no such possibility now."

He almost sounded sorrowful, but she knew better. She could see the glittering thing in his gaze, dark and possessive and very, very male.

"You might as well slam the cage door shut and throw away the key," she managed to get out past the constriction in her throat.

"I am not a cage," Leonidas said with quiet certainty. "The Betancur name has drawbacks, it is true, and most of them were at that gala tonight. But it is also not a cage. On the contrary. I own enough of the world that it is for all intents and purposes yours now. Literally."

"I don't want the world." She didn't realize she'd shot to her feet until she was taking a step toward him, very much as if she thought she might take a swing at him next. As if she'd dare. "And I understand that you're used to ruling everything you see, but I took care of your company and your family and this whole great mess just fine when you were gone. I don't need you. I don't *want* you."

"Then why did you go to such trouble to find me?" he demanded, and the force of it rocked her back on her heels. "No one else was looking for me. No one else considered for even one second that I might be anything but dead. Only you. Why?"

And Susannah hardly knew what she felt as she stared at him, her chest heaving as if she'd been running and her hands in fists at her sides. There were too many things inside her then. There was the fact that she was trapped, in this marriage and in his family and in this life she'd wanted to escape the whole time she'd been stuck in it. More than that, there was the astounding reality of the situation—that there was *life* inside her. That she'd found her husband on a mountaintop when everyone had accepted that he was gone, and she'd done more than save him. They'd made a life.

She thought it was grief that swept over her then. Grief for the girl she'd been and grief for the woman she'd been forced to become. Grief for the years she'd lost, and grief for the years he'd had taken from him.

Susannah told herself it had to be grief, this wild and unwieldy thing that ravaged her, turning her inside out whether she wanted it or not. She told herself it could only be grief.

Because the possibility that it was joy, ferocious and encompassing, might be the end of her.

"I don't know," she said quietly, her voice sounding as rough as she felt. "I didn't believe the plane could go down like that. I certainly didn't believe it was an accident. And the more I looked into it, the less I believed you'd died."

"But you don't need me. You don't *want* me."

He wasn't asking her a question. He was taunting her. Leonidas shifted then. He pushed away from the fireplace and he stalked toward her, making everything inside Susannah shake to hold her ground.

And then he kept right on coming, until he was standing over her and she was forced to tilt her head back to meet his gaze.

"No," she whispered. "I don't want you. I want to be free."

He took her face in his hands, holding her fast, and this close his eyes were a storm. Ink dark with gold like lightning, and she felt the buzz of it. Everywhere.

Inside and out.

As complicated as that mad thing that could not possibly be joy.

"This is as close as you're going to get, little one," he told her, the sound of that same madness in his gaze, his voice.

And then he claimed her mouth with his.

CHAPTER NINE

WHEN SHE KISSED him back, shifting her body so she could press closer against him and dig her hands into his chest, something deep inside Leonidas eased.

Even as something else burned anew, harder and wilder at once.

He kissed her again and again. He dug his fingers into the sweet, shining gold of her hair and he let it tumble down over her shoulders, and still he took her mouth, claiming her and possessing her and marking her the only way he could.

She was his. *His*.

And he was tired of keeping himself on a leash where his woman—his *wife*—was concerned.

She wasn't going anywhere. Never, ever again.

He had never been much of a gentleman, and then he'd become a god. He was the one who'd been acting as if he was in a cage these last seven weeks, but that time was over now.

She was pregnant. His beautiful Susannah was ripe with his child even now. A child they'd made when she'd surrendered her innocence to him in that compound where he hadn't known his own name until he'd tasted her. A child she'd already started building inside her when she'd walked with him through the gates and back into the world.

Leonidas had never felt anything like this in his life.

Triumph pounded through him, wild and ruthless in turn, and he wanted to shout out his savage joy from the rooftops of Paris until the whole world trembled before the child that he would bring into it.

And this woman whom he had no intention of letting out of his sight, ever, was a miracle. *His* miracle. She had not left him on that mountain. She hadn't left him the moment she'd delivered him home. She hadn't left when she'd wanted to do it a month ago, and despite what she'd said on the dance floor, she hadn't left him tonight, either.

And now she'd missed her chance, because he would see to it that she never would.

She was his wife. She carried his child.

Nothing would ever be the same.

Leonidas devoured her mouth, and when her sweet little moans began to sound like accusations, greedy and hungry against his mouth, he lifted her against him and then bore her down onto the thick rug that stretched out before the fire on the floor of his salon. The flames crackled behind their grate, and he laid her out there before the fire like some kind of offering, determined that this time he would go slow.

This time, he would learn her. This woman who had consented to be his right hand all these weeks, when she so easily could have left him to fend for himself. This woman who was not only the wife who had waited for him and stayed dressed in black years after his death, but who was also the mother of his child.

The child who would not grow up the way he did, with a cruel father and a selfish mother, beaten into becoming the Betancur heir they'd wanted.

He would die before he let that happen and for good this time.

But first he intended to imprint himself on Susannah.

He wanted her to taste him when she licked her own lips. He wanted her to feel him as if he was inside her, even when he wasn't.

He wanted to wreck her and redeem her, over and over, until the very idea of leaving him was what made those tears spill from her eyes.

And then he wanted to keep doing it, again and again, until this edgy hunger for her was sated at last. If it could be.

He took his time, exulting in the fact there was no barbed wire here. No followers with an arsenal and no video cameras on the walls.

There was nothing but the two of them. At last.

Leonidas moved over her, touching and tasting and indulging himself, from her lush mouth all the way down to the delicate arch of her feet. Then back again. He stripped off the stunning ball gown he'd insisted she wear, in that bright green that was so unlike the Widow Bettencourt that he expected whole tabloids to speak of nothing else come morning.

But he couldn't wait to take it off her.

He stripped her bare so that he could get to the glory beneath it, all those luscious curves he'd dreamed a thousand times since that day in Idaho. Did he imagine that they were richer than he recalled? He cupped her breasts in his palms, then tried them against his tongue. He worshipped that belly of hers that was still flat, though slightly thicker, perhaps, than it had been that last time.

He settled himself between her legs and bent to taste her fully. Sweet cream and that feminine kick, she went straight to his head. And he did absolutely nothing to stop the intoxication.

He brought her to a shuddering, rolling sort of shattering with his mouth, there where she was wet and needy.

Then he did it again. And only when she called out his name, her voice cracking, did Leonidas finally crawl up the length of her and fit himself to her center.

At last.

Then he finally thrust himself into her, sinking to the hilt, and loved the hitch in the little sound she made as he possessed her completely.

He waited as she accommodated him, wriggling her hips and flushed bright everywhere, more beautiful beneath him than any woman had a right to be.

And when he moved, it was with the knowledge that she had given him the one thing he hadn't known he wanted more than anything else in this world. Again.

His blood was all around him. His cousins, his mother, more Betancurs than anyone could possibly want. They were shoved down his throat whether he liked it or not. They schemed and plotted. They lived sparkling lives his hard work provided them and they still would have been the first to snap at him if they could. They were the part of his life he wished could have stayed forgotten, but it wasn't as if he could escape them. They were everywhere.

It had been that way all his life. His mother the worst of them, demanding and deceitful and never, ever any kind of parent in any real sense. He'd stopped expecting any better of her and he'd stopped wondering why he always felt empty inside when others clearly did not.

He knew why. This was how they'd made him. This was who his family wanted him to be, this harsh creature who felt nothing.

But Susannah hated them all as much as he did. She wanted nothing to do with his blood or what proximity to the Betancurs could do for her. If she saw the emptiness in him, she didn't shy away from it. On the contrary, she was the only person he'd ever met who treated him as if he was no better or different from anyone else.

And she had given him a family.

A family.

Leonidas would do everything in his power to make sure that he never lost what was his. Not to his own memory, and certainly not to those vultures who banked on the fact they shared his blood, assuming that would keep them safe.

He made himself a vow, there on the floor in his Paris townhome, on the night of the Betancur Ball where once again, Susannah had given him the world.

He would do no less for her—whether she liked it or not.

And then he lost himself in her, making her cry out again and again, until he finally lost his patience. He gathered her to him, then reached down between them to help her fly apart one last time.

And he followed, calling out her name as he fell.

Later, she stirred against him and he lifted her up, carrying her through the house to the room he had no intention of letting her stay in on her own the way she'd planned to do when they'd arrived. But there was no point arguing it now. He found a loose long-sleeved T-shirt and a pair of lounging pajama bottoms, and dressed her quickly. She made a face at him while he did it, but then curled herself into a ball on the bed in the last guest suite she would occupy.

And when she fell asleep, she fell hard.

With any luck, she'd stay that way until they made it to the island. Where he had every intention of keeping her until she couldn't imagine any possible scenario that involved leaving him, because that was unacceptable.

She was his.

Leonidas had led a cult for years. Whether he'd been a figurehead or not, he knew exactly how to keep one woman where he wanted her, and he had no qualms about using each and every one of the dirty little tricks he knew to make her think it was the best idea anyone had ever had.

He stood there and watched her sleep for a moment, aware that his heart was pounding at him and that he should probably be concerned that it was so easy for him to slip back into the sort of headspace the Count had always occupied. But he wasn't. The truth was that the Leonidas Betancur who had got on that plane and the man who had been dragged from its ashes weren't so different. Neither one of them had believed in much besides themselves. The Count had possessed a version of morality, but it had all been arranged around the fact he'd believed he was at the center of everything.

Susannah had changed that, as well. She'd knitted him together and made him care about her, too. It should have outraged him. Maybe on some level it did. But more than that was the deep, abiding notion that she belonged with him and anything else was intolerable.

Especially now that she was carrying his child.

It was the beginning and the end of everything, and he'd be happy to fight with her about it on his favorite private island, where she could scream into the impervious ocean if she liked and it wouldn't do a single thing to save her. If he was honest, he was almost looking forward to watching what she'd do when she realized she really was stuck there. With him.

Leonidas smiled, then tucked a strand of her golden hair behind her ear. He had to order himself not to bend closer and put his lips to her sweetly flushed cheek, because he knew he wouldn't stop if he did.

But he forced himself away from her, out into the hall.

Then he called for his staff and his plane, and methodically set about kidnapping his wife.

Susannah jolted awake when the plane touched down and she had no idea where she was.

She knew she was on one of the Betancur jets, though it took her a moment to recognize the stateroom she was in. She clung to the side of the bed as the plane taxied in, frowning as she tried to make sense of the fact that she'd apparently slept through an entire flight to somewhere unknown.

Paris gleamed in her memory. And the doctor's visit. Her pregnancy, confirmed.

And what had happened after that announcement, there before the fire.

But everything else following it was a blur. She had the vague recollection of a car moving through the city in the dark, her head pillowed on Leonidas's shoulder. Then the spinning sensation of being lifted into his arms.

She might have thought she'd been drugged but she'd felt this way before, and more than once these last weeks. This powerfully exhausted. The good news was that she knew it was the pregnancy now, not something that required a hospital stay, or that allergy she'd been half-convinced she had to Leonidas.

When the plane came to a full stop she stayed where she was for a while, then rolled out of the bed, surprised that no attendant—or confusing, breathtaking husband—had come looking for her.

She stepped out into the corridor, blinking in the light that poured in from the plane's windows in the common areas. It told her two things—that the shades had been pulled in her stateroom and that wherever they were, it was morning.

And when she looked out the windows, she could see the sea.

She made her way to the front of the plane and stepped out onto the landing at the top of the jet's fold-up steps. She blinked as she took in the soft light, then looked around, realizing after a beat or two that she was on a small landing strip on a rocky island. She saw silvery olive trees in all directions, solid hills covered in green, and the sea hovering in the distance on all sides, blue and gray in turn.

And Leonidas waited at the foot of the stairs, leaning against the side of a sleek, deep green Range Rover.

It was only then that she became aware of what she was wearing. The long-sleeve shirt she slept in and a pair of very loose yoga pants. And there was only one way that she could have come to be wearing such things, she thought, when she had no recollection of putting them on. When the last thing she knew she'd been wearing was that green dress at the ball.

Although she hadn't been wearing much of anything in front of the fire.

And maybe that was what shivered through her then. The sheer intimacy of the fact he'd dressed her. She imagined him tugging clothes into place over her bare skin, then pulling her hair out of the way...

It wasn't heat that moved through her then, though she thought it was related in its way. It was something far more dangerous. She tried to swallow it down, but her feet were moving without her permission, carrying her down the metal stairs whether she wanted to go or not.

And she could feel Leonidas's dark gaze on her all the way.

She made it to the bottom of the steps, then crossed over to stand in front of him, and the silence was what got to her first. She was so used to Rome. Paris. Great cities filled with as many people as cars. Foot traffic and horns, sirens and music. But there was nothing like that here. There was a crisp, fresh breeze that smelled of salt. No voices. No sounds of traffic in the distance. It was as if they were the only two people left on the earth.

"Where are we?" she asked, and was not surprised to hear how hushed she sounded, as if the island demanded it.

"Greece," Leonidas replied. Perhaps too readily. "More or less."

"What are we doing in Greece?" What she meant was, *Why are we so clearly not in Athens near the Betancur offices if we're in Greece?* But she didn't say that part out loud. It was as if some part of her thought the island spoke for itself.

Leonidas's hard mouth kicked up a little bit in one corner, but something about that smile of his didn't exactly make her feel easy. He did not cross his arms, or straighten from where he continued to lounge against the side of his vehicle. And something a little too much like foreboding moved through her then.

"In one sense, we are in Greece because I am Greek," he said, and his conversational tone only made the foreboding worse. Susannah felt the itch of it down the length of her spine. "My mother is Greek, anyway. This island has been in her family for many generations. There are very few staff, and all of them are some relation to me." That curve in the corner of his mouth deepened. "I mention this because you are very enterprising, I think, and you do not wish to frustrate yourself unnecessarily with fruitless escape attempts."

She blinked. "What are you talking about?"

"I will not insult you by giving you a list of rules, Susannah. That is the beauty of an island such as this. There is no way off. No ferries land here. The plane will leave tonight and you will not be on it, and there is a helicopter that flies only at my command. Do you understand what I'm telling you?"

"I assume I'm still asleep," she said tightly. "And this is a terrible nightmare."

"Alas, you are wide awake."

"Then I do not understand," she managed to say, though she was very much afraid that she did. "It sounds as if you've just imprisoned me."

"I prefer to think of it as an opportunity for you to embrace the realities of your life." Leonidas inclined his head. "An opportunity to spend some time accepting what is and let go of what cannot be."

"That sounds suspiciously like cult talk."

"If that is what you wish to call it, I cannot argue." One arrogant shoulder rose, then fell. "I would encourage you to recall that I was not a follower of any cult. I was the leader." He smiled at her. "I can be very persuasive."

"You need to take me back to civilization," she snapped at him, because that smile lit her up inside and she didn't know which one of them she hated more for it. "Immediately."

Leonidas shook his head, almost as if he pitied her. "I'm afraid I'm not going to do that."

And it was as if everything that had happened and everything she'd seen since she'd stepped off that plane into the wilds of Idaho slammed into her then. The compound itself, after that steep climb. The barbed wire, the cameras, the ugly weapon pointed at her with a few threats besides. Not to mention what had happened inside with her long-lost husband.

There'd been the press storm when they'd left, when Leonidas had been returned to the world that had thought him dead. And these weeks of close proximity, always so scrupulously polite and careful not to touch too much, as if she wasn't spending entirely too much time with the man she meant to leave. The Betancur Ball. His cousins and his mother and then worse, her parents.

And that dance in the middle of all the rest of it, like some bittersweet nod to a life she'd only ever dreamed about but had never seen. It had never existed and it never would, and the fact that she discovered she was pregnant and then fell all over him like some kind of wild animal didn't change that.

She wanted her baby. She didn't want the Betancur baby and the circus that went along with that. She didn't want Leonidas.

Because she couldn't have him, not the way she wanted him, and all of this was just delaying the inevitable. Why couldn't he see that?

"I told you that I didn't want to live in a prison," she said when she was sure that she could speak again, and she didn't care if she sounded distinctly unlike her usual serene self. She didn't care if he saw her fall apart right there in front of him. "I told you that our marriage already felt like a cage. Your name is the key in the lock. I told you. And your response to that was to pack as I was sleeping and strand me on some island?"

Leonidas finally stood. He straightened from the side of the Range Rover, unfolding to his full height, and then loomed there above her. His arms dropped to his sides and his face took on that granite, lethal expression that she somehow kept forgetting was the truth of him. She'd seen it when he was the Count. And she'd seen it last night in Paris. And there been glimpses here and there, across these past seven weeks, of a different side to the man—but she understood now that they were flashes, nothing more.

This was the truth of Leonidas Betancur. Susannah had absolutely no doubt. Ruthless, bordering on grim, seeming practically to burn with all that power he carried around so effortlessly inside him.

This was the man she'd married. This was the man she'd given her innocence to, then made a baby with.

And she had no one to blame but herself, because he'd never hidden any of it. He was a Betancur. This was who he was and always had been.

"I am your cage," he told her, in the kind of voice it didn't surprise her at all had led men to abandon their lives and follow him up the side of a mountain "The marriage, the Betancur name, all of that is noise. The only prison you need worry about is me, Susannah. And I will hold you forever."

She wanted to shake. She wanted to cry—put her head down and sob until her heart felt like hers again. She wanted to scream at him, beat at him with her fists, perhaps. Pound on him until something made sense again, but she didn't do it. That same impossible grief—because it couldn't be joy, not here, not now—rocked through her again.

She sucked in a breath and tried to straighten her shoulders. "If that was meant to make me feel better, it failed."

"You are carrying my child," he blazed at her, and it took everything she had not to jump. "I don't know what kind of man you think I am, but I don't give away what's mine, Susannah."

It was possible the top of her head exploded. She

surged forward, recklessly taking her finger and poking him in the chest with it. "I am not yours."

Leonidas wrapped his hand around hers, but he didn't pull her finger away from him. He kept her hand trapped against his chest.

"I will not debate you on that, my little virgin. But it doesn't change the fact that only I have ever had you."

"I was the widow of one of the most famous men in the world." She tugged at her hand, but he didn't release it. "I couldn't exactly pop into a club and pick someone up to have sex with, could I?"

"But you would have, you think. Had you been a less identifiable widow."

She frowned at his sardonic tone. "I would have divested myself of my virginity before the end of your funeral if I could have. Happily."

She threw that at him, but he only laughed, and she hated him for it. Or she hated herself for feeling so unsteady at the sound.

"I don't believe you," he told her. "You pride yourself on your control, little one. It's obvious in everything you do. The only place you cede it is when you are beneath me."

She shook at that, and she knew he saw it. Worse, he could likely feel it in the hand he still held against the steel wall of his chest.

"I'm an excellent actress. Ask anyone in your company. Or your family."

"Deny it if you wish, it makes no difference to me." This time when she tugged on her hand, Leonidas let her go. And it didn't make anything better. He regarded her with that dark stare of his that she was sure could see all the things she wanted to hide. All those feelings she didn't want to name. "But do not imagine for even one second that I will let you wander off with my child. Do not fool yourself into some fantasy where that could ever happen, prison or no prison. It won't."

"You can't keep me here." Her voice didn't even sound like hers. Susannah supposed she sounded the way she felt—frozen straight through.

Or at least that's what she thought she felt. The longer she spent around this man, the less she seemed to know. Because there was a perverse part of her that almost liked the fact that he wasn't letting her swan off, out of his life. The way everyone else in her life had if she'd proved less useful than they'd imagined she'd be.

"I can," he said quietly.

"You'll have to spend your every waking hour trying to keep me locked up if you want me to stay here," she warned him. "Is that really what you want?"

"I think you'll find that I won't need to expend any energy at all," Leonidas told her. Almost happily, Susannah thought, which she knew damned her even before he went on. "The geography takes care of that. It is an island, after all, in an unforgiving sea." He shrugged, clearly amusing himself. "All I have to do is wait."

CHAPTER TEN

Susannah didn't speak to him for a week.

In that time, she explored every inch of the island. She had access to one of the vehicles parked in the garage if she wanted, but it wasn't as if there was anything to do but drive back and forth along the same dirt road that led from one end of the island to the other, about a fifteen-mile round-trip. There was a dock or two, but they were clearly for swimmers when the weather was fine. No boats were moored at them, or even pulled up on the beaches.

Nothing that could make it across the brooding Ionian Sea, anyway, even if Susannah had been a sailor.

There were olive trees everywhere, growing too wild to be considered a grove. There were beaches, more rock than sand. It was a sturdy island, with no village to speak of and only a few homes clustered together around one of the coves. What few people lived on the island worked in the big house that sprawled over the top of the highest point of the island. It rambled this way and that, a jumble of open atriums and windows that let the sea in and then flirted with the nearest cliff.

She might have loved it, wild and raw something far more intense than the usual whitewashed Greek scenes that cluttered up the postcards, if she hadn't wanted to escape so badly.

"You cannot keep this up forever," Leonidas said a week into her prison sentence.

She'd wandered into the villa's surprisingly well-stocked library without realizing he was within. He usually worked in the office that was tucked away on the far side of the house, which meant she'd gotten used to avoiding him easily when she was inside.

Susannah spent her days driving aimlessly around the island as if she expected a magical bridge to the mainland to appear at any moment. She sunned herself on the rocks if the weather was fine, though it was always too chilly for swimming. Or she took quiet walks among the olive trees, trying to keep her head clear. When she felt sufficiently walked out, she usually moved inside and rummaged around the books that were packed onto the library's shelves, smelling faintly of age and water.

If she hadn't been trapped here, this might have been the most relaxing holiday she'd ever had.

Today she'd gone straight for the huge stack of German novels that had caught her eye yesterday. And she cursed herself for not looking around before she'd wandered into his vicinity.

Leonidas was sprawled back in one of the deep, comfortable chairs, his feet propped up on the table before him and a cup of coffee at his elbow. He had a laptop open on the wide arm of the chair, but he wasn't looking at the screen. He was studying Susannah instead, with an amused, indulgent look in his eyes that drove her mad.

"Why would I speak to you?" she asked, making no particular attempt to keep the challenge from her voice. Or the dislike. "What can you imagine I could possibly have to say to the prison warden?"

Leonidas shrugged. "I told you before that you can

be as stubborn as you like, Susannah. It will make no difference."

"I know you think you can wait me out," she seethed at him. "But you have no idea who you're dealing with. You never actually met the Widow Betancur."

He laughed at that, raking a hand through his dark hair and reminding her, against her will, how much she'd liked sifting her fingers through it herself.

"I'm not afraid of my own widow, little one."

And she didn't know why the way he said that, his gaze trained on her though he didn't rise from that chair, should have echoed in her like a promise.

"You should be," she told him coldly, snatching up her book and heading for the door again—and faster than she'd come in. "You will be."

But the truth was, she thought that evening as she readied herself for another one of the long, dangerous nights she tried so hard not to think about during the day, she was very much afraid that he could indeed wait her out. That he was already halfway there.

Because Leonidas was relentless.

He didn't argue with her. If he saw her throughout the day, he rarely said anything. Maddeningly, he would most often offer her a slight smile, nothing more, and leave her to it while he carried on running the Betancur Corporation remotely. The staff served food in the villa only at specific times, so there was no avoiding him when she wanted to eat, but if she didn't speak to him he did nothing about it. He only smiled and ate, as if he enjoyed his own company immensely.

More, as if he already knew how this would end.

Every night, Susannah readied herself for bed and resolutely climbed into the four-poster in the guest suite she'd tried to claim as her own. And every night she would fight to stay awake, but she never managed it. She fell asleep, and sometimes dreamed of being lifted into a pair of strong arms. Or being carried through the villa with only the moon peeking down into the open atriums to light the way. But the dreams were never enough to wake her.

And every morning she woke up in Leonidas's bed, because they weren't dreams at all.

Not just in the same bed, another massive king bed like the one she'd never slept in back in Rome, but curled around him as if she couldn't get enough of him. As if she wanted to be a part of him.

It didn't matter what she told herself the night before. It didn't matter what promises she made. Every morning it was the same. She woke up feeling rested, warm and safe, and only gradually became aware that she was sprawled over him. Or curled on her side, with him wound tight around her, holding her to him with one heavy arm.

And every morning she fled as soon as she woke. And he let her go, his arrogant laughter following her as she went.

It was an insidious kind of warfare, and he was far too good at it.

Tonight, Susannah sat on the edge of the bed in her room she kept trying to sleep in, but she was running out of steam. More to the point, she was growing tired of her own defiance.

It did nothing to Leonidas if she ignored him, or tried. He didn't care if she stormed off or if she snapped at him. He was like a mountain, unyielding and impassable, and she'd been battering herself against him for much too long now.

Meanwhile, all he did was smile and go about his business, and he got what he wanted anyway. What was the point?

She moved over to the French doors that led out to her terrace, and threw them open. It was too dark tonight to see the sea, but she could hear it, crashing against the rocky shore down below. She'd always loved the waves. She'd always admired the inexorable push of the sea, over and over, tide after tide. But tonight she found that she felt significantly more sympathetic to the shoreline. Battered over and over by a ruthless, unyielding force, whether it wanted it or not.

She let the night air slap at her, chilling her from the stones beneath her bare feet all the way up to where her hair moved against her shoulders. She hugged her arms around her middle, noticing with a touch of awe and wonder the changes that were happening to her every day. She was a little thicker. A little bit different all over despite her best efforts to pretend none of this was happening.

As if her body had picked sides a long time ago.

She turned back toward the bedroom and stopped, the buttery light from within gripping her. She could see the rest of the villa, built to look almost haphazard as it claimed the top of the cliff with bright windows glowing against the dark night, too cloudy for stars. But she didn't need light to see the island any longer.

It was one more thing that was becoming a part of her no matter how little she wanted it. She remembered when that had happened four years ago. The first day she'd walked into the Betancur Corporation offices had been intense. Awful, even. She'd been a nineteen-year-old with nothing going for her but her ability to hold the gazes of angry men and smile politely until they finished ranting. But every day she'd gone back had been easier. Or she'd gotten used to it.

And one day she'd found herself sitting in the office she'd claimed, going through some files, and it had struck her that it was all…normal. She'd made the impossible *normal*.

Leonidas was right, she realized then, pulling in a breath of the cold night air. He was going to win. Because she could apparently adapt to anything, and would without thinking about it.

That night she fell asleep almost before her head hit the pillow the way she always did. But when she felt his strong arms around her, lifting her up and carrying her through the dark halls, she forced herself to wake up. To become more alert with every step. And when he laid her down in his wide bed, she waited for him to sprawl out beside her, and then she propped herself up on one hand and gazed at him.

"Sleeping Beauty is awake at last," Leonidas said in a low voice. "That's when the trouble starts, I'm told. Historically."

There were no lights on in his bedroom, only the last of his fire glowing in the grate. Susannah was grateful for the reprieve. In the almost total dark, there was no need to worry about what expression she might have been wearing. There was no need to hide if he couldn't really see her. So she forgot about her own masks for a moment, and let herself marvel at the lack of his.

In the dark, he seemed approachable. Not soft—he could never be soft—but all those bold lines and harsh edges seemed muted, somehow. And though she knew his scars were there, stamped into his rangy body, she couldn't see them either.

It was as if the shadows made them both new.

"If you didn't want trouble," she whispered, "you should have let me go."

"At some point, Susannah, you will have to face the fact you didn't really want to leave," Leonidas said, his voice barely more than a thread in the dark. "Or why go to such lengths to find me at all?"

"I thought it was what you would have wanted," she said before she thought better of it.

But she knew the truth then. When her words were lying there between them, so obvious once spoken. It was what *she* would have wanted if her plane had gone down. She would have wanted someone to find out what had happened, and when the answers didn't make sense, to dig deeper. She would have wanted someone to send investigators. She would have wanted someone who refused to give up until the truth came out.

She would have wanted someone to care. Just once.

"I always get what I want," Leonidas said, his voice as dark as the room around them. "Sooner or later."

And Susannah had spent entirely too much time working this through in her head. On all those drives, walks through the olive trees, and afternoons on the rocks with a wool sweater wrapped tight around her to ward off the cold while the sea spray made her face damp. Or when she'd sat out by the heated pool near the house and had pretended the sun might warm her more than it did, there where she could smell flowers and dirt and the salted crispness of the bright Greek air. She'd been so furious, and she hadn't wanted to see what was on the other side of it, because fury felt like a destination all on its own.

The island slowed her down. It made her think even when she didn't want that. It had defeated her even if he couldn't.

But it had also given her a new resolve.

"Always?" She reached across the wedge of space between them and traced that hard, unsmiling mouth of his with her fingers. "I know that's what you tell yourself. But I think we both know you don't always get what you want. I saw the compound, remember. I know how you lived there. And how quick you were to leave a place they worshipped you outright."

"Eventually," Leonidas said, but there was an edge to his voice then. He stilled her hand, drawing it away from his mouth. And he didn't let go. "I always get what I want, eventually."

And this was what had happened to her four years ago. First the shock, and a kind of grief that the life she'd been training for all those years was no more. She'd let it take her down. But then she got up again, and when she did she'd taken action.

It was what Susannah always did.

So she would do it here, too. And if there was a part of her that mourned the man who'd held her in his arms while they'd danced at that gala, well. That had only been a fantasy, after all. A fairy tale. This was gritty. This was a baby she hadn't planned for and a complicated life with a husband whose name she knew better than she knew him.

She'd had a fairy-tale wedding with a man who'd scoffed at all her silly dreams and crushed them while he did. She'd lived through widowhood, pretending to mourn a man she'd hardly known and a love that had never existed, except possibly in her head. She'd hunted down a stranger who hadn't known her when he'd seen her, and she'd won back the husband she barely knew with a kiss. And her virginity. Then she'd spent seven short weeks pretending to be a devoted wife and business partner while sleeping by herself in a lonely guest room.

But she had never done *this*.

Susannah had never been his wife in act and deed as well as word. And she decided that she was tired of punishing herself. She was tired of hiding. Most of all, she was tired of fighting wars she wasn't sure she even wanted to win.

If he could do exactly as he pleased, kidnap her and confine her on this island simply to make a point, there was no reason she couldn't do what she liked, as well.

And it was time to stop pretending that she didn't like him, because she did. He was a flame and she was a desperate sort of moth, but there was no need to batter herself to pieces when she could choose instead to simply land. And burn as she wished.

"Eventually will be a long time coming," she told him softly. She moved closer to him then, tangling her legs with his. "If at all."

He let out a laugh that was more warning than anything else.

"I'll have you eating out of my hand sooner than you can possibly imagine," he promised her, perhaps a little roughly. "It's inevitable, little one. You might as well fold now."

"You can't have me," she told him then, her voice as simple as it was stark. A part of the shadows, somehow. "That's how this works, don't you understand? When you keep something against its will, you can hold on to it, but it's never yours."

Then she leaned in close, because it was what she wanted. Because she could do as she liked, surely, since he always did. Because she was much too fascinated with him and her heart went silly whenever he was near, and she'd resolved to embrace that.

To burn of her own volition on that lethal flame of his, again and again, until he tired of her and this game and all the rest of it. The way she knew he would.

She got even closer, pressing herself against him in the dark, and sealed her doom the only way she knew.

With a kiss.

CHAPTER ELEVEN

"I TRUST YOUR cage grows more comfortable by the day," Leonidas said, his voice hardly more than a growl, shoving his mobile into his pocket as he strode out to the pool in the atrium. "You almost look as if you're enjoying it."

Susannah looked up from where she sat in the bright sunlight, wrapped up against the cool breeze in an oversize sort of shawl that looked as if it could double as a duvet, thrown over the flowing, casual dress she wore. Her blond hair was twisted back into the makeshift chignon she preferred, looking messy and yet somehow as impossibly chic as she always did, as if it was effortless.

He thought he couldn't want her more. Every day he thought this. Every night, he was sure.

And then she did something unforgivable, like sit out in the sun on a cold winter's day to read a book with her sunglasses on and her bare feet exposed. What defense was he expected to have against such a thing?

"Comfortable or not, a cage remains a cage," she replied, almost merrily. The same way she always did. As if it was all a joke when he knew very well it was not.

None of this was any kind of laughing matter at all.

The anger that had beat at him all through that last call he'd hated making didn't disappear, but the sight of his wife somehow…altered it. She reminded him that no matter who had acted against him or why, *she* had stepped in and saved him.

He reminded himself that she was what mattered to him. Susannah and the child she carried. This, right here, was all that mattered.

And someday he would find a way to bring back that dancing sort of light he'd glimpsed in her only briefly, now and then. Usually while they were naked. He would make her happy, damn it. Leonidas was always successful at what he did. He would succeed here, too.

Susannah wanted to keep a part of herself separate, and he couldn't abide that—but he could wait. He told himself that he could wait her out, wear her down…and no matter that he was finding that harder and harder to tolerate.

Everything had changed.

She'd kissed him that night and altered the world again, and for the most part, he liked it.

He liked an end to the charade of separate beds. She stopped the pointless theater of marching off to the guest suite every night and took her place in his rooms instead. She stopped giving him her icy silent treatment and simmering anger at every turn.

And she gave herself to him with a sweet fire and wild greediness that might have humbled him, had he let it.

"I am your husband and you are my wife," he had said that first night, after he'd reduced her to a boneless heap. He'd carried her into his expansive bathroom to set her in the oversize tub set in an arched window to look out over the quietly seething Ionian Sea. "And I have no intention of being the sort of husband who creeps down the cold hallway when he wishes the company of his wife. I do not believe in twin beds. I don't believe in anything that gets in the way of you and me, not even a damned nightgown." He'd watched her as she'd settled in the steaming water. "I trust we are finally in accord on this."

"I don't think you know what you believe about marriage," Susannah had retorted, though she'd been sleepy and satiated and had watched him as if she might like to take another bite out of him. He'd climbed into the tub with her, then had shifted to pull her against him, her back to his chest. "Since you've only been married to one person in your lifetime and I remember more about those years than you do."

"I intend for both of us to remember this part of our marriage," he'd murmured into her ear, raking his teeth over the tender lobe to make her shudder. "Vividly."

And there had been no arguing after that. He didn't bother with that anymore. He picked her up when things got a bit fractious, then expressed his feelings about whatever minor disagreement it might have been all over her delectable body. He showed her exactly how little space he wanted between them. Over and over again.

She had spent seven weeks filling in the gaps in his memory. Now, having met her parents, he took it upon himself to fill in any gaps she might have had in her own life thanks to the things they'd obviously not given her. Such as nurturing of any kind. He tended to her headaches. He made sure she ate. He took care of her.

He'd never taken care of anyone in his life, not directly, but he took care of Susannah.

And he taught her that she'd been very silly indeed to imagine that one stolen afternoon in a faraway compound meant that she had the slightest idea what sex was. Because there were so very many ways to tear each other apart.

And Leonidas happened to know every last one of them.

She learned how to take him in her mouth and how to

make him groan. She learned how to crawl on top of him where he sat, and settle herself astride him, so she could take control and rock them both into bliss.

Sometimes when they were lying an exhausted heap, barely able to breathe, he would slide one of his hands over her belly and hold it there. And allow himself to imagine things he'd never imagined he'd want. Much less this badly.

"You haven't had one of your headaches in some time," he said today, coming over to stand at the foot of the lounger where she sat. She set her book aside and peered up at him. Then she swept her sunglasses back and anchored them on the top of her head, narrowing her eyes at him in a way he couldn't say he liked.

"What's the matter?"

Leonidas didn't want to answer that. Or acknowledge that she could see into him like that.

"Perhaps the worst of them is over," he said instead.

Susannah stood, pulling her shawl around her and tilting her head slightly to one side as she regarded him.

"You're not all right," she said softly. "Are you?"

"What can that possibly matter to you?" It was ripped from him. Too raw. Too revealing. And yet he couldn't seem to stop. "As you keep telling me—as you go to great lengths to make sure I never forget—I can never have you. What does it matter whether I am all right, whatever the hell that means, or not?"

Susannah didn't flare back at him. She didn't do anything at all for a moment but stand there and study him, and only when he thought he might come out of his skin did she move. Even then, it was only a small thing. She reached over and put her hand to his jaw, then held it there.

Small. Meaningless, he wanted to say.

But it felt like the world.

"You have this, Leonidas," she said quietly. "And maybe this is enough."

It shouldn't have felt like a storm. It shouldn't have rocked him the way it did, deep and wild, razing what had been there and leaving nothing he recognized in its wake.

But he would think about that later. He would piece himself back together later.

He would try to rebuild all the things she'd broken then.

If he could.

Here, now, he took what she was offering.

"It's my mother," he said gruffly, and tried to hold on to his anger. Because he was very much afraid that what was beneath it was the pointless hurt and grief of the child in him who still, all these years and bitter lessons later, wanted Apollonia to be his *mother*. Just once. "She's the one who had the plane tampered with. She's responsible for the crash."

Susannah's brow creased, but she didn't say anything. She only waited, dropping her hand to her side to hold her shawl to her and keeping her gaze trained to his. And somehow that made it easier for him to keep speaking.

"I never stopped investigating the plane crash. Your investigators led you to me, but I wanted more. Because, of course, if someone tried to assassinate me once it stood to reason that they would do it again."

"What's frustrating is that there are so many possibilities," she murmured. "And so many lead in circles."

And Leonidas felt his lips thin. "Indeed. And it warms the heart, I must tell you, to realize the extent to which I am hated by my own blood."

Susannah's gaze sharpened on his, and her blue eyes were serious. Intent.

"They don't hate you, Leonidas," she said fiercely. "They don't know you. They are tiny, grasping people who long for things to be handed to them, that's all. They are victims forever in search of someone to blame. They look around a world in which they have everything and see nothing but their own misfortune." She shook her head. "Being hated by these people says nothing about you, except perhaps you are a far better person than they could ever dream of being."

"Careful, little one," he said roughly. "You begin to sound as if I might have you after all."

She looked away, and he felt that like a punch to the gut, even when she smiled. Was it his imagination or his guilt that made him think that soft curve of her mouth was bittersweet? And why should he feel that like it was the worst of the blows he'd taken today?

"The truth is that your mother is the worst of them," she said, and he didn't want to do this. He didn't want to talk about his mother. He wanted to trace the curve of Susannah's mouth until her smile felt real. He wanted to wash himself clean of all of this. His name, his blood. "I mean no disrespect."

Leonidas let out a short laugh with precious little humor in it.

"I doubt you could disrespect my mother if you tried." And the air was so clear here, bordering on cold but not quite getting there. The island was quiet. The riot was in him, he knew that. "And still, I didn't think it could be her. Not her. I didn't want it to be her."

Susannah whispered something that sounded like his name. Leonidas forged on.

"My cousins made sense to me as suspects. All they do is congregate and plot. Why not the biggest plot of all?" He shook his head. "But not one of them would actually want the things they claim have been taken from them. They don't want to be in charge. That's responsibility, and they would hate it. They just want money. Money and stature and power. They want the appearance of power, but certainly not the work that goes with it. My mother, on the other hand…"

Susannah's eyes were wide. "Apollonia doesn't like to work. She likes to talk about working and claim she's exhausted from some other sort of work that can never be performed when anyone can see it…" He held her gaze until she trailed off and blew out a breath. "Are you certain?"

"The investigators reached this conclusion some weeks ago," he said bitterly. More bitterly than he should have, because what had he imagined? That a woman like his mother could change? She'd always been selfish. He'd always known that. The only surprise was *how much.* "But I refused to accept it."

"Do they have proof?"

"They didn't," Leonidas said. His jaw clenched tight. "Now they do."

And for moment, they only stared at each other, out in the bright Greek sun, held tight in the grip of that horrible truth.

Susannah didn't apologize for his mother. She didn't express her sorrow for what could not have been, in the end, that much of a surprise to her. Just as it hadn't been for him. Loath as he was to admit that, even now.

It wasn't a surprise. But that didn't make it hurt less.

She didn't apologize, but she didn't look away, either. And he thought that this, right here, was why he was never going to get over this woman. This was how she'd wedged herself so deep inside him that he could no longer breathe without feeling her there, changing everything with reckless abandon whether he wanted it or not. Because she simply stood there with him. As if she was prepared to stand there all night, holding a vigil for the mother he'd never had.

"And now I must face the fact that she is far worse that I could have imagined," Leonidas said, forcing the words out because he was sure, somehow, that it would be better that way. He couldn't have said why. "It is not bad enough that she has never displayed the faintest hint of maternal instinct. It doesn't matter that when she could have protected me from my father's rages, she only laughed and picked herself another lover. It all follows the same through line, really. There is not one single thing surprising about this news." He shook his head slightly, almost as if he was dizzy, when he was not. Not quite. "And yet."

"And yet," Susannah echoed. This time when she reached over, she placed her palm in that hollow between his pectoral muscles and held it there, pressure and the hint of warmth. That was all. And he felt it everywhere. "What will you do?"

"What can I do?" He didn't grimace. He felt as if he'd turned to stone, except it wasn't the stone he knew from before. It was as if he'd lost the ability to harden himself, armor himself, the way he wanted. And he knew it was the fault of the woman who stood there, keeping her hand on him as if her palm was a talisman crafted especially for him. He knew it was her fault that he cared about anything. Because losing the things that had made him harder in that other way felt worth it, he realized, if this was what he gained.

If Susannah was what he had, he couldn't care too much about the things he'd lost.

Something dawned in him then, deep and certain, that he didn't want to know. And not only because he'd imagined himself incapable of such things. But because, as the phone call he just had had proved beyond a reasonable doubt, he didn't know a single thing about love. He never had and he doubted he ever would.

"I cannot haul her before any authority," he pointed out, fighting to sound dispassionate. Analytical. "I don't want that sort of attention on the plane crash, much less what happened afterward. Even if I wanted her brought to justice, it would be nothing but a fleeting pleasure. And on the other side of it, more instability for the company. More questions, more worries. Why permit her to cause any more problems than she already has?" He tried to hold his temper at bay. "She took four years of my life. Why should she get another moment?"

Susannah's eyes flashed. "I admire your practicality. But I want her to pay even if you don't."

And he thought he would remember that forever. Her hand on his chest and her blue eyes on fire while she defended him. He'd never felt anything like the light that fell through him then. He'd never have believed it existed.

"Making her pay is simple," he said, his voice a little gruffer than he'd intended. "She only cares about one thing. Remove it and she'll act as if she'd been sent to a Siberian work camp." He shrugged. "I will simply cut her off. No money, no access. Nothing. She should be humbled within the week."

"Apollonia?" Susannah shook her head, and her gaze was hard. "I don't believe she can be humbled."

Leonidas stepped away then, before he couldn't. Before he took his wife into his arms and said the things he knew he couldn't say. There was no place for that here. That wasn't who he was, that certainly wasn't what he did, and he couldn't allow that kind of weakness. Not now, when all he had in this world was betrayal on one side and a captive spouse on the other.

And a baby who would come into this world and know only a father who had imprisoned his mother on an island.

He had never wanted to be his own father, a brute dressed in sleek clothes to hide himself in plain sight as he went on his many rampages. And yet it had never occurred to Leonidas that when all was said and done, he was more like his mother than he wanted to admit.

What he was doing to Susannah proved it.

His father would simply have beaten a defiant woman. This sort of game was in Apollonia's wheelhouse. Manipulation and treachery were her life's blood.

How had he failed to see it?

"I hope you let her know that you know what she did," Susannah said, frowning. "That she hasn't gotten away with it. That there will be consequences, whether she likes it or not."

But Leonidas was looking past her then. He looked out toward the rocks and the sea beyond. The wild Greek sea that stirred something deep in his bones. It always had. He liked the rawness of these islands, unmanicured and untamed. They spoke to something deep inside him, and he understood in a sudden flash that Susannah did the same.

She had warned him. He couldn't pretend she hadn't. He could keep her, but he would never have her. A cage was a cage was a cage.

And he recognized that now only because he'd broken out of his. At long last, he'd finally seen his mother for who she was. Not an amusing socialite, flitting here and there as the whim took her. But the woman who had ordered the murder of her own son. On a whim.

She hadn't even denied it.

"You were being so tiresome about my allowance,"

she'd told him when he'd called, her voice shifting over into that nasally whine she used when she thought she could plead her way out of a scrape. She didn't seem to understand that this was no "scrape." That Leonidas was done. "What did you expect me to do?"

Some part of him—most of him—might have preferred to stay imprisoned in the last gasp of the lie he'd built a long time ago to explain Apollonia's behavior, because it was easier. It was what he knew.

But this was better. It had to be. There had to be a point to this sort of bleak freedom, he was sure of it, even if he couldn't see it now.

"I have never loved anything in my life," he told Susannah, out where the air was fresh and the sky was blue and none of the stink of his family could taint her. "I doubt I am capable, and now I know why."

"You are not responsible for the things that woman did," Susannah retorted, instantly drawing herself up as if she intended to go to war with Apollonia there and then. "Not a single thing."

"I fear it is in my blood," he confessed. "It's not only the Betancurs. It's every single part of me. Venal. Malicious. Scheming and vile. Those are my bones, Susannah. My flesh. My blood."

"Leonidas," she began.

But he couldn't stop.

"I have been a god and I have been a king, of sorts. I have acted the lover, but I have never felt a thing. I can run a company and I can lead a cult, but I have no idea how to raise a child. How to be a father." He shook his head, not sure if he was dazed or this was what it felt like to finally have perfect, devastating clarity. "I'm not entirely certain I know how to be a man."

"Stop it." Her voice was ragged. A scrape of sound,

and then she was moving toward him again. He hadn't realized he'd stepped away. "Just stop this."

Susannah didn't wait for him to argue as she must surely have known he would. She crossed the distance between them, dropping her shawl at her feet and not bothering to look back. She leaned in and wrapped her arms around him at his waist, then tilted her head back to scowl up at him.

"I want you to stop talking," she told him.

And he heard it then. All the power and authority of the Widow Betancur herself. A woman who had every expectation of being obeyed.

But he had never been anybody's underling. "And if I refuse?"

She studied him for a moment, then she stepped back again. Keeping her gaze fixed to his, she reached down to gather up the loose, flowing dress she wore. It was long and deceptively shapeless while managing to emphasize the sweetness of her figure, and she simply watched him with that challenging glint in her eyes while she pulled it up and off. And then she stood before him in nothing at all save a pair of panties.

She was already so ripe. Her breasts had grown heavier in these weeks, round and sweet. Her belly was beginning to curve outward, reminding him of the baby she carried even now. And the fact that she was his.

No matter who he was, no matter what he'd done, she was still his.

"You can refuse me if you like," she said, all womanly challenge. "Or you can take me. I know what I would choose."

And Leonidas might not be much of a man, but he still was one. And when it came to this woman he had no defenses left.

He hauled her to him, crashing his mouth to hers, and taking her with all the wild ferocity that stampeded through him.

Raw. Hot.

Perfect.

She was fire, she was need, and he was nothing but greedy where Susannah was concerned.

He couldn't get close enough. He couldn't taste her enough, touch her enough.

Leonidas took her down onto the lounger where she'd been sitting, and let himself go. It was a frenzy, it was a dance. It was madness and it was beautiful.

And she was his.

Right here, right now, she was his.

And as he thrust into her, for what he understood even then was the last time, he let himself pretend that he deserved her.

Just this once. Just for this moment. Just to see what that felt like.

He made her fall apart. He made her scream his name. He made her beg, and he knew he'd never hear anything so beautiful again as the sound of her voice when she pleaded with him for more. And then more still.

When he finally let himself go, Leonidas toppled over the side of the world, and he carried Susannah with him one final time.

And later that afternoon, while the bright Greek sun was still shining and the air was still cold, he put her on that helicopter and he sent her away.

CHAPTER TWELVE

IT WAS NOT a good week.

Leonidas spent most of it in his office, because he couldn't bear to be in that damned penthouse, filled as it was with the ghost of the wife he'd sent away.

For her own good, he snarled at himself every time he thought about it—but he never seemed to ease his own agitation. He was beginning to imagine it couldn't be done.

It had amazed him at first that a space he'd lived in with her for only seven short weeks should feel haunted by her, particularly when she'd gone to such lengths to avoid him. But Susannah was everywhere, filling up the soaring levels of the penthouse as if she was some kind of aria he couldn't bring himself to shut off or even turn down. He didn't understand how she could manage to inhabit a place when she wasn't even in it, especially when he hadn't spent the kind of time with her in the penthouse as he had on the island.

They had never shared his bed in Rome. He'd never touched her the way he wanted to here.

And still he lay awake as if, were he only to concentrate enough, he might catch her scent on pillows she'd never touched.

He'd spent his first night back from the island in the

penthouse, restless and sleepless, and he'd avoided it ever
since. It was easy enough to spend twenty-four hours a
day in the office, because there was always a Betancur
property somewhere in the world that required attention.
Leonidas had poured himself into his work the way he'd
done so single-mindedly before his wedding. And he
had his staff pack up all the things Susannah had left in
the guest room she'd stayed in while she was his widow,
and he'd forwarded them on to her new home across the
world from him.

Just as he'd wanted, he reminded himself daily.

He had not asked his staff in the Betancur Corporation's Sydney office to report in on how she was settling
into life in Australia. She wasn't to be tailed and watched,
or have any security above and beyond what was necessary for a woman in her position. He had vowed to himself that this would be a clean break.

"You wondered why you couldn't have me," she'd
said back on the island when he'd informed her that they
needed to separate. That this was over, this thing between
them. That their marriage worked, clearly, only when
they were apart. Her voice had been thick with emotions
he didn't want to recognize or even acknowledge, and
she'd swayed slightly as she stood, as if he'd dealt her a
body blow. "This is why. There was never any question
that you would leave. It was only a question of how and
when." Her gaze had nearly unmanned him. "I expected
tawdry affairs I'd be forced to read about in the papers, if
I'm honest. That's usually how the people we know send
these messages, isn't it?"

He'd wanted to answer her in a way she could not possibly mistake for the usual vicious games of the kinds of
people who glittered in Europe's most prestigious ball-

rooms and viewed the tabloids as their own version of social media. But he'd kept himself under control. Barely.

"It is a big world," he'd said coldly. Hoping he could turn them both to ice so neither one of them could feel a thing. "All I ask is that you choose a place to live that is within reach of one of the Betancur Corporation offices."

"So you can monitor my every move, I presume?"

"So that if the child or you are ever in need, help can arrive swiftly," he'd replied. Through his teeth. "I am trying very hard not to be the monster here, Susannah."

But he'd felt like one. His scars had felt like convictions, pressed into his flesh for all the world to see.

"I want to live in Sydney," she'd told him, her voice a rough sort of whisper. "I not only wish to be on a different continent from you, but across the international dateline whenever possible. So we won't even have a day in common."

He hadn't responded to that the way he'd have liked to, either. Instead, he'd sent her on her way and had a plane meet her in Athens for the flight to Sydney. She'd been as far out of his life as it was possible for her to get without him retreating back to the compound in Idaho.

And now he had exactly what he'd wanted.

Leonidas reminded himself of that as he stood at the window in his immaculately furnished, quietly intimidating office, where he could look out over Rome and feel like a king instead of a monstrous wild man who'd thrived in the wilderness for years. Centuries of rich, powerful men had stood in positions much like this one, looking out at the same view. Rome had been breeding emperors since the dawn of time, and what was he but one more?

An empty king on an empty throne, he thought with

more than a little bitterness today. But that was what he'd asked for.

He hadn't been lying when he'd told her that he always, always got what he wanted. It was only that it had never really occurred to him what a pyrrhic victory that could be, and the truth was, the world without her felt entirely too much like bitter ash.

It will fade in time, he told himself now. *Everything does.*

Leonidas realized he wasn't paying attention to the conference call he was meant to be on, the way he hadn't been paying attention to much these last days. His memory was as good as it was going to get, he'd decided. Too good, since all it seemed to want to do was play out every moment of every interaction he'd had with Susannah since she'd found him in the compound. On an endless, vivid loop.

"I want this settled," he interjected into the heated conversation between several vice presidents scattered around the world, because he had no patience left. Not when he had to spend his every waking moment *not* flying to Sydney. The call went quiet. "Quickly."

Someone cleared his throat. He heard the shuffle of papers, echoing down the line, and what sounded like traffic noise in some or other distant city.

"Of course," the Philippines vice president began carefully. "But it will take a little more time to really—"

"I want the matter dealt with," Leonidas said again, more brusquely this time. "I don't want any more discussion. If you cannot do it, I will find someone who can."

He ended the call with perhaps a bit more force than necessary, and when he turned around to look out through the glass at the rest of the executive floor, he froze.

He thought he was hallucinating.

On some level, he welcomed it.

Leonidas was already starting to think of his time in Idaho as an extended hallucination. It already seemed more like a dream than a reality he'd known for four years—the only reality he'd known at all while he was in it. He'd decided that perhaps he needed to simply accept that he was the sort of person for whom reality was malleable. So it made perfect sense that he should see Susannah marching down the central corridor of the executive floor of the Betancourt Corporation dressed in her trademark inky black.

His widow had been resurrected. And was headed straight for him.

And Leonidas told himself that what he felt as he watched her stride toward him in impossible shoes with an unreadable expression on her lovely face was fury.

The way his pulse rocketed. The way his heart kicked at his ribs. That pounding thing in his head, his gut, his sex.

Fury. He told himself it had to be fury that she had dared contradict his wishes and show up here.

Because he wouldn't let it be anything else.

Susannah nodded imperiously at his secretary, but didn't slow. She swept past the outer desk, then pushed her way into his office as if he'd issued her an engraved invitation to do just that.

And then she was here. Right here. And it had been only a week since he'd last seen her on that island. A week since he'd said the words he knew would hurt her, and so they had. A week since she'd stood before him, her mouth moving in a way that told him she was working her hardest to keep her tears inside. She hadn't let one fall. Not a single one.

He'd felt that like a loss, too.

But today he told himself that his response to her was fury, because it should have been. He didn't move as she kept coming, bearing down upon him where he stood as if she was considering toppling him straight backward, through the window and down to the streets of Rome far below.

A part of him thought he might let her try.

Before she made it all the way to the window, she veered to the left and to his desk. Her blue eyes met his and he felt himself tense, because the look that she was giving him was not exactly friendly. She held his gaze and stabbed her finger on the button that made the glass in all his windows that faced the office go smoky. Giving them exactly the sort of privacy he didn't want.

"You are supposed to be in Sydney." His voice sounded like steel. Harsh and very nearly rude. "Sydney, Australia, to be precise, which is a good, long way from here. A good, long, *deliberate* way from here."

"As you can see, I am not in Sydney."

This woman made him…thirsty. His eyes drank her in and he wanted to follow his gaze with his hands. The deep black dress she wore fit her beautifully, and called attention to that tiniest of swells at her belly. So tiny that he very much doubted anyone but him would know what it signified.

But he knew. Oh, did he know.

And this time, when a new wave of fury broke over him, he knew it wasn't masking anything. He knew it was real.

"Do you think I sent you away for my health?" he demanded.

She let out a noise. "I don't care why you sent me away, Leonidas."

And he had never heard that tone from her before. Not

at all cool. Not remotely serene. Not calm in any way whatsoever. It was so surprising—so very unlike the Susannah he knew—that it almost knocked him back a step.

He frowned at her, and realized abruptly that while she looked as sleek and controlled as she usually did, it was only the surface. The effortless chignon to tame her blond hair, the stunning dress that called attention to its asymmetrical hem and its dark color, and the sort of shoes that most women couldn't stand in upright, much less use to stride across office buildings. All of that was typical Susannah.

But her blue eyes were a storm.

And this close to her, hidden away behind smoky glass in his office, he could see that she was trembling besides.

"Susannah—"

"I don't care," she said again, more sharply this time. She took a step toward him, then stopped as if she wasn't sure she could control herself. "For once, I just don't care about you or your health or your feelings or anything else. My God, Leonidas, do you realize that my entire life has been about you?"

"Hardly." Leonidas scoffed at her. At that notion. At the heavy thing that moved in him, entirely too much like shame. "I doubt you could have picked me out of a lineup before our marriage."

And the laugh she let out then was hollow. Not much like laughter at all. It set his teeth on edge.

"You're thinking of yourself, not me," she retorted. "A rather common occurrence, I think." When he only blinked at her, astonished, she pushed on. "I was a teenager. My parents told me that I was promised to you long before we got married, and believe me, I knew exactly who I was saving myself for. You were Leonidas Betancur. I could have found you blindfolded and in the dark."

He told himself there was no reason that, too, should settle on him like an indictment.

"I am not responsible for the fantasy life of a schoolgirl," he gritted out at her.

Susannah nodded, as if he'd confirmed her expectations. Low ones, at that. "On our wedding day, you took great pains to tell me how little the things that mattered to me matter to you. Like my schoolgirl fantasies that you might treat me the way any man treats his bride. And I accepted that, because my mother told me it was my place to do so."

Leonidas couldn't tell if he was affronted or abashed by that. He didn't much care for either. He decided he preferred affront, and stood taller.

"You were nineteen years old and I was an extremely busy—"

"But then you died," she continued, and there was a shaking in her voice, but it didn't seem to bother her in the least. She advanced another step. "Has it ever crossed your mind how much easier it would have been for me to marry someone else after that?"

"It would make you a bigamist, but I sense that is of no matter in this remarkably slanted portrayal of our relationship."

"I'm not sure *relationship* is the word I'd choose to describe a distant engagement, a circus of a wedding during which you spoke only to your business associates, your death and resurrection, my unwise attempt to help you—"

"Susannah." His lips felt thin enough to cut glass. "I am still an extremely busy man, as you must surely be aware. This harangue could have been put into letter form and sent by post, surely. Why did you fly some sixteen thousand kilometers to do it in person?"

She studied him for a moment, and there was still

that fine trembling all over her. Her mouth. Her fingers. He could even see it in her legs. But she didn't appear to notice.

"Everyone was deeply invested in my remarriage, Leonidas. I was bullied and manipulated, pushed and prodded. No one took me seriously. No one wanted to take me at all, unless it was to the altar. But I persisted."

"Yes, and your persistence makes you a great hero, I am sure," Leonidas said drily. "Given that it made you perhaps the most powerful woman in the world. My heart bleeds for your sacrifice."

"I persisted because of you, you arrogant—" She cut herself off. He watched her pull in a breath, as if she needed it to steady herself, and then her blue eyes were hard on his again. "I persisted because of *you*. Because I had an idea of you in my head."

"Based on tabloid nonsense and too many fairy tales, I have no doubt."

"Because you danced with me at our wedding reception," she corrected him, her voice as quiet as it was firm. "You held me in your arms and you looked at me as if I was…everything. A woman. Your wife. Just for one moment, I believed I could be. That it would all work out."

Leonidas could say nothing then. He remembered that dance, and he didn't know if it was memory or longing that moved in him now. The urge to hold her again, to sweep her into his arms without having to pretend it had anything to do with dancing or weddings or galas, swept over him. It was like an itch, pushing him to the limit.

But Susannah was still coming toward him, that wildness in her blue eyes.

"I carried this company for four years," she told him matter-of-factly. "I made myself into an icon. The untouchable widow. A Betancur legend. And all the while, I looked for you."

"No one asked you to do this," he growled back at her. "You should have left me on that mountaintop. No one could possibly have blamed you. Hell, they would have celebrated in the streets."

"I looked for you and then I found you," she continued, as if she hadn't heard him say a word. "I took you out of there. I even sweetened the deal with the virginity I'd been holding on to for all these years. But like everything else, you didn't seem to realize that it was a gift."

"I beg your pardon." He stood as tall as he could without breaking something, and his voice was so scornful he was surprised it didn't leave marks. And he couldn't seem to stop it. "Have you come all this way to remind me that I owe you a thank-you note? I'll instruct my secretary to type one up as soon as possible. Is that all?"

Susannah shook her head at him, as if he'd disappointed her. Again. "You know your cousins. You can imagine the lengths they were willing to go to get control of me, and by extension the company."

The truth was, Leonidas did know. And he didn't want to know.

"I refused to drink out of an open glass that wasn't first tested by someone else for years," she told him. "Because I didn't want to wake up to find myself roofied and married to a random Betancur, then declared unfit and packed off to a mental institution before ten the next morning so I couldn't object. Do you think that was fun?"

"So that's a yes, then," he said after a moment, feeling more and more certain that if she didn't leave, and soon, he was going to do something he might truly regret. Like forget why he'd sent her away in the first place. "You do want a thank-you note."

But this time, Susannah closed the distance between them. And then she was standing there before him, within touching distance. She was still trembling, and it slowly dawned on Leonidas that that faint little tremor that shook all over her wasn't fear or emotion.

It was temper.

She was furious. At him.

"I wanted to leave when we brought you home from Idaho, but you begged me to stay," she reminded him.

"Begged?" He laughed. Or made himself laugh, more like. "Perhaps your memory has as many gaps as mine."

"The funny thing is that I knew better. I knew that nothing could come of it. That we would always end up in the same place." That storm in her eyes seemed to get wilder. More treacherous. "Right here."

He said nothing. He could only seem to stand there before her, undone in ways he refused to investigate because he didn't think he could be fixed. He didn't think he'd ever put himself back together—but he didn't want to think about that, either.

Because it doesn't matter, something in him asserted. *Nothing matters once she's gone.*

He told himself that life—frozen and haunted and consumed with the company—was better. It was much, much better than this.

"I'm pregnant, Leonidas," she said then, as if the very words hurt as she said them. "Don't you understand what that means?"

"Of course I understand," he bit out.

Then Susannah did something extraordinary. She punched him.

She balled up her hand into a fist and whacked it against his chest. Not enough to hurt, or move him backward even a little, but certainly enough to get his attention.

The way no one had ever dared do in all his life.

Leonidas stared down at her, at that fist she held there between them as if she planned to punch him again, and felt something roaring in him. Loud and long. Raw and demanding.

"I would suggest that you rethink whatever it is you think you're doing," he said. Very, very quietly. "And quickly."

"I am your wife," Susannah said, in very much the same tone. "And I'm the mother of your child. Whatever else happens, those two things remain."

Her fist seemed to tighten, as if she was contemplating hitting him again.

"I take it you have never heard of the divorce you asked for," he said, not exactly nicely. "Perhaps they didn't teach that in your strict little convent where you dreamed of wedding dances and were met with only cruel disappointment."

Susannah punched him again. Harder this time.

"You're a coward," she said, very distinctly.

And that roaring thing in him took over. It was as if everything rolled together and became the same searing bolt of light. Leonidas reached down and took her fist in his palm and then held it away from his chest as if it was a weapon. As if she could do him real harm, if he let her.

And he had no qualm whatsoever pulling her closer, reaching down to wrap one hand around her hip and haul her the extra distance toward him so he could keep her locked down.

"Say that again," he invited her, getting into her face so his lips were a mere breath from hers. "I dare you. And see what happens if you punch me again when you do."

But she had married him when she was a teenager and she'd stayed his widow for years when anyone else would have folded. Maybe it wasn't surprising that she didn't back down.

If anything, her blue eyes blazed hotter.

"You're a coward," she said again, and with more force this time. "It took me too long to recognize this for what it is. I was so certain that you would behave exactly the way my mother said you would behave. Like all the men she knows, my father among them. Faithless and unkind because they don't think they're required to be anything more than the contents of their bank accounts. I assumed you were the same."

"I am all that and more," he promised her.

"Those men are weak," she threw at him, and if she was intimidated by the way he held her, pulled up against him as if he might kill her or kiss her at any moment, she gave no sign. Her blue eyes flashed and she forged on. "If any one of your cousins went down in a plane, they would have died. And not from the impact. But because they wouldn't have it in them to fight. Every single scar on your body tells me a story about the real Leonidas Betancur. And every one of those stories is a tale of overcoming impossible odds. It isn't accidental that you ruled that compound. They could have killed you when they found you, but they didn't. They could have put you to work as a cook. A janitor. Instead, you became their god."

"A god and a janitor are much the same thing in a place where there is no running water and winter lasts ten months," he told her, his voice a harsh slap.

"I told you that you couldn't have me, but I was only protecting myself," she whispered.

"Something you would do good to think more about right now, Susannah."

"But you never told me the truth," she accused him.

"That no one can have *you*, Leonidas. That it's not about me at all."

That struck at him, and he hated it. "You have no idea what you're talking about."

"You are so filled with self-loathing and this terrible darkness you carry around inside of you that you think you have nothing to give anyone. Leonidas. You do."

And her words sat there like heavy stones on his chest. Her blue eyes burned into him, accusation and something else. Challenge, perhaps. Determination.

Not that it mattered.

Because she was right.

"I don't," he heard himself say, as if from far away. "I don't have anything to give. I never have."

Susannah made a sound, small and raw, and the look in her eyes changed. Still electric, though the storm seemed to deepen. Soften.

She stopped holding herself so tightly upright and apart from him, and melted against him. And it was only the fact that it might hurt her that kept Leonidas from hurling her away from him. Throwing her across the room, before that melting softness could tear him apart the way he knew it would.

He knew it.

"You do," she told him, as if it was a self-evident truth, blazing like a fire in the corner of his office. "You have everything to give. You're a good man, Leonidas."

He let out a laugh, harsh and short. "Not only is that not true, but you wouldn't know it if it was. You don't know me, Susannah. I might as well be a stranger on the street."

"I do know it," she retorted, fiercely. "Because I walked into a room in a scary compound on the side of a mountain and met a stranger who had no reason at all to treat me kindly. You could have hurt me then. You didn't."

"I took your virginity."

"I gave it to you and even then, you didn't hurt me," she said hotly. "You didn't remember me and you weren't abusive. And you could have been. Who could have stopped you?" She shook her head at him. "I want you to think about that, Leonidas. When you thought you were a god, you didn't abuse your power. You tempered it."

He felt his grip tighten on her and made himself loosen it. "None of this matters now."

"Of course it matters." She sounded something like frustrated. And raw with it. "You think that you're the same as your parents. Leonidas. But you're not. You think you're just like your cousins, but there's no comparison. You're nothing like any of the people we know."

"That is nothing but a mask," he gritted out.

"The mask wasn't the Count, who lived by his ideals and stayed true to his vows," Susannah retorted. "The mask is this, here. The Betancurs. Not you."

He let her go then, before he did something else he'd never be able to forgive or undo. Like pull her closer.

He put the distance between them then that he should never have allowed her to close and straightened his suit as if he was making sure his costume still fit—but no. She was wrong. This was his life, not a mask. That was the trouble.

"I will support you and this child," he said briskly, ignoring the thickness in his voice. "Neither one of you will ever want for anything. If you wish to remarry, nothing will change. If you wish to retain the Betancur name, you can do that as well with my blessing. It is entirely up to you, Susannah. All that I ask is that you do it far from here, where there is none of…this." And his voice was too rough then. He knew it. But he couldn't seem to stop it. "None of these lies, these games. Make the child a better class of Betancur."

"Him," Susannah said. Very distinctly.

When Leonidas only stared at her, as if everything in him had turned to ice where he stood, she aimed that heartbreaking smile of hers at him. Straight at him as if she knew, at last, what a weapon it was.

"It's a boy, Leonidas. We're having a little boy." And she didn't wait for him to process that. Instead, she twisted the knife and thrust it in deeper. "And you have a choice to make. Will you treat your own son the way your father treated you? Or will you prove that you're the better man? Will you behave like your mother—so terrible that when her only son found out she'd arranged to have him killed he wasn't all that surprised? Or will you make certain that your own child will never, ever believe that you could be capable of such a thing?"

"You're making my point for me, Susannah. Look at where I come from."

"I know exactly where you come from, because I come from the same place," she said fiercely. "And I've been in love with you since the moment I learned that I was to be yours."

And it wasn't the first time in his life that Leonidas had shattered, but this time, he thought the damage might be permanent.

"That's nothing but a schoolgirl's fantasy," he managed to say past the noise inside him.

"Maybe so. But it's still here. And it's only grown, you foolish man. I don't think it's going anywhere."

"You need to go," he said, but his voice hardly sounded like his own.

"I'm going to do something radical, something our

parents never did for either one of us, and love this baby. Our son." Susannah's gaze held him as if she was pinning him to a wall. "Will you?"

He staggered back as if she'd hauled off and hit him. Some part of him wished she would. He knew how to take a blow. He'd learned that young, at his own father's hand—

And the thought of a son of his own taking the kind of beatings he'd weathered sickened him, down deep into his bones, until he felt something like arthritic with the force of his own disgust at the very idea.

"I told you before," he threw at her. "I don't know how to love. I don't know what it is."

But she kept coming. This woman who had saved him. This woman who never saw a monster in him. This woman who called him the worst of the Betancurs, an unparalleled monster, but made love to him as if he was only and ever a man.

"Neither do I," she told him as she drew closer. "But I want to try. Try with me, Leonidas."

He didn't mean to move, but he found himself down on his knees, though he was a man who did not kneel. He was on his knees and she kept coming, and then he was wrapping her in his arms—or she was the one wrapping him in hers—and he kissed her belly where their future grew. Once, then again.

And when he looked up into her face again, tears were leaving tracks down her cheeks and her eyes were as blue as all the summers he wanted to show his son. As clear as a promise. As perfect as a vow.

"I will try, Susannah," he whispered. "For you—for him—I will spend my whole life trying."

"I will love you enough for both of us, Leonidas," she told him, her voice rough with emotion. "And this baby will love you even more than that."

"And I will love the two of you with every part of me," he replied, aware as he said it that she'd changed him. That he was a different man.

Not the invulnerable Leonidas Betancur who had gone down in that plane. Not the Count who'd believed himself a prophet at the very least, but more likely a god. But both of those men and more, the husband who had been loving this woman since he'd kissed her in a faraway compound and she'd brought him back to life.

Life. Love. With Susannah, they were the same thing.

"I will try until I get it right," he told her. "No matter how long it takes. I give you my word."

"As a Betancur?" she asked, but her mouth was curved as if she already knew the answer.

"As the man who needs you, and wants you, and never wants to be apart from you," he replied, smoothing his hands up the line of her back as he knelt there before her. "As the husband who cannot imagine a world without you. As the fool who lost his memory and now sees nothing at all in the whole of this world but you."

And he tugged her mouth down to his, his beautiful Susannah, and showed her what he meant.

Forever.

CHAPTER THIRTEEN

ADONIS ESTEBAN BETANCUR came into the world with a roar.

He had a shock of dark hair and fists he seemed to think were mighty as he waved them all around him in a great fervor.

And Susannah had never seen anything more beautiful, heartbreaking and gorgeous at once, as the way one tiny baby boy with an outsized personality wrapped his ruthless, intimidating father around his perfect little fingers.

Though their life together came close.

Leonidas found he didn't much care for running the Betancur Corporation alone, and especially not when he could have Susannah by his side to do it with him. Leonidas on his own had been a force to be reckoned with. The Widow Betancur had wielded her own inexorable power.

Together, there was nothing they couldn't do.

She was pregnant with twin girls when he came to her, late one night after he'd put four-year-old Adonis to bed with tales of brave Greek gods and stories of grand adventures. Susannah watched him from where she sat, out by the quiet pool in the soft Australian night, in the same Darling Point house in Sydney where he'd sent her to live on her own once upon a time.

Leonidas smiled as he came to her, lit by the soft lights that hung in the trees, and sat beside her on the outdoor couch that was tucked up in the shade during the hot days and offered a fire pit for the cooler evenings.

He rested one arm on the back of the sofa and twisted to kiss her as he rested his other on her huge belly, laughing against her mouth when one of his daughters kicked at him. This was how they danced now, Susannah thought. This was the best dance of her life.

"When you tell Adonis stories of gods, do you mention that you were one?" she teased him.

Leonidas took the kiss deeper for a moment, letting her taste that hunger that had only intensified across all these full, bright years. And when he pulled back his smile had gone wolfish in a manner that boded well for the rest of the evening.

"That is a story he will appreciate more when he is older, I think," he murmured. "When he has forgotten how much he looked up to me when he was small."

He did not mention how little he'd looked up to his own father. He didn't have to; it was obvious every time he did not beat his own son to a pulp. Every time he did not go off on a rampage and use his fists as punctuation.

Every time he did not have to *try* to love his son and his wife—he just did, and well, despite the lack of any parental role models in that area.

Because when Leonidas Betancur decided to do something, he did it well.

Susannah had stood beside him as he'd handled his mother these past years after he'd cut her off from the Betancur fortune, as promised. The world had watched Apollonia's dramatic response to that, played out in as many tabloids as would listen to her tales of woe.

"If you want to see your grandchild," Leonidas had

told her the last time she'd showed up where she wasn't welcome, "you have a great deal of work to do to convince me that you deserve it."

The names his own mother had called him then had been disgusting, but unsurprising. And the last they'd heard of Apollonia, she'd shacked up with one of her many lovers in Cape Town. Where Susannah hoped she'd stay, nicely hidden away, for as long as possible.

Meanwhile, the arrival of Adonis had cracked something open in the heart Susannah would have said Martin Forrester didn't have.

"I suppose you don't have to be a good man to love a baby," she'd said to Leonidas in wonder not long after Adonis was born, when her father had not only insisted on a visit but had chastised Annemieke for her dour attitude during it. Because if she wasn't mistaken, her crusty father had fallen head over heels in love with his grandson.

"No," Leonidas had agreed. "But if you're lucky, loving a child can show you how to be a better one."

Leonidas was more than a good man, Susannah thought. He loved his son so wholly and obviously that it could have lit up the world, if he'd let it.

He loved her the same way.

So much, so deep, it was almost funny to imagine that five years ago, they'd stood in the Betancur offices in Rome and vowed to *try* to love each other.

"Do you know what today is?" she asked him now.

"A Tuesday," he replied at once, drawing patterns on her belly as if sending secret, encoded messages to the twin girls within. "In Sydney, Australia, where I am happy to say we are both on the same side of the international dateline."

"Five years ago today I hunted you down in your office in Rome, pregnant with Adonis and very, very unhappy with you," she reminded him.

"Surely not, when I am in all ways the very best of men. Isn't that what you were moaning into your pillow just this morning?"

Susannah made a face at him. Then reached out to put her hand on his rock-hard thigh beside her, letting his heat and strength seep into her. He made her feel safe and strong. He made her feel as if they were dancing, around and around, when they were sitting still. She was huge with this pregnancy, ungainly and slow, and he made her feel beautiful.

"If all of this is you *trying* to love me, and our son, and these babies we haven't met yet, I can't imagine what succeeding at it will look like," she told him softly. "Or how my heart will take it."

Leonidas turned to her then, his hard and beautiful face in shadow—but she could see him. She could always see him.

"I love you, Susannah," he said, very gravely, so it lodged in her heart like the best kind of steel. "You saved me five years ago. And you've saved me every day since. And your heart can take it, I promise. I'll make sure of it."

"I love you, too," Susannah whispered, as his lips claimed hers.

She felt him smile against her mouth.

"I know that," he told her. "Haven't you heard? In some places, I am worshipped as a god."

But no one could possibly worship this man as much as she did, Susannah thought, even as she laughed. This remarkable, formidable, perfect man. Her husband. Her other half. The man she'd loved since she was a girl, and loved so much more now she was a woman.

So she showed him, right there on their patio while the wind blew in from the water with hints of summer in it.

The way she showed him for the rest of their life, day after day.

It turned out Leonidas was right. Her heart was just fine, if bigger and brighter than she ever could have imagined when she'd walked up the side of a mountain so long ago and located the husband she hadn't lost, after all.

And never would again, as long as they lived.

* * * * *

If you enjoyed
A BABY TO BIND HIS BRIDE
by Caitlin Crews
why not explore these other
ONE NIGHT WITH CONSEQUENCES *stories?*

A NIGHT OF ROYAL CONSEQUENCES
by Susan Stephens
THE ITALIAN'S CHRISTMAS SECRET
by Sharon Kendrick
THE VIRGIN'S SHOCK BABY
by Heidi Rice

Available now!

MILLS & BOON®

MODERN™

POWER, PASSION AND IRRESISTIBLE TEMPTATION

MILLS & BOON®

Coming next month

CLAIMING HIS NINE-MONTH CONSEQUENCE
Jennie Lucas

Ruby.

Pregnant.

Impossible. She couldn't be. They'd used protection.

He could still remember how he'd felt when he'd kissed her. When he'd heard her soft sigh of surrender. How she'd shuddered, crying out with pleasure in his arms. How he'd done the same.

And she'd been a virgin. He'd never been anyone's first lover. Ares had lost his virginity at eighteen, a relatively late age compared to his friends, but growing up as he had, he'd idealistically wanted to wait for love. And he had, until he'd fallen for a sexy French girl the summer after boarding school. It wasn't until summer ended that his father had gleefully revealed that Melice had actually been a prostitute, bought and paid for all the time. *I did it for your own good, boy. All that weak-minded yearning over love was getting on my nerves. Now you know what all women are after—money. You're welcome.*

Ares's bodyguard closed the car door behind him with a bang, causing him to jump.

"Sir? Are you there?"

Turning his attention back to his assistant on the phone, Ares said grimly, "Give me her phone number."

Two minutes later, as his driver pulled the sedan smoothly down the street, merging into Paris's evening traffic, Ares listened to the phone ring and ring. Why didn't Ruby answer?

When he'd left Star Valley, he'd thought he could forget her.

Instead, he'd endured four and a half months of painful celibacy, since his traitorous body didn't want any other woman. He couldn't forget the soft curves of Ruby's body, her sweet mouth like sin. She hadn't wanted his money. She'd been insulted by his offer. She'd told him never to call her again.

And now…

She was pregnant. With his baby.

He sat up straight as the phone was finally answered. "Hello?"

Continue reading
CLAIMING HIS NINE-MONTH
CONSEQUENCE
Jennie Lucas

Available next month
www.millsandboon.co.uk

LET'S TALK

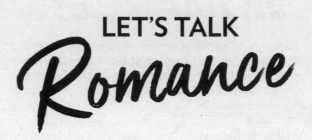
Romance

For exclusive extracts, competitions
and special offers, find us online:

 facebook.com/millsandboon

@millsandboonuk

@millsandboon

Or get in touch on 0844 844 1351*

For all the latest titles coming soon, visit
millsandboon.co.uk/nextmonth

*Calls cost 7p per minute plus your phone company's price per minute access charge